STAR CHILD

T STEDMAN

ACKNOWLEDGMENTS

A special thank you to my much loved readers and my team, Nicky Lovick, Freddy Studart and Jane Harrison.

A tale of magic and evil behind the music industry.

Inspired by real events ...

CHAPTER 1

'Welcome to Metal Beats, the podcast that brings you all the latest news and views in the urban music world, here in LA. Today we have an exciting collective of artists who've been blowing up all over the internet. Literally everyone is talking about them. Welcome, Ballistik, High Hat, Tiny Tears, Duo Tempo, Brain Freeze, Lil Sensei, Pope, Jynskie, Vaggabond and Lil Jace, who make up TRHBDor. Troubadour. Is that the correct pronunciation, guys?'

'Yes, Trent, thank you for inviting us on.'

'What was the thinking behind the name? Does it stand for anything?'

'Well, a troubadour was an olden times poet or singer who travelled around performing in the great houses and castles of Europe, but also in the village squares for the regular people too. We thought it was kind of cool.'

'Yeah, and the letters actually stand for The Restless Hour Before Dawn. It's the time in the day when you're your best self, you know, the most creative and open to the spiritual side of life.'

'That's just fantastic. Why don't you go ahead and introduce what you all do…'

SASHA BOND, aka Vaggabond, sat with their little band as they spoke up one by one. Each showing a little part of their personality in the way they presented themselves and the names they'd chosen.

Ballistik, or Ballsy, as they called him, went first. He was a rapper from Carlsbad. He was a twenty-one-year-old black guy with short dreads coloured blue at the ends, and he wore steampunk goggles around his neck.

Next was High Hat, the surfer dude, with brown messy hair and a tan, from San Diego, who made the beats behind all the music they made.

Tiny Tears was the only other girl and was from right there in LA. She was a black, petite dancer/rapper with tight Bantu knots all over her head. Duo Tempo was her brother and a rapper/singer with short, dyed yellow-blond hair and Lil Jace's best friend. They had a real Bromance going on. Brain Freeze, or 'Brains', was from the Valley, who played on his pale, geeky good looks and happened to be a great poet and even sang a little. Lil Sensei was their graphic artist and rapper, responsible for all the backdrops and light shows, along with Jynskie, an Asian guy the others ribbed as the blackest Asian guy they'd ever met; with his patter, face tats and black wave cap tied around his head.

Then there was her. 'I'm Sasha Bond. People call me Vaga, short for Vagabond. I design the clothes the guys are wearing here. It's kind of a street, urban expression kind of thing.' She thanked Trent Derby for having them. He was an older, balding white guy, covered in more tattoos than any of them, like he should know better. He had already moved on to Jace, or Lil Jace as he was known. Real name Jacek Novacek, who'd travelled there with her from their home in Pittsburgh and who she'd adored since middle school. They'd dated on and off ever since seventh grade and despite not actually knowing where they were at that moment, she loved him, and she was sure the feeling was mutual.

Although she was under no illusions, Jace was no saint. Girls came and went with him. They all loved him. He came across as so vulnerable and cute and he played it to the max. A completely flamboyant dresser, with much of his hair shaven and what remained was a mess, coloured blond and purple this week. It was a full-time job for her simply to stay in his trajectory. Because he was undoubtedly a comet. One that was on a fast collision with Earth.

Her mother warned her several times not to get pulled along in his wake, or she'd crash and burn with him. But it was hard. Truth be told, as troubled as Jace was, he was by far the most talented, charismatic, hypnotic person she'd ever met. And she'd been hopelessly hooked ever since they'd begun to upload his songs to SoundCloud from his bedroom five years ago, just two blocks from where she lived. Even then, he'd smiled into her camera with his goofy smile of uneven teeth and paraded around in her customised clothes covered in pink fur and sequins, completely at home in his skin and sexuality, which was ambiguous at best. Tattoos were already appearing at the edge of his face, making ever getting an ordinary job impossible. By the time they moved to LA and joined the collective founded by Brains, his love of tattoos had spread across his body, even his face. Including a heartbreakingly cute VB from her clothes logo, just below his ear. To any girl's mother, he looked a terrifying prospect for their daughter, but hers knew him as the shy boy who smiled and called her mam through his bedazzled dental grill.

The trouble was that rather than keeping people away, which she was convinced was much of his motivation, girls adored him. If there was ever a special something that stars had, then Jace had it in spades. The girls knew it, his group mates knew it, and Trent Derby, the interviewer, sure as hell knew it, which was why he left him till last. That's why Jace had to beat girls off with a stick and his band-mates shuffled in their seats, irritated at the extra attention he was always getting.

The podcaster droned on, singing Jace's praises, singling him out and making the rest of the collective visibly exasperated. She should have seen what would inevitably happen down the line, even then, but she pushed it to the back of her mind and just felt sorry that he had to continually dumb himself down in front of them. He was with them because he loved being with them. He truly believed in what they produced as a collective, and being an introvert, he much preferred to be with people he knew. The group, however, didn't see it that way. They were growing more resentful every day, because deep down they knew Jace was the guiding light just passing through; the flame that drew the growing fandom to them all. They'd managed to blow up without a single agent or record label between them and they owed much of that to Jace. Out of the whole emo-rap scene, full of young artists trying to rise to the top, it was the tall, almost effeminate, quiet guy at the back, the girls always screamed for on stage.

'Jace,' Trent continued. 'Is it true, you've started to get interest from a major label?'

Jace fidgeted nervously and looked down at the chipped black nail varnish on his fingers. Everyone had gone quiet around him, waiting for him to speak, but the tension crackled in the air.

'I'm currently talking to a UK management company. That's true.'

Sasha saw the pink flush of embarrassment enter his cheeks.

'Will that mean you'll be leaving TRHBDor for the United Kingdom? Does that mean a solo album is in the offing?'

Jace put his hands up in front of him to slow Trent down. 'It's way too early to say,' he said, trying to salvage something in front of his band-mates. He blinked a little slowly with the Xanax he'd obviously taken. It was nothing new for Jace to self-medicate to face something like this. Thankfully, it was Duo who jumped in for him. They'd been inseparable and collaborated on much of each other's music, but even he must feel a little sidelined a lot of the time. 'Ya'll know, where Jace goes, the crew goes too,' he said, laughing easily.

Jace put a hand on his shoulder, laughing as well, clearly relieved. 'That's true.' The pair bumped shoulders and the interviewer smiled knowingly. He knew, rightly or wrongly, it was Jace who'd be going places. Trent was up to the minute on the industry, what was popular in LA and even what went on in their loft. He understood what was going on between them.

However, not even Duo knew him as she did, and they shared most things. You would have had to grow up together for that. To remember the music made for years in Jace's bedroom before it ever saw the light of day. Practising the looks and the make-up, singing all night into a lonely mic, never knowing whether anyone would ever hear what he made, but doing it anyway because it was something he needed to pour out of him. Seeing his mother lose hope that he would ever be a regular guy when the first tattooed butterfly appeared inside the anarchy symbol on his cheek.

Jace now mixed in a world where people always loved to be with him. But it wasn't necessarily a love of *him*, but the hope that some of his star quality would somehow rub off on them. She guessed everyone was a little guilty of that. Like a moth attracted to the light. However true all that was, he was never happy in it. Sasha constantly lived with a feeling of dread in the pit of her stomach. That he was somehow fading and he would leave her one way or another. With his excessive partying: the alcohol, coke, Xans, he was on a path to self-destruction at just twenty years of age. The wilder he became, the more his fans cheered. Because he was a true rock star, living the dream and they were meant to live fast and die young. It was the deal they made with the Devil. Then everyone got to join in with the tragedy and grieve and cry at the waste when he inevitably crashed and burned.

Sasha loved Jace. That was a given, but they'd barely been in LA a year and argued constantly. It forced her to go home regularly for time-outs, where she continually felt neglected. Somewhere along the way, she became the live-in therapist and housekeeper that Jace looked to as his steadying rock. It wasn't enough for her, and, if he was truly honest, not enough for him either.

Every time she went back to Pittsburgh to teach him a lesson – usually when he disappeared for several days with some skank, she'd get a call at around 4 a.m. from him, wasted in someone's bathroom, crying for her to come and show him how to get home. She never entirely knew whether he meant it figuratively. Either way, it broke her heart and she'd travel back on the first flight, bringing groceries for the empty cupboards.

Sasha would be back in Jace's contrite arms within twenty-four hours and they'd eat for a few days, but it never lasted long. He took drugs, consuming little else, disappearing for days and never answering his phone. He was so pale and thin and his soulful brown eyes looked huge in their dark, sorrowful sockets. With his slim build, six feet in height, and his asymmetric, brightly coloured hair, he often reminded her of a sad marionette.

Other girls didn't seem to see that side of him and looked on enviously, often overlooking her talent and what she brought to the group. Determined to see her as some hanger-on or groupie, their looks of hatred were quite scary when Jace pulled her close. One actually asked her what she was doing there, once. 'With your bland face and your nothing hair.'

Sasha had been stunned into silence. She'd never thought about it, as she and Jace had been together for so long. She guessed she was ordinary in comparison to many of the stunning girls. She was kind of average with long brunette hair, often worn in a ponytail, and simple gold hoops in her ears. She prided herself on her clear skin that she covered with very little make-up. Maybe a little mascara just to make her hazel eyes pop. She wore a lot of hats. Her clothes were always black or denim, which was kind of her trademark. Plus, she preferred being in the background. Always there, but not in the madness. Jace loved her, often calling her 'home'. Whispering, 'there are enough plastic girls out there'. It was a weird compliment, but she'd take it.

And so here they all were, on Trent Derby's Metal Beats show. A year ago, she and Jace had dreamed about this. Now, with the collective, they'd grown online, and she was making most of the little money they lived on from designing and selling the merch: T-shirts, hats, jackets, all with the TRHBDor logo of the fairy-tale guy playing a lute. The collective played to bigger and bigger audiences, which paid for the drugs, the rent and the afterparties in their loft. They attracted more and more hangers-on, many who didn't go home for days.

Jace often joked that you could tell who the truly connected people were by the class of drugs they brought along. Sasha remained a skeptic, but she was always there, remaining sober. Worrying.

Until the day Zach Bennington walked into their loft and their lives. It was one of their famous loft parties after a show. A smooth, London-born black guy in a sharp grey suit. He was in his mid to late twenties and looked far too smart for the emo-rap scene to be anything other than a scout. He had music exec written all over him.

Turned out Jace had already agreed to sign with Locke and Key management and Zach had been sent from England to pin him down with a signature and guide him through the process of moving to the UK.

Sasha should have listened to the alarm bells then, but she was simply too shocked and upset. He'd never done anything without her before. Maybe if she'd caused a scene, everything would have ended differently. But Zach said those golden words every artist wanted to hear. Like the Devil himself, he tempted him with one beautiful spell-binding compliment after another, as men like him often did: 'We noticed you… you're causing waves…come with us and we'll blow you up bigger than you can imagine… Massive deals… Talk shows… Money… Everyone will know your name… You'll model… Be on the cover of magazines… Huge concerts… Even festivals… Endless women…' And then the clincher: 'The whole collective can come.'

Sasha should have been ecstatic along with him, but any excitement in her slowly dissolved away. She watched the shy smile disappear from Jace's face as he looked at Zach with hope in his drug-filled eyes. 'Everyone…even Sasha?'

Sasha saw the moment Zach registered the key to signing Jace. A light literally switched on behind his eyes. 'Yeah,' he said, still tidying up what he'd say in his head. 'You'll all live together in a house in London, just like you do here. Then we'll slam the scene with a UK tour with some of our other breakthrough acts. They'll go mad for you…and the guys,' he tacked on.

Jace, being Jace, welcomed Zach into his life right then. He opened his arms and his life and hugged him, leaving Zach patting his back in bewilderment.

And so the deal was struck. Only, despite how it felt, the evil part came much later.

If only she had realised then, just how real it would all become. Instead, she sat feeling numb next to Jace as he talked animatedly of their plans through the night. Party-goers carried on around them. Duo announced it and they all went wild. They'd entered the drop of a white-knuckle ride and it was already too late to get off.

CHAPTER 2

The London house was in Camden, not far from many of the coolest bars and live music venues. It was a vibrant, bohemian place, full of interesting, artylooking people, though it was a little cold and rainy. Clothes stalls and music seemed to burst out of every gap between buildings and doorways. It wasn't unusual to see well-known musicians sitting casually at a bar or cafe. In many ways, it was just like home. The same houseful of artistic, colourful people.

On this particular evening, Sasha came downstairs and stood in the doorway, just observing the scene. Just for a moment, it felt like nothing had changed. It was the Jace she loved and would never forget. They were in the purposebuilt mixing room at the back of the house, an upgrade from a laptop in their loft. Jace and Duo were working on a new collaboration. Both had a mic and were dancing side to side, facing each other, rapping and singing, lost in what they were trying to achieve. Pope was moving around them with his camera phone, filming them, ready to upload to YouTube instantly. Hat was nodding along from behind his desk. He would stop and rewind, and they would go again, and those lounging on the sofa pitched in every now and then, and everything was kept in. It grew into a wonderful, creative, organic beast of its own. It was always such a privilege to see the way they worked.

'Use the TRHBDor one, Hat,' Jace said.

Hat nodded immediately and played, 'TRU, TRU, TRU… light me up like a TRHBDor,' three times over the beat in Tears' clear voice. It was one of his selection of overlay jingles that the fans expected over the top of the songs. Like a little tag or signature of their work.

Then Duo kicked in with a really clever, intricate rap about growing up in the streets of LA and finding himself in the UK, with Jace bouncing off him until he took his own verse. Jace spoke of how they were leaning on each other, no matter what came ahead. Then they both sang the chorus, with many of those watching joining in and Jace taking the highest register. It was great. Sasha loved it.

Without prompting, Jace picked up a bottle of purple-looking liquid from the side and began to dance his way past her, grabbing her hand, pulling her along with everyone else following behind like the Pied Piper. They went out of the back door and into the narrow street of garages and dumpsters behind them. Sasha had never actually been out the back, but it was quiet, it had stopped raining and the road was slick and wet. A single lamppost lit them, and Pope was filming everything like mad. Hat opened the window and the beats continued outside.

Sasha giggled and went along with it. It reminded her of home. This kind of thing happened all the time. Everyone emptied out of the house and, sensing an impromptu music video was happening, they formed a circle and played to the camera, joining in.

Jace and Duo resumed taking it in turns and while they

sang or rapped, they moved forward and back to the lens of the camera. They linked arms around each other's shoulders, and the music sample blared so loudly in the breaks that Sasha was sure someone would call the police. But when the chorus kicked in, even she shouted it at the top of her lungs with the others.

Jace laughed and pulled her between them and she fell in. 'Leanin'' was a great play on words for the addictive purple cough syrup-based drink and two best friends leaning on each other for support. It was Jace and Duo at their best. The melody was catchy, and the subject matter clever; Lean or Purple Drank was a scourge back home. Plus, it had two cute guys who obviously loved each other, making it a sure-fire hit with the fans.

Everyone clapped and cheered when they wrapped it up and Jace and Duo went back inside to finish the overdub. The evening ended with everyone lounging, drinking and smoking, much the same as they did back home.

Sasha sighed contentedly with her head nestled in Jace's lap. She felt his rumbly voice vibrate through him as he absently stroked her hair. He chatted to Duo and the others about old times and people they knew, many of whom had moved on or passed away. Jace was completely relaxed and at home like this. It would be what she remembered most about him. Not the fans screaming for him on stage, but this, among like-minded friends. Drinking, laughing and producing a piece of moving art from nothing, without a single note or word written down. She really felt privileged to be a part of something momentous. A real movement. It was a point in time, in music, that would never be repeated. And it came from Jace so naturally, so organically, he didn't even realise how great he was.

There was no rivalry between Jace and Duo then. They

were an old couple, laughing and finishing each other's sentences, thinking it would last for ever.

THE DAYS PASSED, and Sasha would have almost relaxed if it wasn't for the hard sell Zach was constantly giving Jace. If they'd only let him settle in, it would have stopped much of the trouble that came later. But it was clear for all to see that he only really wanted Jace. All the energy, PR, and budget were only going Jace's way. It was no great surprise. She was more amazed at how far along in the charade they were prepared to go, to include the rest of them. She started to look at it as a paid vacation. Her band-mates, not so much. The shared looks and grumblings were growing.

Jace was quickly introduced to a London rapper on the Locke and Key books, Lexxxlooter, who would be touring with them. He was a mixed-race guy with a rapidly growing fan base they hoped would crossover with Jace's. He and Jace hit it off right away and their campaign to move him away from the collective began.

Duo was pushed to the back – even on their popular collaborations – and Sasha felt desperately sorry for him. He was clearly being benched and much of the tour, interviews and advertising revolved around Lexxx and Jace, even though the apology for what was happening was constantly in Jace's eyes. Zach would be in his ear, smoothing it out with all the reasons why it had to be this way at first. But it was obvious that Jace was simply being schmoozed. Separated. Isolated. And that wasn't good for him. Both she and Duo knew that for a certainty.

The rounds of drug-fuelled parties continued every night. Same kinds of people, bringing more drugs, just in a different time zone. While Jace continued on his same trajectory with Earth and the collective muttering under their breath.

Then, on one rainy night, in the middle of a practice session in the studio room of their house, Zach arrived, barely able to contain his excitement. He was fidgeting and nervous, sweating from being bundled up in too many clothes. It reminded Sasha of someone with a nasty comedown. It was soon apparent that he was dying to tell Jace something, alone, but Jace was deliberately avoiding him. Judging by Zach's whole demeanour, whatever it was was big.

Sasha sidled up to Jace, who was recording one of his silly jingles, 'High Hat on the beats', over and over, which was to be repeated over their songs. He slipped his hand in hers, leaned down and kissed her cheek, still holding the mic in the other.

'What is it?' she asked.

'I don't want to talk to him.' He lifted his head to look at High Hat behind the mixing desk. 'Little more reverb, Hat.'

Sasha didn't allow Jace to push her away. He would dismiss her to get back to what he was doing. It was one of the things she loved about him that he didn't care that his agent was there, clearly excited about something. He wouldn't interrupt his flow. Money, fame, and business were simply by-products for Jace. 'Come here,' she said, pulling him off to the side. 'You have to speak to him, Jace. Otherwise, what are we all doing here?'

He searched her eyes while he lounged lazily against the wall. He slowly blinked in his usual mid-range level of high. He smiled and shook his head as if she was killing him, kissed her and beckoned Zach over with his hand.

Zach was there in about two strides, but before he could launch into his spiel, Jace cut right across him. 'Whatever it is, you need to say it to the group, OK?'

Zach sighed and weighed him up for a long moment before he turned to address the room. Not everyone was there, but most were. High Hat and Duo were behind the desk, quickly shutting off the beat and Brains, Sensei, Pope and Jynskie were squashed onto the old brown leather sofa, opposite, smoking. Ballsy just walked in with a beer, immediately alert to something going on. 'Right, listen up,' Zach said, clearing his throat.

Another couple of hangers-on wandered into the room, still chatting.

'Quiet for the man,' Duo said over the mic.

Everyone found somewhere to perch and listen. Jace squeezed Sasha's hand.

'Locke and Key got a very interesting call this morning from the office of probably the most powerful and influential company in the business.'

Jace looked down at Sasha, puzzled, obviously as clueless as she was and faced Zach again. 'They said that our little crew – this collective right here – has been making waves in the industry and come to the notice of none other than Raziah Faye Carpathian.' Zach turned a circle to take in all the baffled faces. They were all looking at each other to see if they knew.

'If I was to say Star Child, would that ring any bells?'

A few eyes widened and looked at each other, amazed. Sasha had no idea who that was.

'Yeah, you heard right. The reclusive, most sought-after producer on the planet is interested in you,' Zach said, looking each of them in the eye. 'Raziah happens to be her real name. And, believe me, the reason you don't know it is because the family wants it that way. But make no mistake, anyone who has ever had any kind of career in this business, does, and has gone through that company. They are the gatekeepers. Not Sony. Not EMI or any of the labels you've ever heard of, Carpathian is the name that will make you big.'

'So Star Child – this Raz character – the one on the back of every album cover, is a girl?' Duo piped up, amazed.

Others laughed that it was her gender he had chosen to home in on.

Zach just shrugged and smiled. 'It would seem so… Honestly, I've never met her, is the truthful answer to that. I just know that people rarely see her. I know she's not much older than you and plays insane guitar. That's it. Suffice to say, if she decides she wants to work with you, then you're made.'

A pain hit Sasha's chest and she gripped onto Jace's hand as if he'd fly off into this mystery girl's orbit right away. Others whooped and clapped. Thankfully, Jace wasn't immediately convinced. She knew him so well. He loved the adoration as much as the next man, but he didn't take direction well. He loved doing things his own way, at his own pace. Making enough money to make his music and, in his own words, 'buy his weed'.

Or so she'd always thought. Even she was intrigued to see the spark that definitely lit behind his eyes. 'So what happens next?' Jace said, hushing the room that had suddenly got crowded.

'Nothing,' Zach said, now openly talking to just him. 'You just do your thing and we'll hear from them if they want to see you…any of you,' he added, holding out his arm, remembering the rest of the group behind him. 'But I'm telling you right now, nothing about who they choose will be up to Locke and Key. That's just how it works.' He gave it a long moment to let that sink in, then he turned back and addressed Jace more quietly. 'They just said that Raziah had taken a personal interest. That's it.'

Others started firing questions and Jace pulled Sasha into

the heat of his body and rested his chin on her head. She welcomed the closeness but knew the manoeuvre well. It was when he wanted to think without her questioning him.

Jace stiffened as Zach leaned in and whispered. 'Let me know if anyone approaches you. A calling card … anything at all.'

It was all so mysterious. Sasha looked up for Jace's reaction. He just frowned and nodded as he processed what he'd said. 'So we just carry on as normal?' Jace asked, turning away.

Zach nodded and held the top of Jace's arm. 'Just do your thing. You have your first pre-tour show at The Phat Lion on Saturday. Keep your social media presence high. Upload songs, jingles, anything. They'll be watching. I promise you. Then she'll come to us when she's ready. That's how it goes.'

Jace nodded and they both watched Zach make his way out, receiving a few pats on the back as he went. He'd delivered his message and now couldn't leave fast enough.

Jace looked down at her, for once looking as disturbed and puzzled as she was. She simply shrugged. It did feel bizarre. 'What do you think?' she said, gazing up at him.

He slowly blinked and smiled his gorgeous, leisurely smile. 'I think we should go to bed.'

She laughed and nestled her hand in his as he led her through the now-packed room. They'd just got halfway up the small staircase to Jace's attic bedroom when Duo called to him from the bottom. 'Shouldn't we talk about this and get some kind of plan together?'

'Tomorrow,' Jace said, dismissing it with a wave of his hand. Sasha smiled at Duo apologetically. Jace's mind had already moved on and thoughts of wildly powerful families who could change their future had been replaced.

· · ·

Sasha stayed in bed with Jace the whole of the next day. Anyone else would have been up and about, running through the night before with excitement. Not Jace. It was often hard to tell whether he didn't care either way or was just completely cool and confident in who he was. But even Jace had to eat sometime. So they eventually roused themselves, showered and she made them some quick, easy pasta and sauce. Then they packed. The whole house was in a state of excitement. Everyone was rushing this way and that and piling their clothes up in the hallway, pushing past the casual friends that came in just to smoke, unaware they were all going out.

At 7 p.m., the tour bus arrived to take them to their first gig at The Phat Lion – the small warm-up venue nearby. Then they'd be off to Finsbury Park, which would kick off their UK tour. Followed by Brighton, Bristol, Cardiff, Manchester, Glasgow, Dublin and back to Camden to a home crowd to finish and assess their popularity. Even Sasha knew that would be crunch time, where a decision would be made about who stayed and who went home.

Sasha followed Jace out with their bags and hoped he'd be well enough to cope with a different town every couple of days. His pill-taking was constant and he barely ate one meal a day.

The wet roads and noise of the busy London street hit them. The huge silver bus was waiting for them, idling by the kerb. It wasn't Metallica standard, but it was certainly a step up from anything they'd ever had. Well, it was the only one they'd ever had. Most of their shows had been local to LA and they'd piled into a friend's truck for that. They now appeared to even have a couple of roadies who helped load their things.

Two girls giggled and passed them on the pavement, huddled under their umbrella. She guessed they did look an intriguing sight. It was clear they were musicians – albeit modest ones. Jace put up a hand and gave them his grilled smile, completely comfortable shirtless, in canary-yellow holey jeans and a fluffy pink coat. They squealed, delighted, and scurried off.

Spirits were high as they got on the bus, bagsied seats and checked out the bunks that were three high. Jace was already ensconced in a corner seat with half-closed eyes. Sasha felt the familiar pounding in her chest as she worried how many Xans he'd taken to make the journey and then the show. She secretly prayed he'd run out soon. They weren't as easy to come by in the UK.

The bus made a brief stop to pick up Zach. He made them all laugh with jokes, standing up front like a tour guide and then wished them all luck. Then the size of the bus made sense when they were joined by Lexxx and a couple of others she didn't know. They were young, budding stars, all itching to leave their mark on this tour.

Sasha watched the first show from the wings. The troop brought their usual brand of chaos from LA and the crowd loved it. Even their UK counterparts, after their initial shock, just gave up and simply went with it.

Nothing followed an order. High Hat would play a few bars, scratch it and start again, flashing the jingle he'd made with Jace, 'High Hat on the Beats!' over the top. Everyone ended up on the stage at once, pushing whoever's intro came on to the front for their turn. She lost count with at least fifteen artists up there at once, and the stage wasn't that big. The whole collective knew the words and acted as backing singers. Girls were pulled up with them, many already screaming for Jace. Then Hat would flip up the bass, heart-throbbingly loud on the choruses, and the whole place would erupt. A couple of the guys somersaulted into the audience to be carried back again. The whole thing was joyous mayhem, and she didn't think she'd ever laughed so much in her whole life. Jace and Duo were openly crying and hugging each other, to a chorus of "Aw" from a delighted group of girls in the front row. She even ended up in the throng, right in the middle of the stage, and that was unheard of.

It occurred to her then, as she looked out at the ecstatic faces reaching up to them, that this was the pinnacle. Money, fame, or even record deals would never top this for many of those on this stage. Mystery girls from connected families were a million miles away. Her graphics of the name TRHBDor were all over the place, Lexxx and Jace were now hugging and everyone already knew the words to the songs. If only they could have all taken the time to realise the moment for what it was. Then maybe this budding friendship between Lexxx and Jace wouldn't have felt so like the death knell for them all.

She wondered how much Jace knew. He might be high most of the time, but he was frighteningly intelligent. He might have insisted the rest of the collective come, but it was clear that LexxxLooter and Lil Jace had been pushed together for a reason and were the ones the management company would take forward.

THE TOUR TRUNDLED on for the full two weeks. Each night growing bigger and rowdier than the last, as if word had travelled. The crowds loved them. Every night was a party where it felt like Jace never let go of her hand. They were the halcyon days – the ones that wrought her heart in two when she looked back on them. Instead of disappearing with strangers, Jace squeezed into her bunk, whispering, 'I got you,' when she hitched a breath in fear that someone would hear them. It was like sneaking into bed as teenagers, with a real danger of getting caught. But Jace was fearless, making love to her tenderly – well as much as his long limbs and the cramped space would allow. He hovered over her, and they looked deeply into each other's eyes, with nowhere else they'd rather be. Then, as their climax overtook them, it was like he touched her soul.

Then all too quickly the tour was over and her closeness with Jace came to an end. A dark cloud came over her like a premonition of what was to come. They came back to Camden a green and hungover bunch, but most were still riding the high of a sell-out tour. Sasha and Jace slid back into their usual routine, except this time, Sasha felt a little more alone and surplus to requirements. Money had started to come in. Suddenly, Jace's clothes seemed edgier, more flamboyant and expensive. He no longer seemed to wear the old ones she'd painstakingly made.

The last straw came when they were shooting their first professional music video for the first single. It was one of Jace and Duo's many collaborations, made in the early days of their loft. Everyone loved it. It was to be shot over three days and had a full camera crew, make-up, wardrobe and everything. A real production. Duo and Jace were ecstatically happy. So much so, it was like they'd never left LA. The new fans had loved the song and it was an obvious first choice for a hit. Except it was soon clear that her clothes weren't needed, Pope's filming was heavily limited and Duo was relegated to appearing solely on a small TV screen in the background of the shot. Lexxx would be taking his part.

The song was called Hellraiser and was about the two of them landing in hell after their misspent youth. Then, realising there were no rules, no escape, and the demons were fun, deciding to party. It was the track the fans called for most often and usually brought the house down. It was a story about brotherhood, but the director had some supermodel brought in and made it a fight about her and completely missing the point. He was an idiot, and poor Duo's part ended up so small that he had finished by day one of filming and stormed off set. The rest of TRHBDor were relegated to bit parts of nameless demon partygoers. By the end of the three days, they'd all dwindled off and no one they knew was left at the wrap party. Except her, of course. She was there till the bitter end.

JACE WAS quiet and pulled her into his lap while they people watched. Lexxx was there, runners, crew and bigwigs from the agency, but none they could really call friends. Jace was always the quietest in these situations. 'You know what's going on, don't you?' she said, turning his face to look at her.

The joy of the video had dwindled, along with his high and he was left drained and sad. He put his head in his hands and buried them into her shoulder.

'Hey, it will be OK,' she said, wrapping her arms around him to absorb his shudders but not really knowing how that would happen. 'We've been through worse.'

He leaned back and the coal black around his eyes had smudged to emphasise the sad marionette look. 'You don't get it, Sash. They just want me, and I stood my ground, but it's just happening anyway. The guys all hate me and don't realise they're just making it easy for them.'

Jace was shaking. She wasn't sure whether it was anger, frustration, or simply his come-down. It was pulsing through the legs she was sitting on. Whatever it was, it would be bad. Locke and Key had no idea who they were dealing with and how fragile he was. 'They're just hurt. They know it's not you, but they've got no other way of venting. They've all worked so hard.'

'Duo,' Jace said hopelessly, closing his eyes for a second. 'We made Hellraiser together.'

'I know…they totally hijacked it. But this is your shot, Jace. Some never come close. So you have to take it,' she said, running her fingers through the matted purple and blond hair.

They were interrupted by Lexxx. 'We're leaving. We're going for a jam session at Squeak's. You coming?' His eyebrows rose in a question and he flashed a glance at her as a courtesy, but that was all it was. She knew the score here. There would be girls, drugs and music and it could go on for days.

Jace looked into her eyes to gauge her and she was briefly reminded of the boy she once knew. His eyes had held an apology then too, when he wanted to go off with other friends. He would, of course, inevitably go. A small blast of laughter and a complete switch in his mood proved he'd thought of exactly the same thing.

She got up from his lap and kept hold of his hand. He stood with her and kissed her softly on the lips.

'I'll meet you back at the house,' she whispered.

'I'll see you at home,' he said next to her ear.

It hit her straight in the heart, which he knew it would. *She* was home and no one else would understand the hidden little demonstration of his love. She sighed and watched him pull on his new, white, customised leather jacket and walk off until he was out of sight.

Jace didn't return for three days.

CHAPTER 3

Zach ranted furiously, but it came from a place of real fear that something had happened to his biggest investment. 'Where the fuck is he? This is so unprofessional.'

Sasha was the one who had to deal with that and the tantrums from the rest of the guys who were there, ready and able for work. As the closest to Jace, and the only one they could take it out on, she copped the lot. They never got that she was as sidelined as the rest of them when this happened. She wanted to scream what they already knew – that the only reason they were angry was that they didn't have what Jace had, but, in the end, she didn't have it in her to rain on their confidence any more than was happening already. All she could say was, 'It's not his fault, guys. He loves you. You know that.'

They knew she was right, but it was hard – particularly for Duo. It was easier for him to vent that Jace was stealing the limelight on something that should be jointly his. They would have to face that from a business point of view, Jace was a gift from the gods to market. It was in his self-made image. In his music. In short, he had that certain something that nobody else had. A hard fact for his peers to swallow, but true. That was why he would get away with this and anything else he wanted to do.

However, it was hardest of all for her. She was the one alone in their bed, wondering whether he was sleeping at all and who with.

On the third day of Zach calling constantly, she had to admit she was worried too. The house had simmered down to quiet apprehension. Jace was a Cobain scenario waiting to happen. Everyone knew him well and accepted that. It was just a case of when. Then their little jaunt would be over and they'd all be sent back to their old lives. It was a sobering thought, even for the haters. Only Duo had the guts to come out and say it: 'He's a selfish asshole.' And pushed past her in the hallway.

She couldn't argue with that.

SOMETIME LATER THAT DAY, Sasha's phone rang with an unknown number. She put it to her ear. 'Jace?'

The line was quiet, but someone was there. She could hear the uneven breaths. 'Jace, is that you?' Then it sounded like a sniff or a sob. She was positive it was him, but she wasn't sure whether he'd dialled her intentionally or not.

Then he spoke in a cracked and ruined voice. 'Come and get me, Sash.' A sob escaped him. 'I need you. I don't know where I am. I don't know how to get home.' He began to cry, breaking her heart as she listened to him. He was on a come-down from hell somewhere and didn't know what way was up anymore.

'Think carefully, Jace. Where are you?' she said, desper-ately. Not knowing how on earth she would find him. She could hear the faint, rhythmical thud of bass, as if it were in the distance. 'Think, Jace!'

He was quiet for a beat, as if he was looking around him. 'I'm in a closet. There's jackets. Cleaning stuff … I don't know,' he wailed.

Her heart thrashed against the walls of her chest. He'd done this kind of thing before. He'd suddenly feel tired and overwhelmed by all the strange people and slope off somewhere quiet to sleep, like a wardrobe, toilet, or even under the stairs. 'Is the ceiling sloped above you, Jace?'

'Er, yeah,' he said, finally pulling himself together.

'Stay put, OK. Keep the phone on and I'll find you.'

'OK,' he said, fearfully.

She hoped to God he didn't come out of his hiding place or return the phone to its owner. Right then, it was the only thing that she could home in on. She dialled Zach, who said he'd come immediately. 'The phone is somewhere in Islington, just fifteen minutes away,' she said.

Zach swore and said he'd send a car.

Sasha slid into the back seat of the executive car as soon as it pulled up and passed her phone to Zach. 'Let's hope the battery doesn't die,' he said, angrily, looking the most pissed she'd ever seen him.

'Look, don't take this out on me. This is your fault. You're determined to take him away from everything he knows. This is what you get. You're lucky he's conscious,' she said, flashing her eyes at him and then looking out the passenger window at the grubby, congested streets.

Zach sat thoughtfully after that. They came to a standstill outside a row of tall brownstones. 'This is it.'

The door opened and music blared from inside. Two student-looking guys trotted down the steps, leaving the door open.

'Come on,' Zach said.

They both got out. Sasha stayed close to Zach as they climbed the steps and entered through the open door. There were people strewn everywhere in varying states of stonedness, as if they'd been partying for days. Most looked asleep or wasted, even though it was Monday morning and the world was getting ready to go to work. It was nothing new. Except Sasha noted there wasn't a single person she recognised. Even Lexxx was nowhere to be seen. They'd probably been to several addresses and Jace had become separated along the way. No wonder he was terrified.

'Where the hell is he?' Zach said, exasperated, opening and closing a door before she could see what was happening inside.

'I think I know,' she said, continuing down the hallway. She waved Zach over when she found the small white cupboard door. Her pulse was already racing at what she might find. She closed her eyes and snatched the door open.

There was Jace, blinking in the sudden light, hugging his knees in a pile of coats with pupils the size of gambling chips. Curled around him were the arms and legs of a girl fast asleep. She stirred at the interruption and turned over.

Sasha didn't even have the chance to ask who it was. Jace was already crawling out, all gangly arms and legs giving out from under him, where he hadn't used them for several hours. In the end, she just got under his arm and Zach took his weight from the other. Zach said nothing. He'd been terrified and just looked relieved. They'd finally found his investment and he was still in one piece.

Between them, they got Jace out and into the car, where he soon curled up and fell asleep with his head on her lap. Zach got in the front passenger seat and said just one thing. 'I heard you.'

Sasha felt a wash of relief. She looked out of the window,

wondering how long they could continue like this. Any normal person would learn their lesson. But not Jace.

Sᴀsʜᴀ ɢᴏᴛ Jace to eat some toast, then he slept the whole of the next day. Zach used the opportunity to do some damage limitation and got the rest of the collective into the studio with a big producer. It seemed to work, as, without Jace, the grumblings disappeared.

Zach pulled Sasha aside. 'The company wanted me to thank you for what you did yesterday. They care about their artists.'

Sasha just looked at him sardonically, conveying that she knew exactly why they were grateful. Jace croaking before they could make any money from him would be very inconvenient – especially as they'd already heavily invested. 'He's my boyfriend, Zach. What else was I going to do?'

'Nevertheless, the company would like you to stay on as his PA…you know. Keep him on track.'

Sasha just blinked. She was so insulted. Then anger seared through her so fast she forgot to breathe. 'I'm a designer, not a babysitter,' she spat through clenched teeth. 'And while we're at it, if you want my advice, you'll let him go back home. He's a fish out of water here. Maybe even to his mother's in Pittsburgh.' A warm feeling flooded her. Cold nights, holed up in the warm. Her and Jace making music and short films together on her phone. It all came back to her in one lovely flash of memory.

Zach studied her for a moment as if he was actually considering what she'd said. 'Leave it with me. I'll see what I can do.'

. . .

Twenty-four hours later, Sasha sat holding Jace's hand on a plane and the whole collective was with them. Except Zach's good sense, or the company's generosity, didn't extend to them going home to Pittsburgh at all, only to LA. But she'd take it. The studio time that they'd missed could be continued there with only minimal disruption to Jace's schedule. Plus, the others might be a little more relaxed. Buzz was building after their little UK tour and they were in a hurry to release an album off the back of it.

Jace was sombre and held her hand a lot during the journey. Not that she minded. Of course, she didn't. It just showed where his mind was at. That, and the dark lyrics he was scribbling in his notebook. Sasha worried about him more than ever before. They were just twenty years old and she couldn't shake the feeling that Jace's descent was coming frighteningly quickly.

They were given a huge house near the beach, a short ride from the studio. The idea being that the upmarket accommodation in a nicer part of town might somehow calm Jace down. But news travelled and the parties continued, except now Jace had funds.

Sasha called Zach a few times, pleading. But apart from feeling the most disloyal girlfriend ever, Zach just lost his patience in the end, shouting, 'What do you want me to do?'

She was stunned into silence. He was right. Home. Rehab. Jace was never going to change. She was asking the impossible. It was making her a wreck.

Zach ranted. 'You wanted him home. He's home. We've moved heaven and earth, stopped production and shifted everything to LA. I don't know what else you expect. At some point, it just has to come down to him.'

Sasha deflated to an empty shell, exhausted. He was right. She ended the call, barely able to speak, her throat was so closed up. She went to the room she shared with Jace and cried broken-hearted tears. Jace found and held her a couple of times without speaking. He didn't have to. He knew. They were breaking and fracturing and there was nothing either one of them could do. He knew it was his fault, but he was incapable of changing. Both knew that.

Somehow, she'd changed from being his girlfriend to simply a support system. They hadn't been physical for weeks. She'd been relegated and she had to face it. Finally. She'd become obsessive and lost weight. She was wrung out emotionally. It was time to leave Jace and go home. Zach was right. It wasn't fair to anyone to hold Jace up forever.

Jace sensed it and kissed her properly in the creeping, early light of dawn. The first time in ages. She'd barely slept and he'd only just come to bed. 'Come back to me,' he whispered.

Her throat cramped up as she wanted to cry. She wanted to shout and scream at him that it was him who'd left her. That he could forget all this and simply come back with her to Pittsburgh, but she knew it was useless. Jace had been on this path since they were thirteen. Younger, even. 'You know where I am and you can call me any time.' As the words left her mouth, she knew she shouldn't have said them. They both needed to let go and move on. But she was scared. They both were. They were at the crossroads of something final. Unchangeable.

She wouldn't be there to be his advocate with the band. They'd already grumbled they'd lost studio time because of him. It was all about to implode and no one would be there to catch him.

Sasha left Jace's arms to shower. Then steadily packed up all her stuff. Jace watched sleepily, propped up on pillows, with those dark, saucer-like eyes and, just like that, he let her go. No one even came with her to the airport.

CHAPTER 4

ace

Jace reached a strange level of detachment when Sasha left. Like the numbness a person gets after someone dies. Or a lost limb that felt like it was still there, until you went to use it and it had gone. He was in a suspended state of disbelief. He never thought she would actually do it and yet knew it was always going to come one day. Today was that day and it was final.

The next few days were a blur. Drinking the sickly concoction of Lean, taking Xans, and passing out. His usual MO. *No wonder she'd left*. Then, at just another random, everyday party at their place, something monumental happened that changed everything.

The girl just appeared.

Of course, no one knew who she was at first. They'd grown used to Zach sending bigwigs, celebrities and head honchos to meet with them. Anything to create buzz and headlines in the hope of future collaborations. For some reason, she'd chosen that particular day.

To Jace, she wasn't hard to spot. She was so conspicuous in her insignificance. He stopped drinking and shifted in his armchair to watch her. She wasn't dressed up to impress, with any bling or arrow pointed at her head. Dressed in simple, worn blue jeans, black sneakers and a cable knit, buttoned-up cream sweater. She seemed tiny and unobtrusive, quiet and watchful, not talking to a single soul except a tall, military-looking blond guy, who was obviously her bodyguard. In fact, on closer inspection, there were four guards in all, hovering nearby, trying to look relaxed but too straight and alert to be anything else. They were dressed smartly in black and wore heavy gold watches. The type that costs thousands of dollars. She looked like a poor waif in comparison. It was weird. This was California, and she wore a woollen beanie over her long, dark-blonde hair, with a large fluffy pom-pom at the point that made her look about twelve years old. It was hard to see her face because she wore dark glasses like goggles that let in no light at all. All he could see was a perfectly formed small nose, rosebud mouth and caramel skin, punctuated with an array of small face tats to rival his own.

He sat forward and blinked. He couldn't help himself. He'd never seen a girl mark themselves up in that way. It hit him profoundly. He didn't know why. Maybe because he understood. Under all that shit – the hat, the wool, the glasses – she was hiding. She was a spectator on the world. The exact same place he always wanted to be, most of the time. It made him feel like he knew her because she was him. He was so engrossed that he hadn't felt Zach come and sit next to him. 'Strange looking, isn't she?' Zach said wistfully, looking over at her as well. 'Raziah Faye Carpathian…doesn't look a day over fourteen, does she?'

Jace flashed his eyes at him in annoyance. It felt like he

was somehow invading a moment. 'She just covers up in public,' Jace said, instantly regretting opening his mouth. It would just encourage Zach to continue speaking.

Zach bobbed his head. 'Maybe … something like that. Don't let first impressions fool you, though. She's razor-sharp and knows what she likes. She comes from the most powerful family in the world…musically, anyway.'

Jace looked at her again. She was solitary, apart and perfectly at ease that way. Before he'd even put weight on his legs to stand, Zach cut in, 'Don't approach her. It's not what you do. She'll come to you.' Then Zach moved off and Jace relaxed back into his seat, confused.

He went to call Zach back to ask what he meant, but the words died on his lips. He just couldn't imagine her going up to some stranger. By the time he faced her again, she'd gone.

Suddenly alarmed, Jace looked left and right. He stood for a better view across the heads of partygoers. He breathed a little easier and relaxed back down into his seat when he spotted that her four guards hadn't moved. He cursed that he'd taken his eye off her.

Then his heart stalled. She was sitting across from him in an armchair, one leg crossed over the other, looking straight at him. 'Er, hi!' he said, completely lost for words. Despite disliking social situations, he'd never been awkward with a girl before. They were familiar territory to him. Duo had even accused him of using the troubled soul act just to get the girls. Whatever it was, it usually worked. They'd let down their guard around him and he'd swoop in like a falcon and whisk them to his bed.

That was in normal circumstances. Not here. He shivered as if he'd been touched by an icy hand. He continued to stare, struck dumb.

A drunken roadie stumbled, almost falling into her. The

blond bodyguard only just caught his arm in time. He patted her guard's back loudly in way of thanks and sat on the glass coffee table between them. He looked at Raziah and then at Jace exaggeratedly and grinned. She and Jace remained locked in some kind of stare-off.

The guy between them laughed. Then, when he got no response from either of them, he tutted. 'Another groupie for you then, eh, Jace?'

The bodyguard was there in a second, helping the roadie up and easing him along and away. It wasn't till then that Jace noticed that there was no one else near them. In a crowded room, they had an eight-foot bubble around them. The raucous party, a mile away. Despite the throb of bass, a chasm of silence gaped between them. Then she simply leaned forward and put what looked like a business card on the table.

He blinked at it a couple of times and picked it up. There was nothing remarkable about it, just a simple black card with a gold logo of an eye inside a diamond, and it was completely plain on the other side. However, by the time he raised his eyes and opened his mouth to ask a question, she'd already gone and all four of the men accompanying her had gone as well.

JACE HADN'T MOVED when Zach flopped back down next to him. 'She came then.' He was shaking his head like he still couldn't quite believe it. 'You realise how rarely this happens?'

Jace honestly didn't know what to say. He was still reliving the most powerfully affecting meeting of his life and not a single word was spoken.

Zach nodded, dropping his eyes to the card Jace still held in his hand. 'Don't lose that. I've only ever seen it twice before and both recipients became household names within a year.'

'What is it?' Jace asked, turning it over in his hand. 'It doesn't tell me anything.'

'I don't think it's meant to. It tells them … it's your ticket in.' Zach grinned and shook his head, clearly delighted. He gripped his shoulder and gave it a little shake. 'The Carpathians have invited you, so when they call, you come.'

Jace frowned, still studying it in the hope that something else would reveal itself. 'And the others?' Like he was happy and all and he definitely wanted to take his music to the next level, but he hadn't got where he was alone and he liked it that way.

Zach exhaled an impatient breath and fixed him with a hard glare. 'You just do what they tell you to do, OK? This is the big leagues. It doesn't get bigger than this. This is real, Jace. Your life is about to change.'

Zach kept his eyes on him as he took out his phone. 'Yeah, Deb, it's me … He got it tonight.' He got up and wandered off and Jace didn't hear any more. The party seemed lame and pointless after that.

Jace went to his room, kicked out a couple making out on his bed and locked the door. He got into bed, pulling the quilt right up over his head. A habit since he was a kid. Then he dialled the number of the one person he could always talk to. 'Sasha … Can you come?' But it was her voicemail.

JACE WAITED, but Sasha didn't come back and that made him sad. Things had changed between them ever since they'd returned from the UK. He hit his forehead with the heel of his hand at how dumb he'd been. This was his fault. He'd broken her. He'd dragged her down like he did everything. Now she was distant and it wasn't just the miles between them. They'd done the long-distance thing a hundred times. This felt too real, like she was trying her hardest to pull away.

He was making great music, though. Inner pain did that. Some guys had flown in from Florida and it was some of the best he'd ever made. Even Duo and the rest of the guys seemed to relax and became productive again.

They'd all settled into a comfortable rhythm when Jace received the summons. They were sitting at home, bouncing ideas for a new collaborative track when Zach flew through the house to find him. 'Jace … there you are,' he said, sounding out of breath. 'The card … tell me you have it safe.'

Jace was so preoccupied that he had to think about what he meant for a minute. He hadn't long swallowed a Xan, but he eventually nodded, much to Zach's obvious relief. His mind went to the drawer next to his bed.

'Good … that's good,' Zach said, beginning to pace in front of him. 'They're sending someone for you tonight.' Then he stopped and turned to face the others. 'They've asked for me and the rest of you too,' he said with a shrug, totally giving away that he had no idea why, which was insulting.

Zach turned back to Jace to explain. 'She wants to see you in your normal working dynamic, or something.' His eyes were darting while his mind was working fast. Jace had never seen him so agitated. It started to register that this must be big.

'So you think we should just go?' Jace asked. They were in the middle of something and he hated stopping when it was going so well.

Zach looked directly at him like he couldn't believe his ears. 'Should we go?' he repeated. 'I don't think you fully grasp the enormity of what's happening here. Every superstar you've ever known. The biggest. Presley, Hendrix, Cobain. They've all been standing where you are now.' He rolled his eyes while he shook his head and made his way towards the door. Then he stopped and turned before he disappeared. 'Be ready at seven.'

The room remained quiet and stunned. The only thing that struck Jace was that all those great stars were dead.

CHAPTER 5

*J*ace passed the rest of the day in some sort of trippy dream and not in the warm, fuzzy way he was used to. He was jittery and restless and couldn't settle to doing anything. He finally had to admit it was down to nerves. Without Sasha's calming voice of reason, he was a wreck.

The newer, larger tour bus arrived for them at 7:30 and everyone bundled on in noisy excitement at who these people were. Jace remained quiet. Particularly when they arrived at a private airfield and a foreign guy went around with a black bag for them to hand over all their phones and devices. It sobered them into silence. Jace gave his freely; he never answered his phone anyway. He trotted up the steps to the large white jet with a single gold star on its tail. He found his place at the back and took a bottle of water from a tray a stewardess was holding out for him. She and the guy next to her wore matching blue suits and hats that reminded him of Barbie and Ken. He finally relaxed, popped a couple of Xans and settled into his seat. He listened to the lively chatter between the others, all agreeing that serious money was behind something as mysterious as this.

Jace's eyes were jolted open as Zach flopped heavily into the seat next to him. He was yet to learn that he hated sitting next to anyone except Sasha on a journey.

Zach was oblivious and fidgeted, wiping his sweaty palms on the thighs of his jeans. 'Here we go,' he said, nodding manically. His demeanour was not exactly filling Jace with confidence and Sasha wasn't there to smooth it away.

When Zach ignored his irritated vibes, Jace asked, 'Where are we even going?'

Duo and Big Ed from Florida swivelled around in their seats to listen. 'Must be an internal flight. I didn't bring my passport,' Ed said.

'No idea,' Zach said, rubbing his hand over his face like he had no clue how to deal with that kind of information.

Jace paid more attention and frowned at that. Duo and Big Ed stared at him, confused.

Zach rolled his eyes. 'You have to understand that these people are powerful. We're going to one of their homes. No one knows where that is.'

'Have you been there before?' Duo asked, starting to look alarmed.

Zach shook his head. 'I mean, I know about them. People in the industry do, but they're like one of those legends you talk about late at night when you're wasted. But no, I haven't been there. I've never been lucky enough to have an artist they wanted to see…till you,' he said, raising his eyebrows in an obvious attempt to deflect the heat off him. It worked.

Duo and Ed looked at each other and grinned, their egos sufficiently flattered to relieve some of the tension. Jace hunkered down in his chair, closing his eyes again. The door was closed, and the plane moved steadily onto the runway.

Jace wished Sasha was there to calm his misgivings for the millionth time that day.

JACE HAD no idea how long they'd been up in the air because he'd slept. They all did. They could literally be anywhere in the world. No one had any idea. It was dark when they touched down and they could see very little. One private airfield looked pretty much the same as another, he guessed. Ballistik agreed with Ed that they must still be in the United States.

Airstairs were clamped to the side with a clank and Barbie and Ken talked into headsets, nodded at each other and opened the door. Jace got to his feet and shuffled along behind everyone else. He stopped at the top of the stairs outside to look around. The air was sharp and cold, smelling of a mixture of aviation fuel and pine. No surprise as pine trees appeared to line the whole runway. They were literally in the middle of nowhere. Jace looked down and paused at the line of guards wearing guns, forming a line at the bottom of the steps to guide them to waiting vehicles. No tour bus here, just a line of four shiny black SUVs.

A sudden panic gripped him as he realised there was nowhere else to go. The sky was ink black, and there was no sign of anything in any direction to bolt to. He desperately tried to get his bearings. It was cold, and dawn looked like a vague pink blush on the horizon, so he guessed they'd gone north.

Everyone else had moved on, so he felt pressured to do the same. They were certainly quieter than when they left and not just from tiredness of the journey. They were as apprehensive as he was. Jace followed and got in one of the cars behind Zach. He figured he'd stick with him to hear first what was going on.

Unfortunately, the cavalcade moved off and offered no more clues. Each car had a driver and a guard next to him and the windows were heavily tinted. A sideways glance at Zach made him even more uneasy. He looked as nervous as the rest of them. 'Are they the army?' Jace asked, tipping his head towards the two guards in the front.

Zach shrugged and shook his head. 'I guess they have their own.' His look was perplexed and apologetic. His initial excitement was turning to worry as they went further. He was now convinced that Zach was no more in control of this trip than he was.

Jace swallowed and looked out of his window. The Xans he'd taken over the last twelve hours could no longer block out his loss and sense of abandonment. Without his phone, he was disconnected. He didn't even know what time it was. His temperature was rising, his neck constricted and his chest felt tight. He would have completely freaked out if they'd been in the car a moment longer, but they came to a huge hangar-like building and drove right inside. It was empty and they drove straight for the far wall and parked, with each of the other SUVs following suit, side by side. Jace got out to the sound of car door slams as everyone did the same. They looked at each other awkwardly until one of the guards led the way, and they went through an exit into a dark corridor that felt like it was going downwards.

The other guards remained at the rear, making Jace feel like they were being herded to keep them moving and not lose any stragglers. It felt a long way before they reached a spiral, stone staircase and began to climb. It was the kind you imagined led to a castle or an old church. They eventually reached the top and congregated around a set of steel doors that opened to an elevator large enough to fit them all in. It moved up smoothly with everyone looking at each other, wide-eyed and silent. Jace noticed Zach was sweating with his eyes fixed ahead.

The elevator stopped with a small jolt and the doors opened. They were instantly hit with a cacophony. 'Follow the music to the lounge,' one of the guards said, sounding German or something.

Jace put his hands in his pockets and waited for someone else to take the lead. Zach nodded, looked up and down the corridor, straightened his jacket, and decided to go left. Everyone fell in behind him with Jace and Duo exchanging glances, following on at the back.

The walls were of yellow stone and covered in rich red tapestries. Huge oak beams straddled the ceiling above them with lantern-like lighting on the walls. The flagstoned floor had a red carpet runner down the middle, which Jace kept his head down and followed. The air smelled like a church. Jace couldn't help wondering what a group of LA rappers were doing in Frankenstein's castle.

Then, as they progressed down the long hallway, the further they went, the louder the music got. Until they finally walked through some double doors into a sight that blew their minds.

The room that greeted them was as tall and as wide as a ballroom. Music was blaring, but not in any organised way. More like hundreds of musicians competing for air space or tuning up at the same time. Many were seated in circular groups of leather chairs and sofas arranged around a huge, square, raised platform. Some looked like they were camping on the floor on soft rugs, cushions and beanbags. People of all languages and nationalities were singing and playing instruments in every direction. Busy waiting staff were balancing huge trays of drinks and platters of food, picking their way between the furniture to deliver them to the people who'd ordered them.

Jace looked across at his friends congregated in the doorway, and they all appeared to be in shock, their jaws open at the sight before them. He didn't know what they expected, but it certainly wasn't this. Zach, however, had transformed. He pushed to the front and came alive. 'Welcome to Shangri-La, boys and girls. You've made it … come on!' He strode into the room, now in his element of musicians, execs and big nights out.

Jace and Duo exchanged another look and followed along. 'Who are these people.' Duo said as a statement. Jace simply nodded in complete agreement as they walked forward, picking their way through the lounging partygoers. Many were chatting and laughing, some shaking hands.

Jace felt a sharp poke in the back. He turned his head sharply to see who it was. Duo was pointing and nodding with his eyes wide. Jace followed his line of vision as Duo said, 'Look! It's Fazer Light, talking to SaneyT … and Spekter.'

Jace did see. By the time he'd homed in on individual faces and spotted LTS and Sand-E, it was feeling more like being let in a side door of a hippie version of the Grammys. Every single person in the room belonged to some great band or another. This wasn't some lookalikes' convention. The room was literally filled with the real thing.

'Everyone's …'

'Famous!' Jace finished for him.

'What is this place?' Someone else said.

Zach turned around and held out his arms in amazement. 'I think this means you've made it, boys.'

A pretty blonde girl dressed in the black waistcoat and white shirt of the waiting staff tapped Zach on the arm. 'Please can you follow me, sir?' she said, sounding European. 'Raz would like you near the stage tonight.'

They all looked at each other. Zach swallowed nervously

and nodded. Jace couldn't remember seeing him so rattled. They followed the girl farther into the room until they reached a cleared area right next to the raised platform, about a foot high. She held out her arm to the bean bags and scatter cushions strewn over a Persian rug. He guessed this was their spot.

Jace noticed more brightly coloured rugs on the empty stage. It was the only area free of people. Just a mixing desk and a few unattended instruments: a row of great guitars, pedals, keyboards, a drum kit and a couple of amps.

Jace finally sank into a black leather bean bag when the guys stopped goofing around and laughing on the cushions. A girl came along with a huge pitcher of juice, and a guy carried a low table, which he set down on the rug between them. Coffee, fruit, and pastries soon appeared. Jace found himself returning a hand up to Fedder, looking on knowingly, from his group, Masta-Jam, a few feet away. It was too trippy for words.

Jace nestled back into his bean bag. It felt unbelievably comfortable as the air hissed out of it and it hugged the contours of his back. He let his eyes roam around, recognising one huge star after another. He wished Sasha could have been there to share it, because he sure as hell wouldn't know how to explain it. She'd punch him in the arm and tell him to stop kidding. He wouldn't believe it either if he weren't seeing it with his own eyes.

A hand appeared in his face, holding a lit joint. He took it before he followed the dark skin of the arm, straight into the face of Tré, one of his all-time rap heroes. 'Thanks,' he said, in star-struck shock.

'Mad, isn't it?' Tré said. 'I remember how I felt on my first time.'

Jace just nodded, not able to think of a single thing to say.

Tré grinned and squeezed his shoulder as if he understood completely. 'Welcome, anyway. I've been keeping up with your career and what you guys have been doing. It is remarkable, without a label or anything. It's all up from here. Congratulations. You've made it,' Tré said, holding out his hand to encompass the room.

Jace nodded, bewildered, and watched him straighten up and walk away to wherever he came from. His eyes fell on Duo and Ballsy, who'd watched the whole exchange. Their eyes were wide and their mouths still open. 'Punch me,' Ballsy said, to no one in particular. 'I need to know I'm awake for this.'

High Hat obliged, far harder than was necessary. Ballsy scowled and rubbed the top of his arm. Jace lay back and took a long, hard pull on the joint. The calming feeling crept through his body until it left a faint tingle on his lips. His eyelids lowered. The thought did occur to him that it probably wasn't a good idea to zone out too much, but it didn't stop him. He needed something to do in this freaky environment. Someone else nudged him with a beer bottle, which made him grin and swap with the joint. It was ridiculous o'clock in the morning, but what the hell. He eased back, now mellow and people watched.

Something was happening. Musicians were walking up onto the stage. He didn't recognise them. Zach moved over and sat down next to him. 'Fantastic, isn't it? I thought it was all just hype and rumour. But it's all true. All of it.'

'Who are they?' Jace asked, pointing his bottle at the stage.

Zach shrugged. 'Some young Australian band, I think, making their debut like you. Apparently, they've blown up down under.'

Jace sat up a little straighter. 'What's the deal here?' Jace said, holding out his arm with the beer still in his hand. 'What's going on, Zach?'

Everywhere he looked was one famous person after

another and the din of uncoordinated instruments began to sound deafening. Paranoia was setting in, largely due to drugs mixed with imposter syndrome. He was just a simple kid who liked making songs in his bedroom; only Sasha understood that. Now here he was, mixing with the elite of the music industry. It felt out of whack somehow and he couldn't shift the weight of dread he felt on his chest.

Zach turned and looked him dead in the eyes. 'Hold out your hand.'

Jace frowned but did as he was told, flattening his palm in front of him. Zach dropped a round white pill in its centre. 'Take the edge off,' Zach said.

Jace recognised the Xan immediately and threw it straight into his mouth without question and took a mouthful of beer. His eyes stayed on Zach the whole time. He was usually trying to stop him from taking drugs, not giving them to him. 'You still haven't answered my question.' Then he gave up when it was obvious he wasn't going to answer, shook his head and looked out at the room. 'What are we even doing here?' he said, more to himself. He couldn't remember feeling more out of place.

'Honestly … I'm not sure,' Zach said on an exhale. 'I don't know how any of this works. All I know is that card you got, people kill for. Tupac. Biggie …'

Jace scrutinised the agent's profile as he stared out into the crowd and raised his eyebrows. He had no idea.

'It's the ticket into all this.'

Zach wasn't telling him anything new. He didn't seem to know.

'They're the star makers, Jace. Anyone who's anyone in the business knows.' He tipped his head towards the way they'd come in. 'The people that come through those doors become next-level rich and famous…and not just that, Jace.

Talented. Beyond your wildest dreams. Have you heard the term, going to the crossroads?'

Jace shrugged, maybe, vaguely.

Zach leaned on his side to face him. 'It's an old story about a blues musician called Robert Johnson, in the 1930s. He was supposed to have been a lazy womaniser who could barely play until he went to the crossroads of routes 49 and 66. The story goes, he made a deal with the Devil in exchange for his soul, to play great blues.' He leaned back, thinking about it. 'Probably came here,' he said, looking like the revelation had only just come to him.

'What happened to him?' Jace said, now keen to hear the rest of the story.

'Oh, he made it … Some say he was the most influential guitarist who ever lived.'

Jace nodded, impressed.

'Well, for three years anyway. Then, some jealous bloke was supposed to have poisoned him for messing with his wife. So they say … but that's not the point. The point is, the crossroads, Jace. This is your crossroads,' Zach finished, pointing at him in the chest. Then he reached for two bottles of beer from the table and passed one to him. Zach clinked his bottle against Jace's and took a swig, watching him the whole time.

Jace did the same, not so sure. It all felt so alien and contrived, like some awards show or something. He loved what he did. It was natural and grew from inside him. Something from nothing, with friends who felt the same. That was what the collective was all about. Yes, he wanted them to blow up, but because he wanted everyone to know what they did, not for any glitzy Hollywood shit. That wasn't who he was at all. Sasha understood that.

Then, before he could fully register the pain twisting in his gut, a ripple of excitement rolled through the room in a huge wave. The chaotic noise began to die down and people rushed back to their seats from conversations they'd been having all over the room.

'This is it!' Zach said, sitting up straighter.

Jace looked at his friends, who looked as startled as he was. A troupe of people: men, musicians carrying cases, escorted by guards, had entered the room and were making their way towards the stage along a path that had been cleared in front of them.

He felt sorry for the four guys already up there. They looked terrified, as if they were about to face the schoolyard bully and were left with no place to run. It was a weird thought to have for guys about to make their fortune, but he couldn't help it.

The mysterious group reached the stage and four of the guards stationed themselves at each corner. Three tall, dark, Italian-looking guys sat down at a desk like talent show judges. Then, to the right of the platform, was the girl. The one from the party. She stepped up onto the stage and seemed so tiny and ordinary and yet Jace was riveted to every single thing about her.

She was dressed as casually as last time, in tight jeans tucked into biker boots and a jean jacket that she took off, folded neatly, and placed next to the drum kit. She said something to the drummer and he smiled and nodded. Her hair hung loose this time, wavy past her shoulders. She had on a slim-fitting vest that revealed she was no fourteen-year-old. She was confident and perfectly formed. Her seemingly everyday clothes followed the curve of her breasts, her butt and her tiny waist. A raging lust fired up in his belly so strong, he had to grab a loose cushion and hug it across his lap. He looked around guiltily to check if anyone had seen. Thankfully, they were all too engrossed in the unfolding scene.

The four guys on stage looked really nervous as they did a quick soundcheck and tuned their instruments, waiting for the moment when she picked up a guitar and pulled it over her head.

The edges of Jace's view were fuzzing from his Xans, but his heart was pounding uncomfortably in his chest. He hunkered down in the beanbag to ride it out. But there would be no sleep yet. He was completely hooked on what the little woman with the big, grown-up guitar on the huge stage was going to do with it.

Then she turned to face him, looked him straight in the eyes, and struck her first chord.

othing else mattered to Jace after that. The thick glasses she'd worn the first night had gone, and she was flashing the most piercing glacier ice-blue eyes he'd ever seen. Like they'd been backlit for night vision or something. The milky tanned skin he'd only glimpsed was inked right across her cheekbones and down the length of her arms in small symbols and geometric shapes. There were too many to count, in a style and unified formation far superior to the disorganised, haphazard ones of his own. And then there was the way she played guitar, like it was an extension of her arms, crying and wailing an intro like a rock god who'd practised a lifetime.

The room erupted into cheers immediately and they all got to their feet as if royalty had entered the room and he followed. He couldn't help himself. The band joined in their song and it was one he vaguely recognised. She was merely adding her part. Enhancing and weaving the tune with a far rockier, meatier sound.

He guessed it was then he fell for her. That exact moment. He'd never understood love at first sight until then. It wasn't anything quantifiable, like awe, admiration, or even attraction; it was a physical punch to his chest that hurt and took his breath. He watched her helplessly and hopelessly, feeling the need for lungfuls of air to help his thrashing heart. His eyes streamed and he wiped them on the back of his hand and he looked around guiltily, wondering if every male in the room was affected the same way. They all looked fixated, glassy-eyed and were clapping, but none seemed as deeply moved as he was.

After an avalanche of applause and the stamping of feet, she approached the drummer, who looked like a different guy, now happily smiling with relief. The band's moment had passed and they'd played well. Curiously, the drummer got out from behind the drums and she took his place. Then he stood there, looking on and nodding in time while she counted them in on her drumsticks and they went into another song. She did the same with keyboards and bass. Song after song. Four in all, until the whole band looked wrung out and exhausted. The place was filled with their heroes and they were all clapping ecstatically and cheering. The girl played everything like a master.

Jace became aware of Zach next to him. 'What just happened?' Jace asked, partly to himself, his eyes still glued to the girl, shaking hands and saying something to each of the band members.

'Not sure, exactly. Everyone assumes she's just a producer. All I know is this is where the magic happens. It's as if she blesses them with her presence, isn't it?' Zach said, laughing, as awestruck as he was.

But Jace was sure there was some truth in what he said. It did feel as though she'd taken each of their parts in the music and enhanced it, adding her magical approval to it or something. It was bizarre.

The girl escorted the four guys to the table of judges, who

stood, shook their hands and then two of them led the band through the crowd and out of the room. The girl stayed behind, leaned down and said something to the guy left behind.

'Now, I guess, the contracts will be signed that will change their lives,' Zach said, wistfully.

At that exact moment, the girl looked right over at them and pointed.

Jace's heart stopped painfully in his chest. He looked behind him in case she was pointing at someone else, but couldn't see anyone there.

The important-looking guy she was with stood up and looked over as well and started walking towards them. Now Jace could see him clearly; he was tall, good-looking and dark – possibly mixed-race or something, dressed in an expensive pale-grey suit, with a cobalt-blue shirt.

Jace straightened and clenched his fists, instinctively, as the guy came to a standstill in front of him. Jace was tall at a little over six feet, and they were of equal height, but the guy was built with muscle; it was easy to tell. He leaned towards him to say something.

Jace stiffened. His mind racing. The guy had come straight to him. Not Zach. Not one of the others in his group. Just him.

The guy seemed to be searching his eyes for something he might find there. They were glacial like a husky or a wolf's. Like Raz's. *A Brother?* He couldn't be sure.

'Raz wants you next,' he said, in his European-accented English. 'You have fifteen minutes. Don't be nervous. Simply do what you do. Raz has followed your work with interest and thinks your sound is fresh and you could be great.'

Jace listened avidly, straining to hear every word over the noise around him. His heart felt erratic through the cotton-wool haze of the Xan.

The guy smiled, revealing a perfect set of white teeth. Then, before he turned to go back to his seat, he added, 'Bring your crew. We'll hear you all.'

Jace watched him walk back to where one of the others had returned and was already waiting.

Jace didn't move. His insides were liquifying with panic. He'd gone on stage wasted his whole career. Often falling over, even vomiting into a bucket and continuing with the show. But this. In front of her. This felt like the test of his life. It made him question his talent for the first time. *Was he a star? Did he belong here with the elite of all musicians? Was he worthy?*

Zach kicked the side of his shoe to get his attention. 'Don't keep them waiting.'

Jace looked over at the stage. She was already slipping her guitar over her head. His heart felt like it was beating out of his mouth when he called to the others and waved his arm. 'Come on! We're up!' and his voice came out a croak.

Their eyes widened and they remained immobile for a moment, but Jace was already moving towards the stage. People started to clap around them and he felt the others fall in behind. His mind was running at breakneck speed. He had no idea what she wanted. What to do first, last, anything. They were never that organised. All he kept thinking was that they were going to make monumental fools of themselves in front of the best artists in the world, but more importantly, her.

He felt something slip into his hand. Zach was there. He continued to walk, but looked down at the tiny white pill and by the time they reached the mixing desk at the back of the stage, he'd put it into his mouth and swallowed.

Then they were there. Looking at each other, lost, and the room had gone quiet. *Shit!* He felt ridiculous. Small. Under-prepared. *But he never prepared. Ever.* The crowd began chatting again and Jace felt a little better. They were used to this and wouldn't focus until they started to play. *He could do this.* He took a slow breath and exhaled.

Duo nodded as if he understood.

Raz walked over wearing her guitar, low slung over her hips and effortlessly sexy. She held out her hand immediately and shook theirs one by one. Jace couldn't stop staring at her. Her eyes were so piercing, they appeared to see right into you. Then, when she took his hand, he held it way too long, taking in the caramel slimness of her fingers, and the ink that went down to her nails. As did his. He wondered if she thought the same thing. How alike they were. 'Snap!' he said, without thinking.

She grinned, a little puzzled. 'I'm so pleased to finally meet you.' She sounded more British than the guy had, with a twang of something else. But reverent, soft, in awe, like some sort of fangirl.

'Thanks…you too,' he found himself saying, equally star-struck. 'We're honoured to be here.'

She bowed her head, accepting the compliment solemnly, then smiled and gestured for everyone to gather round. It was the first time they'd performed since Sasha had gone and he felt weird about it. Disloyal. Ashamed that maybe he was a little glad she couldn't see this and that she'd been right, that maybe they weren't meant for each other. His rambling thoughts quickly dissipated as Raz began to talk.

'I want you to do a typical set, as if you were at one of your shows. Forget everyone out there,' she said, tipping her head to the huge crowd now sitting and chatting. You're playing this for me.' Then she nodded at the judges' table. 'And those guys over there.

'Just play and I'll jump in where I feel I can. Then you'll go and talk numbers and contracts, OK?'

Jace was still revelling in the sound of her voice, soft, with a tiny hint of a rasp. He bet it sounded fantastic when she sang. He tuned back in. Everything sounded reasonable enough. He glanced at Zach, who was nodding vigorously.

'Why don't you take a seat over there with my guys,' she said to Zach, pointing at the desk of judges.

Zach agreed, nervously, and touched him on the shoulder as he went. 'Good luck.'

Someone slipped a mic into his hand and Jace looked out at the lounging crowd, camped out as if they were at a festival. Lights were facing them right in the eyes and the room was so big, it was easy to imagine that was where they were. The edges were fuzzing as he felt the warm hug of the pill starting to take effect. He relaxed. Zach seemed to have taken his nerves with him and he breathed. His eyes landed on Raz, who winked to encourage him.

It was weird he should think of Sasha right then, but he did. It was so trippy, not just the druggy cloak he wore. He told himself that the collective had already done great things before they came here and they'd done it alone, with no help from anyone. Just the love of their loyal fanbase. Then Zach came and they had an agent. They'd done a small tour. Had record deals in the pipeline. Something in this felt rushed and out of his control. He almost dropped the mic and walked off stage, when Hat dropped a beat and then his jingle, 'TRU, TRU, TTTTRU, TRHBDor… High Hat on the beat!' And Ballistik kicked in with his biggest hit.

It worked like magic.

Jace skipped to the back of the stage, clapping as Ballistik came forward. Everyone else clapped and chanted, and the audience began to cheer and get to their feet. This was it. Familiar territory and Jace let it come to the fore. To hell with thought and negativity. This was what he was born for.

Everything made sense. They'd all do their biggest song, one by one and showcase their talent.

Tiny Tears went next and the beat broke down for a verse of Brain's street poetry, then hit hard for Jynskie and then Duo went into one of their duets and then he was out there, singing, speaking rhyme, doing everything instinctively and without thought. It was their biggest hit and got the place and everyone on the stage jumping. The whole collective seemed to know to put petty jealousies aside and take this as their one chance at superstardom.

It wasn't until then Jace realised that Raz had done very little. She was behind the desk with Hat, turning knobs and nodding along to the beat. He was unsure what that meant.

Then Hat slipped the beat into one of his solo songs that relied heavily on a sampled, popular guitar riff. She stepped out in front of him and played it live, slightly altering it to make it sound bigger and better than before. Perhaps to avoid copyright infringement, but most likely just to make it sound better, and it did. So much so. Once he overlaid his voice and it was looped into the song, he knew she was improving it live, in front of everyone's eyes. It was amazing to see her work. It was a masterclass in record production, except this was done in real time, in front of close to a thousand peers. She was definitely the creative influence of the family and the guys sitting behind the desk were the execs making the business decisions.

He began to rap and they faced each other. She played for him and he spoke to her. Often freestyling. No one else existed. They were in a dreamlike world of their own, he never wanted to leave. Then, in no time at all, the song was over. The song. The Set. Their time together. The lights dimmed and the world felt a colder, lonelier place.

Raz pointed at the men at the desk, just like with the band

before them. 'Go with them,' she said. 'They'll go through the paperwork with you.'

Jace stood there, stunned and confused. Disappointed. Like he knew it was what they were there for, but something supernatural or spiritual had just happened between them and no one was acknowledging it. They were back in the world as if nothing had happened.

'I'll find you later,' she said, as she walked past him.

He swallowed and shook his head to get it back online. Duo nudged his arm and he allowed him to steer him towards the edge of the stage. Zach was beckoning them excitedly. Raz's brothers, cousins, or whoever they were, were already walking away.

Jace followed in a dazed kind of shock.

JACE HAD to wait outside the room for what felt like hours as each member of the crew, including Zach, went in before him.

At last, Zach came out with a handkerchief wrapped around his hand. Where is everyone?' Jace asked, looking over Zach's shoulder to see if anyone was following. His buzz had long gone and he was feeling restless and agitated.

Zach didn't look so good. He looked tired and drained, like he'd just had a shock. He cut the air in front of him with his free hand. 'They went out the other way.' He rubbed his hand over his face and stared at him, making Jace start to dread what might be coming.

'What's the matter?'

Zach straightened and tried to look brighter. 'Nothing … I just came out to go through a few things with you before you go in.'

Jace frowned. 'OK.' He was starting to get really concerned about what Zach clearly found difficult to say.

Zach looked like a man who'd seen a ghost. 'What happened to your hand?' Jace asked, pointing as Zach inadvertently adjusted the bandage. Blood was seeping out of the sides of the white cotton. 'Is that blood?'

Zach lifted his hand and flipped it over and shrugged as if it was nothing. 'I dunno … must have caught it on something. Look, take a seat,' Zach said, pointing to a lone chair next to the wall.

Jace allowed him to lead him and sat down, still thoughtful. His hand was clearly something for him to have to wrap it with a makeshift bandage. Jace leaned forward and looked up at his agent warily.

'I just wanted to talk to you about what's going to happen in that room.' Zach was glaring at him in the eyes, the most serious he'd ever seen him. Like his life depended on it or something.

'I'm not a kid, Zach,' Jace said. 'I'm not going to start demanding pink Lamborghinis and orange M&Ms. He was joking, but Zach's face didn't move, making his unease with the place intensify.

'No, you don't understand, Jace. They will offer you a contract that you will accept. Do you get me?'

Jace went to stand up and just get on with it. Zach was acting weird and paranoid, and he couldn't handle it right now; he was nervous enough. But Zach grabbed his arm. 'A lot is riding on this – the whole future of the group rests on you. Their career … their lives.'

Jace stared into Zach's eyes, transfixed by the meaning in them. It was unlike Zach to talk so cryptically, let alone advise him to think of the collective as a whole. He was always trying to pull him away from them. But this—

'And mine,' Zach finished, deflated, holding up his bandaged hand.

Jace's mind scrambled and he laughed. The whole thing started to feel ridiculous.

'Do you understand?' Zach said, reiterating and still refolding the now blood-soaked handkerchief.

It was like he'd entered some sort of bad dream. Like a horror film where he was being given some dread-filled warning: 'don't talk to anyone, don't look at anyone, just nod and keep your head down and you might make it out alive. *God, he must be losing it.* He needed to sleep off the drugs. 'Do you have any more Xans?' came out before he could think more deeply on it.

Zach sighed, rolled his eyes and held out one from his pocket. 'You need your head straight for this, Jace. Please. This is the contract of your life.' He poked him in his chest. 'Your life. My life. Your friend's lives and Sasha's,' he finished a little more sheepishly.

He lost him at Sasha. She wasn't even there. Then the thought occurred to him, 'What, they want her too?' It was just the excuse he needed to call her and get her to come back. However, his smile evaporated at Zach's uncomfortable body language.

Jace sagged wearily. 'What is it, Zach?' The scare tactics were wearing thin now.

Zach took a breath and Jace thought he was going to say something, but he nudged him instead. 'Just go in. Sign your contract and know that it's a good one. Congratulations! You're about to be one of the biggest stars on the planet.'

Outwardly, Zach looked pleased and Jace allowed himself to be shuffled along, but he couldn't help noticing the tension in Zach's jaw and the raised vein throbbing at his temple. Maybe he was just fraught after working hard on all the negotiations. This was the culmination of his life's work and he was making life harder for him. He pulled Zach into a tight hug. 'Thank you, Zach,' he said, thumping his back. He put him away from him, smiling wryly. 'I doubt that could happen to an emo-rap artist, but thanks.'

Zach smiled stiffly, as if there was so much more he wanted to say, but Jace dismissed it with a wave of his hand, and he went up to face the large oak door and knocked loudly.

'Come in,' a male voice said from the other side.

When he looked over his shoulder, Zach had gone.

CHAPTER 7

*J*ace was initially startled by the room he walked into. It wasn't so much the décor, which was dark and gothic black and reds, in keeping with the rest of the place; it was more to do with there being far more people in it than he was expecting.

The three guys from earlier were there, sitting, facing him at a huge, dark, wooden table and there were at least another four guards stationed around the room. A fire was roaring in the tall fireplace, biting his face and making him sweat already.

'Take a seat,' one of the men said, holding his hand out to the single chair placed directly opposite them.

Jace sat slowly, looking over his shoulder as two more guards came in and stood by the door. He faced front and looked at the three men apprehensively after Zach's pep talk. They were all big guys, tall and far better built than him. They were good-looking and ranged in age from their late twenties to thirties, he'd say at a guess. Their hair was black and oiled back, revealing handsome, shrewd faces with eyes like Raz's. Except for them, they looked icy and predatory.

They had to be part of the same family. *Mafia?* It was hard to tell. They seemed too good-looking to be hardmen, although their aura of menace was palpable.

He was sitting in a solitary carved wooden chair designed to make him feel small and isolated. He coughed and shifted uncomfortably.

The one who'd spoken smiled to reveal his perfect white teeth and pushed an A4 manila envelope towards him. It had to be the contract he was expecting. Jace reached forward, picked it up, and pulled out the several-page document. The paper felt thick and weird, like no paper he'd ever felt before and the ink on it was real. Black with swirly loops, making it difficult to read.

A guard came from behind him and put down an old-fashioned quill in a stand and a pot of ink next to it. Jace looked at it, startled, and then across at the main guy questioningly. He'd never used anything like it.

The guy chuckled and the other two joined him. He waved his hand to urge him on. 'Do not worry. Your fellow band members have all signed before you and your agent has vouched for you all.'

It was a strange choice of words. Jace put it down to his European origins. He looked down at the paper and saw the long list of scrawled, untidy names – the real and the stage name next to them, with Zach and a messy red smudge next to it. *Blood.* His mind shot to the bandage around his hand. They must have hated him messing up their fancy document.

'Mr Bennington's blood, as you see,' the guy said, creepily echoing his thoughts.

The two guys chuckled on either side of him as if they were enjoying an in-joke.

Jace leaned forward and gingerly picked up the quill and looked at it. He guessed it wasn't that hard to use. He'd seen enough films to know roughly what to do with it. He dipped it in the ink pot twice, tapped it on the hard edge to get off any loose drops, then took a breath and held it while he put the scratchy nib to the paper under Zach. Before he moved the quill, something made him stop. 'What do I get? I mean, what do you do for the artists that sign with you?' He knew Zach would have negotiated a deal for him, but it seemed pretty important to ask at that point. The guy in front of him narrowed his eyes and took him in for a moment that felt like an uncomfortable ten, until he relaxed back into his chair. He steepled his fingers as if he was considering something.

The fire was burning the side of Jace's face, although his sweat felt cold. He felt a shuffle behind him, but the guy across from him shook his head slightly as if to stop something. Jace looked startled over his shoulder at the guard now directly behind him. Something was definitely off about this situation. He felt vulnerable, like he had to tell himself over and over that he'd done nothing wrong. He was just an artist about to sign his first contract, a deal that would catapult him to stardom. It was a deal. That was all. 'It's a fair question, isn't it?' Jace said, trying to regain some of his composure and facing the guy again.

The guy inclined his head. 'Indeed, it is. Let us begin again with proper introductions… I am Tegan and these are my brothers, Taj and Rollo. We belong to a very old and distinguished family, with many connections, reaching into every corner of society.'

Jace nodded once. It made sense. He knew they had to be connected, but he still didn't know what any of that had to do with signing a recording contract with him and his friends.

Tegan narrowed his eyes, reminding him of a bird of prey, sizing him up for the kill. 'I can see why you excel far beyond your band-mates. You are single-minded and shrewd.' He held his hand out to the papers again. 'Sign and you will succeed.'

Jace studied the three men watching him closely. They were all smiling but with hunger in their eyes. Like they couldn't wait for him to sign. This felt like so much more than about music.

'You will be courted by the world's media. Your music will reach every home and you will have riches beyond your wildest dreams. You will no longer have to waste your time on the humdrum necessities of life. You will be free to concentrate on what you love best – the creation of your art.'

It was a seductive offer and for a guy he'd never met, he knew him well. Or maybe it was what all artists wanted to hear. 'And what do you get?' Jace said, looking down at the cursive writing in front of him. The legal jargon seemed to go on and on without actually saying anything he needed to know.

'Perhaps Rollo can best explain it for you,' Tegan said, turning his head to his brother.

A similar version of him, in a darker grey suit, began to speak, but he didn't once look down at the paper to read the words he was supposed to be interpreting. He knew them by heart. 'You, the undersigned, do pledge to the Carpathian family, group and all its subsidiaries, for perpetuity. The undersigned will accept management from its chosen agent: Zach Bennington.'

Jace recognised Zach's scrawling signature.

'Merchandise, live tours, recordings, session musicians, collaborations, interviews, endorsements, to be arranged by the delegated agent of the Carpathian group.'

It all still sounded confusing and heavily weighted in their favour. Then he said the one thing he really understood: 'At a rate of fifty-one per cent. Terms of the contract are binding. Artists listed in the collective known as TRHB-

Dor, are subject to compliance from the lead signatory, Jacek Novacek and underwritten by Zach Bennington. In the event of non-compliance with the said contract, by the lead signatory…'

All the while the guy spoke, without faulting once, Jace became more and more convinced he knew the contract because he'd said the spiel so many times. He sounded bored, like a kid reciting tables. Jace hated business talk and the legal stuff that went with it. He just wanted to make music. He'd always left that shit to other people, namely, Sasha. She dealt with everyday life, allowing him to keep his head in the clouds. But even he knew, from the extensive use of many words, they sought to trap and mislead him into something totally one-sided. 'So let me get this straight,' Jace said, when he finally got the opportunity to speak. 'You'll own fifty-one per cent of everything I make. My friends are only included if I agree to sign it and Zach is liable if I break the contract in some way. And this is for my whole career?' Jace said, knowing that that part couldn't be right.

'For life!' The three guys all said together.

Jace sat there looking at the three of them, stunned. The silence was only broken with a knock at the door and Zach entering the room. Jace felt a huge wash of relief. 'Do you know what's in this?' Jace said, still not quite believing he'd heard right.

Zach shifted his feet uncomfortably and the guy, Tegan, just continued like he wasn't there. 'No one is forcing you to do anything, Jacek. You can simply walk out of here and never be bothered by any of this again. Or you can have a forty-nine per cent piece of a multi-million-dollar jugger-naut that will support your family, friends and associates, for the rest of your natural life.'

There he went again with the weird word choices that made it sound like he was being nitpicky. Jace looked over at

Zach for any hint at what he should do. Surely it was his job to negotiate for what was best for him. Instead, he widened his eyes and bobbed his head towards the paperwork on the table. 'Better than a hundred per cent of nothin', Zach said, but he was sweating and looked far from relaxed.

On the surface, it sounded reasonable. Then why didn't it feel right? His gut told him that if Sasha were there, she would have told him to take the time to think about it. 'What about Sasha? She hasn't been included,' Jace said, like a bolt of inspiration.

Tegan smiled as if he knew he was stalling, reminding him more and more of a wolf. 'This is a music contract. We'll look into something separately for a clothes designer. I'm looking forward to meeting her,' he said, his smile widening.

Jace felt a sudden chill. He hated the way he spoke about her, like he'd enjoy corrupting her in some way. He knew it wasn't rational and he should be pleased she'd get something out of this, but something made him want to keep her as far away from these guys as possible. It was the final nudge he needed. 'I'd like to take some time to think about it ... if that's OK?'

Tegan raised his eyebrows and let out a single blast of laughter. He looked left and right at his brothers as if he couldn't believe his ears, but was quite amused by it. Then the smile dropped suddenly from his face. 'I'm afraid our offer is rather time sensitive. I leave for Geneva in thirty minutes.' Then he leaned forward over the table menacingly, making Jace sink back away from him in his chair. 'Make no mistake, Jacek Novacek. This is a once-in-a-lifetime offer to be the artist you always dreamed of.'

'Stop fucking around and just sign it!' Zach said, stamping a foot forward and making him jump. He seemed so angry that the guard put his arm out to stop his progress. It made Jace stare at his whole demeanour in shock. He was cradling his injured hand, and there was more than just anger in his eyes; there was desperation. Fear. *What the hell was going on here?*

Jace looked back at Tegan. 'Will I get to record an album right away?'

'Yes, there will be many.' A slow smile of satisfaction was now creeping over Tegan's face.

'Will I get to work with Raz?'

His wolf-like smile widened even further. 'Of course.'

'Can you write it into the contract?'

Zach rolled his eyes and said something under his breath.

'And Sasha definitely won't be included?'

Tegan looked at his brothers and chuckled. Then he inclined his head. 'As you wish … I can see you drive a hard bargain … Is that everything?' he said, tipping his head towards the paperwork again.

Jace racked his brains. He had him on a roll and he didn't want to lose the opportunity. The other thing that was bothering him was being tied for life, 'And the lifetime thing is a deal-breaker?'

'It is,' Tegan said, smiling regretfully.

Jace could never see past thirty, *shit,* he never saw past twenty-five, but the others were a different story. They could well live long and productive lives and never be free to produce a single note for anyone else. Then it came to him like a bolt out of the blue, so dramatic and ridiculous that even he thought he was being paranoid. Because he was undoubtedly on his come-down. But he simply had to say it. 'So everything in that contract rests on me, you say?'

'It does,' Tegan said, narrowing his eyes like he wondered where he was going with this.

Then can I just add that it lasts as long as I live, then everyone else in it is free? If, like you say … it's all down to me?'

Tegan's eyes narrowed further and the smug smile drained from his face. It felt like a small victory. Jace's heart began to beat hard as the two brothers leaned in to gabble in their language. Jace glanced at Zach and the strange look he saw in his eyes troubled him more than anything. He looked worried, but there was gratitude and maybe even an apology. He couldn't be sure.

'Very well,' Tegan said, dragging him from his thoughts. 'With one proviso: suicide. In a business like this, it simply couldn't be valid,' he said, knowingly. He leaned forward and pulled the papers and the quill back towards him.

Jace ran quickly over the implications and couldn't see himself offing himself any time soon. He'd be unreasonable to labour that one. No company in their right mind would underwrite suicide – especially a rock star.

Tegan scribbled a few lines in the space before the signature line. 'There. All your demands have been met. Sign it now. I need to leave.'

A guard came forward and put the papers in front of Jace again. He swallowed, picked up the quill, and copied the way Tegan had used it. He'd won a victory, but it didn't feel like one. He couldn't shake the thought that he was signing away his life. He let out a long breath, dipped the quill in the ink, and tapped the excess off onto the rim. Then he scratched his name on the paper: Jacek Novacek and then Lil Jace next to it, just as the others had done above him.

As soon as he'd put a dot on the page, it was whisked out from under his hand, and the three brothers were on their feet. 'A wise choice,' Tegan said, just before he went out the door. 'You will stay for a couple of days to settle in and learn what is expected of you.' Then he disappeared with his brothers and the guards, leaving him and Zach alone.

Zach visibly sagged with relief as if an invisible force had been holding him up the whole time. 'Thank God!'

Jace glared at Zach, too angry for words. Even though his gut said he didn't know any more about this than he did, something told him that these guys didn't mess around and if he'd refused to sign, none of them would have been around long enough to talk about it. 'I don't think God has anything to do with it.'

CHAPTER 8

*J*ace found his way back to the huge lounge and flopped back down on the bean bag he'd left no more than an hour earlier. A girl quickly brought him a tall alcoholic drink, which he accepted gladly, gulping the whole thing down without knowing what it was. He was unbelievably thirsty.

He relaxed back into the bag, knowing he should feel elated or at the very least happy after signing such a huge deal, but he felt hollow and sad, like something had been taken away from him, not given.

Zach had sheepishly disappeared right after the meeting, and the rest of his troupe were nowhere to be found. They should all be celebrating. Instead, he was alone, and where earlier the lounge seemed full of cool musicians strumming and relaxing, now everything seemed different. The mood had shifted and it had escalated into a raucous party, right out of his nightmares.

A death metal band began playing ferociously and the audience he'd once recognised had become anonymous faces wearing white masks. They were laughing hysterically, shrieking and falling about on the floor and pulling the struggling waiting staff down with them. The light breakfast trays of earlier were now heavy with bottles of hard liquor being grabbed by arms in a tangled mess on the floor. Others were laden with bowls of different coloured sweets that he soon realised were pills, when another followed, piled high with vials of white powder.

Every direction he looked, people were kissing and writhing like some sort of Roman orgy. He'd been to some wild parties in his time and nothing usually shocked him, but he'd never seen anything like this, on such a large scale, by the people looked up to like gods. Maybe he needed to process the meeting, or maybe he hadn't had enough drugs and he was down to his raw nerves. He couldn't tell. The large drink he'd downed was definitely fuzzing the edges, but he couldn't stand it – this place, the hundreds of wailing, faceless people. His head hurt and he tried to block it out by closing his eyes for a few moments. This was the point where he usually took himself off to hide. The idea appealed. There must be hundreds of rooms, so he quickly got to his feet. He picked his way through the moving bodies, careful not to tread on a writhing arm or someone's hair.

He got to the corridor and breathed, but he still couldn't relax as he wasn't alone. Couples and even threesomes were entwined against the walls, groaning and gasping in door-ways. It seemed like behind every door he tried to open, he was greeted by people having sex. All of which he wouldn't mind betting had appeared on MTV at some point. It was beginning to hit him the sheer scale of what he'd got himself into. If the wolf cousins got fifty-one percent of everything made in this room, then no wonder they were so rich and powerful. This place was a castle. He even found the indoor pool, where the party was continuing in the water. People were cavorting on mats and sun loungers, while some off-his-face hippie strummed guitar. He was crazy good and if he wasn't so creeped out, he would have stayed to listen.

As he turned for the door, a waitress passed with her tray. He lightly tapped her arm and pointed at the bowls she was carrying with his eyebrows up in a question. She balanced the tray on her hand and pointed at each of the bowls with her other. 'BlueBoys, Ket, Doves, Coke and some Golden Leb,' she said while she chewed her gum.

Jace's eyes lit up at the light-brown cubes of resin. 'I'll take that,' he said, quickly.

'Do you have papers?' she asked, while she pulled out a pack from a gun belt full of them around her waist.

Jace patted his back pocket and, realising he was out, smiled at her and took the pack she was offering.

'Enjoy!' she said, quickly moving off before he could ask how much he needed to pay.

He raised his eyebrows and guessed that was his first company perk.

He wandered back to the maze of hallways and corridors and took the route where the noise became quieter, until the party became non-existent behind him. He eventually came out into a huge red-and-gold atrium. Its centrepiece was a large chandelier the size of a small car and a sweeping stair-case that split in two directions and met at the top. Something told him he shouldn't be in this part of the house, but the alternative pushed him onwards. Besides, he needed a place to build his joint and think. It had been one crazy day.

Jace felt tired and decided to venture upstairs, with no clue what time of day or night it was, or even if he would wake up from a dream. He kept going. Huge paintings of lords and ladies adorned the cream-stone walls, and the deep red and gold carpet runner continued down yet another hall-way. He followed it, figuring that at least it was quiet up here.

Nagging at the back of his mind was the constant feeling that he'd made some monumental mistake in signing that contract. He told himself it was fear of commitment. He was an artist and if he wanted to eat, then he'd have to sign one sometime. He and his crew had reached as far as they could on their own. This was the leg up they needed to take them to the next level.

He slowly wandered past door after door, each with a pedestal and a white statue, or a plant pot in between. As he walked, his thoughts churned. *And that was another thing. Why all the secrecy?* If they were an old and successful family, why did they need to hide? He started opening doors and peeping inside. They were all bedrooms. Each one was lavishly deco-rated like some high-class hotel and appeared unused.

'Going somewhere?' a female voice said from right behind him.

He whirled around and there she was. *Raz.* The tiny, perfectly formed doll of a rock star who played insane guitar that no one had ever heard of. Even that didn't make sense. She was Hendrix-good. She should be fronting her own band.

This close, and in the light, he got a perfect look at her. Her mousy hair was quite long and wavy with flecks of blonde, as if it had been caught by the sun. Her skin was smooth and tanned, but he became stuck on her tattoos. They were grey symbols or writing that accentuated her cheekbones, disappearing under a bundle of necklaces, into the open neck of her tank top. Then they continued down in Japanese-like columns, to her small, well-formed breasts and down her arms. He wouldn't mind betting they went on past her tiny, belted waist and under her weather-beaten jeans.

Everything about them was deliberate and well-placed. Whoever had inked her had been a master of the contours of muscle and bone. They were breathtakingly good.

'I asked you a question,' she prompted, making him aware he was openly staring at her. 'You shouldn't be here.'

Even her voice, with its sexy rasp, he could listen to all day. 'Sorry,' he said, finally snapping himself out of it. He opted for honesty. 'Just being nosy. I just wanted to find a quiet spot to smoke this,' he said, holding up the small cube of resin.

She narrowed her eyes as if she were considering whether to believe him. Then she overtook him and, taking a key from her pocket, went up to the next door. She turned the lock, pushed the door open and looked back at him. 'Come inside. You'll get into trouble if someone finds you out here.'

Without a second thought, Jace entered the room. Not only was she the most interesting girl he'd ever met, but he couldn't think of a single person more qualified to talk about any of this with. It was a perfect opportunity.

However, when he got inside, his jaw dropped open. The room was movie-set huge. Like a film he'd seen from the 90s of some billionaire kid, or something. It had a basketball hoop, juke box, circular bed that he had no idea really existed and rich velvet-red curtains at least thirty feet high.

She followed him in, closed the door and began taking off the many beads and necklaces around her neck. She hung them over a rack on her carved dressing table that was at least ten feet long. Then she went to a drawer, took out some clothing and disappeared behind a Chinese screen. He turned a circle, taking in what was clearly her bedroom.

There was a ladder that took you to a library of books near the ceiling, you could reach no other way, and a wall bracket displaying at least six electric guitars and countless acoustic ones underneath.

Although it was the far-right wall that made him approach to examine it. Floor to ceiling, there were hundreds of photographs, mainly black-and-white, with a few in colour. He skated over them all; they were so unexpected. He imagined they'd be filled with every famous rock star she would undoubtedly know personally, but they weren't. Every photo was of some spectacular natural place or a study of wildlife, flora and fauna. A single bee caught covered in nectar or a tiny bird hovering next to a hole in a tree. A waterfall over some exotic lagoon, a mountain range, or a field of wildflowers. Even an old junkyard overrun by weeds with handwritten scrawl in the corner, 'Nature always wins'. Each one was solitary and peaceful and without a single person in them. It was a huge window into her personality.

'Do you like nature?' she said from right behind him, making him jump and whirl around.

He was about to answer truthfully and say that, with his lifestyle, he rarely thought about it or got to see it, but she'd changed into the cutest little girl pyjamas he'd ever seen. They were short-sleeved, white with tiny pink flowers all over, with her brown, little tattooed feet poking out from the ankle of matching trousers. Her hair was now scooped into a high ponytail on top of her head like a cheerleader's pompom. She'd gone from rock chick to cute chick in sixty seconds. 'Yeah, the photos are great,' he said, coughing away his broken voice. 'Do you know the photographer? They're crazy good.' They really were. He was no expert, but even he could see that.

Her face brightened into the most brilliant smile, wrinkling the corners of those unusual feral eyes. 'I took them … all of them. It's a hobby of mine…I don't get to escape much.'

He widened his eyes in amazement and looked back at the wall. They were expert-level good. The kind that appeared in *National Geographic. Was there nothing this girl couldn't do?*

He turned his head back to praise her, but her face had fallen as if he'd said something to offend her. She turned and walked away, sadly and he followed. 'Wait! … what's wrong? They're fantastic. Honestly,' he said, desperately racking his brains for what he'd done to make her think he didn't like them.

She dismissed it with her hand and went and sat on her huge circular bed that made her look even younger. 'No, it's OK. It's not your fault. You're just thinking the same thing everyone does. 'She's so lucky…she can do everything.' Everyone says it, or at least thinks it. No one understands, that's all.'

Jace looked around for someplace else to sit. He didn't want to get on the bed with her. It seemed too presumptuous, somehow. He opted for a small armchair next to the dressing table. He sat, put his long legs out in front of him and, crossing them at the ankle, clasped his hands across his abdomen. 'OK then. Enlighten me. Explain to me why people thinking that you're good at everything would upset you so much. I kind of like it when people think I'm good at something." He raised an eyebrow and gave her a lopsided grin when his mind shot straight to sex.

It worked as she smiled and crossed her legs to get more comfortable. 'If I tell you a secret, will you promise not to tell anyone?'

Jace frowned, trying not to smile at her cuteness and nodded, completely intrigued as to what it could be.

Then she looked him stonily in the eye and delivered the blow that could have only been surpassed if she'd admitted to secretly being a guy. 'I have never done an original thing in my life. I am incapable of it.'

Jace just stared at her, struggling to sift through the words to understand what the hell she was saying.

'I mean, I can play … anything … any instrument, really well. I can take photos and portray what I can see. But that's just it. I copy and enhance what is already there. I can't make anything up right from the beginning like you guys do. I add my part and the magic happens, that's it.'

Jace looked at her, dumbstruck. She was playing with her fingers in her lap like she'd just revealed a secret she'd carried for ever. He looked over at the rack of guitars and then at the wall of superb photos. He didn't understand why she thought she couldn't create anything. Her talent was undeniable, and he'd only just met her. 'You don't understand just how fantastic you are, do you?' he said.

She looked up sharply and then shook her head as if he didn't get it.

'Art is about interpretation. All of it. Your take on a book, what you see in a painting. I don't know you that well, but I can tell you that what you see is amazing.' He strode over to the wall of photos and pointed out a particularly good one, capturing a simple rabbit looking out over a barren range into a sunset. 'This one! This isn't about a cute bunny or even a great sunset. You saw and captured a moment where the rabbit looked out in wonder. At nature. At its future and whether it would see another day. You caught it and printed it and kept that moment for us all to see for ever. That's a pretty marvellous thing. And you do the same with the music. You're amazing. You take a simple track and you weave your magic and enhance it into something even the creators didn't see. You're kind of awesome.'

He walked back over to the bed and came to a standstill and studied her. Her eyes stayed on him the whole time, but they were glassy with tears. 'Thank you … for saying that,' she said, quickly wiping away a tear as it fell with the back of her hand. 'But you don't really understand—'

Before he could say anything, there was a knock at the door and the huge blond soldier-looking guy he recognised put his head inside without coming in. It annoyed Jace instantly, as he hadn't waited for permission. His eyes immediately flicked to Jace in surprise and then went back to Raz. 'Oh, you've already found each other. Good! Your cousins wanted you to spend some time together, that's all.'

The guy's eyes rested on Jace again and he nodded once. 'I'll leave you to it.' Then he disappeared. It was the weirdest, totally one-sided, non-conversation Jace had ever witnessed. It got his back up as it was clear in just a couple of sentences that Raz was ordered around and controlled by those bigger, older cousins who didn't have an ounce of her talent. 'Who was that guy?' Jace asked, not able to hide his annoyance.

'Oh, Steve, he's OK. He looks after me. He's like a big brother.'

I bet. His mind was already whirling on possible family connections and who was what to who. 'Does he always keep such a close eye on you?'

She brightened instantly and nodded, not seeing his barb at all. It made him instantly ashamed. It was becoming clear that she was incredibly sheltered and had experienced very little of the real outside world. It made it very easy for the unscrupulous men around her to manipulate her. 'So,' Jace said, quickly, to change the subject. 'They want us to spend time together ... Do you normally do that with your newly signed artists?'

She shook her head and lay down on her front, picking at a flower on her bed throw. 'No, never really. I choose them and I only get to meet them on the stage, really ... and the studio, after. I picked you. You're the first I've sneaked in here,' she said, grinning.

Something twisted in his gut at the innocent girl grinning at him. How was it possible when she was surrounded by all this debauchery? 'So you don't get involved in the artists' contracts.' He just knew that for a fact, before she even said anything. She was all for the music, like him.

She shook her head, taking it as a question. 'No, I have no interest in any of that kind of stuff. I leave business to my brother.'

Brother? Now Jace was totally confused. 'I thought those guys were your cousins?'

She nodded, sitting up, facing him again. 'And they are. They sign all the bands and musicians. My brother, Demeter, is like me. He helps corporations and financial institutions. He finds them struggling, weaves his magic and makes them bigger and richer. Just like me!' she finished brightly.

She was so endearing, and yet there was something raw and almost primal about her. Maybe it was just the tattoos, he wasn't sure. It was starting to make a little sense now, though in a far more disturbing way than he first thought.

There were two of them: a brother and a sister. One took care of the music industry and the other one, commerce. It was all far bigger than he ever imagined, and off. So far off that he had to question his level of paranoia because a word kept bouncing around in his head: evil. That was it. He couldn't shake off the feeling.

He took in the innocent girl fidgeting in front of him and it was hard to think of her as anything other than talented and beautiful. She was a prisoner; *she had to be.* Forced to work for her evil cousins.

Then she said the words that stopped his heart dead. 'I think you should stay here tonight.'

Jace simply stared at her. *Did she not know who he was – his reputation?*

'You're trying to fight it, but you can't.' Her face dropped and she looked genuinely sorry. 'You're stuck now. Sorry. You may as well stay with me and we can be trapped together.' she finished with a sly smile spreading over her face that looked sexy and gorgeous. 'Two trapped birds in a cage,' she said, laughing and looking at her wall of photos.

Jace laughed along with her, but now understood a huge part of her – the music, her photos. They were all her way of setting herself free.

CHAPTER 9

ace now felt beyond tired. 'What time is it?' *What day is it?* More to the point.

Raz tapped a small box on the nightstand next to her bed. '3 p.m.,' she said.

'Saturday?'

'No, Sunday,' she said, smiling. 'You lost a day,' she said, laughing. 'I do that all the time,' she said, with an adorably puzzled look on her face.

Jace shook his head. Somewhere between leaving LA, travelling, the time difference and the party, she was right.

Her look turned sympathetic, as if she hated it when that happened. It made him wonder if it was self-inflicted, like him, or whether they did something to her. It made no sense, but he felt suddenly protective of her. The feeling was strange. Unchartered. He'd never protected anything in his life before. He felt a sudden jab of shame when he remembered Sasha. That job had fallen to her.

'Do you want to sleep a while?' she said, making him study her closely for any hidden innuendo, but there wasn't.

He was beginning to realise she said exactly what was on her mind. No games. That was rare. He had to admit that he was in the presence of someone truly honest, with absolutely no guile at all. It was sobering. 'I could use some,' she said with a small frown as if she was scared she'd offended him in some way.

It made him feel instantly unworthy. He stood up from his chair and looked around for somewhere else for him to sleep. He felt her eyes on him the whole time. 'Do you know where my room is? I'd like to find the others, settle in. That kind of stuff,' he said, not meeting her eyes. When he glanced at her again, she was lying down with her head on the pillow, watching him. 'OK. Steve will be outside. He can show you.' She turned over and faced the other way.

He stood there for a long moment, wondering whether he should apologise or not. She was clearly disappointed. He felt bad about leaving her so alone here, but not as bad as he'd feel if he got into that bed and took advantage of her. He hardly knew her and yet he felt responsible for her somehow. He scratched his head and made for the door. It was the lack of sleep and the strange place. He'd feel better in the morning. He just needed to get back to his friends. 'Bye!' he said, just before he opened the door.

'Yeah, bye,' she said, sounding half asleep already. Then, just before he disappeared, she added, 'Don't worry, Sasha will come soon.'

Jace came to a sudden halt. 'Sasha?' he repeated, looking back at the bed over his shoulder. 'She's in Pittsburgh.' A pain twisted his gut in a knot. He hated the idea of her coming here and mixing with all this. He wanted her far away, where he felt everything was cosy and safe. It was controlling and illogical, but he thought it just the same. Then he thought of the boardroom of wolf cousins. That made his skin crawl and he knew he'd never change his mind. 'Why do they want her?' he said, turning round to face her properly. 'She left the collective and she's not a musician.' His jaw tightened as his anger gained momentum.

'Don't worry,' she said, dreamily. 'My brother, Demeter, is going to meet her especially.' He wanted to stride up to the bed and shake her awake to explain, but he was conscious of the door now open and Steve giving him the evil eye from outside. Instead, he strode past him, angrily, barely able to look him in the eye. This close, he was built and would flatten him with one open palm. 'Can you take me to my room, please?' he had to ask, when he realised he had no idea where he was going.

Steve took a walkie-talkie from his belt. 'I need someone to take our new boy to his room, over.'

His words cut through his anger haze.

'Roger that!' came back immediately.

Steve's stare penetrated him with its steely-blue directness.

Jace pushed his hands deep into his pockets and shuffled his feet. He wasn't too tired and wasted to know he'd have nothing useful to say.

Thankfully, a girl in the staff's black smock and trousers came quickly and asked him to follow her.

He nodded a thank-you and registered the hostile look from Steve as he walked away. *Shit, this place was messing with his head.* He needed to call Sasha and keep her as far away from it as possible.

He followed the girl silently, churning the strange night and day's events over and over in his head. Thankfully, the girl didn't try to start a conversation. She was obviously used to being around musicians and was no longer star-struck. Or maybe she'd been instructed not to and it was more than her job was worth. He wondered then if everyone stayed over for days as he had. His mind buffeted around like that, all the while, as he tried to map the way as he went. Although in the end, with all the lefts and rights, upstairs and down in elevators, he soon lost track. Whatever he thought about, his thoughts always drifted back to Raz. *Who the hell was she?* How could someone that beautiful and that talented seem that tragic? But that's how he felt about her: desperately sorry that she seemed so lonely. He barely knew her and yet he could already tell she wasn't just cosseted and protected but guarded and watched like some prized possession. It didn't feel right.

And the other thorn in his side: why send for Sasha? Why now? Did they really need a designer, or another way to control *him?*

They came to a stop outside a door. 'This is yours,' the girl said, pushing the door open and leading the way inside. 'The bathroom is in there,' she said, pointing to another door. 'There's TV, a stocked fridge and a phone next to the bed you can use anytime for room service.' It was so normal that he wondered if he was actually losing his mind. He thanked her and she went, leaving him convinced he just needed to sleep off the drugs and the strange day. He sat on the bed and pulled off his shoes. He could be in any hotel room anywhere in the world. There were closed red drapes with a matching throw on the bed. An abstract painting was also picking up the red theme. Everything was clean, simple, and serviceable as it was undoubtedly reproduced similarly over several of the rooms.

His eyes rested on the phone and, remembering Sasha, he scooted across the bed and lifted the receiver. 'Hello,' a voice immediately said. 'This is the housekeeper. I'm happy to take your order.'

'Can I get an outside line, please?' Jace said, feeling his heart race as if he were running away.

'I'm afraid I can't give that to you, Mr Novacek. It is company policy to keep the Carpathian estate location secret.'

It sounded reasonable enough as he replaced the receiver. They'd taken their phones as soon as they got on the plane. Then why did he feel so trapped? His heart was tripping, he was sweating and the room felt small. Too small. He had to get a grip. He slowly lay flat on the downy quilt and his head sank into the incredibly soft pillows. It was OK. He'd warn Sasha as soon as he got out of this place. His eyelids felt suddenly heavy. She was safely away and they'd take a while to find her. The world finally, slowly, drifted away.

JACE WOKE up to a towel thrown over his face. He lifted his head, and an ache slammed into his forehead, forcing it flat again. He blinked, taking a moment to remember where he was.

'What are you doing in here?' he said, realising the room invasion was Zach.

Zach was muttering and buzzing around the room, looking for something, until he felt the bed shake as he dumped his bag on the bed. 'Good! You didn't unpack … Get up! We're leaving. The cars are leaving in ten.'

The agitated tone in Zach's voice, rather than what he was saying, was what snapped Jace out of his just-woken grog. He pulled himself up on his elbows. 'What's the rush? Can't I get a coffee first?'

'You can get one on the plane. You've slept for ten hours, Jace. We can't wait any longer. We need to leave.'

'Didn't we just get here?' Jace grumbled, sitting up and throwing his legs over the side of the bed.

Zach was throwing his clothes at him, one by one, as he picked them up off the floor.

It would have been nice to have had a shower and a change of clothes, but Zach was hot and flustered and completely unmovable in his decision to leave, so Jace began pulling his clothes together.

The guys aren't happy and we're about to have a mutiny if you don't hurry up. And don't forget my neck's on the line. We need to leave NOW!' Zach shouted when Jace paused to take in the panic on his face.

'OK…OK,' Jace said, finally getting up and padding to the bathroom. He used the facilities and took a two-minute shower, letting the water soothe his pounding skull and wash into his sandpaper-dry mouth. *Ten hours.* He'd somehow lost another day. 'Why aren't they happy?' Jace called out, wrapping a towel around his waist.

'Get dressed and I'll explain on the way.'

Jace dropped the towel and pulled on yesterday's jeans, t-shirt and Vans. Then, finally, his oversized biker jacket with a Day of the Dead skull on the back. Then he overtook Zach, throwing his bag over his shoulder and with his hair wet and unbrushed, he left the room. Another staff member showed them through the endless corridors. Guards soon joined them, and they went downward in a lift to the underground car park, where everyone was waiting in a noisy group.

Ballsy was shoving Brains, and Brains rarely argued with anyone. Duo was coming between them to break them up.

Zach immediately strode up to them and bellowed: 'Get in the fucking cars, now!' Then he glared at them all until they sorted themselves out into groups and got into the SUVs, parked in a row, with their engines running.

Zach nudged Jace along to the one in front and got in behind him, muttering, 'It's not your lives at stake, it's mine. Now move!'

Jace got in the backseat, stiffly, looking at Zach's intense expression, wondering if he was still asleep. If he was, this wasn't pleasant and had all the markings of a bad trip. He thought for the millionth time, thank God Sasha was far away. Then he remembered Raz's parting words that she was on her way.

He sat forward, alert, with a sharp intake of breath, and grabbed the door handle.

'What is it?' Zach asked immediately.

'Stop! I need to get out.' Jace pulled and pushed, but the door wouldn't budge.

The car moved off and Jace attempted to wind down the window, but that only went down a few inches.

'We've got to go, Jace. What is it?' Zach said, pulling on his arm to sit back.

'You don't understand,' Jace said frantically, now bashing on the window with the heel of his hand.

The guard in the front twisted around and pointed at him. 'Stop that! Calm down, or I'll put you down.'

Jace blinked back at him in shock, then looked at Zach again. 'You heard that, right?'Zach just closed his eyes.

The car built up speed and screeched out of the building into the light. 'Sasha is coming,' Jace said, frantically, watching the building disappear behind them. 'I can't leave her alone with those people.'

Zach's expression softened to one of sympathy. 'Don't worry. We can call her as soon as we can. We had to leave. It's not a choice. I know they won't hurt her.'

Jace looked deeply into Zach's dark eyes in anguish and asked himself in what universe would someone even say something like that, and at the same time knew that he meant it. And he knew why: because she was useful.

'You have my word,' Zach said, bringing his attention back to him.

This whole thing had gotten so out of control. He didn't understand any of it, but he knew how he felt and that was scared. Signing a deal should not feel like this. That much he did know. Something was very wrong here and Sasha was walking right into it.

'What's going on, Zach? Why is everyone fighting?' He tried to remember the course of their visit. It was a little hazy, but he hadn't been that out of it. They'd played their set for Raz. OK, the contract signing had been weird. He'd found Raz and gone to her room. 'What did I miss? I didn't touch her, I promise,' Jace said, suddenly panicking, that it was the only thing he could be accused of.

Zach looked irritated and rolled his eyes, like he didn't know the half of it.

Slightly relieved, Jace dropped his gaze to Zach's hand resting in his lap, now dressed in a proper bandage. 'Well, what the hell happened then, Zach?' Jace said, finally allowing himself to relax back into his seat and wait for an explanation.

Zach glanced nervously at the guards in the front. 'On the plane,' he said quietly.

'Plane!' Jace repeated, loudly. 'Where the hell are we going?'

'Back to LA,' Zach said through tight lips and eyes that told him to shut the hell up.

'But Sasha—'

'Will be fine,' Zach cut in. 'You just have to trust me on that.'

Jace shifted in his seat, moodily. He knew when it was pointless. The rise in blood pressure was pounding his head like a piston.

The drive was short and they soon pulled into the airfield. It was manned by men in the same uniform, indicating it was for the Carpathians' sole use. He had to close down Sasha thoughts before they sent him mad and the big guy put him down like he promised.

The plane was waiting for them, its high-pitched whistle and the acrid smell of running engines. Everyone got out of the cars and went straight to the metal airstairs. Guards pulled out their bags and Jace followed them at the back in silence.

It was now Tuesday; they'd left on Friday, and he literally had no idea what happened to the time in between. It felt like they'd only just got there. It was obviously due to the time difference, but it still felt weird. And judging by the sombre mood of his friends, they all felt the same.

Jace made sure he sat next to Duo. He needed to know what was going on. He flashed angry eyes at him and faced his sister, who was sitting opposite. They exchanged an in-look between siblings that felt like a slap in the face. Now he'd had enough. 'Is someone going to tell me what's wrong?'

'Like you don't know,' Tears said, rolling her eyes furiously.

'I just woke up to be told we're leaving. I don't get it?' Jace looked across at Zach, who flopped into his seat across the way and fastened his seatbelt.

The staff in their sky-blue uniforms were busy closing the doors and doing final checks. Duo leaned across him to glare at Zach, too. 'Why don't you tell us what that was back there, because it was sure as hell was no signing I've ever known.'

'Not for our benefit,' Tears added, with the grumbled agreement of a few of the others.

Jace's eyes widened in surprise as Zach bit and spat back so suddenly and venomously; 'Do you think it was for mine?' he said, holding up his injured hand.

The plane moved off to taxi to the runway, and Jace had to swivel in his chair to look more squarely at Zach. 'Whoa, whoa, whoa … back up.' He took in a few of the guy's faces and they were all fuming and averting their eyes. 'You've got to explain this to me, Zach,' he said, more reasonably. Real fear was beginning to creep up his spine.

'Where did you spend last night?' Ballsy called out.

'Yeah, where did you sleep?' Jynskie echoed.

It started to seep through that the anger was directed at him, more than where they'd just come from. 'In my room, out cold,' he said, frowning, like it should be the most obvious thing in the world.

The engines revved and Jace gripped the arms of the chair as they built speed for take-off. A few minutes later, after some belly rolls, they climbed into the air and the plane stabilised. 'I swear, I was asleep,' Jace said, now his heart had stopped fluttering.

Ballsy kissed his teeth.

'No, before that. After the contract signing?' Duo said more reasonably, next to him.

Jace looked into his eyes and there was no anger in them, only hurt and that cut most of all.

Jace looked over at Zach for some sort of help or explanation for what they thought he'd been doing, but Zach just looked down at the palm of his injured hand. Everyone else had become deathly quiet. Jace cast his mind back to retrace his steps. 'I don't understand. I went back to the party and it had turned a little wild. I couldn't find any of you. They were passing out coke, pills and smoke like candy. I took some Leb and went to find somewhere quiet to smoke it. That was when Raz found me and I went back to her room.'

Several tuts and grumbles made him pause.

'No, seriously, guys. Nothing happened. We talked, that's it. Then someone took me to my room.'

'What was your room like?' Jynskie threw in, which puzzled him a little. There was an edge to the question he didn't fully understand. 'The same as yours, I guess.' Jace looked into each of the cold faces of his friends and it was like he never knew them. They'd completely turned against him. 'What is this?' he said, for what felt like the hundredth time, but he faced Duo this time in the hope that at least he would tell him what was going on.

Duo flashed his eyes at his sister, who tutted and sat back in her seat as if she was washing her hands of the whole thing. 'The contract we all signed back there; it was bad, man,' Duo said.

Jace went to agree, as he'd felt it had been off, but Zach cut in, 'We're not supposed to be talking about it.'

Jace looked over at the cabin crew. Thankfully, they'd left the soldiers behind. 'That's so we don't compare,' Jace said, now a little more bravely.

'That's true!' Tears said.

Jace looked around at them all. 'I felt the same. It was heavily weighted in their favour.'

'In their favour,' Jynskie repeated, flatly.

The seat belt sign finally went off and Duo got to his feet. 'Stop, Jynsk! You can see he's got no idea what happened. It's not his fault.'

Although he felt the wash of gratitude at his friend's defence of him, he couldn't stop the cold, hard grip beginning to constrict his heart.

Finally, Duo faced him, rested his weight on his hip and began to explain. 'They brought us all in together, to the three weird-looking guys.'

Jace followed perfectly and nodded for him to continue.

'We didn't even get to sit down. He shoved the contract in front of us on the table and just told us to sign.'

Jace nodded again, a little more dubiously this time. Apart from the sitting part, it appeared to be the same as him.

'He said our success as a collective was solely dependent on you as an artist. He asked whether we thought you could deliver. And knowing you as well as we do, Jace, we had to say, we couldn't be sure.'

Jace frowned, now completely confused at the direction they were taking.

Ballsy cut in. 'That's when they brought him in,' he said, pointing at Zach, who tutted and rolled his eyes, still cradling his hand. Always the hand.

'And that's when they gave you that?' Jace said, not able to keep quiet about it any longer.

Zach swallowed uncomfortably and nodded. 'I swear I had no idea what we were walking into, Jace. They called me in before all of you.' He shrugged, shook his head and looked out of the small oval window as if the answer would be somewhere out there. 'At first, it seemed like any other contract negotiation. But then…the things they said sounded strange – and not just because of language differences.'

'Like what?' Jace prompted, his heart pounding. Zach seemed to have drifted off into his memories.

'Like, for instance, "for greatness there must always be sacrifice. One life for another, time for time, death for death. And then they asked, was I so sure of you, Jace, that I was willing to offer mine as surety for you?"' Zach said, turning his head to look Jace straight in the eye.

It stopped Jace breathing; it was such a direct, no-nonsense look.

'At first I couldn't get my head around what they were saying. Then I realised they were serious. They spelled out that once you'd received an invitation and been there, no was never an option. They had to keep their organisation secret, and people who said no were a liability. By then, I'd lost all track of what they were offering and to who. They sent me out to think about it and called everyone else in – except you, Jace.'

'That's when we were all called in,' Duo explained. They

intimidated us. We wanted to get the hell out of there, so they pulled Zach back in.'

'And nailed his hand to the fucking table!' Jynskie shouted.

Jace's eyes widened with shock and he looked from Jynskie back to Zach in disbelief. But the hand injury and Zach's whole demeanour suggested it was true. 'Why, though? We could just go to the police. It doesn't make sense,' Jace said, panicking and yet knowing he was grasping at straws.

Zach was watching him sadly. 'Which police force? What country, Jace? We've got no idea where we even were. And people like that own them.'

Jace just stared at Zach, letting what he'd said sink in. He was completely right. 'What then? What can we do?'

'I think it was just shock tactics, to get everyone to fall into line quickly.'

'So you're saying we should just do what they want?' His pitch had risen with panic as he looked around at all the hopeless, angry faces around him. 'We just give up? We can go to a lawyer as soon as we get home. See what we can do to break the contract,' Jace said desperately, thinking surely it was the only thing left to do.

Zach just shook his head wearily. 'Won't work,' he said, barely audibly, as if he'd thought of it already.

'So we're letting them get away with it,' Jace said, throwing his hands up, exasperated.

'You weren't there, Jace. We thought they would kill Zach – we thought we might all die,' Duo's sister, Tears said, almost crying.

Brains gave her shoulders a squeeze from his standing position behind her.

Jace swallowed and tried to calm his heart, which seemed out of rhythm that day. 'So what happened next?' he said.

'They took us to a big room in the basement. I don't think they wanted any of us talking to you. We stayed there until just now, when we left for the airport,' Duo said.

'They let me go to get you,' Zach said quietly, as if he was ashamed he hadn't been stronger. 'Reminding me that sacrifice was expected, and they owned me if I said anything out of place.'

Jace sagged in his chair, bewildered. He knew they were telling the truth and it sounded like Zach had been put in an impossible situation. Even he had thought his meeting was strange enough to add his own death caveat. It had felt strained and definitely held an undercurrent of menace. Now it made sense.

He also remembered the time he'd spent with Raz and how she'd reminded him of a caged bird. He put his hand to his forehead. Using his brain this early was making it thump. He was probably dehydrated and he couldn't remember the last time he'd eaten. He let his hand drop wearily. 'Why, though ... why would they need to do all that? Isn't that what artists desperately want, to be signed?'

Everyone stared back at him blankly or shrugged, as if there was no answer to that.

'And Raz...she's so nice...she'd never knowingly be involved in anything like that.' Then, even before he finished speaking, he guessed they could easily keep that part from her. He hoped that was the case.

Just then, the stewardess came along, pushing a trolley laden with breakfast stuff: pastries, juice, and coffee. It all felt so normal in contrast to what they'd just told him. He shook his head wearily.

'Maybe she ain't,' Zach said, bringing him back with his strong London accent. 'Strikes me, she's just a golden goose.'

Jace stared at him. He'd never heard that expression before.

'Like in the fairy tale,' Brains added, obviously under-standing more than him.

Jace still didn't get it. 'What fairy tale?' His mind went to Raz in her cute PJs, alone in the great big room full of stuff, with nothing but her photos to keep her company.

'It's the story of the man who finds a golden goose that brings luck, or grants wishes, or something, to whoever owns it,' Brains explained

'Doesn't it lay golden eggs?' Tears asked.

'That's a different story, but still works, I guess.'

'This one lays gold bars – musical bars,' Zach said, thoughtfully. 'Worth millions of dollars… Those guys know she's the secret to their success. A licence to print money. Think about it,' Zach said, looking at them all one by one. 'Without her, what do they have?'

He was right. Jace let out a single blast of air. 'Just a multi-billion dollar corporation.' His mind was shattered by all the conflicting information. It was a weird setup, that was for sure. He relaxed a little. At least they were away from the place. The menace held over them seemed far away. 'What now then? They just let us all go. What do we do now?'

They all looked at Zach as if he knew all the answers. Jace already knew what he would do. As soon as he got back to the US and civilisation, he'd be warning Sasha.

'London!' Zach said, halting his thoughts in their tracks. 'They're ramping up the PR, starting with a round of inter-views in London.

Jace was already on his feet and everyone else started arguing. 'You lied!' Everyone assumed they were going home. 'Sasha!' Jace said, pushing through a heated argument to get to Zach. 'They said they were going for her next. Getting her signed to a different contract, or something.' Jace started pacing, pulling at the roots of his matted hair, while Zach watched him from his seat, a little fearful at what he would do.

'I had to get you out of there fast,' Zach said.

Jace was almost in tears. 'She'll go to that place all alone,' he said, covering his face with his hands, while fear and panic racked his body, until he felt someone pull his hands away from his face.

Zach was now standing in front of him. Everyone seemed to have gone quiet and was watching them. 'She's at home in Pittsburgh, isn't she?' Zach said, still holding his wrists, grounding him with his eyes.

Jace nodded and then groaned. They'd been away for days. Anyone could have got to her by now. 'I've got to stop her.'

'We'll call her from London,' Zach said, pulling him into the heat of his much bigger body. Jace was so strung out and scared that he allowed it. 'There is no difference in calling her from London than LA. You can warn her, don't worry,' Zach was saying, but he sounded like he was convincing himself. His voice was trembling and so were his hands.

They were all scared. Jace just had to pull himself together. He straightened up and ran a shaking hand through his knotty, unbrushed hair.

'Here!' Zach said, dropping a pill in his hand. Relax, we'll be landing soon.'

Jace reluctantly went back to his seat, where he swallowed the pill with some water. All the while, his eyes stayed on Zach. A man he barely even knew. Pills were the answer to everything with him. Sasha would have wanted his head straight. For the first time in a long while, he doubted Zach's motives around him. Then he looked around him at everyone else. Some were in quiet conversation. Others were trying to sleep. No one looked happy. His mind churned, drifting back to Raz and how sweet she was. There was no way she was involved in anything that had happened to them. Then his mind shot to Sasha and his blood pressure leapt up. All he could think of was the wolves' eyes and the cousins ' predators' smile, and he felt physically sick. He couldn't get that image out of his mind when he tried to imagine Raz's brother.

CHAPTER 10

Sasha always enjoyed going home and being cosseted and spoiled by her mother. She made Sasha chicken soup and tucked her in bed with a hot water bottle. She was always so glad to simply have her home. It was what Sasha needed after the emotional tatters she was left in after time spent with Jace. Her mother instinctively knew that.

Despite knowing Jace forever, she was a homegirl at heart and an introvert. Preferring a quiet dinner to wild parties any day of the week. Nevertheless, she worried about Jace; she guessed she always would.

'You have to learn to let go,' her mother said, after a few days of her moping around. 'If he's going to fall, he's going to fall, whether you're there to lean on or not. You just have to make sure he doesn't pull you down with him when he does.'

It was the most candid her mother had ever been about the Jace situation. She guessed it was a testament to how bad it had got. It was also true. So much so, she couldn't answer. She simply hugged her mother so she couldn't see her cry.

Useless, she knew, as she would feel her sobs. She had to get stronger, for everyone's sake.

Then, out of nowhere, the call came. It was a woman – a representative from the Carpathian group. She explained that the collective had signed with them and one of their execs from the corporate side wanted to speak to her about a job offer.

Sasha's heart flipped. An opportunity was just what she needed, a new start. Then she remembered that the whole point of leaving was to get away from Jace, not to work for the company that had signed him. Still, he'd be hard to escape once he was a household name.

The woman sensed her reticence. 'Hey, just talk to our guy. What do you have to lose?'

She guessed she was right. 'OK, where do I need to go?'

'Don't worry. I'll call him now and let him know you're open to discussion, and he'll contact you directly.'

Sasha thanked her and replaced the phone. She wondered how she'd got her number, and then guessed it was probably from Zach. So Jace had signed. Something big was always going to happen for him. It was no real surprise. She was just glad they'd signed them all. Now, she had to get it straight in her head what she'd say now that opportunity was coming her way. Maybe she could still do it and stay separate from Jace. She clung to that, but knew it was unlikely. It was too soon and she was still too raw to be around him.

It was another day until the call came. At first, she had no idea who it was. 'Sasha?' the deep voice said, and then she fell in.

'Oh, hello … Sorry, I didn't realise it was … sorry!' she said, knowing she was babbling and coming across as unprofessional.

He lightly chuckled. 'No problem at all. I'm sorry that it took this long to call you.' His voice was soft and sounded very European. Where, she couldn't place. 'I have been in New York on business. I should like to fly down and see you if that's OK?'

He sounded gorgeous and she was blown away that he was willing to go to all that effort just to offer her a job. 'Yes … of course … I mean, I can come to you if it's easier or videocall?' she said hopefully.

He chuckled again, as if he found her most entertaining. 'No need. We will talk over dinner. A car will call for you tomorrow at seven.'

Her heart stalled. It wasn't what she was expecting. 'What! Where? What should I wear?'

He laughed this time. 'Wear something nice,' and then he was gone. She was left staring at the phone, her heart thumping. But she felt alive. The most alive she'd felt in a very long time.

The next day, her mother helped her choose the right dress. With a few alterations, it was simple yet elegant in deepest blue. It gathered high at the neck, was to the knee and sleeveless, showing her shoulders in a diagonal V. Classy and not revealing, yet a little bit sexy.

Sasha preened in the mirror, waiting for the car.

'You look beautiful, honey,' her mother said, coming up behind her. 'Your life is going to change tonight. I just know it.'

Sasha smiled sadly at her mother in the mirror. 'You don't have to worry, Mom. I won't go back to Jace. I've made up my mind.'

Her mother smiled, knowingly. 'You have a big heart, baby. You might not be able to help yourself.'

Her phone beeped. 'I have to go,' Sasha said, pulling her coat off the stand and picking up her huge, flat portfolio case by the door. 'Don't worry. I'm stronger now.'

'Be careful, love,' her mother said, watching her all the way out to the waiting, sleek black car.

Sasha was surprised when a chauffeur in full black uniform got out to open the door for her and even more surprised when she found the back seat empty.

'Mr Carpathian will meet you at the restaurant, Miss Bond,' the driver explained, taking her large folder, stowing it in the footwell next to her and closing the door.

He got back in his seat and the car moved off. Her heart was beating wildly as she looked around at the expensive grey leather interior. Butterflies swirled with abject terror when she realised she must be meeting someone very important. 'Do you know him? Mr Carpathian, I mean.'

The driver's eyes met hers in the rear-view mirror. He was really quite handsome in an older guy kind of way. Clean-shaven and well-groomed, she put him in his mid-thirties.

'A fair, straight-from-the-shoulder kind of guy, I guess,' the driver said.

'Are we going far?' she asked.

'Not at all, Miss?'

'Sasha,' she filled in for him.

'Sasha,' he repeated. 'The Attic, I believe.'

'The Attic at the DeSeers Tower?' she said, flatly. It was the most expensive restaurant in town. The list to get a table was, like, forever. It was supposed to have one of the best views of the city.

Jace had always promised that when he'd made it big, he'd take her there to celebrate. Now she would be fulfilling their ambition with someone else. It felt hollow and hurt like she'd been robbed. She felt disloyal and that made no sense at all. She had to get a hold of herself to sparkle for this guy, as he'd be buying into her as much as her brand. It was the chance of a lifetime.

She looked down at the dark-blue satin of her dress doubtfully, then at her cumbersome portfolio, which he'd never mentioned to bring. Maybe she should have thrown a little more money at the dress and bought something new. The imposter list was growing in her head at why this was such a bad idea, when the car pulled up outside the red canopy of the DeSeers building.

Too late to run. They were there already.

'Here we are, Miss,' the driver said cheerily as he got out and opened her door for her.

Her legs didn't seem to want to move, but she forced herself out of the car, with her coat over her arm.

'Good luck, Miss,' the driver said, passing her case and smiling knowingly down at her.

She wondered if she looked as terrified as she felt.

He nodded and disappeared back inside the car. She turned, hesitantly, and walked up to the entrance. She coughed, not knowing what to say to the doorman.

'Name?' he said, looking down at his clipboard.

'Sasha Bond,' she said, croakily.

'Of course,' he said, with a little bow of his head, making her think he had her confused with someone else. She followed the line of the arm he held out for her and went inside.

There was a short corridor that ended at the steel doors of an elevator. Two couples joined her and stepped into the lift. The doors closed and it moved quickly upwards.

One of the couples looked younger and they were giggling, obviously smashed already. The other two looked middle-aged and faced the front in silence. All of them looked rich and well-dressed, like something out of a glitzy magazine.

Sasha gripped the handle of her large case and looked down at her own feet, at her flea market silk slippers. They seemed such a good idea at the time, as they matched the colour of her dress perfectly. Now they looked cheap and flimsy and she wished again that she'd spent a little more money on the occasion.

However, there was no more time. The lift pinged, the doors opened and the embarrassing silence lifted immediately with the warm sounds of dinner jazz, gently clinking silverware and soft chatter of beautiful people.

She walked slowly into the room, allowing the two couples to go ahead of her, but a young man in a black waistcoat and white apron approached her immediately, whisking away her coat before she could stop him. 'Come this way, Miss Bond. Mr Carpathian is already here.' His accent sounded very French.

She had to walk hazardously fast to keep up with him as he sashayed through all the circular white-covered tables. She dodged statues, pot plants and various carts laden with food, trying not to hit them with her case and yet not able to keep her eyes from the huge bank of windows that looked out over the city spectacularly and ran parallel to her on the left. Until they finally reached the furthest corner, filled with foliage, creating a far more secluded dining area. It was a prime spot with a corner view of the city, obviously reserved for the super-rich or famous.

Sasha was still in awe of her surroundings when the waiter stopped and held out his arm. '*Et voilà.*'

She lost track of whether she had thanked him after that. Her eyes found and stayed riveted to the man already seated at the table.

She wasn't sure what she'd been expecting. Some middle-aged corporate exec, she supposed. Possibly balding. In a good suit. But the guy seated was nothing like that. There was no other way to put it; he simply punched her with raw sex appeal and masculinity. She'd never felt anything like it.

He noticed her right away and put his phone down on the table. He got to his feet, unfolding to his full, above-average height, showing a perfect physique in a fabulously fitting pale-blue shirt, adding to the already swooning impression she had of him. Then he smiled the most open and warm smile, drawing her into those eyes. The cold, arctic, mesmerising eyes of a bird of prey, or wild animal. She couldn't make up her mind which. She swallowed and blinked in what felt like slow motion, taking in the dark lashes below the immaculate arch of his expressive brows, which immediately drew together, concerned by the effect he was having. His hair was black, wavy, and a little long, brushing the open collar of his shirt, which he had neatly tucked into his expensive, belted, navy pants.

He walked around the table to greet her and, for a moment, she had the overwhelming urge to run, or at least jump back, as the attraction for him was so strong. Except he stopped at a good distance, as if he knew, and simply held out his hand for her to shake.

She looked at it, dumbstruck for a second, examining the good hand. Definitely unused to manual labour, and yet revealing small, inked hieroglyphs poking out from just below the cuff. Tattoos were the absolute last thing she expected from an exec, but strangely not from him. It seemed to go with him perfectly: discreet but dangerous.

He leaned forward and picked up her hand, as she was leaving him hanging and drew her in to kiss her cheek. 'Welcome, Sasha,' he breathed next to her skin.

She instantly broke out in goosebumps. In that one nanosecond, her senses came alive. The warm sandalwood smell of his closely shaven skin and its softness made her want to nestle in his arms far longer than the couple of seconds it took before he pulled apart. She was losing her mind; his effect on her was that strong.

He towered over her, looking down with those piercing blue eyes, pale blue and ringed in deepest indigo. 'Wow,' she said, not able to help herself.

His smile widened to a grin that lit his whole face.

She came to her senses with a jolt. She was still gripping his hand. 'Sorry,' she said, quickly letting it go and blasting red.

He laughed gently and held out a hand towards the chair. When she finally moved, she leaned her case against the leg of the table and he pulled out her chair for her to sit. 'What a stunning dress,' he said in a deeply accented voice she couldn't place. 'We are colour coordinated this evening,' he said with a grin as he walked back and sat back down in his own seat

Sasha blushed. She simply couldn't help the way she reacted around him. She stopped herself from saying '*like your eyes*' before she made a complete fool of herself. 'I made it today… Well, re-designed it, actually. I made it a while ago. I'm not used to places like this – shit!' He'd turned her into a jabbering wreck. Her eyes darted about until she gave up and looked at him wearily, resigned that he must think she was an idiot, so why fight it.

Strangely, he wasn't laughing at her. In fact, he looked like he was scrutinising her every expression. Instead, he said, 'Of course. I should have known; you are an excellent and fresh designer.'

Now he was talking stuff she knew and was confident with, so, with a wash of relief, she went for her case leaning next to her leg, but he held up his hand. 'No need. I have followed your work. I know what you can do.'

She could only stare at him. They were interrupted by the return of the waiter and her guy gabbled something to him in perfect French. The waiter bowed slightly, thanked him and left.

'You're French,' Sasha said, realising she'd spoken aloud.

'Romanian, actually,' he said, his full lips curving into his knock-out grin. 'But I speak several languages … communication is kind of my thing.'

She exhaled on a sigh. She couldn't help herself. She bet there was nothing he couldn't do. He was so sophisticated and accomplished. 'Wow!' she said. 'How many do you speak?' too curious not to ask.

'All,' he said, his smile dropping and his eyebrows drawing together in a gorgeously insecure expression that took her breath away more than what he'd actually said. 'Apart from a few dialects, but I pick them up quickly.' His eyes never left hers, serious and direct, until she realised that he wasn't joking.

Then he seemed to snap out of it. 'I have taken the liberty of ordering for you, along with some champagne,' he said, straightening as the second waiter arrived with a beautifully presented basket of rustic sliced bread, quickly followed by the original guy carrying a swaddled bottle he quickly uncorked and poured into the flutes in front of them.

When at last the waiter left, he lifted his glass for her to do the same. 'Forgive me. You are very affecting. I have not introduced myself. I am Demeter Carpathian, head of acquisitions for the Carpathian Corporation.' He held out his arm to clink his glass with hers. She responded in a daze, not understanding why someone as high up as him was taking the time to meet with her. It made no sense, even if he did say she was affecting, *whatever that meant.*

'Here's to a long and successful collaboration together.' He smiled and watched as she took an unladylike gulp of her champagne. It was good and not the cheap stuff.

'So,' he said, easing back into his chair. 'You are the famous Sasha Bond, founder of the Vaggabond label. Great brand name to market, by the way,' he said, flashing his grin again.

Sasha still hadn't moved past sitting at the table with one of the actual board members of the Carpathian group to take too much notice of his flattery. The restaurant, the expensive champagne, *god,* the actual guy himself, were all too good to be true. She couldn't help wondering why they were rolling the red carpet out just for her.

In a swarm of waiters, extra condiments and cutlery arrived, and some sort of consommé was placed in front of her. With the weight of disappointment landing in her stomach and her mind free-falling as it began to make sense, she picked up her spoon and shakily scooped a little of the clear liquid.

His eyes burned into her the whole time.

She was glad the food was light; she wouldn't have been able to eat much at all with the fisherman's knot in her stomach the size of a fist. She was hot with fury and it was hard getting the soup down with her jaw clenched in bitter anger. 'So you signed the rest of my collective?' she managed to say, vaguely registering the delicate, fishy flavour of the soup. 'And you want me to keep Jace stable.' She let her eyes rise, angrily, to Demeter to see his reaction.

He picked up some bread, watching her shrewdly with no sign of discomfort at being called out on his little ruse. 'That is another arm of the company.'

She huffed and put down her spoon. 'But you wouldn't be interested in me if it wasn't for them,' she persisted.

He bobbed his head and took a bite of his bread as if he was genuinely considering her point. The charade was infuriating.

'Because you're wasting your time, if you are, as I left it. I'm not with Jace anymore. I think it's only fair to warn you.'

Then he smiled, satisfied, as if she'd walked nicely into his pre-sprung little trap.

'What?' she said irritably.

He gave nothing away except the obvious scrutiny behind those eyes. She wanted to scream at him. Especially when he laughed heartily and shook his head as if he hadn't had so much fun in ages. 'This is not how a high-powered corporate interview is meant to go, Sasha, even an informal one,' he said, looking at her sardonically.

She was mortified and quickly gathered herself together. He was right. She'd blown the best chance she'd had or ever would have.

He seemed to relent. 'You will be on a completely different contract, with very little to do with the rest of them – except maybe fittings, if you want it that way. You don't have to see … Jace, is it? This is strictly a business transaction,' he said deliberately, sipping his champagne and holding her eyes the whole time.

Sasha sat back in her chair, feeling foolish. She was obviously so overwrought with the whole Jace thing that she was not thinking objectively. 'Sorry,' she said, feeling utterly embarrassed and exhausted. She wished she could explain, but it wasn't appropriate. 'I'm really grateful for the opportunity. I'm just working through some personal stuff, you know?' And she was grateful. It was exciting and thrilling, but a huge part of her was terrified that once she saw Jace again, old habits would creep in and they'd drift back together just like they always did. The only reason she was able to be strong was the thousands of miles between them and that Jace almost never used or answered his phone. She had to salvage something out of the heartache she'd gone through.

'I think it will be OK, Sasha,' Demeter said, looking genuinely concerned. 'Come to my family chateaux and we will finalise the contract. You can meet the other board members and you can get a feel of how we run things. We are a family business at heart. What do you have to lose?'

He seemed so kind and sincere, particularly as she must have come across as completely unprofessional. 'Will Jace be there?' There she went again, with the inappropriate, unbusinesslike questions.

Those eyes bore into hers again, calculating, surmising, gathering intel from her body language alone. She knew it instinctively and she was sure he was good at it.

Then he said the words that froze the blood in her veins and changed everything.

'As we have veered into personal matters, I think it's only fair to warn you that there are rumours that Jace and my own sister are forming a connection – a bond, shall we say. And I tell you this, not to hurt you, but to strengthen you in your resolve, to make decisions that benefit you alone now.'

She could scarcely breathe. He was right, and she knew without any doubt that he was telling her the truth. She didn't know Demeter, but she knew Jace.

The jagged stone of hurt scraped down her chest and hit the pit of her stomach with a dull thud. The one thing she'd been dreading was finally here. Jace had never actually been faithful in the true sense of the word; it was part of his butterfly nature, but this – this was different, she could tell. She felt it in the marrow of her bones. If the sister had one quarter of the pulling power of the guy sitting opposite her, then Jace was lost. The idea of a female version of Demeter scared her half to death and sickened her to her stomach, as Jace would be powerless to resist it.

Demeter immediately understood and attempted to soften his blow. 'Of course, they are just rumours at this stage. I didn't mean to upset you.'

Part of her was sure he did. He was trying to get her to

make a decision and, after finding her weakness, was using her emotions to make it. A solitary tear escaped her eye, which she scraped quickly away with her fingers. He was an excellent reader of people and was just as good a manipulator. Because he absolutely knew from that moment that she would need to see for herself. She would have to go to his family's mansion to prove that she'd been replaced and that everything was finally over.

Demeter had done her a favour, really, as it showed that, until that point, she secretly assumed there was a way back. Now, it seemed, there was not. 'When do you want me to come?' she said, barely able to speak, watching him closely for any hint of satisfaction she knew he felt at having manoeuvred her.

He never even broke stride. He lifted his glass. 'You've made the right choice. Tomorrow ... A car will come for you at eight.'

'Will you be coming with me?' she said, feeling suddenly clingy, panicking at going so far on her own.

He smiled kindly, as if he understood. He gave her the eerie impression he understood everything. 'Don't be afraid. You will be looked after. I have some business to take care of first and I will arrive shortly after you to show you around. Your real life starts now,' he said, tilting his head and holding up his glass.

Sasha watched him for a long moment, wondering if he was right. Then their food arrived and he took his first bite from his silver fork. A chill went through her like an icy draft. 'I haven't signed anything yet, you know.'

He chewed slowly and inclined his head. 'That is correct. It will be my great pleasure to convince you that it is a good idea that you do.'

CHAPTER 11

Sasha spent the next day in a state of excitement that her life was finally changing, turmoil about Jace and despair. It hadn't helped that Jace had left three messages on her muted phone the night before and even phoned her mother, begging her to get her to call him.

She ignored them all. Despite thinking that his actually picking up his phone was new, she had to remind herself that this was what he did. He found a chink in her armor and reeled her in. He was probably just insecure with his new girl, or wasted and paranoid somewhere and needed the feeling of safety only she could bring.

She packed and repacked her case several times, having no clue what she needed. In the end, she guessed and chose a cold climate, hoping she was right.

It was nearly time and her mother came up behind her while she did the final touches to her make-up and hair in the mirror. She'd opted for a simple black sweater and pants. 'Will I do?' Sasha said with a ragged breath.

Her mother squeezed her shoulders. 'You look perfect,

honey.' However, her smile faded and she began to look worried.

'What is it, Mom?' She turned around so she could look her mother directly in the eye.

'I never told you all of Jace's last message, because I didn't want it to affect your decision, but I'd feel terrible if I didn't tell you and something happened.'

Sasha's heart was thumping as she grabbed the tops of her mother's arms and gave her a little shake. 'Tell me!'

Her mother sighed, rolled her eyes and shook her head. 'He just said, whatever you do, don't sign anything. Then he made me promise over and over to tell you. There... I've done it. What you do with it is up to you. But I tell you, honey, I can see why you can't help yourself with that boy, he's like a wounded puppy. Who could say no to that?'

Sasha looked at her mother for a long moment while she processed the information. *Did he mean with Demeter? Did she even want to sign?*

Her phone beeped and a message came up that the car was outside. It seemed to bring some sense to her and she broke out of her daze. Whatever Jace was warning her about, she'd figure it out on the way. Whether he was just scared of her moving on, or he knew something she didn't, she was single now and had to start putting herself first.

JACE WAS BACK at the LA beach house feeling on his last nerve. They'd done a day of interviews in London and got on the first commercial flight back to LAX. He was exhausted and irritable and couldn't stop thinking about Sasha and what could be happening to her all alone. 'We need to go back!' he demanded, standing toe to toe with Zach. It was unlike him to get so riled up about anything, but this was Sasha.

'Be reasonable, Jace. We don't even know where that place is. They won't worry about her. She's nothing to do with the music side of things.'

Jace sneered, remembering the looks on the cousins' faces when they talked about her. Zach was just shitting himself at the thought of going back there. Then, as a final insult, he took out a small brown pill bottle from the inside breast pocket of his jacket and shook it in front of his face. Jace snatched it from his hand, annoyed that he thought he could be bought off so easily.

'He's right, Jace,' Duo said, lazing with some girl on the daybed. 'You don't know she's even gone there for sure. They must have loads of places.'

Jace tutted and began tapping on his phone and put it to his ear. 'Patricia? … Is she there? Did you tell her?'

'Is that you again, Jace? No, honey,' Sasha's mother said kindly. 'You gotta stop calling. I did tell her, but she's gone. You just missed her.'

Jace groaned in pain like something ripped open his chest and his heart fell out on the floor. 'Do you know where she's gone? Did she go with that guy – the one offering her the job?' Jace said, barely able to speak, his throat constricted so much. This was his fault. He'd ruined it and pushed her into the orbit of these kinds of guys. The thought of her out there like a kitten amongst wolves threatened to send him insane.

'I'm not sure, Jace. You just have to give her some time.'

But time was what they didn't have. 'Do you think she will take it, the job I mean?'

Sasha's mother let out a loud sigh. 'To be honest, I don't know. I don't think she's even made up her mind yet. She's not sure the two of you should be working together so soon.'

His heart lightened a little at that, followed by mixed emotions. Sasha was sensible and strong enough to say no to an opportunity like this. Even one that would make her career. But if she did take it, they'd be together again, side by side, working on projects and he could look after her. He wanted that so badly. 'That's true, she's right,' he said, while his mind raced over what they could offer to get her.

'But the guy really wants her and it's a great opportunity for her, Jace.'

Jace thanked her and ended the call, now more confused than ever. The fact that she was dubious about working together meant that she really thought it was over and that was a new feeling he was yet to process. He wanted her out of danger, but he couldn't stop the embers of excitement of being around her all the time again.

'What did she say?' Zach said, rousing him from his thoughts.

Jace shrugged and took out one of the pills he'd just given him. Then he picked up a beer and took it with several glugs. 'Leave me alone. I'll be in my room.' He turned and pushed his way through a group of people just making their way in and made his way to his room at the back of the house.

The rest of his band sure forgot their fears quickly. Maybe normality made it all seem ridiculous. They were all at various stages of wasted and enjoying the attention from the girls as a newly signed band. It was easy to feel a sense of security now they were away from the madness and out of harm's way. Jace wasn't so sure. Sasha was flying right into it and she was all alone, around those cousins, circling her like a pack of hungry wolves.

There was no lock on his door, so Jace pulled a heavy chair in front of it. If anyone came, at least it would wake him up.

His room was large and on the ground floor. It had glass doors that opened directly onto the pool decking, which was great when he wanted to party, but not for his current mood.

Squealing and splashing were coming from right outside, and two girls came running in to escape whoever was chasing them. They dripped pool water onto his white-tiled floor.

Jace was so angry, he couldn't even speak. He just glared and pointed at the way they came. Their eyes went wide with fright and they froze. They obviously recognised him and were just star-struck fans. Then they regained their motor skills and ran back out, arguing over whose fault it was as soon as they got outside.

Jace strode over and closed and locked the doors after them. Then he pulled across the monochrome-patterned curtains and switched on the matching lamp. He checked his phone for the hundredth time for any message from Sasha, then set it down on the bedside table. He took a step, his sneakers squeaked and the next thing he knew, he was seeing stars on the ceiling. *Fuck!* He wanted to kill those girls. He would have them thrown out of the house if he only had the energy. Instead, he pulled himself up and flopped face down on the bed. He felt dazed and woozy and just had to close his eyes for a second.

His mind wandered over the last few days. Most of it seemed so exaggerated and unreal. It had to be his mind playing tricks after days of pills and no sleep. He reminded himself that everyone had been scared – especially Zach and he was the one who'd dragged them into all this.

Then he heard a crash and laughter outside and everything felt so normal and everything before seemed so unreal. This was why he needed Sasha. She would have made sense of all this. It was business as usual. He just had to get used to it. *Sasha, Sasha.* Somewhere along in his ramblings, he must have fallen asleep.

·   ·   ·

Sasha didn't sleep throughout the whole journey, even when, by her reckoning, it was the middle of the night. She was just too wired and excited, with bouts of sheer terror. She'd said goodbye to her friendly driver, who'd wished her luck and handed her over to a guy who looked like secret service. He led her by the elbow, up the airstairs and onto a private jet. In the end, she had to suspend disbelief that she hadn't entered the set of a Bond film. *Pun intended.* A beautiful Barbie hostess showed her to her cream leather swivel chair, with a table between her and her stern escort opposite. Looking around, she guessed the plane held no more than around twenty people, including crew.

There was no hanging around. The hostess helped her with her seatbelt, the doors closed and the plane took off, leaving her stomach somewhere behind them on the runway. They began to climb, and she was immediately offered a glass of champagne, which she took gratefully to steady her nerves. The hostess smiled as if she understood and told her to ask for anything she needed.

'How long will it take?' Sasha asked.

The hostess smiled and, in a very strong European accent, replied, 'The journey will take around ten hours, if the winds are good.'

'Where are we going, exactly?' Sasha asked, now she'd managed to get her talking. Sasha looked at the guy opposite and then back to the hostess when no one answered.

Barbie looked uncomfortable and flashed her eyes at the guy for some help, who finally said, 'Europe! To the Carpathian family home.'

Sasha continued to stare at him, hoping he'd elaborate, but he didn't, and she didn't feel like she could ask again after that. He hadn't even told her his name.

Demeter had revealed he was Romanian, so she guessed she was probably going there.

She was brought some food at intervals, some sort of chicken in a cream sauce and rice, then bagels and cream cheese, which she guessed counted as breakfast, but she didn't eat much. She would have listened to music on her phone, but she'd been asked to turn it off. Plus, it would have just reminded her of Jace, and she didn't want to risk seeing a message from him. It was all too little too late. She did try to close her eyes to sleep, though, and managed a light doze.

It was very disorientating when they finally touched down. It was dark, and at home, it would have been morning, but she guessed, going east, it was probably early evening, but what did she know? She had no real idea where they were.

A long silver car met her at the foot of the steps and her guy stuck with her like a bodyguard. He opened the door for her and she looked around before she dipped her head to get in. They were surrounded by a forest of tall Christmas trees, as far as she could see. There were no buildings, just a control tower and the runway and nothing else.

She got inside and her bodyguard got in with her and said something to the driver in what sounded like German. Nothing was making it easy to pinpoint where she was.

They went through some kind of checkpoint and out onto a deserted road that seemed to go on for ever. They passed through steep gorges and several pretty villages with chocolate box gables, until they were out into the black countryside again. At least it looked like that, with no lights.

After about an hour, they drove through some iron gates and followed a windy lane and pulled up outside what could only be described as a fairy-tale castle. It was lit from the outside, made of pale-yellow stone, and had several circular towers with conical roofs. Pale-blue shutters framed every window and delightful flower boxes with pastel flowers hung underneath. It was so enchanting that she reached for her phone to take a picture.

'No,' the guard said, putting his hand over hers, holding the phone. 'I must take this until you leave,' he said, pulling the phone out of her hand. 'It is policy,' he said, sounding more German than ever.

She had a sudden need to at least read Jace's messages, but his face was implacable and she knew it was useless to ask.

'Get out,' he ordered gruffly.

She hesitated for a moment and then slowly got out of the car. The building seemed much bigger up close. *Who were these people?* They had to be super-rich or even royalty to live in a place like this.

Her guard nudged her forward by the small of her back and she went up the small flight of curved steps to the large oak door. Inside was a magnificence she'd only ever seen in films. This was definitely a princess's castle.

A butler and maid met her in the huge, vaulted hallway of cream stone walls, oak beams and magnificent oil paintings. They asked her to follow and began to climb one side of a double sweeping staircase of white marble. Sasha followed, awestruck. Her feet sinking into the soft, scarlet and gold carpet that ran down the middle. A crystal chandelier hung in the stairwell, lit like a thousand little stars, perfectly downlighting a classical white statue of a naked couple below.

They continued along a corridor of more paintings and statues, then, after several right and left turns, they reached a bedroom so large, she was sure she could fit her mother's whole house in it.

The maid quickly drew the red velvet drapes across the huge windows on the left and turned down the king-sized bed on the far wall.

The butler said, 'Dinner will be served in your room this

evening, Miss Bond, to allow you to settle in. Mr Carpathian will breakfast with you in the morning.' Then, with a low bow, 'If that is all, I bid you goodnight.'

The whole thing felt bizarre. Like she'd entered a Princess Diaries film. 'Good night … Thank you,' she said, in a daze. She was grateful for the time to herself to process it all. She wished she had her phone so she could at least call her mother. She stood in the middle of the huge space and took a ragged breath. This was it. Her new life. She had to get used to it. It was strange and exciting, but also lonely and scary. Her mind shot to home and Jace, and she had to stop herself, otherwise she'd cry.

Her case was by the bed. It was bulging because she hadn't known what to bring or even how long she'd be staying. She hefted it up, laid it flat on the ottoman at the foot of the bed and opened the zipper. She couldn't be bothered to unpack, just a few of her toiletries. She wandered over to the windows and peeped between the curtains. Everywhere was in darkness, just the twinkling lights that lined the drive. They disappeared into nowhere, and she thought of Jace. 'I hope you're OK,' she whispered.

JACE WAS WOKEN by a scrape of furniture and 'Get up! barked at him from his doorway. 'It's noon. Zach has called a meeting,' Jynskie's croaky voice said, proving he hadn't long been up himself.

Jace groaned and hauled himself out of bed, regretting it instantly with the pounding at the back of his head. Then he remembered his fall the previous night and swore under his breath. There was a lump at the back of his skull, but no blood, *thank God.*

He pulled on yesterday's clothes of grey track bottoms and an old grey t-shirt with 'Just Geekin'' across the front.

He padded to his full-length mirror and pulled a face at the sight of himself. Yesterday's eye black had smudged, making his dark circles now look like the living dead and his purple and blond hair stuck out in all directions in dreadlock-like clumps.

He found the others in the living area and flopped down into an empty chair. He began picking at his chipped nail varnish and realised he had the shakes.

He was the last to assemble, so Zach began, telling any hangers-on to 'Get out!' as soon as they tried to walk in. 'Go home. This is business.'

He turned to face them all again. 'Right! Now we're all back, we get the benefits of all the shit we put up with the other day. You're going to Ruff Noize studios today to start work on your first album.'

They all looked at each other, then cheered. Some whistled and others clapped. It was a welcome release from all the tension that had built up.

'I know you were scared. I was scared. But now we put it behind us and get to work.'

'Yes!' somebody whispered, loudly.

'Raziah is flying in to work with you. I don't have to tell you to do whatever she says. There'll be a music video for the single and some more TV and radio interviews. This is it, guys. The bigtime!'

Jace listened to it all with blobs floating before his eyes. He had a killer head that could only be cured by cocaine. He had to do this. He was excited to see Raziah again. It was the only thing keeping him sane. Maybe she could give him some answers about what was going on with Sasha. And he was drawn to her, even though he wasn't over Sasha. *Was he?* Maybe he just had trouble letting go. *Would he be interested in Raz otherwise?* It was a troubling theory. Raziah was beautiful and dangerous in a way Sasha could never be. He was fascinated by all that perfection. He wondered what she thought of him. It was hard to tell whether it was more than just business. Still, it was a pleasant distraction.

He got up and went back to his bathroom, making sure he got some coke from Brains on the way. After cutting and snorting it from his mirror, he stepped into his shower. He intended to look every bit the rockstar when he met Raz again.

She'd been the little girl lost in her bedroom; now, he would party with the rock chick. The thought alone made him hard.

CHAPTER 12

Sasha woke with a start and took a few moments to work out where she was. Excitement flickered through her stomach, followed by a weight of dread.

She lay there in the warmth of the soft quilt while she woke up properly, realising how completely exhausted she must have been to sleep as heavily as that in a strange bed. Light was now escaping the edges of the curtains, meaning a new day. Which one and what time, she wasn't sure.

Now sufficiently awake, she swung her legs over the side of the bed and stood up. Then she padded over to the windows and drew them aside with a scrape as the curtain rings ran across metal.

The sight that greeted her took her breath. This was surely a palace. There was the long drive she had travelled down the night before, but in daylight, set a few feet back, stood a tall hedge and walled alcoves, each with a different white marble statue. Behind that were manicured lawns, walled gardens with clever topiary of various animals. There was a huge chessboard with pieces the size of a person and what looked like a maze at the far end. It was stunning and went right up to the forest on either side. More of those spruce trees she'd noticed as soon as she arrived. Dark and foreboding, a complete contrast to the grounds.

Her feelings of dread returned. This place was beautiful, but totally isolated. *Where the hell was she?* She still had no idea of the nearest town or even what country she was in.

A light tap on her door brought her round sharply. 'Come in,' she said, with a croaky voice from lack of use.

The maid from yesterday came in and smiled. She was young and pretty, cute in her maid's uniform with a mass of blond curls squashed under her small white cap. She looked around twenty-five. 'Ah, you're awake. Mr Carpathian has arrived and said he will breakfast with you in around forty-five minutes, at nine. Is that OK for you, Miss Bond?'

'Er, yes. Of course,' Sasha said, still trying to place her accent as a clue to where they were. The maid went straight out, leaving her wondering how she would ever eat with her stomach turning cartwheels at seeing Demeter again. She hoped the daylight would make him more normal and less – she couldn't even quantify what it was. Scary, intimidating, masculine, desirable. *Shit!* She headed for the shower.

It was a wet room, plain, clean and completely serviceable in floor-to-ceiling white. She turned the large dial and was soon enjoying an excellent shower. The shower gel smelled of lemons and the shampoo of grapes. It pounded the last of the knots away in her tense back. When she finally rinsed, she turned off the faucet with a squeak and wrapped one large towel around her body and one around her head. Then she brushed her teeth and examined herself in the mirror over the sink. Dark circles shadowed her eyes, making her feel immediately ugly. She had to remember the reason she was there. As handsome as Demeter was, he was interested in her brand and what she could bring to the company. She must remember that. Not what she looked like. At the very least, and a whole lot more likely, she was a tool to keep Jace in line and productive. Either way, it wouldn't matter what pants she put on today.

She walked out and went over to her case. After pulling everything she'd brought with her out in a heap, she sagged with a sigh. Then why did everything seem so drab and shapeless? It really felt important to make a good impression.

In the end, she opted for black loose pants, a long-sleeved fitted black t-shirt, and a sleeveless denim tunic over the top. It was her trademark thing: clever slogans and brightly coloured accessories. This one said 'Brains are the new black' in small writing over her left breast. The placing was meant to be ironic. She hoped he got it. It was the kind of thing the fans expected from her, so she would give him that.

Then she went to her mirror and put concealer under her eyes. She set it with a pale foundation and completed her doll-like look with black lashes and nude lip gloss.

There!

She felt better about herself now. More her. After blow-drying her hair, she scraped it back into a tight ponytail and felt ready for business. Neat and serviceable. Her personality entirely. A terrible match for Jace.

She tried not to let thoughts like that shadow her day, but her resolve was incinerated by the vicious jealousy she felt as soon as she thought of Demeter's sister. She imagined her beautiful and confident, like him. *Were she and Jace together now?* Did Jace compare the two of them? *Was he falling for her?*

Thankfully, her downward-spiralling daydreams were interrupted by the return of the maid. She knocked, came in and asked if she was ready.

Sasha nodded, nervously, and whispered, 'As I'll ever be.'

Then the girl said, 'Follow me. I'll take you to Mr Carpathian.'

Nerves twisted her stomach, but she followed behind the

girl, soon grateful for her showing the way. The smooth stone corridors all seemed alike. Door after door of closed off rooms, punctuated by tapestries and oil paintings of landscapes, battles and knights.

'Where are we?' she called out, jogging a little to catch up.

The girl turned her head and smiled at her. 'I'm afraid I'm not at liberty to say, Miss Bond. The family likes to keep their family home a closely guarded secret.'

'Oh,' Sasha said, instantly sobered. They probably had their staff sign a non-disclosure agreement. She guessed it was flattering, really, to be invited at all, but all she kept thinking was that no one back home had a clue where she was.

They finally went down the huge staircase she remembered from yesterday. More knights on rearing horses festooned the walls. They followed the corridor that ran directly beneath until they came out into a large, elegant conservatory.

It was bright and delightful with potted trees and various hanging plants. In its centre was dainty white iron furniture to match the intricate ironwork of the building. The whole thing felt like a work of art in iron and glass.

And there he was. Already seated at the white wrought-iron table. The same soft black hair and perfect physique. This time, he was dressed a little more casually in a blue plaid shirt and dark blue pants. He was reading a broadsheet, with a pot of coffee and a jug of orange juice on the table in front of him.

'Mr Carpathian,' the girl said to announce their arrival. She held out her hand for Sasha to step forward.

She went to take a step, but those eyes landed straight on hers and froze her. They captured and held her. She had forgotten just how spell-binding they were. He seemed to feel the moment as keenly as she did, as, for ages, they didn't move. Each assessing the other for changes. Then he abruptly closed his newspaper, beamed that heartbreaking smile, and stood up. 'Good morning, Sasha,' he said, approaching her. 'I trust you slept well.'

She felt unable to move, like a petrified rabbit, until he pulled out her chair and indicated she should sit. She was breathing in his wonderful, newly showered smell until she jolted herself awake to move.

'How lovely and fresh you look this morning,' he said.

She took her seat, conscious of his arms still on either side of her, guiding the chair into the table, his hair brushing her cheek. 'Thank you,' she managed eventually. 'I slept unbelievably well.' It still amazed her.

He went back to his seat, sat and studied her with that warm, breathtaking smile. It was utterly fascinating; she could just stare at him all day. Then, as if he had mirrored her own thoughts, he said, 'You are a real natural beauty, Sasha.' He leaned forward and began to pour her some coffee.

It completely took her by surprise and she frowned. It wasn't exactly the level of professionalism she was expecting. She couldn't help the blush that heated her cheeks, though. She wasn't used to getting compliments like that, from anyone.

'All the more refreshing as you don't appear to know it,' he said, pushing her cup closer and taking his with him as he sat back in his chair, smiling.

They stared at each other. She didn't know whether to be angry with him. Every gaze he gave her, however small, was penetrating and knowing, as if he knew exactly what made her tick. What made him uncomfortable to be around was not the fear of sexual harassment, but that it was impossible to put on an act around him. And that kind of exposure, she now realised, made her feel small, insecure and pathetic. It made her heart sink, like she wanted to cry.

'How do you like the house?' he said, changing the subject and pulling her out of her nosedive.

'It's beautiful,' she said, coughing to disguise her emotion with irritability. 'Can we get on with what it actually is you want from me?' It came out rather more rudely than she intended, but it was out there now and she was forced to follow it up by looking directly into those mesmerising eyes.

He regarded her for a moment, slightly mocking with the slight raise of his eyebrows. His lips twitched as if he wanted to smile, but decided against it. She was glad because she honestly didn't know what she would have done with that and would undoubtedly have blown her career prospects.

His eyes remained on hers, watchful and alert, as if it were some interesting game.

Suddenly, she felt so weary with it all. 'Is Jace here?' she said, finally. 'Because I'm sorry, but I just don't buy that you got me here as a designer. You haven't even asked to see any of my designs.' She knew she was blowing it, but, in that moment, she didn't care. Now emboldened as he hadn't said anything: 'And while you're at it, do you mind telling me where the hell we are, because no one wants to tell me?

His eyebrows rose and then knitted together in a frown.

Her tirade had left her shaking.

He inclined his head once, as if he allowed her the first shot and then it was his turn. She swallowed hard.

'First, why wouldn't I want you as a designer? Your work, continually modelled by your band-mates, is exciting, fresh and very marketable. However, I can see you are a no-nonsense businesswoman, and I can respect that, so I will give it to you straight. Jace is not here…You were contacted because the music side of my company wants to sign your whole collective. It is necessary for the protection of the brand.'

That sounded a lot more like it. It was to stop her from using her designs anywhere else. She rolled her eyes and went to cut in, but he continued. 'Unfortunately, I cannot tell you your location because I must safeguard the safety of my family.'

'Against what?' she blurted.

'Against many enemies: organised crime, the media, crazed fans. You have to understand, Sasha, that when you are as rich and as powerful as we are, there are always those who would take your place.'

She was stunned for a moment. His eyes drilled into hers to convey how serious he was. And it was reasonable. It was proof of the old saying: money brought its own problems – one she'd never experienced, so hadn't thought of it. She felt instantly foolish.

He seemed to relent as if he understood. 'Perhaps, when I have grown to know you better and you are more comfortable around us, I may be able to trust you a little more. But, believe me when I say, it is safer for you if you don't know.'

Sasha looked at him, startled. She hadn't thought about people trying to get to them through the people they knew. Suddenly, the world he lived in seemed terrifying.

Dishes began to arrive of eggs, bacon, toast, fruit and pastries, along with a fresh pot of coffee. 'Eat!' he said, cutting the silence. 'You must be famished.'

His phone rang. 'Excuse me. I have to take this.'

She nodded awkwardly as he stood and walked away, out onto the walled terrace. She spooned some eggs onto her plate and picked up a croissant. She watched him pace outside, speaking a foreign language and gesturing with his hands. It was a grey day, and while it wasn't too warm, the gardens still looked beautiful in the light. It really was another world here. It was scary and alien and so different from everything she knew. Maybe that was why she was so suspicious. It even occurred to her that she was self-sabotaging because deep down she didn't believe she deserved a break like this.

Demeter came back and snapped her out of her maudlin thoughts. He sat down and immediately began piling food onto his plate. 'It's good?'

He seemed completely relaxed and, thankfully, not offended by her earlier comments. She tried to smile in apology and poured herself some juice. 'It's lovely, thank you.' She took a sip of her juice and ventured, 'So Jace isn't here, then?' She couldn't help herself. It was hard to imagine Jace in all this opulence, and yet, he was absolutely destined for greatness.

Demeter watched her as he chewed a mouthful of food. He always seemed to find her fascinating, which she found weird. She'd always thought she was rather boring, really. 'He went home a few days ago,' Demeter said, eventually. 'He is back in LA working on his first album. My sister is producing it, I believe.'

He studied her closely and she was sure she went red under his gaze. She was so thrilled for Jace and her friends. It was what they'd always dreamed of. It was what any artist worked for. So then, why did she want to cry? Pain twisted in her chest, making it almost unbearable. She guessed it was the realisation that it was finally over. Jace had reached his goal and had no further use for her. Demeter's sister would take over from here, and in her deepest heart, she knew that was true.

She dragged her tear-filled eyes to his. Of course, he was analysing and gauging her, measuring just how hurt she was and whether she was still a viable proposition. It didn't feel great to be replaced so quickly. 'I'm pleased for him and the band. It's a dream come true,' she said, gruffly, having run a finger under her eyes to disguise and hide her tears.

The whole thing felt like a test, so he could see her reaction. It angered her a little. She decided she could use it to her advantage. 'So what's your sister like? Is she like you?' She was hoping for more big and butch and less fascinating and beautiful, but she wasn't banking on it.

Demeter narrowed his eyes and bobbed his head in respect as if he'd understood right away her thought process. He was so unnerving like that. 'She is the opposite to me in every way,' he said, stirring his cup and smiling wistfully.

'I am large, she is petite. I am very dark, she is fair. She is gifted with music … I … am not,' he finished, clinking his spoon down on the saucer and bringing his cup to his mouth. He was no longer smiling. He fixed her with his enigmatic stare, looking devilishly handsome, and took a sip from his coffee to draw her eyes to those full, sensuous lips.

She had to swallow because she was sure he continued in his head, *she is good and I am bad*. It did something to her insides and they immediately went to liquid.

'Surely you must be alike in some things … You're brother and sister,' she said in a voice gone deep and husky, like she hadn't used it for a week.

His face immediately brightened, and he grinned as if their little moment had never happened. 'I can see you are interviewing me,' he said, with a single blast of laughter. 'We share a father,' he said with a shrug meant to explain all.

Sasha continued to watch him as he looked out into space as if something had never occurred to him before. 'I guess we are both very good at seeing the potential in something and getting the best out of it. With her it is music, with me it's business … I am a dab hand at corporate takeover,' he said with an evil grin.

He was totally playing with her and she liked it. It was

showing her a little of the real him, but he had walked into her little trap. She seized her chance; 'So why does a big bad businessman like you need to waste his time with small fry like little ole me?' The comparison to Little Red Riding Hood almost made her laugh; it was so absurd.

He laughed loudly at that. Then he narrowed his eyes and pointed at her as if she'd got him with a good one. He nodded as if he was only just getting the true measure of her. Then his face dropped and her blood froze as he turned into the hard businessman of earlier. 'Because you are good for business; my sister wants Jace, and, to have him, she must have you.'

There it was, total honesty at last, delivered straight from the shoulder with both barrels. She was so shocked she couldn't even speak.

Then, before she could pull herself together, he delivered another blow. 'And you are fast becoming a mission for myself, Sasha Vaggabond.' He narrowed his eyes playfully again. 'Not many people surprise me in this world. Well done! Very well done. You are hired.' He stood, the meeting apparently over.

Her mind stalled and she spluttered, 'Hang on … I haven't even agreed to anything yet?' Her mind scattered, grasping at all the questions she should have asked if she'd been aware that this was the actual interview: hours, pay, where she'd actually work, for instance. But in the end, she had to ask herself why she'd even come if she didn't intend to take his offer. 'OK,' she found herself saying, feeling completely beaten.

Demeter held out a hand, which she gingerly took. He pulled her to her feet and kissed her cheek. It became a brief hug where he whispered, 'Welcome, Sasha.' In that single moment, she had time to feel the tautness of his muscles and smell the low notes of his cologne that stirred something deep in her pelvic floor. Then he said something low, in another language, right next to her ear.

It affected her deeply in ways she didn't understand. It melted her and any resolve she had to resist the railroading she was undoubtedly getting and with a final, 'Stay and finish breakfast. My legal assistant will come and go through the contract with you.' He pulled apart, but seemed reluctant to let go of her.

It felt weird, like she didn't want to let go of him either. It was irrational and unprofessional, but she couldn't help the feeling. She really felt like she was losing her mind. 'Then what happens?' she said, suddenly emotional, like she wanted to cry. 'I thought you were going to introduce me to the family.' Her mind had already shot to his sister.

He stood looking down at her and all his playfulness had gone. The game was over and they were back to brass tacks. 'In time... I have to fly to Germany. Spend the day. Ask for anything you want. A plane will take you back to Pittsburgh this evening. You will be called when you're needed.'

She stared up at him in a weird state of shock as he turned and walked towards the door. She felt immediately lonely and almost used, which she knew was ridiculous. 'What, that's it? You got me all the way out here for that?'

He turned and grinned and continued to walk backwards. 'Don't worry, Sasha Vaggabond. We shall see each other again.' Then he winked and pointed as if he hadn't forgotten that she'd got one over on him earlier, then turned and disappeared out of the door.

Sasha flopped back into her seat and wondered what the hell just happened. She was more confused about the job than before she came. Well, at least she had the job. He'd told her that much. Now she had to wait to see what he really wanted from her, because it certainly wasn't her clothes.

CHAPTER 13

A black stretch Hummer arrived to take the collective to Ruff Noize's recording studios and they all appeared to have forgotten what it had taken to get there.

Jace let everyone get in ahead of him, laughing and whooping for joy over the stocked minibar and telling the driver to pump up the NAS he was playing up front. It soon became the party car.

Jace sat quietly at the back next to Zach and marvelled at their short memories. Zach flexed his bad hand, proving he was thinking the same thing. The signing never happened and they were determined to live in the now.

Jace took a beer. Maybe they had the right idea.

'Kids in a sweet shop,' Zach said, shaking his head.

'They're here, aren't they?' Jace said.

Thankfully, the journey was short and they couldn't get too wasted on the ride. It was still before noon. They came to a stop and everyone piled out, this time with Jace going first. He squinted in the bright sunshine and pulled his dark goggles up from his neck. They were in a square parking lot, surrounded by painted yellow buildings. One had a red-and-black mural of the Ruff Noize logo: a black vinyl record with a clenched fist on the label.

A girl came bounding out of an open doorway with pigtails bouncing, her under-boobs flashing from her crop top at one end and white panties showing under her mini skirt at the other. She wore Britney socks down to her knees and, when she grinned, she had two purple studs in the dimples of her cheeks.

Jace smiled weakly, not in the least interested and not wanting to offend her.

'I'm such a fan. This way, guys,' she said, giggling and skipping, reminding him of a cheerleader. He expected a backflip any minute. 'Everyone is so stoked to meet you. I'm Rachel, your Ruff rep. 'I'm the one who can get you everything you need.'

Duo laughed next to him as her eyes fell on Jace last. 'Happy days,' he started to sing.

'Is Raz here yet?' Jace asked, not meaning to shoot the girl down, but there was no point in her wasting energy. He wasn't interested. He guessed he'd changed. Before, he would always flirt, making the girl feel special, even if he had no intentions of going there. Most times, sex was the conclusion to a good day. Nailing some random girl made him feel like he was giving back and gave an edge to a druggy haze.

The poor girl deflated immediately as she shook her head. Jace followed her through the open fire escape, used by the artists to enter discreetly, then down a long red corridor, through a door at the end that opened into the main studio and mixing room. Everyone recognised Daren and Keven Macafee, two of the best producers and sound engineers in the business. The two Irishmen immediately stood and clapped hands and hugged everyone.

Jace's spirits lightened. It meant Carpathian was pulling out all the stops for them. He looked out through the glass at the studio, feeling like he was still in a dream. He'd wanted this for so long. It was smaller and less impressive than he'd imagined, but not intimidating, which was good, as it would be home until the album was finished. There were music stands, a drum kit, pedals, and amps for session musicians and an enclosed booth to the left for vocals.

Hat was already chatting beats with the two producers. Jace wandered out into the recording space to the booth. This would be where his voice would be recorded for posterity. He absorbed the feeling for a moment. This was a landmark. The thing that he and Sasha had worked so hard for. Tears welled in his eyes. The moment he'd always dreamed of and he was doing it all alone.

'Hello again, Jace.'

Jace turned to see the owner of that silky voice through the glass. *Raz.* She'd arrived with her pet, Steve, next to her. 'Come, let's talk strategy and get started,' she said, sounding more British than ever.

The mixing room now felt crowded with people. There were his troupe, now nine without Sasha, Raz, Steve, the Macafee brothers and another two sound techs from Ruff. That made fifteen squashed in, by his reckoning.

Raz smiled when she saw him and pointed to the arm of the black leather sofa, already occupied by four of his bandmates. Jace went and leaned against the wall next to it.

'Hello, everyone,' she began.

Her voice receded as Jace watched her closely. She was exquisite. She moved confidently and easily, gesturing as she spoke. She was far above everyone else in the room. It was nothing tangible. She was dressed super casually in a washed-out blue vest with 'Grime Warp' over the front and faded jeans tucked into biker boots. Her hair hung loose in messy curls past her shoulders. No make-up. Just a light tan to showcase those eye-catching tattoos. *Wow* was the only word that came to him when he looked at her. There was something so powerful that just radiated out of her. He wondered whether everyone else felt it.

'Is that OK with you, Jace?' she said, pulling him from his thoughts.

'Er...' He hadn't listened to a word she'd said and he shifted uncomfortably against the wall.

She didn't seem angry; in fact, she smiled a little. 'Never mind, we'll go with the flow and simply tidy it up afterwards. I want it organic and raw, like one of your shows.'

Jace nodded, getting it right away. It was exactly how he would have done it if he'd organised it himself. She had great instincts.

Someone nudged his arm and passed him a beer. Then a joint. He soon slid onto the arm of the chair, then into the seat. The techs talked tech and Raz talked directions and Jace managed to relax. People chatted and got up and down from their seats, just like a creative session in their old loft.

Jace watched Raz interact with the Macafee brothers. He wasn't sure if she knew them, but they sure as hell respected her, he could tell. She included Hat in the conversation and they were soon talking beats and running order for the songs. Then she talked overlay of real instruments and jingles she wanted over the top.

Time slowed down to warm and fuzzy. This was where Jace liked to be. Not the live shows or the interviews, which of course were great, but this was where the magic happened. This was where he felt most at home. It was cool and laid back and nothing else existed except the music and the people in this room. It was a cocoon. Food, drink, weed, and anything they needed were all brought in.

Beats were laid down. Then session artists, one by one. Each of his troupe members took their turn in the booth. Jace was mellow and wasted by the time he took his. Every time he opened his eyes, Raz nodded and directed him. No matter where he was, he found her watching him. It felt good. Reassuring. She was the consummate professional.

Then she took her turn for the shredding guitar solo on his track, 'I die young', and he was lost, in absolute awe of her. The coolest girl became the only girl for him.

Days must have passed. He couldn't be sure and Steve, Raz's buzzkill, was nowhere to be seen. There was a loft space with a bed and a sofa, where everyone took turns passing out. From there, they'd surface and carry on where they left off. Then, at last, the recording stage was over and just the mixing part was left for Raz and the Macafees. They would do that later when they'd had some sleep.

They all walked out into the head-splitting sunshine. Jace could barely open his eyes. It felt floaty and unreal. Raz was wearing his goggles and offered him her Ray-Bans. He felt vaguely sick after days of drinking and smoking. He needed to eat.

Somewhere between the studio and the street cafe they ended up in, he was holding Raz's hand. It felt little and perfect in his. Everyone was in a great mood. He couldn't remember feeling this happy. People spotted him and shouted a greeting. Guys whistled and he felt proud of who he was with. They were the perfect couple. She was perfect for him.

Selfies were taken and Jace made sure he stayed close to Raz. In fact, it occurred to him later that, from the time he set foot into that studio, he hadn't thought of Sasha once. Then, sometime after the cafe and several bars, they must have found their way home to the beach house, and he fell asleep. In his room. In his bed – with Raz.

He blinked at her sleeping body. Then up at the ceiling, where he attempted to scramble his thoughts.

Nothing had happened. *He was sure of it.*

He vaguely recalled them getting back there and him stumbling through the door. Falling face-first onto the bed, where he must have passed out immediately and slept like he'd never slept before. Deeply. Soundly, securely. It left him with a weird feeling. Like he'd been unfaithful in just doing that. No dreaming, just rest.

Passing out was nothing new. Nor were memory blanks. He could barely remember a single thing after they left the last bar. It was who he was with.

He couldn't help staring at her. Raz was still sound asleep next to him. He could feel the soft brush of her breath on his shoulder. He lifted the quilt and spotted the boxers he was still wearing. She, on the other hand, wore nothing but a thong. She held the sheet under her tanned arm and he had a great view of her tattoos that disappeared onto her back in crafted lines.

Jace studied the markings up close. They were exquisite, like her. Tiny, detailed, little hieroglyphs of stick men and squiggles in columns that followed the contours of her body. It was clearly writing and he wondered what language they were in.

It disturbed him that any girl could pull him away from his preoccupation with Sasha. But after the last few days, it was clear that she had. He couldn't help himself. She was perfection. Beautiful. Talented. Beyond belief. He ached to run a finger along the soft skin of her arm and when she moved towards him, kiss down the curve of her neck. She was so close to him already, on the pillow.

Jace inched down so his mouth was level with hers. He had an unbelievable urge to kiss her. They'd been together for days and from what he could remember, they'd even held hands. It was unlike him. He had a killer high score with the girls.

Her eyes fluttered open and he was staring into those

feral eyes. At first, she didn't speak; she just looked right at him, making him wonder if she was trying to remember what she'd done just like he had. But there was a strength inside her that made him sure she never completely lost control.

Then she completely surprised him by brushing her lips with his. It was barely a whisper, but it sent shock waves through his body. 'Are you scared of me, Jace?' she said, switching his heart rate up to full pelt.

His eyes widened at the playful taunt. She was probably right. She excited and terrified him. 'I didn't want to take advantage,' he said, gruffly.

'You were a tough nut to crack. It took me a lot of alcohol to get you here,' she said, with the same crafty look in her eye.

Jace frowned, half smiling. He could remember very little: a lot of bars, a restaurant, a couple of street cafes. It came to him like a lightning bolt. 'The pool!' He'd kissed her in the pool.

They hadn't gone straight to his room like he first thought. He had a flash of memory of her beckoning him from the centre of the pool – wet hair, bare shoulders and glyphs. He couldn't remember losing his clothes or even getting in the pool with her. Just the next frame of him bobbing in the water in front of her. Then her arms were around his neck and they were kissing. A kiss that replayed in a loop in his head in its affecting softness. He couldn't remember any more. Just a hello with promise.

He had no idea who put the brakes on it, or whether they were just too wasted and incapable of going further, because the next thing he knew, he woke up there. 'I'm sorry, I was pretty wasted.' He was genuinely embarrassed that he'd missed whatever had happened between them. It wasn't good for his reputation.

She was smiling. 'It's OK. I think it's cool that you still think of your girlfriend.'

His embarrassment sank even lower into his abdomen. 'Sasha?' It shocked him. Not what she'd said, but that he was sure he hadn't thought of Sasha for several days. And for the first time in living memory, it occurred to him that they might have made the right decision. 'We're not together anymore.'

Raz looked deeply into his eyes, gauging whether he was being honest, looking so gorgeous and trusting. But he meant every word – he wanted to mean it. Part of him would always love Sasha for what they'd shared. Where they'd come from and what she'd done for him. But she wasn't his lifeline. It wasn't fair for her to be. He just had to learn to let go. This wasn't being unfaithful. It was simply a part of their relationship that was over. They would become something else to each other.

It should have occurred to him then that his thought process alone meant he wasn't over it properly, but lying there, feeling the most beautiful girl's breath on him must have overruled his judgment. All he knew was what the right thing to do was. He shouldn't need to own Sasha anymore. They should be free.

It felt new. Like a revelation. 'I think I just got over her,' he said in complete amazement. He should have taken the time to process it, but he didn't.

Raz closed the small gap between them and finally put her mouth on his. She used her weight to roll on top of him and they were kissing, him loving the strength and dominance in such a tiny girl.

With the momentum, he continued the roll so he was back on top, tongue venturing, tasting, nipping down her neck, ripping the thong from her legs. His own boxers went next, with her hands and feet helping him. It was rushed and frantic and he was forced to take a moment's pause before he plunged into her bare, hairless body. Hovering above her, taking his weight on his elbows.

Her eyes were half-closed and she was utterly beguiling. *He shouldn't think.* This was always going to happen from the moment he saw her. It was inevitable. He wondered if she felt the same. How many times had she done this before? How many other wild and dangerous musicians? The little girl in pink pyjamas, in the lonely room, seemed a long way away.

'What about you?' he found himself asking, knowing he should shut the hell up.

The sexual tension in her body relaxed and ebbed away as she fully understood what he was asking. His arms were aching as he searched her eyes, now working hard to look at him. 'It's been a while,' she said, looking away.

He'd insulted her and he felt instantly bad, but he couldn't help it. She had such enormous power over him; he had to take some of it back.

'I'm choosy and you sleep with lots of girls.' She went to turn and push him off her, but he didn't move. She looked back at him defiantly.

She was right. He was a sap, overthinking this. He was the envy of every man who'd ever met her. He dropped down and kissed her again. Long and powerful enough to expel any resistance. Until he found and pushed straight into her and they both let out a breath. His body took over and his brain shut down. Each pistonning thrust pulled Raz closer and pushed Sasha further away, until there was no sane thought. Only the two of them, in the moment, having the most erotic morning sex of his life.

They rolled and moved together until she was sitting in his lap with her legs wrapped around him. Holding him to her, pulling his mouth to her neck and breasts. Her lithe hips kept moving, pushing, pulling him, stroking him smoothly. Bringing him higher. 'Ah, fuck. Raz!' he called out, not able to help himself as he soared to his climax.

She was quiet, but she went right along with him.

This was it. They were coming. It was big and nothing on this earth was going to be able to stop it. They built to an animal, frenzied speed. He groaned loudly and she was panting, until they both cried out together as the world of sensation swept over them. He dug his fingers into her buttocks and ground the last of her to him and rode several waves of pleasure that rip-curled and washed right through him.

Their hips slowed to a stop, his grip loosened, and together they fell onto their side. For a long moment, they lay amongst the cool sheets and just breathed. His eyes remained closed, and he savoured the completely comfortable, sated feeling. He couldn't move. He didn't want to move. Neither of them spoke for a full five minutes.

When he felt the cool air of Raz pulling apart, he opened his eyes and they both studied each other. They were checking each other for regret. What they'd just done was huge. They both seemed to know it. This wasn't just sex with some random girl. It wasn't even that he'd nailed the most desirable girl in the world. Or that she was related to the wolf cousins and the producer of the company holding him and his friends to ransom. No, this went far deeper than that. Raz was the girl who had ended him and Sasha, and while he would always love her, this was too good and too big to go back.

'How do you feel?' she said, turning her head to him, looking curiously insecure and concerned.

She seemed to have razor-sharp instincts in all other things. He let out a breath and almost laughed after the sex of his life. 'Good,' he said, truthfully. 'Amazed and a little sad,' he finished, smiling. His body was still cooling down and he remained immobile, exactly where he'd landed in the sheets

Her small brows knitted together, absorbing and analysing every word.

'What about you?' he said, teasing her a little. 'Am I your plaything, or what?'

Raz laughed and he laughed with her. She ran a thumb across his lips as if they were still a wonder to her. 'Isn't that supposed to be my line?'

He tried not to give away how exposed and vulnerable he felt. She was right, but he doubted she was anyone's booty call. Then she surprised him.

'It's never just sex, Jace. Whether it's to get over a person, a hard day, or simply to feel loved. It's never just sex.'

He lay looking at her, thinking about that for a long moment. She had such a strange, alternative take on things. It occurred to him that she might be telling him off for past transgressions or simply letting him down gently. He couldn't tell. 'What about love? Can't sex be about love?' His cheeks heated as he spoke, making him more exposed than ever.

'Why are you so intent on heading for the cage, Jace? You artists are all the same. You have all the freedom in the world to create beauty from nothing. Then you want to throw it all away by hemming yourself in with restraints and boundaries. I never understand it.'

Anger reared inside him while he scrambled over what she'd just said. He felt pissed and confused in a way he never had before. He thought they were talking feelings and she'd turned it into work. He was embarrassed because, if he pushed aside sappy thoughts, she was perfectly right. It was her cousins who had captured and chained him, and what she was saying wasn't fair. 'A musician's gotta eat,' he said snarkily, his face burning red. 'We were lucky we had a growing fanbase online, but to play bigger crowds and hit the mainstream, we had to sign with someone. Everyone always does.' He was really angry by the time he'd finished speaking, because she'd dared to call him out on something so close to home. It felt like an attack from someone he thought he was getting closer to.

'Why, though – why do you need to be a household name? Why not be content with being a cool underground movement?'

He was sitting up now, glaring down at her and she was looking up at him, face hot and eyes alive with excitement. Almost like she was feeding off his reaction. She was enjoying it. No one had ever challenged him in this way and he wasn't sure he liked it. He wanted to shout at her to shut the hell up and storm out. To leave her feeling as raw and vulnerable as he felt. She attracted and infuriated him at the same time, but he instinctively knew that the more he reacted, the more she would enjoy it. 'Why are you insulting me? We just fucked. Are you deliberately making an argument?' he said, scowling at her.

She laughed loudly, sat up and hugged him as if she was delighted. He allowed it, stiffly, and had to wonder what had become of the innocent girl of her bedroom.

Raz pulled apart and, still holding him closely, searched his face. She kissed him on the mouth, solemnly, while his eyes remained open in a dazed kind of shock. 'Don't stay angry with me, I'm just reminding you who you are, so you don't get lost.'

He studied those strange, hypnotic eyes that were way too direct and honest. 'What about you? Why do you let your cousins push you around?' He narrowed his eyes, now hardening. 'The business is nothing without you.'

She let him go with a sigh and leaned back against the headboard. She didn't seem hurt, but considered it for a moment. As if he'd made a very valid point. 'Everything around me is for my protection.' She frowned as if she had become lost in her thoughts until she was looking at him again. He guessed it was an argument she'd convinced herself of a very long time ago.

'And your brother…he has the same…protection?' Jace said, now his turn to watch her closely.

His arrow flew true and she looked the most vulnerable he'd ever seen her. She looked down at her hands in her lap and Jace felt guilty for attacking her. Then, when he didn't think she would answer, she surprised him. 'No, but he's a man and he's stronger than me and able to look after himself.'

It was logical and exactly what he guessed was the case, until she followed it up with: 'And I'm the good one.'

It stopped his thoughts in their tracks. She looked defiant. As if she'd given it a great deal of thought and that's what she'd decided on. *The good one. What was that supposed to even mean? Was she throwing that out to hurt him because her brother was after Sasha? Was that it?* He was scowling at her again.

'Don't pull that face,' she said, immediately brightening. 'Sasha is fine. We'll see her tomorrow. We're going home. She'll be there.'

His mind went into freefall. Not just because of her obvious little game with his emotions, but they'd all be together in their changed status and that would be weird. He wasn't sure he could handle it. 'Why will she be there?' he snapped, already dreading the answer. 'I don't want to work with her.' He did and he didn't. *Fuck!* He didn't know what to think.

'You know, silly. Demeter wants her and he always gets what he wants. She signed the other day.'

Jace was left reeling at the malicious glint in Raz's eyes.

CHAPTER 14

Sasha didn't want to go home that day. In fact, she never felt the same again. Her innocence was gone. It was a weird thing to say, from a girl who mixed solely with artists, rappers and musicians and all the debauchery that went with it, but she guessed it was because it had only ever been her and Jace and she'd felt shielded from a lot of it. She'd remained the same girl he'd first met as a kid.

Now she was in a foreign country, signing deals of her own with wildly exciting people. Demeter sprang easily to mind. She felt very grown-up.

She sat alone in the conservatory, finishing her breakfast, mulling over the strange interview she'd just had. It was so peaceful with just the clinking of her cutlery and birdsong chirping through the open doors to the garden.

'Good morning,' a female voice said, bringing her head around.

A smart redhead in a rust-coloured trouser suit was walking towards her. Her hair was rich brass, pulled back into a tight ponytail and her skin was alabaster white with a spattering of freckles across her nose. She was extremely pretty. Like a runway model. A perfect silhouette in tall black heels. Her eyes were brilliantly blue and wrinkled at the corners as she greeted her with a bright smile. Sasha was already in awe of her perfectly arched brows and palest-pink lips before she even spoke. She was all businesswoman, with the perfect splash of sass.

She sat down opposite her and held out her hand. 'I'm Margaret. We spoke on the phone. I'm Dem's attorney and you could say PA,' she finished with a smile.

Dem. Sasha couldn't imagine being close enough to call him that. Margaret seemed confident and at ease, which meant she had been with him some time. She was such a perfect-looking woman, Sasha couldn't help wondering if she'd made the classic mistake of sleeping with the boss. The thought alone made her blush. It was inappropriate and none of her business, anyway. 'I'm Sasha… Sasha Bond,' she said, hurriedly, realising she had left her waiting.

'Yes! Great to finally meet you. Dem's told me all about you.'

Sasha's emotions ranged from sheer annoyance at being discussed with a stranger to excitement and wild curiosity at what had been said. 'What did he say?' she blurted. 'All good, I hope,' she said quickly, to cover herself.

Margaret smiled brightly and appeared to search her face as if she was making up her mind about something. 'That would be more than my job was worth,' she said, still studying her. 'But I can tell you, he was determined to get you.'

Sasha's heart was thundering in her chest. She had no idea why the mere mention of him and her in the same sentence made her react like that. Her palms were damp and her mouth had gone sandpaper dry. She put it down to no one ever being determined to get her in her life. It was so flattering.

Margaret scribbled something down in her notepad.

'Was he like that with you?' Sasha said, wanting to clamp a hand over her own mouth, but kind of glad her question was out there. Why couldn't she just shut the hell up and nod in all the right places?

Margaret looked at her shrewdly and put down her pen on the table. 'Look, I am going to give you the advice no one ever gave to me. Yes, Dem was like that with me. He knows what he wants and, rest assured, he always gets it. The Carpathians are rich and they're powerful and if you work for them, you're made. This contract...' And she held the envelope up in her hand. 'Is the best you'll ever get, anywhere.'

Sasha gingerly took it from her, as if it contained a bomb, and removed the contents. It seemed like any other contract of employment, except it was on surprisingly thick, yellowed paper. She skimmed the pages until she found the numbers: $250,000 per annum. 'Two hundred and fifty thousand dollars. Is this right?' she said, looking over at Margaret, shocked.

'I know, right?' Margaret said, nodding excitedly. 'And forty-nine per cent of the profits of any future clothing lines or merchandise. It's a dream offer. The best I've seen, actually. He must really want you.'

Sasha looked down at the pages again, not sure how anyone could turn down an offer like that. She scanned for any mention of Jace or the collective, but there didn't appear to be anything anywhere. She checked twice. 'I don't get it. I thought I was being brought on board purely for Jace. You know...to make sure he flies right.'

Margaret bobbed her head a little. 'And you kind of are. You'll be nearby, so to speak. But you'll be on the business side of things, not the musicians'. You work for Demeter, not Raz. Is that clear? Because that's really important.'

Sasha nodded, frowning, not sure what advice Margaret was giving her, exactly. 'So are you saying to sign it or not to sign it?' Sasha asked, a little confused.

Margaret grinned. 'I can see you're getting it. If you don't, Demeter might up his offer slightly, but he will get you in the end. He always does. I just wanted you to be aware that this is a life, not a job. We live for the company twenty-four hours a day. Do you understand?'

Sasha was nodding, but she was still running through it all in her mind. She guessed that for two hundred and fifty K, they would expect their pound of flesh. 'OK,' she said, eventually.

Margaret's smile was one of concern, as if she completely sympathised. 'It's not at all bad,' Margaret said, obviously to bolster her up. 'You'll get to travel the world, mix with the world's most influential people and have more money than you know what to do with. Dem's very generous.'

Rather than jumping for joy, Sasha found herself wondering whether Jace's offer had been like this and how he had dealt with the caveat of no freedom. It would be far harder for him.

'Can I take some time to think about it, please?' Sasha asked.

Margaret laughed out loud and held out a pen. 'No, I'm afraid not. Dem was very clear on that. He wants it tied up today.'

Sasha reached out her hand slowly for the pen, not fully understanding why she was resisting and searching for a reason to say no. Her life wasn't exactly full at the moment. Living for an exciting job could be just what the doctor ordered.

She looked down at the pages and scanned them again. 'There is no notice period,' she said, like a bolt of inspiration that made her heart flutter at the convenient excuse. 'What if I wanted to leave?'

Margaret laughed again, as if she was really quite amazed by her. 'I promise, you won't need one. If Dem no longer needs you, you will leave right away, fully compensated.'

It still wasn't an answer. Surely that should be written down. 'But what—'

'You won't want to leave,' Margaret cut right across her. 'People just don't,' she said with a shrug and an expression that said it was still a source of amazement to her.

'OK,' Sasha said, bending over the paper. Her mind was still racing for something to stall her. It didn't help remembering Jace's panic in trying to contact her before she came. *Was she holding out for that? Some misplaced hope that he wanted her back?* 'Can I just add something small?' she asked, still formulating in her head what that could be, exactly.

Margaret bowed her head, 'Shoot!' she said, as if she was humouring her and she was just prolonging the inevitable.

'As I'm going to be primarily employed because of Jace—'

'You're not—' Margaret went to say, but Sasha held up her hand to finish.

'Yes, I know what you said, but can I add the option to leave, for whatever reason, should Jace no longer be part of the collective?' It was sketchy, she knew, but it was the best she could come up with at a moment's notice to give her some breathing space. 'You know...shouldn't be an issue if you're right and no one ever leaves,' she finished, not able to look Margaret in the eye.

They would undoubtedly want Jace to pursue a solo career, or he may even end up flatly refusing to work at all. That would be the sticking point, she knew.

Margaret was smiling knowingly when she finally had the courage to look at her again. She held out her hand for the document, which Sasha gathered and handed back to her. 'I can see why Dem wants you. You're a shrewd business-woman. Leave it with me. I'll go over it with Dem and get back to you later today.'

Sasha finally sat back in her seat with a wash of relief. It really felt like she'd dodged a bullet and, for the life of her, she had no idea why.

SASHA DIDN'T KNOW what to do with herself after that. She guessed she'd just have to wait.

She was shown back to her room by the maid, where she grabbed her bag and a book she'd brought with her for the journey. Perhaps she'd take a stroll in the garden, where she could find a nice spot to read.

The maid gave her directions to get back and left her at the conservatory doors. It was near the busy kitchen. Raised foreign voices and the crash of pans were easily carried through an open window. It made her wonder how many people it catered for in a house this size. The number of staff looking after one family was mind-blowing. It was like a hotel.

She needed some space to clear her mind. She took a step out onto the patio and her tension left her on a long sigh. For the first time in days, her heart lightened to something resembling optimism. She could finally spend some time on her own to absorb all this.

She ventured further out onto the neat grass, mown with tennis-court-line precision. It felt warmer and the air smelled marvellously of cut grass and spring flowers. Birds chirped from the trees, and a small plane went overhead. It felt a million miles from the nocturnal, drug-fuelled musicians' life of Jace. This could be her life if she wanted it.

She kept walking. Past wonderfully maintained flower beds, with colours cascading a rainbow, white marble benches and fruit trees with white blossom, until she came to the maze of crisp and angular hedges as tall as a small house.

She followed the path that urged her to go in. It could be fun. She looked to either side of her and ventured inside. The path of lumber wood chips was easy to follow. The temperature dropped inside as it was in the shade and made her shiver. The further she went, the more the hedge grew over her head, making it harder for the sun to penetrate. It got darker, quieter and lonelier.

A crow squawked and made her jump. She held her chest, breathed, and quickened her steps. Left and right, she went. Faster and faster, until she was jogging. Coming to dead ends and retracing her steps. She was now sweating and getting out of breath. It was darker, with the hedge a complete roof over her head. She'd been in there a long time. Her heart started to race and her head pounded in panic. She was getting to the point of shouting for help when she turned into an avenue with light up ahead. She sprinted for it and suddenly came out into a large square clearing.

It took a moment for her eyes to focus in the sunlight. She closed them and allowed her painful breathing to come back to normal. When she finally opened them, she was surprised. She was in a grassed area with a white marble fountain in the middle and a bench placed right next to it. A bench that was occupied.

Sasha hitched a breath.

A man was sitting on the bench and not just any man. He was strikingly similar to Demeter, lost in thought. He was staring into the falling water of the fountain. She thought he hadn't seen her until he said, 'Congratulations. You solved the maze,' in the now- familiar European accent.

Her mouth was dry from running and dehydration. Her voice came out gruff and croaky. 'Sorry to disturb you. It was just such a lovely day.' She went to turn back. 'I'll leave you to it.'

'No,' he said, a little curtly. 'Come and sit. I've been waiting for you.'

Sasha's feet dragged in the slightly overlong grass. There was something a little scary about this guy. He looked like Demeter, but he seemed harsher and sterner somehow. 'How did you know I'd come here?' she asked, her heart now speeding up from fear. Maybe it was the place and how isolated she felt.

'Just a hunch,' he said, laughing a little. Then he tipped his head towards her. 'Everyone ends up here in the end.'

She smiled, feeling foolish, and guessed he was right.

'No magical divination, I promise,' he said, fixing her with those piercing predator's eyes. It was strange, as they seemed so much crueller on him.

She ventured closer as she didn't want to offend him.

'Sit!' he prompted. 'I am Tegan. You have already met with my cousin, Demeter, I believe.

'Yes,' Sasha said, sitting down, conscious that she was perching at the furthest point of the bench without falling off. 'He's offered me a job.'

Tegan chuckled. 'Ah, yes, a job… And will you take it?' He was still looking ahead of him until he turned and held her with those husky dog eyes. Demeter's eyes; keen, sharp, deadly.

She studied him for a moment. He was very dark and striking like Demeter, except his face seemed harsher and his hair was greased back, away from his face, so it fell in sharp arrows down his forehead. He was looking at her and waiting.

She thought back to the question and answered honestly. 'Probably. I mean, I think so. Margaret is making a few small changes.'

He laughed lightly again. A laugh that didn't really lighten his face.

'What?' she asked, unsure what she'd done.

'Oh, it's nothing…just that your boyfriend did something very similar.'

'Just the mention of Jace felt like a stab to her heart. 'You saw Jace?' she asked, sitting up straighter to face him. Then, a little more calmly, 'Actually, he's not my boyfriend. Not anymore.'

He narrowed his eyes on her shrewdly. 'Yes, I'm on the board of acquisitions for the music side of the company.'

Sasha nodded, taking it all in. 'So he signed then … in the end.' She couldn't keep the hint of sadness out of her voice. Strangely, her sadness had nothing to do with her or the breakup. It just felt like Jace had lost a part of himself somehow. It was illogical, she knew, but that's how it felt.

Tegan was watching her closely. Knowingly. As if he'd followed her every thought. 'Don't worry, Sasha. They will be huge and make us all a lot of money.'

That was it, she guessed, smiling wanly. The bottom line. It was called the music business after all. It was one of life's cruel ironies that by their very nature, art and business didn't mix. 'I hope you're right,' she said, more to herself.

'That is where you come in.'

Her eyes shot to his. In that single moment, it hit her; she was still being interviewed. He was smiling benignly, knowing she finally understood that this chance meeting had been designed.

'You are a clever girl and a good designer. You will make money, but we both know that Jace's somewhat fragile nature will need careful handling.'

Her mind shot to Demeter and the breakfast meeting that morning. He'd known all along that this little meeting was going to happen when he left. She felt conned. It was ridiculous, she knew. She didn't know the man, but she guessed she expected better than this. He'd hooked her in, Margaret had done the pitch and this guy had been sent in for the close. *Unbelievable.*

'Don't be angry. Demeter genuinely sees a business opportunity in you. But he is a pragmatist and will always look at the benefit to the company overall.'

Sasha felt beyond pissed and looked at him flatly to get on with his spiel. 'What do you want from me?' she said, through clenched teeth.

Tegan laughed loudly at that. 'I can see that Demeter will be kept very busy with you.'

She didn't know how to even process that comment and continued to stare at him blankly.

He seemed to relent. 'All we ask is that you simply be available. Don't close yourself off to Jace. Be a friend when needed, so to speak.'

'We *are* friends,' she spat, shifting in her seat in annoyance. 'So I was right all along. You want me to babysit him.'

Tegan shrugged and bobbed his head slightly, in a non-committal kind of way. 'I wouldn't call it that.'

Sasha didn't know why she felt so bitterly disappointed. Deep down, she knew what the score had been here. But she guessed she hoped that, for once, someone actually saw her for who she was. Ironically, it was only ever Jace who did that. 'Do you have any idea how hard it is for us to get over a relationship we've been in since we were kids? ... Seeing each other might not be the best thing for Jace right now.' She tutted, shook her head and looked around the small garden.

Tegan smiled tightly. 'I can imagine.'

She doubted that very much.

'All I'm saying is why rip the band-aid off in one go? My

cousin Raziah is taking a special interest in him. Let's just ease him into his new life slowly, shall we?'

His words sounded reasonable enough, and on the surface, she guessed she really couldn't argue with the logic, but she recognised that look in his eye. It was implacable, leaving her no real choice. 'Why do you want Jace so badly? Surely there is a queue to take his place."

Tegan searched her face with a strange expression, as if he was amazed by something she didn't get. 'Everyone wanting success and fame comes to us in the end.'

She stared at him for a long moment after he finished speaking. Something in those words made her shiver. She guessed it was the inevitability in them and the absolute confidence that he was telling the truth. It made her feel dreadfully sad.

Tegan certainly didn't dwell on them. When he realised she'd got the point, he nodded once like a full stop and got to his feet. He was a taller, slimmer version of Demeter, right down to the expensive black shoes. Except he reminded her more of an undertaker than a supermodel, dressed completely in black. 'I'll leave you to think it over.' He made his way towards the way out.

Sasha watched him until he'd disappeared. Despite confirming her fears, she was now more in turmoil about the job offer than ever. What he was suggesting only benefited Jace in the short term and was definitely not the best idea for her, emotionally. But it was still the job offer of a lifetime; she had to remember that. She would get to spend time with Jace and be paid a lot of money for it. But for Jace, this was a patch job, not a fix, and the artificial limbo would cripple her. She was sure, in the end, it wasn't good for either of them. But Jace had already signed, and she was about to. *Could she really say no? Would she?* Maybe she had to stop kidding herself.

By some miracle, with a confused and heavy heart, she found her way out of the maze quite easily. Or perhaps her preoccupation made it seem like that. She still hadn't fully made up her mind by the time she made it back to her room.

Then, as if on cue, the phone by the bed rang. It was Margaret. 'Meet me in the boardroom at five.'

Sasha slowly replaced the receiver. She didn't have long to decide.

CHAPTER 15

It was the longest day of Sasha's life. She'd read and re-read the same paragraph of her book maybe fifty times. In the end, she showered and changed into something more business-like in the hope of finding inspiration.

When at last the light knock at the door sounded, her time was up, she let out a ragged breath, nodded, and followed the maid out in silence. Preoccupied, the maze of corridors passed quickly, until she finally walked into the impressive boardroom at five minutes to five, still not a hundred per cent sure what she'd say.

The room was large, dark and decorated in a claret red. Display cabinets and dark-wood-framed paintings lined the walls, continuing the antique feel of the whole building. However, it was the huge, heavy oak table, lit by a large black chandelier, that dominated the room. Margaret was already seated there, in conversation with the guy, Tegan, from the maze, who nodded when he saw her.

Sasha swallowed and her feet dragged. An old clock on the mantelpiece chimed the hour and made her jump. This was already harder than she thought.

'Ah, there she is. The woman of the hour,' Margaret said, her smile brightening when she saw her. 'Please take a seat. I think you've already met Dem's cousin, Tegan. He's looking after Jace's interests.

Sasha already felt out of her depth. The only jobs she'd ever interviewed for were a cash register operator in Speedimart and one summer job as an intern for a clothes label no one had ever heard of. This was nothing like that. It was more like signing away her life.

By the time she sat down at the impossibly large table, an acre away from Margaret and Tegan, she was convinced she had no business being there at all. Suddenly, working at a shop for bosses younger than her or dressing mannequins felt warm and fuzzy.

Margaret passed her back the envelope she'd seen earlier. 'We've made a few changes as you suggested after running them past Dem. He agreed them in principle, with just one small adjustment.'

Sasha slid the contents of the envelope free and studied them. Her eyes felt blurry, as if she were reading Chinese. Luckily, the amendments in darker black ink were easy to find. 'What is it?' she asked. It all seemed to be in order. 'Immediate release should Jace leave for any reason … I don't see the difference.' She looked across the table, from one to the other, for the answer.

Tegan remained silent, watching her shrewdly with heavy-lidded eyes. Margaret spoke up immediately. 'That's good. All it is is a small change from leaving the collective to leaving the Carpathian Group.'

Sasha let that sink in. Demeter was very crafty. The small change allowed Jace to have a solo career, and she'd still be tied.

'It is still a very generous offer,' Tegan piped up for the first time. His penetrating gaze bore straight into hers and he gave her his tight smile, which looked like an effort.

He was right, though. What was the alternative? Go home and stay closeted with her mother? Even she was pushing her to get a life, and she loved having her home. It wasn't like she had job offers lining up.

Sasha let out a ragged breath. She felt damned if she did and damned if she didn't. She picked up the heavy gold pen Margaret had passed her and signed her name in full: Sasha Victoria Bond. Her heart physically ached when she dotted the paper, as if a knife had twisted in her chest.

Her eyes went straight to Tegan. He was still watching her closely. He nodded once as if he was impressed. 'You have made the right choice,' he said, as if he knew full well how hard it was for her.

'What now?' Sasha asked, leaning back in her chair.

Margaret was sliding the contract back into the envelope before she could change her mind.

'Am I still going home tonight?' It would be nice to decompress things and get her head straight.

'No … Dem thinks it's a good idea to put you to work right away. TRHBDor have a world tour coming up after the release of their first album. A team will be arriving to work with you tomorrow. So stay the night. Relax. And celebrate,' Margaret finished, with her characteristic bright smile.

Sasha smiled weakly, a little overwhelmed. She hadn't spoken to her mother in two days. Everything was moving so fast.

Tegan gabbled something in his own language as he stood from his chair. Then he turned and bowed his head slightly towards her. 'Good evening, Sasha.'

'Good evening,' she replied lamely.

As soon as he disappeared, Margaret slid her mobile

phone across the table. 'Be quick! You have two minutes to phone your mother.'

Sasha stared for a long moment, not sure she'd heard right, then she snatched it up. She put it to her ear as Margaret reached the door. 'I'll wait outside … Oh, and by the way, the phones are monitored. So don't go ringing anyone else,' Margaret said before she disappeared.

Sasha didn't have time to process that before her mother answered. 'Sasha?'

'Hi, Mom, sorry I haven't called. Been so busy and with travelling and the time difference and everything.'

'Oh, don't worry, honey, you're calling now. Where are you?'

'Can you believe it? I'm overseas. Romania, I think?' she said, sounding upbeat, not sure she was convincing her mom or herself. 'It's a bit hush-hush. I just wanted to check in and let you know I'm OK. It might be difficult to call for a while. Is everything alright at home?'

'Yes, of course. Don't worry about me. So you got the job? I knew you could do it. I'm so proud of you, honey.'

Sasha's heart swelled with the selfless love emanating from her mother. Her life was very small and lonely without her there and she still wanted her to get out and live. 'Yeah, I did. I signed the contract just now. It's a lot of money, but it will be a big commitment, I think. I might not be home that much.' It made her feel guilty for playing it down. By the sounds of it, she'd hardly make it home at all.

'I'm not in the least bit surprised. That nice handsome man was so keen on you getting it.'

'Wait! Say that again. What nice handsome man?' Sasha's heart was beating in her chest. She knew exactly who it was, and yet dreaded hearing the words.

'Dem-Demetrius, was it—'

'Demeter?' Sasha said, cutting across her. 'Demeter called you?'

'No, dear. He came here just the other day. Just after you left to go there. He said he wanted to meet me and reassure me before you started work. He told me that you would be working away a lot, that his company would look after you, and that he would personally see to it that you were safe. Then he gave me a package of full medical insurance. The highest level money can buy. I mean, I was blown away. You hadn't even got the job at that point. He said he didn't care and that he had confidence in you. He's so generous, honey. He must have been so sure of you to do that.'

'Yeah, he must have,' Sasha said weakly, while her brain scrambled on what it all meant. Maybe she should have been pleased or, at the very least, flattered, but all she felt was shocked. He'd grossly overstepped into her private life and she was left reeling.

Margaret put her head back inside the door and mouthed the word, 'Time.'

'Gotta go, Mom,' Sasha said, feeling immediately relieved. She didn't want to give away how alarmed she felt. Her mother seemed so happy about it.

'OK, honey. I'm so thrilled for you. Oh, and before I forget. Jace called again and said he'd see you at the chateau in a few weeks… Chateau, eh? What a life you kids lead,' she said, chuckling.

Sasha closed her eyes. 'Thanks, Mom.' She clicked off the call, not sure she could deal with Jace on top of everything else.

'Jace is coming here,' she said, passing the phone back to Margaret.

'Yes, I heard. Hopefully, in a couple of weekends' time, if they get finished in LA. There's a music festival thing the family puts on here. Raz organises it. It's entirely up to you whether you attend, but I think Dem will want to see you there so the media know you're still with the brand.

'And this Raz … Do you know her?'

'Not personally, no. She's Dem's sister.'

Sasha was immediately struck by the usually bright smile, clouding at the mention of Raz's name. It sent alarm bells ringing.

'She's stunning. Well, you'll see for yourself. The whole family attends. She's an accomplished musician as well, I believe.'

Great. Jace was already lost. And when they got there, she'd have to see them together.

JACE AND RAZ had been inseparable. She'd been insatiable since they'd had sex and they were soon having it anywhere and everywhere: in public bathrooms, the back of cars, the beach. It was dangerous because the paparazzi had cottoned on and followed them everywhere and headlines of Lil Jace and his mystery girl started to appear in the music rags. Despite the threat of her cover being blown, she couldn't get enough of him. He was bowled over and flattered that such an exquisite creature could be so into him. However, what started off as a wild ride began to feel like he was losing more of himself every day. Raz was siphoning his energy as sure as an enterprising teenager siphoned off petrol for a joy ride. Except the petrol was his freedom and the joyride hers.

With only the minor security of Steve and a car nearby, as long as she was with him, she seemed able to do pretty much what she wanted. Her drug-taking and partying eclipsed his, easily. Until he wondered if the little-girl-lost persona of her bedroom was just an act. She was out of control and reckless. Far more than he was, dragging him to one superstar party after another. Many tucked away in the Hollywood hills or on the beaches of Malibu. They were the new power couple in town that everyone wanted to be seen with.

Jace often looked at Steve to intervene, but he never did; it was as if he expected it. He simply looked on benignly and scanned the area for hidden dangers.

In the end, it felt like nothing they did was his idea. Jace went along, blocking out the fake people with more and more drugs. There was no one there from his troupe. Only film and rock stars and people he knew from TV. All the while, Raz held his hand and kissed him shamelessly in public, showing the world they were in an intense relationship. Which they were. All-consuming. Twenty-four hours a day.

The looks he got were envious. All the while, behind the eyes, the men were asking themselves what he had that they didn't. He sure as hell didn't know. Something in the whole situation felt off. He didn't know how, he just knew.

They'd played a kick-ass show that night. It was a small, intimate gig for their most loyal fans and industry crowd to showcase the album material before the tour. It went brilliantly. It was their usual brand of chaos on stage, but the fans loved it. The girls screamed for him, as they always did and Raz, who normally stood in the wings, remained at the back of the room with the suits. Until she came on and shredded her guitar on the track that was to be the single. It took off the roof and reminded him of what he saw in her. Every time he wanted to pull away for space, he'd see her work and was so proud she was his, she would reel him back in. She was, without doubt, the coolest, most sexy, high-maintenance girl he'd ever met.

Jace came off stage and went straight to the dressing room he shared with the troupe. He came across Raz with two female fans. They were always at his gigs and he knew them well. He put up his hand and smiled, but it faded when he realised they were crying. Raz was standing over them while they huddled together on the sofa. Raz whirled around, shoving him in the chest as she stormed past. He only just caught the pen and pad she let drop from her hand. 'Scribble your name and get rid of them,' she hissed.

Jace frowned at the ferocity of it. It was uncalled for and unkind. He watched Raz flounce off out of the room and turned back to the girls, who were getting to their feet. They looked at the door and he smiled reassuringly. 'It's OK, she's gone. What do you want me to say?' he said, holding the pen to the pad.

Their faces lightened, although their eyes were still red. 'It's for my sister, Kate,' one said. 'She's in the hospital and couldn't come.'

Jace smiled and scrawled his untidy handwriting across the page while he spoke. 'Kate. Look forward to meeting you at my next show, love and best wishes, Lil Jace,' and he finished it with a big heart. An idea he got from Sasha. His heart ached a little as he dotted the page. 'Do you want a picture?' he said, trying his best to hide his sadness.

Both girls clapped and squealed and, without a care that their eyes were red from crying, they crowded in with him in the middle and took a selfie on both of their phones.

'Thanks, girls. See you next time I'm in town. I'll see you get tickets at the door.' They both bounced and clapped. Then they looked at the exit, a little unsure. They were scared of Raz. 'Go. It's OK. I got you,' he said.

The girls literally swooned into a fit of giggles, which made him laugh. Then they headed for the door, much happier.

Duo nudged him with a beer. Jace took it absently while he waved at the girls. One stopped and called out over her shoulder, 'Please be careful, Jace.' He nodded, not completely sure what she meant.

'What was that all about?' Duo asked after they went.

Jace shook his head, relieved they'd gone. 'No idea,' but, weirdly, his mind went straight to Raz.

He looked for her after, but she'd gone, which was unusual. She normally dragged him to some party or another. Very often, she ended up on guitar, which the party-goers always loved. Tonight, it felt like a bonus, so he used the opportunity to go home. It made him chuckle ruefully how the tables had turned. Sasha would have loved that just once in a while.

THE BEACH HOUSE was in darkness when Jace got home. He went through the house, switching on lights and stopped dead when he went into his room. Raz was sitting on the bed, staring into space. 'You OK?' he asked a little apprehensively when she didn't turn around.

She turned her head to look at him and rolled her eyes. 'You don't care,' she said, bitterly, in a low voice so he could barely hear her.

'What do you mean? Of course I care,' he said, taking off his heavy leather jacket and gathering himself for the inevitable scene.

She got up and stalked towards him, only stopping when she had to crane her neck to look up at him a few inches away. 'Do you, though? Enjoy shagging your fangirls, did you? That's sure as hell caring, isn't it?' Her volume increased the more she said, until she shoved him in the chest and went to pull back to punch and kick him, but he was too fast and hugged her over her arms, drawing her to him so she couldn't move.

'Stop this…stop!' he shouted, crushing her struggles and trying to calm her, while he spoke soothingly into her hair. 'You know I didn't fool around with those girls … talk to me.

Please, Raz.' Even as he said the words, it struck him what a strange statement that was. Alien on his lips. Because they almost never talked. They communicated over music, in the studio, or when he was writing a song. They played music, danced, drank and took copious amounts of drugs. They had off-the-scale, unbelievably hot sex together, but in the few weeks of knowing each other and being together all the time, they'd never talked. They knew almost nothing about each other because it hadn't mattered. That had been the appeal.

Raz was the antithesis of Sasha. Closing that thought as quickly as it came, he prompted, 'Come on, tell me.' Jace walked over and sat on the edge of the bed and pulled her onto his lap.

Raz turned into him and linked her arms around his neck, staring at him with those otherworldly eyes. 'I'm sorry,' she said.

Jace was shocked to see them fill with tears. She immediately went to pull away, but he wouldn't let her. His conflicting thoughts were quickly replaced by an overwhelming urge to comfort her. He guessed it was because he'd assumed she was always so strong. But she wasn't. It was clear she was extremely insecure. Ridiculous but true.

He sat with her in his arms and, to his horror, she actually cried brokenheartedly into his shoulder. 'What is it?' he said, looking out over her head while he rocked her. His mind scrambled. This couldn't possibly be just because of those girls. 'You can tell me. Please, Raz.'

She sniffed and straightened up so he could see a little of her tear-stained face. It devastated him to see her like this. He broke girls. It was what he did. He never meant to, but it happened just by being him. He'd wrongly assumed that just because of who she was, she was impervious. She wiped her eyes and nose on the cuff of her denim shirt.

Jace put a finger under her chin and brought it around so

she would finally look at him properly. 'I know almost nothing about you, Raz. It's time to talk, isn't it? I want to know everything.'

She nodded and closed her eyes as if the moment she'd been dreading had finally come.

Jace was completely baffled, watching her intently. He caught a tear before it fell on the pad of his thumb.

'You still love her,' she said, wearily, as a sad statement, not a question.

It took him a moment to catch up with what she was saying. 'Who, Sasha?' He was shocked they'd headed straight in that direction. He wasn't expecting it. 'Well, yeah. Of course I do.' Her eyes widened, but before she could erupt, he continued, 'I'll always love Sasha.' He shook his head and frowned. He was forced to analyse stuff about himself he normally avoided. 'It's nothing like us, though.' He and Raz were a tornado and he and Sasha were comfortable sunshine. 'I've known her for like, forever.' Then, before he could get lost in uncomfortable comparisons, he deflected the subject. 'I don't understand. Why are you saying all of this now?'

She looked down sullenly, picking at her fingers in her lap. Jace found himself following her delicate grey tattoos down the length of her forearm to the nailbeds of her fingers. It occurred to him then that it would have been excruciatingly painful there.

'Everybody loves you, Jace. They can't help themselves. Your friends, your band-mates – even though they're jealous of you – Sasha, fans, those two fangirls tonight.'

Now it became clear what all this was about. He sighed, exasperated with her. She, of all people, should know what the business was like. 'Is that it? The two girls in my dressing room tonight?'

She looked away, confirming he was right.

'You think that I – those days are gone, Raz. I never

thought they would be, but meeting you has seen to that. I don't need that anymore.' The revelation blindsided him. Because he absolutely didn't. He adored his fans, but the days of getting off with fangirls, or boys, come to that, were over. Despite all his regrets about Sasha, it was being with Raz that had changed him. Then, with exhausted resignation, he said, 'You're everything I need.' It was the finality of it that floored him. 'You'll be the death of me, but it's true.' He frowned. He wasn't necessarily happier, but it was Raz's high-maintenance, not Sasha's easygoing nature, that he needed to grow up.

Her eyes went to his as she studied him for any tells of bullshit. He nodded in all seriousness. 'It's true. You've made an honest man out of me. I can't see anything after you.'

He arranged her more comfortably on his lap, into his body, but it was really to hide the panic hurtling through him. He kissed the side of her face and buried his nose in the crook of her neck and spoke next to her skin. 'Raz, you outshine me in every way. You outplay me, outparty me, outsex me,' he said incredulously. 'You even out-fuckin'-tattoo me. You're better than me at everything. As long as there's breath in me, you'll never lose me. I promise.' He hugged her to him tightly, but, strangely, his mind went to the clause he'd had added to his contract. The one that released everyone on his death. He felt raw. He'd never poured himself out like that. Not even to Sasha. No, because Sasha always knew. He didn't have to.

Raz proceeded to kiss the side of his neck, sucking a little of the skin to draw blood. She was always preoccupied with it. What it symbolised. A person's life force. What made them them. She wanted it as keenly as she wanted him. And it was hot. Hot like her. 'You shouldn't make a promise you can't keep,' she said huskily.

Jace pulled her face around roughly. 'I can keep it!' His

eyes dropped to her full lips. She was driving him wild as she always did.

Her eyelids lowered, not missing a thing. She rummaged in her jeans pocket and pulled out a vial of powder and the small razor blade she always had on her.

His blood was already pumping like a train.

'Are you willing to bleed for me?' she asked, her voice almost completely gone.

A rod of lust shot right through him. This was why he could never leave this girl. She could lead him through hell on a leash because she owned him in the sack. That was the power she had over him. His mouth crashed into hers. Their frantic hands dispensed with clothes and he was pumping into her like a man possessed.

Raz pushed him off her roughly and mounted him, cutting lines of coke on a small mirror as she worked him slowly and deliberately. The anticipation quadrupled his endorphins, heightening his excitement as she passed him a rolled ten-dollar bill. 'Don't stop!' she ordered, as he leaned forward to sniff his line.

Jace thought he'd have a heart attack as the rush mowed him down. He flipped her over as soon as he regained motor skills, pounced and renewed his thrusts. He became wild with only one thought. *Her.* Nothing else mattered. Only her. Fucking her. Snorting coke with her. Blowing his mind.

The next thing he knew, she was picking up the blade from the discarded mirror and holding it next to his face. He was hot and sweating, looking up at her straddling him. But despite her obvious threat, he couldn't stop his hips gyrating. 'You'll never leave me?' she asked, her eyes wild and dilated against her red, overheated face.

She clenched her inner muscles, and he hitched a breath and shook his head. 'Never,' he said, barely holding himself together.

Are you prepared to make a pact?'

Serious vibes were threatening to break through his buzz and he frowned a little, but circled his hips to move things along.

Raz took that as a yes, picked up his arm, made a shallow cut across his wrist, and brought it to her mouth. He stopped moving to watch her tongue licking and circling the small line of blood. Then she did the same in two lines down the pecks of his chest. His cock flexed inside her when he thought of how tribal the scars would look. She answered by dragging her tongue up the full length of the cuts to catch the blood.

Strangely, he was so far gone down the sex slave track that he didn't have an ounce of fear when she took the blade to his neck. He was utterly spellbound when she did the same with her own. He had to be bruising her; his hands gripped her hips so hard.

'Take this and I own you,' she said, throwing the blade onto the nightstand.

All he could think about was how wrong it was, but how completely turned on it was making him. She leaned forward onto her hands and began working him again. Small, warm drips – a mixture of blood and sweat – began to land on his face. It was completely unfair. He was unbelievably close and he threw his head back and groaned.

Then she was there, kissing him fiercely. Biting his neck hard, and before he knew it, he was at hers. Tasting the salty, metallic mess while his hips pumped and he came, the hardest, most all-consuming climax of his life. It came over him so fast and so strong that he lost all idea of who or where he was. Sane thought had abandoned him. Nothing else mattered but the two of them riding that final, heart-crushing wave of pleasure.

At last, they slumped together in a slap of wet skin,

completely exhausted. So completely replete that neither spoke for a long time. They lay there so long that his damp skin became goose-bumped and cold, and the joy he'd felt during the act was replaced by an overwhelming feeling of sadness. Like a junky who'd given in to his addiction and some part of him had been taken away instead of gained. Loving Raz was always so extreme. Soaring highs, followed by soul-crushing lows. Nothing was making any sense anymore.

Jace turned his head to the large patio doors and the heart-warming orange of morning was still a suggestion in the distance. The blue grey he saw made him think of the name of his collective: The Restless Hour Before Dawn. It should now be the damned hour because something had died that he would never get back. He was lying with the hottest girl he'd ever known, but felt utterly forsaken. Alone.

This was how it was with them. Just when he managed to pinpoint why it was not working between them, she'd hit him with her crushing vulnerability, and his resolve would crumble by having soul-possessing sex as they'd just had.

They were inseparable but apart, like train wheels on a track.

He wrote songs trying to quantify it, shared drugs and his hazy world with her. Strangely, it was him who got them to the shows and TV interviews. Late, but he got them there. Their notoriety was growing even faster than their record sales. They were the power couple in town, but they were just about holding it together. *Power couple?* More like a lost-in-the-abyss, just-about-functioning couple. That's what tonight had been about. Two hopeless people trying to glue themselves together with coke and blood.

The last thing he felt was powerful. He was the guest actor appearing in his own life. A helpless spectator. He'd entered the roller coaster on the drop and now there was no way off.

Duo saw it. The whole band started to notice. That was the real reason their jealousy had subsided. None would swap places with him now. They were used to Raz always being around. They'd become the Sid and Nancy or the Kurt and Courtney of the group. *How did he become this fucked up?* The album was finished. He should be happy – especially as they were going back to the chateau and he'd finally get to see Sasha. But even that he was dreading. She would see him like this: a shell of a man.

He left Raz purring in sleep and wandered out to the decking by the pool with just a towel tied around his waist. Everyone had crashed and it was far too early for them to be up.

He flopped down at the edge and dangled his feet in the cool water. The chill grounded him and helped with his feelings of aimlessness. His nose was running, his arms and legs weighed a tonne and it was all he could do to hold himself up.

Someone approached. Jace turned his head and saw it was Duo. He was dressed like he hadn't been to bed. Duo gave him that look he reserved only for when he was wasted. Jace was forced to say 'Stop!' before he got the lecture.

'What?' Duo said, half laughing. 'I haven't said a word yet.'

'You don't have to,' Jace said, more to himself.

'What the hell happened?' Duo said, sitting down next to him, removing his shoes and rolling up his jeans.

It took Jace a moment to catch up, then he remembered his chest. He looked down and saw the red, angry tracks down his body. They seemed the least of his troubles. 'I should be happy, shouldn't I?' Jace said, looking at his friend and frowning.

Duo shrugged, not committing himself either way. 'It's

been intense. No one has really had time to touch the ground yet.'

'Are you happy, though, D?'

Duo gave him his lopsided, gold-grilled grin. 'Sure … beats washing dishes or flippin' burgers.'

Jace nodded. That was certainly true. Maybe he was just a whining baby with nothing better to do. 'It's just that I expected … I expected to feel … more, you know?'

Duo laughed, no doubt thinking of the amount of drugs he took so he didn't feel. Even he had to smile a little.

'What more could you want, Jace? You just cut your first album, you're signed to the biggest production company on the planet, you're about to start a world tour, supporting Tré. We're in the top twenty of the Billboard charts before the album is even released. And you have a banshee in your bed?'

Jace tried to look angry at his friend for his last comment, but even he had to smile and nod along with it. Raz was a wild spirit and he did have the dream life. Then why did everything feel so flat?

Duo touched him on the shoulder and used it to help himself up. 'Gotta sleep. Sun's coming up and we'll be on a plane in a few hours.'

Jace nodded and the familiar ache twisted in his chest. Maybe he was just burnt out and needed to recharge. He would see Sasha; he had to remember that. Even though he had no idea whether he could handle it.

His come-down would hit hard.

CHAPTER 16

Sasha spent the next few weeks at the chateau. Her misgivings receded, and she began to feel quite relaxed. She soon found it hard to remember what it was she was even worried about.

As promised, the next day, an experienced designer, Julius Calcarni, and a team of pattern cutters and seamstresses arrived. They got straight to work on new looks for the collective to take on tour. It felt like she'd gone to heaven. Every kind of fabric was delivered for her, no matter the cost, and everyone treated her like she was already a name. She'd never felt so good about herself. She'd earned this, all on her own.

She glimpsed Demeter a few times. He stalked in, confidently, and talked to Margaret or Julius and his eyes would meet hers just for a second. Enough to make her wonder what was being said.

She found herself grazing over his trim physique. How wide his shoulders were and how well they sloped into his neck. How his back tapered into the waistband of his Italian pants in a perfect V, proving he was fit. She bet he ran every day. It was obvious he was athletic, without being muscle-bound from hours in a gym. He moved fluidly and yet seemed powerful, as if violence was only just below the surface.

He affected her completely, taking over her thoughts, like no one ever had. Not even Jace. She would lie awake at night thinking about him and wondering if a man like that ever dated. Somehow, girlfriends seemed too mundane for him. He probably just had conquests. Margaret came to mind and she wondered if she'd been one of them. How she wished she could ask. He'd kept her loyalty and that said a lot about his character if she had.

Then her mind would drift to Jace and what he was doing now. He was finally coming to the chateau. It had begun to feel like a carrot dangled to keep her on edge and in her place. However, fittings were needed if the clothes were to be ready for the tour. The album was due for release and the tour would start next week. So the day she'd yearned for and dreaded equally was coming and she would finally see him with the girl who'd taken her place.

SATURDAY MORNING WAS D Day and Sasha was woken with a start. 'Miss Bond ... Miss Bond!' her maid said, pulling the curtains across with a loud jingle and a swish. 'You only have two hours to breakfast and get ready. The helicopter leaves at ten.'

'What helicopter?' she said, blinking herself awake. 'Why? Where are we going?'

'It's the Vamp festival today. Chop-chop! I will bring you your breakfast in an hour. Be ready, please, Miss Bond.' The maid whisked out on a gust of wind, leaving Sasha stunned, sitting up in her bed.

'Vamp festival?' she said to herself, vaguely remembering

Margaret mentioning a family thing, but she was sure this one was a huge deal. It was German or Polish, or something. It made her wonder, for the millionth time, where she actually was.

She swung her legs over the side of the bed and padded into her bathroom on autopilot. After turning the shower dial, she stared into the spray as it warmed up. By the time she got in, she felt confused, disappointed and a little annoyed. They hadn't been upfront and honest, leading her to believe Jace was coming. They must have known about the festival for weeks, and the only time it had been mentioned, it had been played down. Jace was supposed to be coming for fittings; she'd got all worked up and mentally prepared for it, and now it was clear that he wasn't.

She hitched her breath and stopped breathing. *Maybe he was heading to the festival too. Perhaps they were performing. Shit! Were the tour clothes meant to be ready?*

Sasha showered in record time and hurried out, dripping a trail of water on the floor. She dialled Margaret's room on the phone by her bed. 'A festival, Margaret. Really? Why didn't anyone warn me?'

'I did mention it early on. The collective was a last-minute booking and we didn't want you choking up with nerves. Don't worry. It's all good.'

'But the clothes…are they wearing them?'

'Don't worry. Just the leather jackets and the seamstresses worked through the night on those. It's mainly getting the merch out there today and that's already been shipped. Don't worry. Eat a nice breakfast and I'll meet you out on the helipad.'

'Margaret!' Sasha yelped, panicking. 'Jace will be there with Raz, won't he?' She couldn't help how incredibly lame and child-like that sounded. Her heart felt like it had a jagged hole in it.

'Sure … you should see everyone today. Even Dem usually puts in an appearance with the cousins. The family is the main promoter. It generates a lot of cash for the sponsors.'

The way she said it left her feeling weird, as if she'd deliberately mentioned Dem right after Jace, as if he was replacing him. It was the weirdest feeling. 'Oh,' was all she managed to reply. She promised she'd be ready, said goodbye and put down the receiver.

Now it was Jace *and* Demeter. It propelled an already terrifying prospect into a nightmare.

JACE WAS in a semi-coma-like state on the Gulf Stream jet all the way to Europe. Raz had literally passed out and was draped over the front of him. He wanted to push her off onto her own seat, but she clung like a cat. There were at least four empty seats and she had to be on top of him on his one.

Zach tutted, and his bandmates laughed at the state of them. He could only manage to open one eye. They'd gone straight to the airfield from a club and stumbled straight onto the plane. *Why was he even awake?* He'd taken enough pills to knock out a horse. He'd gone hard that night, even by his standards. He guessed that seeing Sasha for the first time after their split was enough to break through even the most robust knock-out cocktail.

It was weird because he never once worried what she'd think of seeing him and Raz. All he could imagine was Sasha with one of those devious coyote cousins and his blood boiled. No wonder he couldn't relax.

Raz stirred and shifted on his chest. He tightened his hold around her and she groaned and snuggled into him. He kissed the top of her head. *This was real. It was now.* He was getting used to it. *Wasn't he?*

The next thing he knew, they were being woken to transfer to a helicopter. He followed and climbed in, stumbling, half asleep. It made his stomach roil and churn so much so that he had to close his eyes or be sick. He saw none of the journey. He remembered flying over wilderness, the smell of pine and the stench of fuel. That would always remind him of the Carpathians. Not a feel-good association.

'We're here!' Zach said, making him blink awake.

Jace sat straighter to see out of the window, making Raz's head fall into the gap behind him. There were fields of people, covering acres, as far as the eye could see. This was huge, like Coachella or Glastonbury.

'Hell, you guys … Have you seen this?' Duo said, excitedly, from the opposite side. 'This is a big deal.'

The others began to whoop, forcing Raz awake.

It certainly was. Jace whistled in wonder as they descended to the chalked-out area with 'Welcome' across it. He'd scarcely ever been to a festival, let alone played to one this size.

'Don't worry,' Zach said next to him. 'You won't be on the main stage. I think they have the Kings headlining. You're in one of the tents to give the club-like atmosphere the fans are used to.'

It seemed logical and a lot less scary for him. He relaxed back into his seat as they landed with a slight bump. Pain immediately gripped his stomach. 'Is Sasha here yet?' It was what his real nerves were all about.

Zach glanced at him nervously and then at Raz, who'd resumed her position with her head on Jace's shoulder and her eyes closed. He nodded, a little exasperated, with a look that said, 'Do you really want to ask that now?'

Then, when Jace didn't look away but stared at him stonily for his answer, he eventually said, 'She will be with the organisers. This is a Carpathian event.'

Jace looked out of the window, knowing he had to get out. The scope of these people still amazed him. They must be making millions from this one weekend alone. And Sasha was here in the heart of it.

He let out a long, ragged breath and freed his matted hair from the knot on top of his head. Today it was white blond, tipped in pink. He always travelled with his hair up like a pineapple to stop it going flat. He smoothed his sweaty palms on his holey, bleached jeans and looked down at the t-shirt he'd chosen especially today. It was one of the few items of clothing he kept from his time growing up in Pittsburgh. One of Sasha's early designs. It had a small glow-worm logo on the front that glowed in the dark, and Radioactive Trap Boi across the back. It was so cool. It could mean his drug-fuelled lifestyle or his music. He'd always loved it and even wrote a song about it with the same name. He wasn't sure why he was wearing it now. He'd been told what to wear. He guessed he wanted to send a tribute to the contribution she'd made to his life and where he was now.

He blinked away a tear before anyone saw it.

They finally got out and, with his arm around Raz's shoulders, they ran clear of the blades. She hadn't said much. Just looked up at him, concerned, studying him for tells. Any fool could see he was as jittery as a box of frogs, so he had no hope of hiding his terror from her. 'Where will she be?' he said, immediately, opting for bluntness.

She answered just as honestly. 'VIP area … It's behind the main Volcano stage.'

He nodded, sending an apology with a simple look. No point dragging this out.

'We're heading there now,' Zach said, overhearing and leading the way.

The whole group moved forward with several of those Hitler Youth-type guards he remembered from the chateau.

A lot of acts had security, but none were in the full uniform of the Carpathian army. It made everyone stare at them like they were super VIPs.

Jace kept his head down, dying for a corner to tuck himself away. He felt remarkably alert for someone who'd had little sleep. Just sick. His stomach sloshed with the empty feeling that followed days of drugs, beer and cigarettes and little else. He'd just need to throw up before he went on stage, then he'd be good to go.

Raz gripped his hand and he looked down into her eyes, now covered in shades. She smiled up at him weakly. He felt guilty at how nerve-racking this must be for her. He pulled her in close and kissed her. Even chronic bed-head looked super-sexy on her. 'Will you play today?' he asked, close to her ear.

'I doubt it. I'll have to spend time with my family. My brother will be here,' she said, glancing at him a little sheepishly.

Joy, Jace muttered. This day just got better and better.

JACE WASN'T there when Sasha arrived, so it gave her a chance to acclimatise to all the people and get inwardly prepared. She even had a glass of champagne to calm her nerves and it was barely midday.

She helped Margaret oversee the setup of the band merch at the mouth of the tent where TRHBDor were due to perform. It was in an area of the festival called Boho village, which she was determined to use for the name of a clothing line one day. She made a mental note to talk to Margaret about it. Then they ambled back to the heavily cordoned-off, strictly VIP area to the right of the main stage. It was behind the huge bank of speakers, so it was not too loud and was mainly reserved for the Carpathian family.

Her heart actually skipped when Demeter was already there, smiling and chatting with the three cousins and some equally handsome men she didn't recognise. Any one of them could have been a runway model. They were all dressed beautifully in expensive suits. They were all tall, their hair and skin dark, with the gold in their rings and watches glinting in the sunshine, against their darkness.

Today, Demeter was completely in black, as many of them were, but not casual. He rarely did that. His black shirt was tucked into perfectly pressed black slacks, and his dark grey silk tie was a tight knot at his neck. She couldn't make up her mind if casual clothes would make him seem more or less dangerous. Either way, she couldn't keep her eyes off him. The way he interacted with his family: the easy way he chatted and even smiled, as they caught up on news.

Then a smaller, fairer girl appeared and Sasha could barely breathe. Her throat closed up so much she had to cough. She had mid-length, mousy-blonde hair and a perfectly proportioned figure. Dressed in simple blue jeans, a grey vest top, and a tatty biker jacket hanging off a shoulder. She was obviously a musician. Cool amber wraparound sunglasses and hundreds of chains around her wrists and neck completed a look she couldn't have designed better herself. She was fascinating, with countless tiny tattoos on her bare arms that crept up her neck and even spread to her stunning, heart-shaped face. She pushed up her sunglasses to reveal those eyes – a perfect mirror of Demeter's, who hugged her tightly.

Sasha's blood began to pump in her chest and temples, painfully, as that confirmed who it was.

Demeter said something in her ear and she turned immediately to look straight at her. They stared in a deadlock, like nothing else mattered. Demeter kept a hold on the girl as if she'd fly off at any minute. It was like he was talking her down, or telling her off. All the while, they just stared, not even blinking, for what felt like an hour.

Then, thankfully, jolting her out of it, the others came into the enclosure. Duo, Brains, Tears, Jynskie. All there except – there he was. His tall, unmistakable gait, like he didn't give a shit about the world. *Jace.*

Sasha had to breathe, otherwise she'd pass out. Jace sauntered in, went directly to Raz and shook Demeter's hand.

Jace was thinner, if that was possible. His hair was a little longer at the top and blonde with girlie-pink tips and the sides and back of his head were newly shaven. His fingernails were in the same shade of pink and so was the studded dog collar around his neck. He was so in touch with his feminine side that it made her smile. He was casual as ever, in his faded, ripped jeans and black t-shirt – her shirt; that almost broke her heart. A huge lump rose in her throat, that he'd obviously worn that for her. There was no other reason with that old thing.

Demeter pointed and all three of them looked straight at her. She would have run in the opposite direction if Jace hadn't started straight for her. Demeter caught Raz's arm before she could take off right after him.

Then all that existed was Jace. Striding towards her as if nothing else mattered. She couldn't swallow or breathe; his look was so intense. Until he snatched her up and lifted her right off the ground and she bathed in his warmth and his wonderful Jace smell that hadn't changed a bit. He let her down slowly, but still held onto her tightly. 'Sash,' he said in a broken voice. He said it at least three times. She wanted to cry with the force of it; it so far exceeded all her dreams of seeing him again. All she could do was return his grip, so relieved that she finally held him.

He had to let her go eventually. Even she became aware of what a spectacle they were making. People were whispering and pointing. Jace gazed down into her eyes, she looked up into his and they searched each other for changes. 'You look good,' he said.

'You look like shit!' she replied, making them both laugh. It broke the tension.

Her eyes darted behind him to see Demeter in conversation with another good-looking man she'd never met, but Raz was standing there, looking squarely at them. It was a strong dare that told her everything she needed to know. If ever she'd wondered what the status of Jace and that girl was, it was answered in that proprietary stare. She was in a full relationship with Jace and her message was 'hands off'. The, 'I'll allow you this once, but it will never happen again' was received loud and clear.

It felt like a slap in the face. Or a grab to her throat. A shock to see it so blatantly. It was like being back in school. 'You'd better go back to your girlfriend,' Sasha said, smiling back at Jace, trying to keep the ache in her chest off her face. This was always going to be hard. The word girlfriend had only ever been associated with her.

Jace hugged her again as if he'd never heard her, but then he glanced back at Raz and nodded. 'We'll talk later.'

Sasha nodded, knowing that was never going to happen if Raz had anything to do with it. But as he strolled back to Raz with his long, lolloping strides, he looked back over his shoulder at her a couple of times to check she was still there. In that look was the same boy she'd always known. She wanted to cry, but managed to hold it together. Raz was never going to let them anywhere near each other. It was in the razor-sharp look she gave her as she kissed him in front of everyone and kept her eyes on hers.

Sasha felt scared for the first time. She loved her job, now she'd got used to it, even though she knew she'd been brought in for Jace. How could that possibly work with Raz acting like a lioness prepared to maul her if she came too close? She was utterly alone.

Then Demeter seemed there to catch her when she didn't even know she was swaying. She was swept up in a wonderful cloud of testosterone and spiced cologne. He held her firmly by the shoulders, forced her gaze to his, and locked her to him. 'You are alright. You'll be fine,' he said, grounding her and bringing her back to the present.

She swallowed and nodded, but she was far from alright. He was saving her from dissolving into the pathetic ex and she was grateful for it.

'Come…let me whisk you away from all this madness.'

She was so relieved that when Demeter took her hand, she let him. She allowed him to lead her away from everything and everyone she knew in a daze. The world and its noise receded. Strangers were staring at her. Duo pointed and Tears' eyes were wide. She continued out of the enclosure with the guy who'd literally enthralled her from the beginning and every eye followed her, including Jace's.

Jace looked into Raz's thunderous face, watching her lips move but not hearing a thing that came out of them. Just blah blah: 'You're with me now…disrespecting me … my family … killing me … kill her.'

'Fuck!' he screamed back in her face. He had no idea what she was saying to him, only that she was poking him painfully in his chest in the place his heart should be. He knew that much. His mind wandered to a tree he could rest and fall asleep under, while everyone else went to hell.

Then she held his face and pointed to where he'd come from. 'Look! See! I told you!'

Jace slowly turned his head to see Sasha looking adoringly up at the impossibly handsome guy. He was squeezing her shoulders, caring for her, comforting her in a way he'd never done.

It was the look Sasha gave him that ripped out what was left of his heart. She was in awe of him. He'd never seen it on her before, not even when they were kids and certainly not for him. She'd rather punch him in his arm than worship him like that. The way she always looked at Jace was a mixture of love, impatience and exasperation. Rather like a wayward brother.

It was then it truly hit him; it was over. She was falling for this guy. Who wouldn't? He was caring for her. 'Who is it?' he asked, to no one in particular.

Raz spoke from next to his shoulder, cheerfully delivering the blow. 'My brother, Demeter. You just met him.'

Jace stood motionless and watched helplessly as the brother picked up Sasha's hand and led her off to God knows where, to do God knows what. He wanted to scream to the heavens to stop them. The remnants of his chest cavity felt like it bled out onto the floor, and in the hole that was left, a pickaxe had taken root.

However, the last thing that finally gave it a twist was the look the guy gave him before he turned away. It lasted only a second but conveyed everything he needed to say: 'You've had your chance, now it's my turn and I fully intend to go there.'

Jace wanted to run after them and punch him in his face, and he was never usually violent like that. The guy would probably flatten him. It was desperation. Frustration. He wanted to pull out his hair until he felt a hefty shove in his back.

He swung around to the glaring scowl of Raz.

'You asshole,' she spat. 'She's gone and you'd better get used to it!'

CHAPTER 17

Sasha didn't speak. She was in a suspended alternate reality. Where everything had gone mad and everything was the opposite of what it should be. Jace was in a fully committed relationship with somebody else. Someone far more beautiful and interesting than she'd ever be, and she was being led away by a handsome, deeply sexual being, so far out of her league; it was the final proof that none of this could be real. All she could do was allow herself to be pulled through the crowds, where she checked behind them several times to make sure she hadn't lost her mind.

The day had been ruined as far as she was concerned. She had no idea why Demeter was bothering. There was no cheering her up after a bombshell like this. At least he kept silent, pushing through the crowds of excited people, until they came to the field where his helicopter was parked.

The pilot hurriedly folded his newspaper and switched on the engine as Demeter helped her inside. The blades began to gather speed above them in a whip of rhythm while Demeter strapped her in like a small child. She let him, unable to even speak; she was in such shock.

Gradually, as the helicopter took off, her mind came back online, and she looked down at the hand he still held. She realised he hadn't let go of her since they'd left Jace. She looked up into his face. His concern gave way to a sympathetic smile. Without speaking, he said all that was needed.

'Thank you,' she said, not sure if he could hear her.

He simply nodded once.

The crippling grip around her heart seemed to loosen the further away they got. The sea of people beneath dispersed to a patchwork of green fields and eventually forest, until the helicopter landed in a clearing a few miles away.

Sasha felt a lot better once the mess was far behind her. Now she felt embarrassed that her feelings had been exposed for everyone to see. Namely, Demeter. She kept her eyes on him, saying something to the pilot, who handed him a backpack, then Demeter helped her down from the helicopter, and they ran clear of the blades. It gently rose, almost blowing her off her feet and disappeared into the distance.

She looked warily up at Demeter, watching her curiously, and then around her, and the absolute silence hit her. They were in the middle of nowhere. No civilisation. No phone. Just the two of them. 'Where are we?' she said, already knowing she wouldn't get a straight answer.

'Not too far from home. I thought you could do with a break.'

Sasha just stared at him. She was grateful, but unsure why he'd taken it upon himself to help her.

'Come, I want to show you something.' He turned and began to walk and she went along with him, conscious that he was still holding her hand. It felt odd and alien and their hands were hot, but there was no way she wanted to let go. He was her anchor, the one thing stopping her from falling apart.

They entered the dark forest. Bird song stopped and

everything felt smothered and quiet. Even their steps and the breaking of twigs sounded dull and dampened, like it was soundproofed. She began to wonder where the hell he was taking her. She was a city girl, where there was always someone a few feet away. For the first time, she was miles from everyone. Everyone, that is, except Demeter.

Thankfully, the green up ahead appeared brighter until the sun finally broke through, and she felt warm with relief. Running water was nearby and her spirits immediately lifted.

And then she saw it.

The most beautiful pool she'd ever seen. It was fed by a waterfall from a crop of rocks high above it and was framed by tall reeds and lush grasses, scattered with purple and white wildflowers. The air was filled with the fragrance of it all. 'It's beautiful,' she said, coming to a standstill with wonder.

'You like my place? It's where I come when I want to escape the world. You are the first person to see it,' he said, taking out a blanket and putting down the bag. 'Are you hungry? I have food.'

She didn't know what to say. She was overwhelmed by the fact that he was sharing such an intimate part of himself with her, a virtual stranger.

He was watching her curiously, as he seemed to always do with her. 'Would you like to swim?' he said, his face transforming into a fabulously cheeky smile. A playful side she'd never seen on him before.

A single blast of laughter left her on an exhale. 'What, in there?' she pointed doubtfully. She wasn't that great a swimmer. 'Won't it be freezing?'

He shrugged. 'A little. But a little cold is good for the soul,' he said, smiling wickedly again.

She started to panic when he began to undo the cuffs of

his shirt. 'I don't have a swimsuit,' she said, a little higher-pitched.

'We'll improvise,' he said, now laughing, taking off his expensive watch and throwing it down on the blanket.

She crouched down to take off her boots, keeping an eye on him the whole time. His shirt came off and then his shoes, socks and trousers. She couldn't articulate after that. It was the first time she'd seen the perfect physique she'd only dreamed about outside of his clothes. He was beautifully tanned, muscled and smothered in tiny tattoos. The same type of tattoos as his sister. She blinked away the pain associated with that. It was too much to process right then.

He, on the other hand, grinned, fully aware of how gorgeous he was. 'Come,' he said, turning.

She wasn't getting away with this, and, with her blood heating through her veins, she wasn't sure she even wanted to. *Why shouldn't she? She was a free agent.* No one as completely attractive as him had ever paid any attention to her. She'd spent so long imagining what he was like that it felt like one of her dreams. That's what she told herself, anyway, as she followed his every movement. Watching in the flesh, all that exceeded expectations.

She stood gaping as he reached the pool's edge and executed a perfect dive. He glided in an arc and came up grinning. 'Don't make me have to get out and get cold,' he said, laughing.

The mischievous threat made her quickly step out of her trousers and pull off her shirt. Until she was left in nothing but her simple black bra and briefs.

He didn't politely look away as she would have expected. Instead, he looked at her openly and directly, as he would a new suit he was about to try on.

It was terrifying and exciting. Her heart thrashed painfully.

'Are you coming in?' he said, raising his eyebrows playfully.

She stood awkwardly, forearms together in front of her chest. 'I'm not great at swimming.'

'Jump! I've got you,' he said, coaxing seductively.

Her insides went to liquid at the suggestion in those simple words and he couldn't look more dangerous. She'd be mad getting in there with him. But she was mad. Hurt, mad and reckless. '*Yes you have,*' she muttered, suddenly not caring if she never came up again. She looked out at the waterfall, stepped over the edge, and dropped into the water.

The water gurgled and swirled around her in searing white cold. The shock slapped her and took her breath. She was sinking rather than rising as her limbs froze and stiffened.

Large hands caught her under the arms and hauled her to the surface. She turned and clung to him, gulping huge mouthfuls of air. As her heart slowed down, she realised he was holding her in the circle of his warm body, and she gradually relaxed. She allowed herself to open her eyes and she was no more than a few inches from his. 'OK?' he asked, looking genuinely concerned.

She nodded, breathing more normally now. All she could think was how close they were. That her legs were literally clamped around his waist and she could feel the strength in his treading water powerfully beneath them. Her arms were in the only place they could go, which was around his neck.

Her teeth chattered uncontrollably. The water was freezing.

'OK, now?' he repeated.

She nodded, not convinced. Despite the cold, the concerned way he looked at her and held her in his strong yet gentle grip made her feel safe. No one had ever taken care of her like that. She didn't think she'd ever felt more protected than she did right then.

There was nothing sleazy or contrived about it. In fact, it was she who began a slow meander of his soft skin, marvelling how it felt under her fingers. 'So many tattoos,' she said, without thinking. And there were. None no bigger than a fifty-cent piece. She'd known he had them, but seeing them uncovered like this, they were stunningly good, and a lighter grey than she thought.

'Not so unusual for you?' he said, bringing her eyes back to his.

His eyelids were low, as if he'd been watching her the whole time. The inference to Jace made her frown. Because, despite what happened earlier, Demeter had managed to completely distract her, and since stepping out of the helicopter, she hadn't really thought about Jace once. 'Thank you,' she said, averting her eyes by dropping them down to his perfectly sculpted chest under the waterline. 'For getting me away from there.'

'You're welcome,' he said, his deep voice vibrating against her hands.

She looked back up at him and he was studying her with those calculating eyes, now acutely aware of just how much skin she was touching. She was skin-to-skin with her boss. One she'd been ogling for weeks and barely knew.

Then, as suddenly as the thought came to her, he was kissing her. Closed-mouthed at first. Soothing and bolstering her confidence. Saying it was all OK without words. That he was right there and she didn't need to worry.

His arms tightened around her and she relaxed and parted her lips. Everything flowed as he was completely tuned into her. Nothing felt awkward or fumbled. He took her mouth, gently seeking and tasting. Swirling his tongue with hers, his hands holding her backside.

Her numb fingers and toes warmed and prickled with the new surge of blood. He felt perfect under her hands and mouth, like soft silk over granite.

All too quickly, he set her free and the icy cold water swirled around her. 'Come with me,' he said, starting to swim away, pulling her along by the hand.

Sasha did her best, but all feeling had gone in her lower legs. The thought of the temperature getting closer to the waterfall's flowing water terrified her. The cold would surely kill her.

'Trust me,' he said, feeling her wavering. He always managed to hold eye contact and melt her resolve when he spoke like that.

He was grounding her with those eyes again. Somehow, she absolutely trusted him. He seemed to give her confidence whenever she was around him. She swallowed and nodded and they continued.

She could no longer hear anything above the tumbling water. Demeter turned to face her and pointed downwards, under the water.

'Oh no,' she said, trying to pull away to go back the way they came. The thought of diving beneath the water terrified her.

But he refused to let her go. 'Trust me,' he said again, with that seductive, lulling tone. He motioned for her to hold her breath. He'd already started counting before she could complain that there was no way she could do it. Then they were underwater, going downward at least six feet. She struggled, but he held her fast until they entered a natural tunnel in the rock.

She would have completely panicked had she not felt a definite rise in the water's temperature. She stiffly allowed him to pull her through the space, no more than three feet across and the further they went, the warmer it got.

She didn't think she'd ever gripped onto a person so hard as she did his hand right then. It was paralysingly scary. She was about to lose her mind completely, trapped in the space, and nowhere to breathe, when his arm came around her and encased her, guiding her through the tunnel and her fear.

Sasha was sure she would have died if a green glow hadn't appeared up ahead. The water warmed even more, the nearer they got, until they started upwards and it became a hot bath. Finally, she gasped for air as soon as they breached the surface and she went limp in Demeter's arms. All she could do for a few minutes was stare up at the strange green ceiling and allow relief to slowly seep through her and bring down her pounding heart rate. Breathing felt so good, although the air smelled sulphurous.

'OK?' Demeter asked, turning her to him, to resume their locked position of earlier. It was strange just how naturally her legs found his waist and her arms wrapped around his neck. As if they'd been doing it for years. She didn't let go, even though she was sure she could put her feet down in places. She simply revelled in the feel of him and the marvellous water temperature that relaxed her tensed muscles.

'It's a volcanic spring that flows into the river,' Demeter explained. He pulled her with him while he perched on a low ledge and she straddled his lap. It was a position of lovers and soon sent a pool of heat to the lower half of her body. It felt strange and yet inevitable. She barely knew him, but, deep down, she always knew it was going to happen. *Hadn't she secretly wished it?* Now here she was, up close and personal with her wildly attractive boss whose family had the world at their feet.

'Relax,' he said, pushing strands of hair from her face with a finger. It always felt like he knew what she was thinking. 'You trusted me to lead you away from everyone you know and to get into the freezing water. Then to dive into the tunnel with no air when you aren't a strong swimmer. Shouldn't you feel safe now, relaxing in the comfort of this warm pool?' He made it all sound so natural. Soothing away any argument, however feeble, with lulling tones. Gently pushing back her hair and stroking her lower lip and throat with his thumb. His words were hypnotic. Everything he was saying felt true and reasonable, but she was also aware that he was no ordinary man. Nothing about this was normal.

'Don't overthink it,' he said, tapping her temple with a finger. His eyelids were low. 'Go with it. Everything can stay within the walls of this cave.'

She watched, riveted, as he absently bit his lower lip. He was right. Surely she could suspend reality for a little while. She began a slow meander over the many tattoos of his chest. They covered every inch of his smooth olive skin. 'OK,' she said, breathily. Gathering her courage: 'You know almost everything about me, but I know nothing about you.'

'OK. What would you like to know?' His eyelids were low and he looked completely at ease.

'OK,' she said with a swallow. 'Why do you have all these, for instance?' She couldn't help running a finger across the tattoos following his collarbone. 'Why are you single? What do you want out of life? You have everything ... are there any goals left?'

He laughed loudly, sending echoes around the dimly lit cave. His eyes smouldered as they rested on her again. 'I'm not sure you would ever believe the truth.'

She frowned, not liking him patronising her like that.

He could barely keep the smile off his face and looked so infuriatingly gorgeous she wanted to thump him.

'OK,' he said with a small shrug. 'But the answer will only bring more questions ... I didn't choose them; I was born with them.'

Strangely, her mind immediately went to Raz, meaning she was born with hers, too. 'Your cousins?'

He nodded and smiled a little sadly. 'You see what I mean?'

He was right. She was already forming a line of questions, but he rearranged her on his lap, which made her hitch a breath when she became aware of what she was sitting on.

His lids lowered and his eyes dropped to her mouth. 'Isn't there something you would rather do than ask me questions that are not easily answered?'

She knew he was skilfully avoiding them and she was dying to ask him about Margaret, but knew she'd be overstepping a line. What line, at that moment, she wasn't entirely sure.

'OK, what do *you* want to talk about?' Her voice cracked, knowing she sounded childlike.

His answer was to pull her in closer, so she felt his hardness flex underneath her. He simply grinned into a kiss. Even though it felt like emotional suicide, she couldn't help herself. The man was pure sex. She parted her lips and welcomed him in, both prophetically and in reality, like a willpower-sucking vampire, needing permission to enter and take it all.

He soon twisted and switched places, so she was on the ledge. Now she was wedged and couldn't move. 'I will demonstrate my immediate goals,' he said, grinning. He kissed her so deeply and thoroughly that every part of her sizzled and woke up. Her voice of reason was screaming it was folly, but was soon throttled by his tongue, and there was no walking away. Even if she knew where the hell she was. This was no ordinary fling. He took great care of her, systematically worshipping and caressing every part of her, from her head to her feet. Massaging, kissing, disappearing for so long beneath the water, she was sure he would drown. But it felt good. *So good.*

Every time her good sense attempted to surface and whisper for him to stop, his tongue would swirl, or his teeth would nip and she would dissolve around him. It was futile. She simply gave in and he had her in his power.

Just when she felt there was nowhere else for him to go and she was no more than a pliable mess, he came up from the water and searched her eyes. She was reminded how strange and alien his looked. She'd never seen the like on another single person other than his family. In them held a question of where they went from here. 'Are you stopping?' she asked, a little high-pitched with disappointment.

He picked up her hands and placed them on him, standing proud between them. She had to swallow. He was so hard and his skin was pure silk. His eyes went up into his head for a moment as she ran her hands over him and took him in her grip.

He hissed his approval.

All the while she held him, she wondered what the hell she would do with a man like this. He was no inexperienced youth. Fear must have made her pause as he opened his eyes.

She felt his hand at the small of her back and he pulled her closer to the edge of the ledge so she became transfixed by those eyes. His hand rose out of the water and cupped her jaw and the back of her neck. Her heart fluttered at what he would do next and she realised she was shaking.

He searched her face for a long moment as if he were deciding on something. 'There is no relationship with me. Do you understand?'

Her mind scattered, gathering together his meaning. *No strings, got it.* She simply nodded. Her eyes widened as he was already nudging at her core. Pushing, tempting with only the thin fabric of her panties as a barrier.

'But I will look over you and see you want for nothing.'

While she sifted through the meaning of that, he began nipping down the column of her neck. In one adept move, he ripped the panties from her and he was there, slowly, gradually filling her a little more with every nudge. Tempting, pushing, driving her wild, with just the tip. Pushing, retracting, pushing, retracting.

Even then, as wildly turned on as she was, her common sense told her he sought to own her without offering her anything real in return. But she wanted him so badly, and he was halfway already; her hips were moving involuntarily to meet his. She ached to pull him deeply inside. He felt so perfect. His strong arms had encompassed her completely and the top half of their bodies grazed temptingly together, her nipples hardened next to his skin. She felt herself already coming apart. 'You're not being fair,' she cried, already feeling herself drift.

He pushed her further still.

'I'm …'

'Not yet!' he said. The strain was evident in his voice as he held still.

She whined with disappointment, thinking of nothing but the pleasure he held a hair's breadth away from her.

And then he was there, holding her gently by the throat and guiding her backwards, to lie flat. He drove himself into her, over and over, until she literally saw stars. Like she'd heard people talk of that and she'd never really believed it, but she lost count of the multiple times her orgasm swept through her. All the while her sheath gripped him and she clung onto him with her life.

She and Jace had had a hectic and varied sex life at one time, but she could never remember him having this kind of stamina. Before she registered what was happening, they'd swapped places and she was facing him, riding him mercilessly, with her legs firmly gripped behind him, while he kissed, sucked and marked her breasts, until his climax eventually came. She became completely lost, still holding him tightly to her shoulder, where he breathed loudly next to her skin.

Eventually, her mind cleared and her thoughts went straight to her pill. Deciding to continue on it had been the best idea she'd ever had and she shuddered at the implications if she hadn't.

After a few minutes, he drew his head off her shoulder but still held her in his arms while he studied her. 'Are you OK?' his deep voice rumbled.

She nodded, already losing herself in those inquisitive eyes, always trying to read her. She really was. She didn't understand how he'd managed it exactly. She'd gone from literal heartbreak and humiliation to having pure animal sex with her wildly attractive boss in just a few hours.

He smiled sexily, eerily reading her as he always did. He kissed her chastely with those full, sensuous lips. 'Good!' He moved her slightly to free himself and arrange her more comfortably on his lap.

'Haven't we committed the cardinal sin between employer and employee?' she said, trying to sound upbeat and playful and not as doubtful and scared as she was starting to feel. *Where the hell did they go from here and still work together?*

His answer was to kiss her forehead. 'Please don't worry. Desperate times call for desperate measures.'

Had he really done that to make her feel better? 'So, you took care of me,' she said, weakly, not sure why a lump formed in her throat, but it did. She wasn't sure what she wanted him to say, or what he could say. She guessed no one had ever really taken care of her before, outside of her own family.

He frowned and studied her as if her reaction puzzled

him. 'I am not that chivalrous, I'm afraid. You intrigued me from our first meeting,' he said with a crafty smile.

He always seemed to know just what to say as she ended up grinning back at him. He had quite the sense of humour and a wicked streak a mile wide.

'Well, thank you, anyway,' she said, goofily, making him laugh loudly. She ran her fingers through his tousled hair, drying in perfectly curled clumps. 'We have to swim back out into the cold, don't we?' she said, shuddering at the mere thought.

He kissed the inside of her wrist and shook his head. 'There is a shaft we can climb. It lets in air and light. You don't need to brave the water again.'

'You mean we didn't have to swim at all?' she scowled, thinking of the terrifying tunnel, while they both got to their feet.

She hadn't realised just how tall he was until he grinned down at her. 'You wouldn't have clung onto me that way.'

She went to punch him playfully, which he dodged easily, laughing. 'Come, brace yourself for the cold air. There is a hunters' cabin nearby.'

Sasha's heart skipped several beats. It meant she didn't have to go back to face Jace just yet, and their sexy little getaway was by no means over.

Jace wanted to give in and descend into chaos as he stared down into Raz's glaring face, but something made him cling to a tiny thread of sanity. He would have kicked and screamed, smashed things, passers-by, anything, if he hadn't caught the absolute desolation in her eyes. The betrayal and abandonment; she was teetering on the precipice of her own madness and it somehow kept him from succumbing and falling into his. Something told him that her fall would be something far deeper, more terrifying and far more dangerous than his own. She had an innate power that, once it exploded, none of them would ever be able come back from.

But he couldn't be there for her. Instead, he withdrew before he did any more damage and drank like he'd never done before. Brains always had coke and today he was his drug buddy. The two of them scored and hit all day. All the time, Raz looked on scornfully, joining in at times, then shaking her head and walking away. But detonation was averted for the time being.

They managed to complete their performance, more

raucously and chaotic than ever. Several of the collective fell into the audience and had to be rescued by security numerous times and Jace threw up in a bucket at the back of the stage more times than he could remember.

However, the fans loved it. It was the special brand of anarchy only TRHBDor could deliver.

In the end, he could barely enunciate his words; his lyrics just slurred into the next. He'd taken several Xans, and somewhere between the first and second encore, he fell into the drum kit already set up for the next band. Through the hazy bank of lights, he tumbled through a pile of amps and landed face down in the grass and somehow woke up in Raz's bed back at the chateaux.

At first, he was scared to move, convinced he must have broken several bones. He chanced a slight turn of his head and saw that Raz was not in the bed. His heart thrashed in panic or low blood sugar; he couldn't tell which. There was a bottle of water on the nightstand, which he lunged for quickly and glugged down before the pain hit.

He flopped back down into the pillows and waited for the waves of nausea to pass. Memories of the festival were a disjointed mess.

Raz wandered out from the bathroom in just a towel. He took one look at the way she moved and knew she was pissed. He closed his eyes, not wanting to deal with it now.

'You're a cunt!' she said, simply, which would have made him laugh if his brain wasn't burnishing his skull. He brought his forearm over his eyes and swallowed the spit that was forming in his mouth, ready to vomit. 'Not now, Raz,' he croaked. 'Please … I beg you. Leave a poor guy alone.' His attempt at humour masked a genuine plea. He needed to process feelings himself. He hadn't exactly faced what happened with Sasha and he needed to get his thoughts straight.

The next thing he knew, his arm was yanked from his eyes, and she was screaming down into his face. The words were lost. His ears were ringing, but the ferocity was loud and clear. Her eyes were bloodshot with her own hangover or crying, and she looked demonic, like he'd never seen her before. Veins protruded on her forehead and her face contorted in pain. His mind tuned back in just as, 'I fucking hate you,' hit his frontal lobe and she flopped down on top of him in sobs.

His arms slowly came around her. He hated that he'd turned her into this. 'I'm sorry … I'm sorry,' he said, over and over, while he stroked her hair and let her sob herself out into his chest.

'You love her … you still love her,' she said, stiffening and revving up her anger again.

But he held her fast. His head couldn't take another barrage of abuse. 'Shh,' he whispered, calming her again. 'I don't … not like that. Not like you. It was a shock, that's all. Seeing her with someone …' His mind went to Demeter; the absolute perfect specimen of a man and his gut twisted even then. It wasn't like he hadn't imagined her with someone else because he had. He always assumed he would die young and she would meet a nice guy. A regular guy who would give her the stable family she wanted. Not this dangerous machine that she would fall hopelessly in love with. That wasn't the plan at all. 'That was all it was. It was the first time, that's all.' He knew he was repeating himself, but he needed to believe it, too.

Raz lay quietly in his arms, absorbing what he said, while he did the same. He hoped she was buying it because he wasn't sure he did. He and Sasha had history, it was true, and that was never going to change. He and Raz were real, for the person he was now. She was beautiful and talented and didn't deserve any of this. Any man would give his right arm to be where he was right now. Sasha was strong and caring, but she came from the past, the place he'd left behind. And despite all she had going for her, Raz was insecure and fragile, needing constant reassurance. It defied belief.

'I was angry too, Jace,' Raz said, eventually.

He nodded and ran his fingers through her hair. 'I know and I'm sorry.'

'No, you don't,' she said, leaning up on her elbows to look at him. 'At Demeter, not you. He knows about us and went there with your ex-girlfriend anyway, not giving a shit about me and what problems it would cause.'

Jace listened to her speak and finally understood. He'd been so wrapped up in himself and what he was feeling that he'd put it down to plain old jealousy. Not only did she have to put up with the fear that he might still have feelings for Sasha, but the asshole brother Raz obviously adored and looked up to, was into the same girl as well. Flaunting it in her face and to the world like a double endorsement of her fears.

Jace hugged her close to his chest and kissed the top of her head. 'I won't go back,' he said, more to himself and he meant it. The thought left him raw and exposed because it was new territory. Sasha was always his safety net. But he knew it absolutely. It terrified him. Everything was easy with Sasha. It was warm and comfortable. This thing with Raz was uncharted and volatile. Neither knew what was around the corner next week, let alone in the future.

'You have to swear on our blood pact, Jace,' she said, leaning up to look at him again.

Jace touched her cheek and saw the raw emotion there, like an untamed animal. This wasn't a game. God only knew what Raz would do if he ever did go back. So, as daft as it sounded, he found himself saying the words, 'I swear on our blood pact, that I will never go back to Sasha.' He knew it wasn't exactly what she wanted, but it was all he was willing to give. She wanted to hear that he would never leave her, but he couldn't promise her that. He couldn't give anyone that promise.

Looking into those otherworldly eyes, he already understood he was on his countdown. And he was OK with it. It was always going to come, as inevitably as breathing.

DEMETER TOOK SASHA TO THE HUNTERS' cabin, hidden in the woods nearby. It was a one-room, single-story building made completely of logs. 'We used to come here as kids,' Demeter explained.

He pushed open the stiff door, which looked as though it hadn't been used for a very long time. She followed him in and watched as he pulled dusty sheets off an old sofa that faced a fireplace with a stove and a double bed near the far wall. There was a kitchen table and a cupboard, which he opened to reveal a few old tins. 'There is a water pump outside,' he said.

It felt like she'd stepped back in time to the wild west.

Sasha sat cautiously on the sofa, not sure what else to do, while Demeter started a fire. He disappeared, came back, and put a kettle on the stove. He began to unpack the bag and placed a large loaf, a lump of cheese, a pie and a carafe of wine on the table.

She was pleasantly surprised.

'What?' he said, smiling.

'I just never had you pegged as the domestic type.' Something shifted in her chest at the thought of all that gorgeousness being practical too.

Demeter laughed. In fact, she realised that she'd seen him laugh a lot that day. 'What are you saying?' he said, making her scared she could have overstepped.

'Oh, nothing … I was just thinking how relaxed you looked, that's all.' It was close to the truth, minus the lusting after his hot body bit. 'It suits you.'

He completely disarmed her with one of his full-on stunning smiles and brought over a plate for them to share. He sat down next to her on the floor and pulled her down with him onto a fluffy bear rug. It was comfortable with the sofa as a backrest, facing the warmth of the fire. 'I think it's you,' he said, nudging her with the plate to take more. 'You have no expectations. It is easy to be myself around you.'

Sasha smiled and took a huge bite of her bread. 'Mmm,' she groaned. It tasted wonderful. The perfect fluffiness surrounded by a thick, crunchy crust. She was starving.

It made him laugh and she laughed along with him. 'I feel like you saved me today,' she said. 'Thank you.'

'It was my pleasure … believe me,' he said, with his devilish grin.

They both laughed, then she got a little more serious. 'What happens now … I mean,' she stuttered, remembering his warning about a relationship between them. 'When we go back … won't it be awkward?' She didn't just mean as a boss and employee. There was Jace to consider and the girl who hated her on sight and whose brother she'd just been with all weekend.

Demeter looked thoughtful as he poured them some wine. 'You want to know how it will work?'

It was partly true. Oversimplified, but true, she guessed. She nodded. 'I'm not good at this.' She didn't want to say she was completely inexperienced and had only ever been with Jace. She'd never dated or been out in the wide world at all, really.

'I can't promise I'll be there for you,' he said, with all the apology in his eyes.

She nodded and swallowed, guessing as much. 'I get it. You probably have to marry some heiress or something.'

He laughed loudly. 'Nothing as simple as that. I'm afraid I can't divulge my family's secrets. But I can promise you that you will come under my care.' He put his hand over his heart, dramatically. 'I so swear it.'

It felt real and solemn, bringing a lump to her throat. She didn't understand why. He was effectively saying she would be his kept woman, but there was something heartfelt about it, as if it was the best he could do.

'What is it?' he said, wiping a tear from her cheek that she didn't know had fallen. 'I'm sorry I can't offer you more.'

'It's not that,' she said, swallowing, desperately trying not to cry. She didn't know why she was so emotional. 'I guess that apart from my mother, no one has ever offered to look after me before.'

He looked at her for a long moment as if he was stunned. He took the plate from her and stood, pulling her with him. He cupped the side of her face while she looked up at him, a little dazed. He bent his head and kissed her soundly. It encompassed everything she felt in that one action.

He lifted her and her legs were back around his waist, while he carried her to the bed. 'I will. Of that, I can promise you.'

Sasha had no idea how Demeter had contacted them, or whether he had cheekily prearranged it, but the helicopter collected them from the same clearing, early, the next day. She was forced to let out a ragged sigh, that their magical little interlude was at an end. They held hands all the way back. The ache in her chest surprised her. It was more than a fear of going back to the unknown. It was for the loss of the closeness that she wasn't sure they'd get back.

However, she did feel restored. Stronger, even beautiful, and sore, after several bouts of very attentive and thorough sex. So much so that she became sure that Demeter Carpathian very definitely knew how to take care of a woman.

It was confusing, because it was the first time she'd ever felt loved, and by a man who'd made it categorically clear it was the one thing he couldn't offer. So she worried about that and what life would be like when they got back to reality. If you could call the chateau reality. It was a fairy-tale castle. The place where she'd have to face Jace again and the woman who felt like the Wicked Witch who'd bewitched and ensnared her best friend.

Friend.

She'd said it. Admitted it. Finally. Because that was now what he was. Her dearest and oldest friend, but a friend nonetheless. She would always love him, but being with Demeter had proved to her there was more. Maybe that was what Demeter had intended all along. He was crafty enough.

Sasha gripped his hand and he smiled down at her, sadly. 'We will land soon.'

She nodded, registering the meaning behind the words and mirroring his sadness. She wanted to grab onto him to keep him and knew that she would have to take her cues from him from now on. Everything was now in his court.

She faced front, letting out a long sigh. Her immediate problem was Jace and how far down the spiral he'd gone while she'd been away. And whether Demeter's sister had the power or the inclination to save him.

Jace remained in Raz's bed for the whole of the day. Food was sent up and they ate, slept and had their usual brand of drug-fuelled sex, many times. It was as if Raz was determined to stamp herself so hard on his psyche that he could never think of anyone else.

He was cool with it. He was already hers and let that knowledge wash over him like seawater.

At some point, the maid came in and announced, 'They're on their way back.'

He hadn't realised Raz had requested the warning. He kept his eyes closed but felt Raz sink down into the bed. She remained quiet and gently simmered.

Something had to be done to manage this situation. Sasha was in definite danger. He felt it in his bones. They all were. Another one of those initiation parties was coming up at the weekend and he didn't want Sasha anywhere near it.

CHAPTER 19

$\mathcal{J}$ace was at the window when the helicopter touched down. Raz was in the shower and he was glad of the alone time. He didn't want to justify what he felt right now. Something twisted in his gut as the tall, incredibly good-looking guy helped Sasha down and held her under a protective arm as they ran clear of the blades.

A butler ran to greet them, took a bag from the guy's hand and the two of them followed him into the main entrance beneath him and out of sight.

Jace was left rooted to the spot, staring as the blades slowly died and the pilot left the scene in another direction. All the little tells had been there. Intimate touches that showed they were more than just friends. Certainly more than a boss and employee, that was for sure.

His blood pressure had risen to a dull thud in his temples, but he had to manage this so they all didn't implode. He had to get a hold of his emotions for everyone's sake. His logic told him that, in a lineup, it would still be Raz, but that didn't help his feelings of ownership when it came to Sasha. He'd never had to share her before.

He certainly didn't want to hurt Raz, but her brother was like the cousins; on a whole other level of bad news. He was never going to give Sasha the family and home life he knew she craved. But he couldn't interfere, either. Otherwise, he'd drive Sasha right to him and Raz to murder.

He sighed and turned away, just as Raz came out of the bathroom. 'I've arranged for the rest of the guys to meet early. We need to prepare for next Saturday's induction and for you all to have your clothes' fittings for the tour.'

Jace tried to manage his features, but his heart hammered and he felt his cheeks get hot. That meant Sasha would be involved. He couldn't see any way out of it. 'What do we need to prepare for?' he said, completely deflecting. He didn't give a shit about Saturday, really. 'Will we be performing?' His eyes remained on her hips, shimmying into her tight jeans as she dressed. He'd become very good at distracting, as she never missed a thing.

She grinned with satisfaction. 'No, but all the newbies will be affirming their contracts. You will be called to do that from time to time,' she explained. 'It's the ceremony after the inductees have gone.'

His mind flipped back to the first night he'd spent in her room and Steve came in to check on her. The look of relief when he saw them together had never made sense, and all his bandmates had been kept in one room. *Was there something else they were never meant to see?* 'Ceremony?' he repeated, frowning, thinking of Zach's injured hand. Nothing made any sense. 'Everyone?' he persisted.

She just nodded, a little more guarded than she was before. She put a gun-metal necklace over her head. 'Everyone still alive, who's ever signed, does it periodically.'

Jace didn't ask any more. The cryptic routine was driving

him mad. It was obvious he wasn't going to get a straight answer. This was what drove him mad about her. In all other ways, she wanted a stifling closeness, which he tried to go along with, but when anything came up involving the business, she'd close ranks with her family. She had to make up her mind. He decided that when he saw him, Zach might be able to shed more light on it.

In the meantime, he had bigger things to take care of. Like hiding his distrust and hatred for Demeter.

SASHA WENT STRAIGHT to her room and waited anxiously for any sign from Demeter. A call, a note, a clandestine visit, anything that hinted that she was more than just a passing fling. But after jumping at the slightest noise in the hallway and staring and willing the phone to ring, it was clear she'd be eating alone. She tutted at her pathetic behaviour and showered and ordered some food.

While she tore into her club sandwich, she wondered about Jace. Was he there and what state was he in? Would there be a scene when they finally saw each other?

It was getting dark when the maid came to collect her plates. She put down a silver tray on the nightstand. 'A note from Mr Carpathian,' she said, then went out.

Sasha stared at the envelope with her heart beating hard. So he hadn't completely forgotten her. He couldn't leave it unsaid any more than she could. She tentatively picked up the envelope and opened it with shaking hands. She devoured the cursive writing, not at all surprised he could write as beautifully as that. However, the more she read, the more her heart sank at the very ordinary, practical message that hinted at nothing of their magical time together. Everything was over now they were back.

· · ·

Sasha,

I will be leaving for Brussels in a few hours. Raz has arranged fittings for the collective tomorrow. They will remain until after the weekend, when there will be one of her A&R gatherings. I will do my utmost to return before that, so you don't have to deal with it alone. If I run late, my advice is simply not to go.

Demeter

SASHA READ it and re-read it several times. *Deal with it,* she repeated in her mind over and over. Did he mean her emotions with Raz and Jace? How about the lack of it from him?

She felt very hurt and let down, even though he'd been very honest from the start. She screwed up the note and threw it on the floor, then she immediately scrambled for it, smoothed it out and put it back on the nightstand. She had to grow up and be an adult over this. She had to be more like Margaret. She was so strong and graceful about everything related to Demeter. She was his trusted rock. She wanted him to see her like that. It wasn't like he hadn't warned her.

She got into bed and tried to come up with a plan for the best way to deal with Jace. That was her immediate problem. Demeter would have to wait.

JACE FINISHED and flopped heavily onto Raz. Their sex that morning had been claiming and relentless, with her carving her initials into his shoulder with her razor blade. Which, considering he often performed shirtless, was a major big deal. He managed to change the RC to RIP as soon as he was alone in the bathroom.

She took scissors to the sleeves of his white Anarchy t-shirt, so the red, angry letters showed. 'There,' she said, with tight, spiteful lips. 'Ready to face an ex.'

He didn't reply. She was spoiling for an argument. He'd already put on another shirt and simply drank down his coffee and headed for the door.

Jace sauntered into a room buzzing with people. His crew and others he didn't recognise, all seemed to be chatting animatedly over the sounds of the sewing machines. Several mannequins lined the left side, wearing their new clothes for the tour, with a bank of windows at the opposite end. A fireplace was to the right and a line of sewing machines went around and back to the door. A large open space for fittings was left in the middle and that was where he soon spotted Sasha.

She looked fine. Great even. On her knees, adjusting the hem to Duo's low-slung cargo pants while he perched on a circular platform. Nothing seemed any different about her. She still wore her hair pulled back, revealing a clear, if slightly pink, face from the heat. She was in a simple white T and black leggings that showed the shape of her great legs. Showcased perfectly when she stood up and stepped back to appraise her work. She'd even filled out a bit, it seemed. In a good way, in all the places that mattered.

He paused, let out a slow breath to get it together; he had no right to have any thoughts like that. He took another deep breath and continued into the room. Breakfast had been laid out on a trestle table and he went straight to the urn of coffee.

Sasha saw him and he immediately looked away.

'Jace,' she called out. 'I need to check the length on the hockey shirts.'

He nodded, took a deep breath and, grabbing a pastry, wandered over to her.

Duo nodded and squeezed his shoulder as he jumped

down to vacate the space. Sasha introduced him to a designer called Julian something. He tuned out after that. He was taking in her flushed face. She was hot, but there was something else. Something like shame – *no embarrassment.* Discomfort. Like she had her own secrets she was hiding. It kind of hurt that she no longer seemed angry for what he'd been doing. 'So you and that guy,' came out before he could help himself.

She threw the orange hockey shirt at him, and he was forced to catch it. 'Put that on!'

He pulled it on over his head. 'We need some time alone to talk,' Jace said, pushing his arms into the sleeves, still trying to get eye contact with her.

'So you can tell me all the reasons why I should remain a nun and wait for you?'

He laughed and then hissed when she checked the fit of his shoulders and touched Raz's handywork from earlier.

She immediately rolled back his sleeve to look. 'Seriously, Jace?' she said, rolling her eyes and shaking her head.

He pulled his sleeve back down, a little embarrassed. It did seem a bit juvenile in the cool light of day. 'I've been worried about you,' Jace said, steering the conversation back to her. It was disturbing how little effect he was having on her. 'You really like this guy, don't you?' The words came out like an accusation, and he didn't mean for them to. They were just words he never thought he'd say to Sasha. Yes, he'd expected her to end up with someone else, but a good guy. A respectable, dependable guy, he wouldn't mind leaving her with, knowing she would always love him – Jace, the real love of her life. Not this dangerous, unknown quantity that scared him half to death. 'Raz says he's bad, Sasha. You need to be careful.'

Sasha flashed her eyes angrily at him and roughly pulled the shirt up so he had to take it over his head.

'This is the same Raz that appears to be a female version of you,' she said, dryly.

In his mind, he couldn't help saying, *worse actually,* but all he could do was frown. That just meant the guy must be more trouble than he first thought.

Sasha walked off.

'Sasha?' he called after her.

'We're done,' she called back, over her shoulder.

He was left stung while she moved easily onto another of his crew. He hovered a while, wondering if he should try again. In the end, he sloped off to be alone. He had to process the fact that he had really lost her. It was easy to be strong when he was with Raz, but when he came face to face with Sasha, the shock left him bitch slapped. It was just him and Raz and he was the sensible one. It was too crazy to even think about the consequences of that.

That just left Demeter, simmering in his mind, and that Sasha liked him enough to get over Lil Jace. The thought was suddenly terrifying.

SASHA WENT through several of the crew's fittings with idle chit-chat and her mind churning on the last conversation with Jace. She had to keep apologising that she didn't hear what they said, until she could finally breathe and get her head on straight. It was never going to be easy seeing Jace again. He looked terrible and was even carving his skin.

Margaret came over to her as she was putting away her pins. 'You OK?' she asked, with a smile, but she was clearly concerned.

Sasha just shrugged. 'I'm worried about him.'

Margaret looked around for him and nodded, but he'd left. She seemed worried, too. Well, they should be. They had to get him through a world tour.

. . .

RAZ'S FINGERS were bleeding by the time he got back that evening. He'd heard her guitar from down the hall. He marched straight in and pulled the plug from her amp. 'Fuck, Raz!' he said. 'How long have you been playing like that?' It was clear she'd been playing hard since he'd left her that morning. There was blood all over the body of the guitar.

He clamped his hand over hers and managed to pull the guitar over her head with the other. He grabbed her wrist and pulled her with him to the bathroom. He ran a tap and pushed her hand underneath it. Thankfully, although it must be very sore, it looked worse than it was. 'You've got to find a way of dealing with this that doesn't involve you hurting yourself.' *They both did,* he finished in his head.

Tears were streaming down her face as he gently dried her hands on a towel. 'You don't understand,' she said, trying to turn away from him, but he wouldn't allow it.

'Talk, now! What is it?' he said, losing patience, forcing her to look at him.

'You don't understand,' she repeated and began to wail.

Jace's mind was already racing to what drug she'd taken.

'It's me … don't you get it? I thought I was good, but I'm the bad one. I'm the bad one, Jace.'

The look in her eyes was desolate and lost. It was what scared him most of all. He'd never seen anyone look like that. Her words weren't the ramblings of a crazed person; she genuinely believed it. He gathered her to him and hugged her tight. 'Shh, I'm here,' he whispered into her hair. She must be hallucinating; otherwise, what the hell could she mean?

'You'll see … this weekend. Then you'll hate me.'

CHAPTER 20

The next few days felt like living in a cauldron. Jace had to walk a tightrope between Sasha and Raz, as well as his friends. They all seemed on their last nerve. Sasha literally braced whenever he got near her and so he kept well clear. Just close enough to make sure she was OK and that her shaking hands were to do with him, not anyone else.

Raz was watching him so closely, a target burned on his back. Despite his constant showering of her with attention when they were alone, she complained that he hid it from Sasha. She guessed she wasn't wrong about that.

Then there were his friends. TRHBDor. They were as jumpy as hell, remembering their treatment the last time they were there. He couldn't blame them. They couldn't relax at all.

Zach came back a few days in. Strangely, he was the one who worried him the most of all. He'd barely spoken since he arrived and disappeared for several hours with the cousins. That couldn't be good. Then he reappeared, grey and washed-out, like he'd seen a ghost.

'What is it?' Jace asked, over and over. It was clear, whatever it was, he didn't want to share.

'Is everyone here?' was all Zach said.

Jace nodded, waiting for more.

'Pope?'

Jace frowned and nodded a little again. Something was wrong. Very wrong.

FRIDAY CAME and all the fancy cars and helicopters began to arrive. One after another, depositing huge stars of the music industry and then leaving right away. Each was met by an army of staff and whisked straight off to their rooms.

Whatever this induction evening was, it was big. Jace hated big and was already trying to find a way to avoid it. He took a Xan and decided to escape into the gardens. On his way down, he fell into step with another guy he vaguely recognised.

'I know you, you're that Lil Jace fella from that LA rap outfit,' the long-haired, rocker-looking dude said in a thick Australian accent.

Jace immediately remembered who he was. 'You were in the band that went on right before us at the induction,' Jace said, immediately holding out his hand.

The guy grinned and shook it. 'That's right. I'm Josh. The band's HeltaSkelta. Great to finally meet you. Crazy, isn't it? Things have been mad and really happening for us ever since.'

Jace nodded. He was right. Despite all the shit, the Carpathians had kept their end of the bargain. 'Yeah, we're just starting a world tour.'

'Congrats,' the guy said, looking genuinely impressed. 'Guess that's why we've all been called back so soon to affirm. Who have you chosen? Or are you letting your manager do it?'

'Manager,' Jace said, his mind racing to Zach, closeted with the cousins. This guy obviously knew a whole lot more about what was going on than he did. His heart was beating in his chest and his head hurt.

'Right-o,' the guy said, suddenly eager to move on. 'Good luck with it,' and he went to move off in another direction.

'Wait! … Do you know what they're being chosen for?'

Josh turned, shrugged and carried on walking backwards. 'Some big honour or something. Everyone has to nominate someone, they said. Even the megastars.'

Jace put up his hand weakly and the guy grinned and walked off. *A huge honour.* Zach had asked about Pope. He loved the guy, but he hadn't exactly been at the forefront of their creativity lately. He would really love it if he got the boost of an award or something, but he couldn't imagine he'd choose him. Something felt off about the whole thing.

Instead of the garden, he stopped a passing female member of staff and had her show him to Zach's room. He knocked and didn't miss the surprise and the shifty look of apprehension as he reluctantly let him in. 'What's happening here, Zach? And no bullshit. My head-fuck is at maximum and I just met some guy from another band who asked if we've chosen someone. Chosen someone for what, Zach?' Jace finished with his head hung low and his hands on his hips.

Zach steadily poured two drinks from a decanter, even though it was barely midday, but Jace nodded and took the one offered to him.

Zach took a huge gulp as if it were OJ and swallowed and nodded once, as if he'd decided on what to say. 'You have to remember that these Carpathians have been around a very long time…and they have these weird, very old…customs.'

Jace's unease grew by the second. It was clear Zach was building up to something.

'We have to choose someone out of the collective to be honoured. Everyone nominated must do it and everyone invited has to witness and take part. It's just what they do here. After the new inductees, it happens in the honour ceremony afterwards.'

Jace's heart lightened a little. That didn't sound so bad. Then why was Zach so uncomfortable about it, refusing to look him in the eye?

'It's a big decision. I don't want to put anyone's nose out of joint, you know?' Zach said, as if he knew he was coming off weird.

Jace nodded, running through all the members of the collective who deserved an award. 'Duo has probably made the biggest contribution,' Jace said. He would love to honour him to make up for the way he'd been pushed out recently.

But Zach cut in with, 'No!' a little too loudly and abruptly, making him widen his eyes in surprise at how forceful he was about it.

'I was thinking, Pope. He's been there from the start.'

Most of them had been there from the start. 'What's going on, Zach. You need to tell me.'

Zach let out a ragged breath that didn't go with what he was saying. He should be happy, not nervous. He shrugged, 'I just thought that Pope has been almost completely redundant lately. There's only so many home videos for social media a band your size needs. I thought he could do with a lift.' He averted his eyes and walked back over to the window and pulled back the net curtain.

Jace frowned. It didn't make sense. It sounded more like they were preparing to fire him, but he was giving him a leg up. He was confused. 'So you're not firing him?' Jace asked, just to clarify.

'No…no,' Zach said with a half-smile, walking back to the decanter and pouring himself another.

Jace felt a wash of relief. On top of everything, he couldn't deal with the guilt of losing Pope. 'That's great. Pope hasn't been happy with nothing to do.' He took a sip of his drink. 'So what happens at this ceremony then?'

'Not much. I give them the name we've chosen. They make the arrangements. They have one of those parties where they sign new bands, and after they go off to sign their contracts, they do the honour ceremony,' Zach said, wandering around the room like he was practising a speech, gesturing with his hand. His behaviour was bizarre.

Jace had to question the strength of the Xan he hadn't long taken. On the surface, it sounded fair enough. He bobbed his head and left it alone, on face value, and pushed down his feelings of impending doom. After all, it wasn't an unusual emotion for him. It just all seemed weird and a lot of trouble for everyone to go to.

'They seem to be into a lot of old symbolism, religious traditions and that,' Zach said as if he sensed his misgivings.

Thankfully, the scotch he'd just drunk was mellowing his mood, so he didn't question him anymore about it. He decided to go back and rest for a few hours before the madness began.

THE LAST WEEK had been awful for Sasha. She was tetchy and nervous and could barely eat or sleep. It was as if the last weekend never happened. Instead of gaining confidence after her whirlwind with Demeter, she now felt foolish and needy. Jace was always there in the background like a harbinger of doom and Demeter was conveniently absent.

However, she still couldn't help keeping an eye out for Jace. She'd caught sight of him a few times. Always with Raz, like she never left his side. The girl was sickeningly beautiful and talented, yet she inveigled herself into him like a vine. One that crept and tangled itself with every aspect of his life. And Jace was affectionate and attentive to her as if he were caring for some sick puppy. It was a fascinating dynamic to watch because it was so different from theirs. Despite what a train wreck Jace and Raz were, it only served as a stark reminder of how lonely she was. In a way, she would have been pleased for him if he hadn't looked so ill.

A lump came to her throat. Now it wasn't even her place to chide him and get him to eat.

The costumes were now done and she saw Julius and his crew of seamstresses off with big hugs. She was genuinely sad to see them go. They had been her lifeline over the last week. Now she'd be completely alone.

The TRHBDor guys were still her friends, but it felt different now that they'd signed separate contracts. There was a definite divide between them. She'd been relegated to Make-up and Wardrobe now.

That was why she was surprised to receive the invitation:

YOU ARE CORDIALLY INVITED to the induction of Lexxxlooter and G-Raj in the Ballroom at 7.30 p.m., followed by the honour ceremony of Carpathian artists, past and present.

IT SEEMED a strange thing to have a ceremony for, but she guessed it was like the awards they gave to legends at big things like the Grammys, which seemed to be the thing these days. Then her next panic was what to wear.

However, she was interrupted by a knock at her door. She opened it and a maid brought in a large box and laid it on the bed. She thanked her and waited for her to leave with a buzz of excitement in her chest. Carefully, she took off the large lid.

Inside was the most spectacular Grecian-style black gown with silver trim. It was gorgeous and she couldn't have chosen better herself. Her heart thumped that Demeter might have sent it. It had to be him.

She wasted no more time and began to get ready. Dressing and piling her hair in coils on top of her head, making sure she left strategic curls to frame her forehead. There. She was ready. Duo and Tears collected her on their way down, so she didn't have to arrive alone.

All three of them stood on the threshold of the room. Sasha had no idea it would be this big. She'd missed the collective's induction and wondered if it was as amazing as this.

'I know. Crazy, isn't it?' Duo said for her. 'Every single one of them is a major player in the music business.'

He was right. Household names were laughing, drinking, strumming guitars, or simply walking past to go and talk to someone in another group. She was seriously star-struck.

'Well, I hope we get treated better than last time,' Tears said.

Sasha would have asked what she meant, but Duo nudged them into the room. A waiter came over immediately and asked them to follow him to their allotted area, suggesting there was some order to the outward chaos. The competing tuning up and playing of various instruments was deafening.

Sasha followed along, trying to take everything in and smiling at a couple of her favourite artists, who were friendly enough to wave back.

Then her excitement nosedived when she saw they were heading straight for Jace. He was lounging on a beanbag, laughing and bleary-eyed already, in his usual state of worse for wear.

Seeing him still held her heart in a vice. It probably always would, but strangely not in a heartbroken kind of way. Not anymore. It was more like the pain you got from nostalgia. A reminder of a time and place lost, never to come back to experience again. Like lost youth, she guessed.

His laughter stopped and drained from his face when he saw her. It was gratifying to see a similar effect on him. He scrambled clumsily to his feet and immediately started towards her. For one brief moment, she thought he would hug her, but instead, he stopped short and glared. 'What are you doing here, Sasha?' He sounded uncharacteristically angry. It was an emotion he rarely displayed, usually being too wasted.

Her own temper fired up at his nerve. 'I was invited, Jace,' and she went to shove past him to sit down.

He grabbed her arm as she passed and she whirled around. 'Let go!'

'Listen to me,' he said, hushing his tone as they were drawing attention. 'It's not safe for you here. You have to go.'

She snatched her arm out of his grip, turned and slammed straight into a firm chest.

She looked straight up into the face with an apology and realised it was Tegan, looking as aristocratically cool as ever. So like Demeter in a way, but with a much more severe edge. He caught her by the arms and, with low-lidded eyes, said something in his language. Then he inclined his head. 'It is I who should be careful where I'm going. Although it is a pleasure to bump into such a beautiful woman.'

She didn't miss the look he flashed across her shoulder at Jace, who she felt keenly there.

'Forgive the intrusion,' he said, resting his hypnotic eyes on her again, appreciatively. 'My cousin asked that I see you and offer you a seat at our table.'

Sasha's heart flipped that Demeter should have

mentioned her ahead of time. The dress and now this. It was the most she'd heard from him all week. She couldn't help but glance around in the hope that she'd see him.

'He is not here,' Tegan said with a knowing smile. 'Perhaps you would allow me to be your escort for the evening?'

She smiled nervously, terrified of what that could mean, yet knowing she couldn't insult him with a no. She nodded. 'Thank you,' she said, conscious that her mouth had gone sandpaper dry. Tegan was stern and creepy, but it would be a relief to get away from Jace. She daren't look at him. Plus, she'd get to sit in a proper seat in her dress. She smiled an apology to Duo and Tears, and, feeling Jace's eyes searing her back, she allowed Tegan to lead her back to his table, next to the stage.

Two handsome versions of him stood immediately and Tegan introduced her to his brothers, Taj and Rollo. Then they sat all along one side of an oblong table as if they were presiding in court.

She people watched after that. The place was fascinating. Her eyes always drifting back to the place she'd just come from, in search of Jace. Tegan was in deep conversation with his brothers. She strongly suspected it was about her and Jace's little exchange.

Some pretty big stars came and shook hands with Tegan and his brothers. One actually gave her a kiss when she told him he was her mother's favourite. Kenny something. She couldn't remember his last name.

However, her eyes were pulled back to Jace, over and over; she couldn't help herself. He was a good fifty feet away, but, like a magnetic force, he kept drawing her head around. She wished she knew what he was thinking. He wasn't talking to anyone and looked stiff and uncomfortable. Like he was pissed.

She felt bad that it had come to this, but he had to understand that he couldn't order her around like that anymore. Maybe he and Raz had argued. She was certainly nowhere around.

At last, something appeared to be happening on the stage. A buzz went through the room as everyone sensed it at the same time. Lexxx came on with his beats guy and there she was: *Raz*. Walking towards the stage with an entourage surrounding her as if she were royalty. She guessed she was in the music industry.

Sasha tried to remain objective, but she couldn't help it. She didn't like her. She watched as the perfectly formed girl slipped her guitar over her head and commandeered the stage. She wanted her to be rubbish, but knew that wasn't going to happen.

Raz went over and chatted confidently with the two guys already up there like a seasoned pro. This wasn't simple jealousy of someone so talented and perfect. It was because out of all the desirable people in the world, falling at Jace's feet, she was possibly the worst one he could have chosen. Raz controlled and manipulated him – in a way she never could, with an influence that made him feel a duty to protect her and that was not good for him. He was trapped.

When she looked at Jace again, he was looking straight at her. Then he clearly mouthed the words, *Go home.*

Hurt scorched through her that he wanted her out of the way. She shook her head and looked back at the stage, trying not to cry. She blinked and swallowed, hoping it wasn't obvious.

Lexxx finished his performance and everyone clapped and cheered loudly. Raz hugged him and accompanied him off the stage, straight towards her.

For a moment, she contemplated running, but Raz captured and held her gaze. 'You think you have the stomach for this?' Raz said with real spite in her eyes.

She wondered if this was a side Jace ever saw. How she'd love to expose her. She had no idea what she meant. She simply replied, 'Time will tell.'

Raz let out a single breath of derisive laughter and ignored her, speaking to her cousins instead. They got up and two of them led the way out of the room with Lexxx following along. Tegan apologised, 'I won't be long' and caught up behind them.

Raz was soon back on the stage with another guy Sasha didn't know and she was left sitting alone. She scanned the room, taking in the scale of the place. It was hard to believe that so many A-list artists were signed to the same company. It proved just how rich and powerful the Carpathians were.

'Good evening, Sasha,' the deep and familiar voice said.

She quickly turned her head and hitched a breath. In one single moment, she took in the blackness and the expensive cut of his clothes and those mesmerising eyes staring down at her.

Before she could check herself, she squealed, 'Demeter!' and was on her feet hugging him. She hadn't realised how oppressive the atmosphere had been until the wave of relief flooded through her at seeing him.

After his initial shock at her open display of emotion, she felt his arms come around her and he kissed the top of her head. 'You look stunning,' he said next to her ear, making her heart twist in her chest.

'I didn't think you were coming,' she said, looking up at him.

'I told you I wouldn't let you face this alone,' he said, smiling, but his look was intense.

It seemed overkill, but she would take it. She really had to learn how to deal with Raz and Jace at social occasions sometime.

'He pulled her closer and whispered seductively next to her cheek, 'I have come to whisk you away to escape.'

She grinned up at him, loving this playful side to him. Maybe she should have paid more attention to what he said, but she was oblivious. She was just too pleased he was showering her with attention again.

He placed a protective hand at the small of her back and steered her out of the room. Everyone could see. Some were wide-eyed with surprise, others whispered behind closed hands. Either way, there was no mistake in the effect they were having being seen together.

She floated all the way along the corridor. Her last thought was of Jace, before she banished it for the evening, and it was the hope he'd be OK.

JACE CLENCHED and unclenched his fists. He wanted to scream and break things in his frustration. Beat up a random passer-by. Instead, he gritted his teeth and sat there simmering. The only thing he could salvage was the thought that at least the bastard had gotten her out of the place.

Something dark was in the room, and it was getting darker by the minute. The mood was changing from mellow and chilled to suppressed excitement. He couldn't shake the feeling of dread that something bad was coming.

A small part of him niggled that maybe it was his mind playing tricks because of the amount of hard alcohol he'd been drinking, but somehow it still didn't cut through the doubt. Instead, he scoured the room for Zach until he remembered he was Lexxx's agent too and would be in with the cousins, going through all that shit again.

His crew didn't look that great either. There were no high spirits this evening, as if they all sensed it too. They were barely speaking, tense and waiting. Everyone was drinking plenty and smoking a lot. They were all sensing the same thing; something big was about to drop. Duo was in a heated conversation with his sister. The others were lounging, but still looked watchful and alert. Only Pope was relaxed enough to sleep as he'd taken Ket.

Jace felt a nudge at his shoulder and he turned to see Zach. He had a grey pallor to his skin and seemed disturbed, like he'd had a shock. He guessed a meeting with the cousins would do that. His eyes dropped to Zach's hand. Intact this time.

Zach rolled his eyes. 'They need only make that point once.'

Jace nodded. He was probably right about that. 'Everything go OK? Where's Lexxx?' Jace asked, looking around.

Zach shrugged. 'They normally keep the new inductees away from what happens in here.' Jace's mind shot back to the party he'd stumbled into last time and the nightmarish orgy it became. Then, later, to Steve, the bodyguard, and his relief to find him with Raz. It had seemed odd at the time. It didn't fit with a bodyguard finding someone of his reputation, alone with his innocent charge. He'd looked relieved. Now it made him wonder if it was because he'd been missing and they didn't want him to see something he shouldn't.

Now he was just grateful that Demeter had got Sasha out of the way.

A massively successful band was now on stage. Another and then another. They were from back in the day. The 60s and 70s, or something. It made him question what drew them back here. They were already successful. The whole room was successful. *Was it just an excuse to pat themselves on the back?*

'They have to reaffirm themselves, like paying allegiance or something,' Zach said, answering his unsaid question.

Jace watched Raz looking as powerfully sexy as ever, not

really understanding what 'affirm themselves' meant. Raz was having a great time.

He couldn't be bothered to question him further. He was too tired, and his head seemed to hurt him continually these days. He shelved the Sasha thing and hunkered down in his beanbag to relax, following Pope's lead, but it was no good. He was too wired. 'Be back,' he said, struggling to his feet.

'Don't go far,' Zach said a little too quickly. 'It starts in a minute,' his eyes darting furtively.

Jace frowned at him. 'I'm just getting something to smoke.'

Zach was as jittery as hell, but he nodded and looked away.

Geez, he wasn't doing his own paranoia any good. Something was going on. He had no idea what it could be; all he knew was that he could only face it stoned. A storm was coming. Everyone sensed it and everyone was on edge.

CHAPTER 21

Jace stood near one of the double doors, waiting for one of the waiting staff to pass with their tray. All the big stars that had been relaxing and chatting easily earlier now looked charged and awake.

A girl carrying a tray at shoulder height was a little way off. He whistled and held up a hand to get her attention. It worked, as she immediately turned her head, changed the direction of her steps, and headed right for him. 'What do you need?' she asked, lowering her tray for him to see what she had.

He pointed at a bowl of dried buds, like the heads of long-dead flowers, and he raised his eyebrows in a question.

'Sensi?' she said.

He nodded. 'And papers,' he said, pointing at her gun belt full of them in various sizes.

She put a handful of buds in a large baggie that would have cost a fortune back home and after he thanked her, he went and stood against the wall by the door. It was a good place to keep an eye on the room while he put his joint together. He grabbed a beer from a passing tray and put it on the ledge next to him.

The band was playing something he knew and he began to relax, keeping half an eye on the waiting staff wheedling their way through the lounging crowd. He sparked up and took a huge inhale of his joint, holding it for several seconds before he let it out in a long funnel of smoke. His eyelids lowered, his lips tingled, as a wave of relaxation swept down his body to his toes.

He was just about to admit to himself he had probably been paranoid when something shifted in the air. The waiting staff began to file out. Not slowly, but as if they'd received an order over their headsets to evacuate without running.

Jace straightened up from the wall as the last girl disappeared and the doors were pulled shut and locked with a heavy clank from the outside. His eyes shot to the other doors and all were being closed in the same way.

His heart thundered at being trapped, making his blood pump and his head scream in pain. The chatter in the room died down and people straightened, wide-eyed and awake. He decided to get back to his crew. He needed to be with people he knew, just in case. Of what he didn't know. All he knew was Sasha had thankfully left.

Raz was walking off the stage with the last of the band members. Her eyes immediately found his as if she had a sixth sense. She pointed to their area to hurry him, but there was no need. The feeling to run was only just kept contained.

As he rushed and picked his way through, tripping over rugs and sticking out feet, a voice came over the mic. 'Find your places. You've been gathered to honour our god and give thanks for the gifts and talents you possess and the success he gives you. Without whom you would remain in a sea of obscurity. Instead, he allows you to rise and live like gods in his place, for the world to worship.'

Jace arrived back with his crew, and, seeing they were all there, he hurriedly sat down and faced the stage, with uneasy breaths like he'd been running. It had to be some big production, like the beginning of a show, or something.

None of his friends were talking. Duo locked eyes with him as if he'd offer up some sort of explanation. All he could do was shrug.

Zach looked more scared than all of them 'What is this? What's going on?' Jace asked. Hoping he would say they were actors and it was a Broadway show.

'Some weird ceremony,' Zach said, shifting irritably, looking shiftier than ever. 'I'm not sure.' But his actions said different.

There was a loud crank and clicking of a mechanism and the rectangular stage began to sink into the floor. It was like a movie-set change as a huge circular one rose in its place. Towards the edge, at three-foot intervals, were small circular podiums that went all the way around. Except near the judges' table, a staircase had opened up in the floor and disappeared into the basement. 'What is this?' Jace asked again, looking from the stage to Zach and back again.

'It's just the affirmation ceremony.'

'The affa— what?'

The guy who'd been speaking walked out to the centre of the stage. He was in white robes and had a tall hat like a priest and continued to speak into his mic as if he was telling a story. 'Please can your nominated beloved, your chosen friend, family member, or colleague, make their way to the stage.'

Jace looked fearfully at Zach, then at Pope. His heart was now jumping; he was so scared. Something was terribly wrong here. The mood of the room was at fever pitch and the sweat trickled down the sides of his face. This wasn't happiness. It felt like something very different in this place and he couldn't understand what it was.

Zach didn't say a word. He just looked at Pope, who must have sensed the music had stopped and the change in the air because he was now sitting up, bleary-eyed and awake. Zach nudged him with his foot and nodded towards the stage. 'You're up…you were nominated.'

It took a moment for Pope to make the connection to what he said. A slow grin went across his face. 'What me … really?'

All of them clapped, Jace included. Some whooped and others slapped him on his back as he scrambled to his feet. Everyone stood with him and Duo squeezed his shoulder.

Inside, Jace felt the worst kind of traitor. His blood was racing and he was panicking. 'Don't go,' he said. For some reason, he didn't want him to get on that stage.

Pope looked at him strangely and frowned as if he hadn't heard properly.

'Don't be sore, man,' Ballistik said, having heard perfectly.

There was nothing he could do but let him go and watch helplessly as he went happily through the crowd to the stage while the clapping grew louder and louder. By the time all the candidates were on the stage, the noise of clapping and stamping was thunderous.

Jace's heart was literally in his throat. So bad he thought he was on the verge of a full-on panic attack. He told himself he was being irrational, that he was often filled with feelings of impending doom, but somehow this situation felt different.

A hand slipped into his and he looked down into Raz's eyes. They held a sad apology, but grounded him at a point where he would have lost his mind. He looked deeply into them, concentrating on slowing his breathing.

'Don't hate me, OK. It's not me. It's just the price everyone has to pay for fame.'

He listened to the words, but he didn't really hear them then. It was only after that they had any real meaning. He looked back at the stage again, but held her hand tightly like an anchor to the earth.

They were putting a white robe over all the nominees' heads, followed by a garland of flowers, like a crown. They were guided to a podium by three guys in white monk-like robes. One stood directly behind, and one stood on either side of each one.

Jace looked anxiously back at Raz, his panic rising again. 'What's happening?'

She just nodded back to the stage for him to watch.

The priestly-looking guy was talking again. 'Today, many of you offer one of your number. One you hold dear in the hope to please him and be permitted to continue on your charmed path.'

At the edge of Jace's consciousness, he knew what this was, but he didn't want to face it. He didn't want to accept what could possibly be happening. He clung to that one shred of sanity that said, it couldn't be that. But his fear grew with every chilling word. Ice crept up his spine like tentacles of a vine. It was a nightmare, where you knew you were in a dream, but just couldn't wake yourself up. He wanted to shout NO, but nothing came out of his mouth.

Those in the crowd began to chant words he didn't understand and stamp in rhythm with their feet. Their faces were ugly and contorted with lust and rage and it merged with the ugly noise around him.

Pope was laughing, never happier. He wanted to run and get him, but it was already too late. It happened like a slow-motion car crash. One, you were too far away and in too much shock to stop. Becoming a grizzly scene that would haunt his nightmares for ever.

Each of the monks behind hopped onto the podium of their candidate and, in one practised, efficient manoeuvre, pulled a curved knife across their throats.

Jace and all his bandmates leapt to their feet with a collective scream, 'Noooo!' but remained glued, frozen, wide-eyed in terror, as each victim immediately collapsed to the waiting monks, who caught them and tilted them forward. Their gushing blood flowed into a carved gully that funnelled into a larger one that ran all the way around. It was appalling and unspeakably fascinating, like the fall of dominoes, the perfect crimson irrigation system, mixing with the next and the next, until it grew and disappeared in a grizzly scarlet waterfall to the room below the stairs.

Jace's gaze was frozen on Pope's face. His unseeing eyes were open wide in terror and his mouth contorted into a silent scream. His skin had gone grey and his lips were turning blue. It was an expression that would stay with him until his own dying day.

He turned to Raz, blinked in complete disbelief and faced the scene again.

The blood flow finally dwindled to a stop and each pair of monks carried their charge away and down the stairs, in the same direction as the blood. Their victim's feet were dragging and bumping down the steps, unnaturally, behind them like a dummy. All around them was stunned silence.

The priest began to speak again, offering up some kind of prayer Jace couldn't listen to. He refused to. It was a foreign language, but everyone seemed to know the words and joined in.

Jace swung around on Zach and screamed, 'What have you done!'

Zach stepped away to the side and flinched at his ferocity,

but then he recovered a little. 'It had to be someone,' he said, sounding desperate.

Deep down, Jace knew he wasn't responsible, but he needed to blame, to rant, to demand answers. He looked around at his friends. Duo closed his eyes and reached out for Tears, who turned and cried in his arms. Jynskie, Ballistik, Brains, everyone looked at each other, traumatised, in shock, in tears.

'It's what's expected,' Zach said, trying to explain something there was no explaining. 'Ask her, not me,' Zach said, pointing at Raz.

Jace had forgotten her; she'd been so quiet. He whirled around and glared, horrified and astonished at her. No wonder she'd pleaded not to hate her. He was speechless, in shock and couldn't even begin to articulate what to say to her. 'I'm getting out of here,' he said gruffly. He managed to push his way through the now stunned and grieving crowd to get to the door, where he ran and kicked at it, over and over. 'Open the fucking door!' he shouted.

He felt his friends gathering around him. None of them spoke; they all began to join in. Security guards were soon there. 'Stand down,' one of them shouted, but Jace took no notice.

Other people started to try other doors and the mood in the crowd began to turn. They were starting a riot. Newer bands like themselves who'd realised too late what this was. Only the old, seasoned performers remained quiet and sombre in their place. Shame was etched on their faces, revealing they'd seen this many times. They looked at the floor or the ceiling, anywhere but at them. It was the price they were willing to pay to keep what they had.

But no one opened the doors. No one came to their rescue.

Instead, tens of serving girls spilled out from the staircase under the floor, holding trays of red wine and began to hand them out. At first, Jace couldn't believe they thought a party and alcohol could buy their silence. His heart stopped and vomit came up into his mouth. Suddenly and violently, he realised what the glasses contained. *These people were animals – no worse than animals – monsters.*

Jace lost his mind and gave himself over to instinct, kicking, punching, screaming at anything that got in his way. Even biting when he could. Something soft grabbed him around his mouth and the world went dark.

WHEN JACE finally opened his eyes, he was in Raz's bed. His memory immediately crashed in and he tried to carry on where he left off, but his limbs screamed in pain and when he went to speak, so did his throat. His voice came out as a barely audible croak. Then it made sense. He was restrained because of all the kicking and screaming.

Raz was sitting cross-legged in the armchair next to the bed, wearing her cute pyjamas.

'What the fuck, Raz?' he said, grimacing, pulling his hand up from one of his restraints, making the chain jingle.

'I'll unchain you if you promise not to go mad.'

He rolled his eyes and she got up and retrieved the key from the drawer by the bed. She turned the key in the padlock and the chains fell loose, allowing him to slowly sit up. She kept her eyes on him warily and passed him a bottle of water. He guzzled it, feeling the instant relief from his raging thirst and sore throat. He hoped it would help with the headache thumping his skull like a train.

He went to put the bottle down on the nightstand and his eyes fell on the wine glass containing the dark-red liquid. He instantly recoiled and whirled around on Raz in accusation. 'Who the hell are you people?' he spat, wide-eyed in panic.

Raz put out a defensive hand before he could shout and knock it on the floor. 'Stop it, Jace, or they will kill you. Believe me, I love you and I don't want that to happen. You just have to drink it to honour the family and your friend.'

Jace just blinked in horror. 'Who the hell are you people?' he repeated, having to swallow down bile that had come up into his mouth. The horrific ceremony kept playing over and over in his head and the river of blood. Pope's blood. Mixing with all the others like no one gave a shit. The last look on Pope's face. Happy, honest, lovable Pope, who just liked making short films with his friends, and none of them had done a damn thing to stop it. He despised himself and he hated them. 'They killed him,' was all he could say, angrily. 'Why? Why did they have to do that?'

'It's just the price, Jace … simple as that. It's always been this way.'

The boiling rage of earlier began to rise in him again. 'I need answers, Raz, otherwise, I swear to god—' He wanted to despise her for being a part of all this, but even then, when he was angry enough to kill someone, he instinctively knew she wasn't the instigator and was a captive as much as he was – albeit a willing one. 'Are they doing it for the blood, like vampires or something?' Tears filled his eyes as Raz watched him sadly. He could no longer hold it in and cried hopeless tears that were hot as they streaked down his face. 'Pope …' he said on a sob. 'He thought he'd won something – he never won anything.' Then great sobs racked through his body.

Raz's arms came around him 'Nothing as simple as that … it's much worse.' she said quietly. He cried brokenheartedly into her shoulder while she rocked him gently, saying, 'I'm sorry … I'm so sorry, Jace.'

. . .

'WHAT'S GOING ON?' Sasha said, soon concerned at the speed they were walking. She had to skip to keep up.

'Nothing! I just hate those things.' His face seemed unreadable and stern.

It just seemed like a disorganised concert to her. However, she was grateful to get away from Jace's dark looks and Demeter had finally made the effort to see her for the first time since they'd left the cabin. She just didn't understand the rush.

A car was waiting right outside the main entrance with the engine running and Demeter got the door for her to get in. It felt like an escape. 'Where are we going?' she asked, still trying to gauge his face as he got in after her.

He held her hand and looked out of the side window, even though it was blacked out, and it was impossible to see. She sensed something new in him. A sense of urgency she'd never seen. He was always so confident and relaxed. Today, he was wound tight, like it wouldn't take much for him to explode.

'Are you OK? … Is everything alright? … Is it your sister?' she asked, grasping at straws in an effort to get him to speak.

He let out a single blast of air derisively, squeezed her hand and finally looked at her. 'Believe me, Raz will be fine.'

His hair was tousled and still damp from a recent shower. His eyes gleamed as arresting and beautiful as ever. But there was something else in them tonight. Something sad. Something troubling him.

'I can't tell you what you want to know, Sasha. But please know that I have a high enough regard for you to protect you from it.'

He wasn't making much sense. 'From what?' she persisted, turning to face him in her seat and holding his hand in both of hers.

He brought her hands to his mouth and kissed them

gently. His smile held so much regret, she thought she was going to get the 'we can still be friends' conversation. Instead, he gently cupped the side of her face and stroked her cheek with his thumb. 'In another life, I would settle down with you. We'd have a brood of kids and grow things on a farm.'

Her heart twisted in her chest and she suddenly wanted to cry. 'Is that your dream?' she asked, swallowing down the huge lump in her throat. 'It's mine too,' she said, as tears overflowed down her cheeks.

Instead of answering, he looked at the driver, concentrating on the road, and shifted back into his seat. He wasn't going to say any more.

'Where are we going?' she asked, to help him change the subject.

'To a small guest house I own. It isn't far. It's quiet and has more amenities than the cabin.'

'I liked the cabin,' she said, her heart fluttering, while she continued to watch his profile and he remembered the idyllic time they'd spent there.

'Me too,' he said, almost under his breath.

He didn't look at her again, but she looked at him, while the car headed deeper and deeper into the mountains.

JACE DID what Jace always did when there was a problem to face. He drank hard and he took pills. He tried to get away from Raz, but she followed him around the room. He wanted to go and find Sasha, but by the time Raz was wasted enough for him to escape, he was too wasted to make it out of the door.

'You have to drink it,' she kept whining. 'You can't honour the pact without it.'

'Are you insane?' he spun around and shouted at her. 'I will never drink it, it disgusts me. You disgust me even asking me … Just tell your psycho cousins I refuse, or I drank it … I don't care. They'll never know whether I did or not.' It seemed a great idea. He didn't know why he never thought of it earlier.

'They will, Jace. We all will …' Her voice trailed off and he stopped pacing and turned and stared at her. She was deadly serious and remarkably sober. She seemed apprehensive, like she didn't know how he would react, but was scared because she knew what would happen if he took no notice of her.

'How? How will you know?' he asked, trying not to sway. His heart was quickening, making his temples pound.

'There is power in it, Jace. Magic,' she said, sounding defeated. 'You might think it's crazy, but it's true. It's in your contract and in the ceremony you saw downstairs. You don't understand it, but it's what my family uses to charm your life. And without it, my father will know.'

Father? It was the first time there was any mention of a father. Jace narrowed his eyes sceptically, 'And he's OK with all this – you being trapped here?'

Raz put her head in her hands as if she was so tired of it all and went and sat on the edge of her bed. 'It's just the way it's always been – how he's always wanted it. A family here, to control like a rod of iron,' she said, looking up at him with weary eyes, letting her gesturing hand drop into her lap. 'To trap fame-hungry people with despicable acts they would never want the outside world to find out about and too proud and desperate for riches to ever notice they only bring him money and power. Then, by the time they realise the price is too high, it's all too late and they're too far in. It's worked for centuries.'

'And no one challenges it?' Jace said, nonplussed, pacing a few more steps and stopping again to glare at her. 'Who the hell is this guy?'

'*Hell*,' she mimicked, laughing ruefully. She looked down

at her fingers. 'Some do …' She shrugged. 'No one ever sees them again. They appear in the media having died young or in mysterious circumstances.' Her eyes looked desolate then. 'The twenty-seven club. The whole world romanticises it, but it's all just a bunch of young people refusing to be a part of it … Or they hit middle age and die mysteriously in some hotel room of an overdose of doctor-prescribed painkillers or some sex game gone wrong. Riddled with guilt and shame, all of them.'

Jace was stunned. 'Are you? … Are you riddled with guilt and shame?'

She just looked up at him hopelessly without answering.

It would all sound too ridiculous and fantastic if he hadn't just lived through what he had. He grabbed his head and wished it was straighter so he could think more about it, but it was way above his brain capacity right then; it took such huge concentration. His eyes were now squinting from the pain. 'So let me get this straight. So you're telling me you're like the Devil's child, or something?' The words sounded ridiculous on his tongue as he said them.

Raz simply looked up at him with those weird eyes that seemed to prove a point. She shrugged. 'The Star Child, actually. There has been one in every generation. I've never met my father. I don't think Demeter even has. He moves around constantly. All I know is that we're different. My family has been in these mountains for thousands of years and we help him secretly control everything.'

Jace tried to sieve through it. It was all so fantastical and yet somehow logical. Like, no wonder rumours of vampires and fairy stories of monsters came from this part of the world. He felt kind of foolish having to put some fantasy label on it, when it was probably more like some sort of elite crime family or something behind it. He swayed with the weight of it all.

Raz got up off the bed and closed the gap between them slowly and seductively as if she sensed his anger leaving him. 'Devil's child … Demon kid … Whatever … I've been called worse.' By the time she finished speaking, her lips were against his neck to nip a path downwards and she began digging her fingers into his back. It instantly relieved his pounding head and eased his knotted muscles. He breathed in sharply, and she moved down, over the taut muscles of his stomach, while she opened his belt. By the time she released him and took him into her mouth, he let out a long breath and released it from his mind. He was in too much pain and he was too tired to hold it all.

She adeptly managed to transform the whole thing into the topic of one of their sex games. He soon became jumbled and didn't know what the truth, paranoia, or the game was anymore. Then, when she looked up at him seductively through her lashes, he didn't care. In his pain and fatigue, it was easier just to let go.

He allowed her to steer him and push him backwards onto the bed, where she was soon on top of him. Dominating and overrunning his senses as only she could. His fight had gone. He'd never be able to resist her, anyway. It was futile. She had such complete power over him in the sack. She began riding him mercilessly and he became lost in her. In those wolf eyes. He didn't want to be found. Any spark of reason or fear was simply pounded away as she drove him higher and closer to the edge.

Just for a moment, he allowed himself to be wild with her. He watched with barely open, lust-filled eyes as she sat up straight and dragged wet fingers down and across his chest. Down his face like war paint. *Red paint.* From his forehead down to his chin. Across his lips, pushing her fingers into his mouth one by one. The metallic, salty taste, dancing on his taste buds like an alarm bell to wake him up from a dream.

At the furthest point of his mind, he knew what it was. It was struggling to surface, but something wouldn't let it. With every advance, she beat it back. He wanted to push her off to show his repulsion, but he was too weak. She simply pinned his arms next to his head and kissed him, filling his mouth with the coppery liquid. His stomach clenched, making him want to retch and expel it, but all the while his hips took on a life of their own and kept pumping. Just like she knew they would.

His mind was thrown back to the times she'd used a razor blade on him and he knew she'd been preparing him for this. Building muscle memory, so his body would remember and he would be helpless in his reaction to it. It didn't matter what his mind said; his body said different, and that was what was in charge right then.

Raz was wrenching and drawing out of him the final and total disrespect of his friend's death, and, what was more, he was absolutely sure it was the whole point. That was what was getting her off, his doing that for her. The orgy going on downstairs, the writhing bodies going on now in that huge room, was all because of this. The blood represented giving away every moral thought to something as basic as sex. He couldn't think of anything more demonic.

Jace hated himself more than he'd ever done in his whole life and self-sabotage was his specialty. Because he was despicable, because he couldn't stop even now, because it sent him completely over the edge.

'Yes, baby, yes,' Raz cried triumphantly.

While he helplessly and hopelessly came over and over again.

CHAPTER 22

By the time they reached the perfect little rustic inn, Sasha was really worried about Demeter.

He was always contained, but completely present. It was one of the things she loved about him. But today it seemed like he had a huge weight on his shoulders and was a thousand miles away.

Their driver brought two bags into the small wooden hallway and Demeter thanked him as he left them alone. 'I had the maid pack you some things,' he explained.

She had wondered about that.

A cheerful elderly woman greeted them with a huge smile. Her white hair was scraped back into a bun at her nape and her face was pale and wrinkled but kind. 'Welcome, Ursuleţul,' she said, wiping her hands on the neat white apron tied around her waist and kissing him on the cheek roughly, while he hugged her.

It was astonishing in that it changed his whole demeanour, like he was greeting a beloved grandma or something. She'd never seen him greet anyone like that. He returned the kiss and gabbled something while the woman nodded at her as if she'd been the subject of what they'd been saying. 'This is my nana,' Demeter said proudly. 'The woman who raised me … I was explaining who you were.'

Sasha was so astonished at the first real piece of information about him that she wasn't quick enough to follow up with any questions. The woman's smile lit up her perfect bone structure and she picked up her hand, gave it a squeeze and welcomed her warmly.

Sasha was aching with curiosity, but returned the smile as graciously as she could and followed. Demeter had already picked up the bags and was walking towards a narrow wooden staircase.

They went up six flights of creaky stairs. The whole house appeared to be made of polished pine, cut from the surrounding forests, which seemed so abundant there. There were a few faded oils on the walls, but mostly carved plaques of farming scenes made of the same wood.

The woman spoke to Demeter in his language the whole way up. She itched to know what they were saying. So he hadn't been brought up by his parents. Maybe that's why he was nice and not at all like his cousins or his sister.

At last, they came to a door right at the top of the stairs. Demeter opened it with a key the woman passed him and she waited on the threshold while Demeter went in and Sasha followed. She was speaking fast and pointing, she guessed, where towels and extra blankets could be found. Then she said 'Goodnight' in English and left them to it.

Sasha stood just inside the room, clutching her purse and looking around. It was cosy and old-fashioned, with deep-red curtains, a large bed with a patchwork quilt in matching colours. The window had shutters that were open wide, letting in the smells of the forest.

Demeter put the bags down on the blanket box at the end of the bed and pointed to a door on her right. 'There is a bathroom in there, but you won't need to bathe tonight,' he said with a mysterious smile. He walked over to a door that was tucked away in the corner, behind the curtain. He opened it and pushed it wide. 'I thought we could relive our last time together,' he said, now grinning playfully.

Completely intrigued, she walked past him to take a peek outside. She giggled and surveyed in wonder. Outside was a delightful decked roof terrace with a gazebo decorated in colored lights and inside that was a jacuzzi tub with steam rising from it.

If ever she had wondered where their non-relationship went after their last meeting, then this was the answer. As if to prove a point, Demeter came up behind her, put his arms around her waist and kissed the crook of her neck. 'I have been thinking about this all week.'

Sasha turned in his arms in surprise and looked up at his beautiful face. She was so amazed and happy. After seeing Jace and the awkwardness at the party, it was hard to believe the evening could change to this. She had no idea their time together had been anything more than a passing fancy to him. 'Really?' she said, terrified she was coming across as needy. 'I'd forgotten.'

He laughed loudly, bent his head, and kissed her. It was drugging and sent heat waves down to her feet. The only detail she'd forgotten was just how utterly he affected her. However, it was tinged with fear. He was becoming important to her. Like she wanted to keep the feeling, even though he was honest about offering her nothing. She guessed, after Jace, that made him the most dangerous person to be around in her current emotional state. It was committing emotional suicide and she was powerless to resist, particularly when he whispered, 'Relax with me, Sasha. I will make it my sole responsibility to look after your every need.'

What girl could ever say no to that?

He picked up her hand and put it around his neck, and while kissing her deeply, lifted her and carried her over to the large tub. Conscious thought stopped after that. Her clothes were soon gone and so were his and they stepped into the deliciously warm water. He pulled her into his lap as he sat on one of the ledges and looked mischievously into her eyes. 'More comfortable than the cave, no?'

She felt so at ease with him, like she was drugged or drunk or something. She guessed she was just happy, and she hadn't felt that for a very long time. 'I have fond memories of that cave.'

He laughed. 'I thought you had forgotten?' he said, playfully. 'Permit me to remind you.'

They were kissing again and before she knew what was happening, he was nudging against her until she sank onto him with a contented sigh. He was warm and familiar and she felt perfectly safe in his hands. She clutched him to her and he nipped down the side of her neck while she began to move purposely against him.

It was astounding that she barely knew him and had this kind of sexual trust. Remarkable as she'd only ever been with Jace. She loved the way he held her, even when she was on top. He was so strong and protective, he cushioned her from the world. Even then, she knew he was addictive. He was experienced and thorough, working every muscle, lavishing every nerve in her body. And when at last he drove her to climax, it was always him in control. He held her and teased her, driving her insane, until he finally relented and set her free.

It was then she realised just how dangerous he was for her. She was falling for him and she couldn't help it, any more than a boulder could stop rolling down a steep hill. As she floated back down to earth after the orgasm of her life, she understood that it was inevitable with a powerful man like Demeter. Not only was he the most desirable man she'd ever met, but she'd been emotionally neglected by Jace for so long. She was low-hanging fruit. Easy to get.

'Don't be sad,' Demeter said, guiding her face around so he could look into her eyes.

'I'm still learning to let go,' she said honestly. There was no point in lying; he seemed to know everything anyway. 'I'm terrified of the future.'

He studied her for a full moment as if he recognised the honesty in her revelation, then he nodded and kissed her chastely on the mouth. 'I will ask nothing from you,' he said eventually.

She smiled sadly at the truth in that. No ties. No promises. She'd got that loud and clear from their last meeting. She was cast adrift. No anchor. No feet on the ground.

'You want chains and expectations?' he asked. He was holding the side of her neck and stroking her throat with his thumb, but there was no accusation in his words. Just a little surprise at a concept alien to him. Even when he was delivering a blow, he managed to put her at ease.

And he was right. You couldn't get hurt if you expected nothing. The self-sabotage monster crept over her and she said the words that were impossible to take back and would be the death knell for the two of them. 'But when love comes, it chains you whether you want it to or not. It's painful and makes you needy and miserable and a shadow of the person you once were.' She wasn't sure if she was talking about her time with Jace or the damage Demeter would undoubtedly wreak on her. She didn't care.

He squinted, suspicious, as if he saw what she was doing. 'You are wise for one so young,' he said, hedging.

'I was taught by the best,' she said, bitterly, trying to work out how old he was. She put him at early to mid-thirties. 'Are you happy?' she asked, as the thought occurred to her.

He looked surprised, as if she'd caught him off guard, and he thought about that for a second. 'Stolen moments, maybe,' he said, tilting his head at that gorgeous angle to the side. 'Isn't it the same for everybody? Snatches of happiness in a world filled with problems.'

She hugged him tightly to her and felt his arms respond slowly, until he did the same. As if he wasn't sure what was happening. He had everything, but she instinctively knew those moments for him were rare. 'Why did you take me away from the party?' she asked, drawing back to look at him.

He frowned a little, making her wonder what he was thinking. 'It's not a good place for you to be,' he said, shifting his weight awkwardly. His whole demeanour changed and he went to stand up. 'Come. I'll get some food sent up.'

She got out of the tub with him, sorry she'd pushed the conversation until his barriers went up. They grabbed towels and dried themselves, their moment of intimacy clearly over, but it angered her too. 'Do you want me to be another yes person? Who agrees with everything you say and doesn't have their own mind?' she asked moodily, rubbing her hair dry with a towel. 'My crew was there too, you know. Why is it OK for them and not me… And Tears is a girl,' she finished, flashing her eyes angrily at him.

His lips twitched as if he was trying not to smile. She dared him, raising an eyebrow and watched aghast as he broke into laughter at that.

'What? What's so funny?' she said, giving him a hefty shove.

He shook his head wearily and pulled her to him by the knot of her towel. 'You … you're funny. You have no idea. People call me the antichrist in the corporate world,' he said, chuckling to himself. 'And you talk to me like a hen-pecked husband.'

She began to laugh with him, liking his playful side. He took her hand and led her back inside and over to the bed, where he sat her next to him and held both her hands. 'You must understand that the music side of the business is handled in a very different way to mine. It works by certain energies ...' He paused as if he wasn't sure quite how to put it. That wasn't a party but an old ritual that can get quite wild. I have no taste for it and I am male.'

She frowned, listening intently but feeling irritated by his condescending tone. 'Your sister ... does she like it?' She knew she was being spiteful, but it was a valid point. *And didn't he know what the LA rap scene was like?*

He bobbed his head, conceding the point right away. 'My sister lives for the music ... I don't think she has much of a choice.'

She felt angry and confused and would have got up and walked away if he hadn't pulled her back into his lap and put his arms around her. She felt instantly sorry. He seemed so sad and resigned when he touched on anything to do with his family. 'Can we just enjoy this oasis of happiness for one night?' he said, putting his head on her shoulder.

She couldn't say no to a request like that. She swallowed and nodded, tightening her arms around him. This vulnerable side pulled her in more than any of the money or power. A pain twisted in her gut. She was in love with him. She could no longer run or hide from it. 'Can we stay for two?' she whispered.

He simply groaned, pushing her down and relieving her of her towel.

CHAPTER 23

The party was a scene from Jace's nightmares. Raz had dragged him back to it after their shameful sex session. She always loved that. Becoming messy and relaxed and then mixing with people who had no idea what they'd just been doing. He usually went along with it, but this was sick. Despite his protestations, she explained forcefully that they had to be seen so her family knew they'd complied with the ritual. He was speechless. The crowd was a writhing sea of limbs and blood. They literally bathed in it. He couldn't even articulate to ask why.

He tried to look for his friends, but, in all honesty, he didn't think he would recognise anyone even if he wasn't slaughtered by drink and drugs.

Raz got under his arm and stumbled trying to hold him up. She took him to a smaller chillout room that was marginally better. Less boisterous, where the people sat bewildered, in shock, looking as if they'd been mud fighting in a pit of red mud.

He found his crew there, conspicuous in that they were reasonably clean of blood, huddled together for comfort on a group of sofas. Zach was there too, looking as traumatised and as fearful as the rest of them.

The next thing Jace knew, he was hit by a train and was trying to pick himself up off the floor. He waggled his jaw to make sure it was still attached to his head and looked up into the angry face of Duo, contorted with rage.

Raz was quickly between them. 'Back off!' she said, shoving Duo hard in the chest. 'The trouble with you types is that you expect it all to come for nothing. Everyone wants the same thing you have, and you think you're special!' she shouted.

Jace scrambled to his feet to intervene before it got too ugly, but Duo simply looked stunned. He guessed Raz had never said more than work stuff to his friends and definitely nothing as honest about their situation there.

Duo's sister, Tears, started crying into Sensei's shoulder and the rest were glaring straight at him as if he had some sort of control over all this. 'What?' he screamed, trying not to cry himself. 'I had no more of an idea than you did.'

'Look at the state of you!' Duo yelled and pointed at the large mirror over the fireplace. 'I don't know you, man.'

Jace staggered with the shock of his harsh words and walked towards the mirror to see what he was talking about.

'You see. Covered in blood. Our friend's blood.' Duo's voice wavered with emotion. 'You're no better than the rest of them.'

Jace wanted to argue back to defend himself. To say there was no way of knowing whose it was, but he couldn't, because it died on his lips at the sight of himself. His face was striped in a warpaint of blood that streaked his neck and arms. Duo was right. He'd sold Pope for fame. They all had. Everything looked startlingly ugly and clear now. He'd sold his soul.

Jace collapsed to the floor in a heap of sobs, crying

broken-hearted tears. It was for Pope. His joy at winning something for the first time in his life. For the simple life they had loved and lost in their loft before they came there. And Sasha, his rock. Who was in the arms of another man, doing God knows what to her.

He felt a sharp pain in his ribs. Then again. He looked up to see Raz drawing back to kick him again. 'Get up, arsehole!' She turned on the others and screamed, 'Don't you dare turn on him! You all wanted this. No one else wanted you. You're all guilty.'

Jace felt her angry footsteps through vibrations in the floor as she marched off. Everyone else went silent as he lay curled in a ball, wishing he could call Sasha to come and get him and show him the way home. But there was no more Sasha. No friends to call and, what's more, no phone to call them on. Pain welled up in his head and he let the darkness take him with an ear-splitting scream.

WHEN JACE NEXT opened his eyes, he was back in Raz's bed. It was happening a lot lately. He guessed her room was now recognised as his. Not so long ago, he would have got off on the status it gave him, but now it just made him a pet.

He knew he was sick. He had to be. The headaches were now incessant and were from more than dehydration, which was what everyone kept saying to him. In another life, he'd have told Sasha and she would have insisted he go see a doctor. He'd argue and make it hard for her, but it was part of their routine and he would have gone in the end.

Now he didn't care about anything. He didn't care if he ever got out of bed. New music hadn't come to him for a very long time because the only thing that eased his pain was copious amounts of cocaine. It went straight up his nose and gave him a break from pain for about twenty minutes each time, before it came crashing down like a hammer. Now he was trapped in a cycle of tequila, pills and coke. Even he recognised he was in a nosedive, about to hit the ground hard.

He turned his head. Raz was still asleep, next to him, still smeared with dried blood all over her. He lay back and stared up at the ceiling as a wave of nausea swept over him.

The phone rang next to the bed. He waited until his stomach settled, swallowed the water that had accumulated in his mouth and reached out without lifting his head.

'Boardroom now!' Zach ordered before he could even say hello. 'I've been knocking on your door for ages.'

'OK,' Jace said, before he dropped the phone and scrambled to the bathroom to vomit.

Raz was sitting up by the time he flushed the toilet and came back. She always seemed to escape the rigours and ill effects of the night before. She just looked messy and tired. He was twenty-one going on ninety today. He went along mechanically as she got up and led him to the bathroom.

'Are you with me, no matter what?' Raz asked, holding the sides of his face when they got in the shower. He was. He had no place else to go. There was no escaping and he had no energy to run anyway. Raz pulled him to her and hugged him fiercely. It struck him that she was the only person more fucked up than him, because she didn't even know it. A performing bird in a cage that was brought out by the family on special occasions. He kissed the soft part of a shoulder. He wouldn't abandon her while there was life left in him.

Raz put on a soft tracksuit and slippers, looking cute as hell. Jace pulled on the first things clean he could find. He was being hurried and his brain wouldn't work, so that it consisted of a beanie to cover his wet hair, his dark goggles to shield his streaming eyes, boardshorts and a pink fluffy dressing gown of Raz's. He almost left with bare feet, but Raz reminded him just in time. 'Can you help me with my sneakers?' he asked pitifully. 'My head's banging and I'll throw up.'

Raz rolled her eyes and crouched down. 'You look like a joke,' she said, pulling them on his feet without tying the laces.

Jace didn't care. They were lucky he was going at all. Raz went on ahead grumpily, refusing to talk to him. He concentrated, one step at a time, pausing and leaning on the walls of the hallways when he had to. Waves of nausea threatened to knock him off his feet, filling his eyes with tears and mouth with excess water, which he spat in the potted plants. 'That's truly disgusting,' he heard Raz say.

He was just thankful it wasn't vomit. He guessed there was nothing left in his stomach to expel.

They finally got to the boardroom, and his whole collective was already there. Apart from Sasha, that is. A pain stung his chest. He guessed he'd always look for her. But he was glad she was gone. If Raz's brother was prepared to look after her, then he was OK with that. He seemed stronger and steadier than his sister.

As he sat gingerly in his chair so as not to jiggle his head, a strange feeling of calm and resignation settled over him. It felt like a relief, like a halo of protection, and for the first time in living memory, the pain subsided.

Raz must have sensed it because she forgot her bad mood, gave his hand a squeeze and studied his face in concern. He leaned and kissed her on the lips to put her mind at ease.

The cousin, Tegan, strode in just ahead of his brothers, Rollo and Taj. 'Welcome. Apologies for the early hour,' he said, eyeing Jace's attire. 'Thank you for coming.' He slammed his briefcase down on the table, making Jace flinch as it shot painful vibrations right through his head. 'I wanted to congratulate you on coming through your first confirmation ceremony well. There are no more secrets now. You are full inductees of the Carpathian society and will enjoy all the benefits it has to offer.'

Jace felt Duo's body stiffen next to him and his hard stare on him. They locked eyes for a moment and he was forced to look away. Duo's were cold and empty. There was nothing in them anymore. No friendship, no bond or affinity. No nothing. Simply disgust and blame. It felt like another nail driven into his heart. Their tight friendship of several years was over. It felt so unfair. Duo didn't seem to understand that he would have gone back to their loft in a heartbeat. To just the crew – Sasha and Duo. Poor as mice, simply making their music. Now his energy had been sapped right out of him, leaving him nothing left to fight with.

'Mourn your friend. Honour him. He gave his life so you might succeed. We've just confirmed your world tour. Eighty dates. Ten countries. Interviews on the top shows in every country. By the time you come home, you will be household names, and you will have achieved your wildest dreams. Something very few artists can truly say,' Tegan went on, like some sort of politician.

Jace's mind wandered. For the head of a music company, he had very little idea how a true artist's mind worked. He never had any wild dreams beyond people loving his music. To be able to perform and have enough money to not have to go in, day after day, to a soul-destroying real job. He'd achieved that back in LA.

He had wanted to travel, maybe. So there was that. And he would get to perform to thousands – the only place he felt truly happy and alive. But it didn't matter whether it was a stadium or a small club, so long as he was creating music and doing it with his friends.

Now they didn't even want to look at him. They hated him. Mainly because of his connection to Raz and, by association, the regime they were tied to. Because of that, they blamed him for Pope and the mess they found themselves in.

Jace became aware of the weight of Raz's head on his shoulder. She'd fallen asleep. The soft purr breathing of genuine sleep. He envied her. The girl could literally sleep anywhere. And didn't that say it all? She was that relaxed because she was numb to it. She didn't react, not because she was naive, but because she'd grown not to care. All these things were necessary hoops to jump through and she'd seen it many times. It galvanised something deep inside him. Only one word came to mind: Escape. The most honest thing he'd thought in weeks and the only thing that made any sense. And making sure Sasha did too.

Tegan finally stopped talking with a 'Well done!' and left with the other two.

Raz stirred and mumbled something. Then, making him jump, she sprang up and ran after them as if there was something important she'd forgotten to say. She didn't need to listen to Zach's pep talk. Jace was already thinking of going back to bed.

The door slammed and they were left in an uncomfortable silence.

'I don't know what to say,' Zach said, eventually.

It made Jace sit up and break through his fog. It was unlike him to be lost for words. It wasn't his fault. It wasn't anyone's fault, but it was obvious he felt guilty.

'Did you know?' Brains asked, cutting across his thoughts.

'No … well … no, I didn't,' Zach spluttered, making Jace alert to the conversation. 'They just asked me to nominate someone as a sacrifice.'

There was a brief moment where everyone froze in their seats, stunned. Then the room erupted. They were all on their feet, except Jace. He remained in his seat, his eyes squinting with the pain of the added blood pressure. Half the room seemed to want to beat down on Zach and the other half were pushing them back, telling them to keep calm till they got some answers.

'Calm down!' Zach shouted. Flattening the air with his hands to get them to quieten down and resume their seats. 'Please, guys. We'll have the guards in here.'

The jostling stopped, but they refused to sit down. Each set of eyes glared pure hatred at Zach. 'When they said sacrifice, you think I knew they meant that? I thought someone had to get kicked out, and bastard move though it was, I thought Pope. He was a filmmaker and not directly involved with the music. I just thought he was the obvious choice to go. I had no idea they would kill him, for God's sake. What do you take me for? I'm as trapped in all this as you are.'

There was a moment where they all considered what he said, turned to each other and grumbled. Jace understood right away. Even if Zach did know, what choice did he have if he didn't want it to be him?

'Look, I'm as gutted as you are. You're in shock. We all are,' Zach continued. 'Get your heads on straight. We get to leave for the tour tomorrow. Let's just get away from here, regroup and think. We'll be gone for months. We'll come up with a plan and maybe we'll be able to get past this.'

'And what about the next time?' Jace said, the vibrations in his own voice sending saliva into his mouth.

'Yeah!' Duo chimed in.

'Who will it be next?' Ballistic shouted.

Zach looked at the ceiling and let out a loud huff of exasperated breath. He shook his head. He didn't have the answers. None of them did. 'I dunno. I honestly don't know what to say to you. Except we're here. We're alive. We have a world tour and there is no exiting an organisation like this. Not outside of a wooden box, anyway.'

Jace's heart stalled on that. They were the truest words

he'd heard all day. He couldn't think. He needed to go back to bed. 'Did anyone see Sasha last night?' he said.

No one would look him in the eye, but several shook their heads. Zach came closer to keep his voice down. 'I asked one of the staff last night and they said she left with that bloke – the brother – and would be coming back today or tomorrow. They weren't sure.' He looked genuinely sorry and his eyes dropped away guiltily as he knew it would be a blow. It was clear now that Sasha was in a relationship with this guy.

'Thanks,' Jace said and nodded. He had mixed emotions about it. Primarily, relief that she'd been away from all this.

'You OK?' Zach said, touching his shoulder with concern. 'You look terrible.'

Jace raised an eyebrow and would have laughed if he'd been able.

'More terrible than usual,' Zach added.

'Headache. That's all. I'm going to go sleep it off.' As he attempted to stand, he longed for his own room, where he could get away from Raz and her constant demands. He needed to be still and quiet, where he could lie in the dark and not be reminded of how everything had gone to shit. Zach helped him out to the hallway and he felt his eyes burning a hole in his back as he hobbled off. He would have attempted to find an empty room, but after finding the first two locked, he gave up and went back to Raz's.

Raz was comatose in bed when he got back. He got in with her and slept fitfully for a full fourteen hours. Waking several times to take codeine and vomit, not necessarily in that order. Even he was now sure it was more than a regular hangover. His lifestyle was finally taking its toll.

When he woke up, Raz had gone. Probably to organise stuff for the tour. He welcomed the peace. Then, after ordering and managing a little food, he showered and dressed a little more conventionally and set off to do the thing that had burned in him for two days.

He found a young bellboy who took him to the room he needed. He knocked loudly, twice, and waited, trying not to sway.

'Who is it?' a deep, accented voice came from inside.

'Jace!' he said, heart thrashing in his chest, making his head pound.

'She's not here, Jace,' the calm voice said.

Jace straightened to his full height. 'It's you I've come to see.'

CHAPTER 24

There was a pause and the door opened.

The guy, Demeter, stood tall, good-looking, and healthier than any decent man had a right to look. Certainly more of an athletic build than he remembered. He was freshly shaven and showered, dressed in something smarter than he'd ever worn to church. He even smelled great, of good clean man and cologne. In other words, everything Jace was not.

'What do you want, Jace?' Demeter said, when he hadn't said anything.

'Can I come in?' Jace said, feeling conspicuous standing out in the corridor with three days' growth on his chin and dressed like a rag-bag.

Demeter let out a long sigh, pushed the door wide and held out an arm for him to enter.

Jace went in slowly, taking in the room. It was far grander and more antique-looking than Raz's. More like a suite than a room. It had sofas, a table, and chairs, and a huge fireplace on one wall. It was obviously the master bedroom as its huge bay window had prime position over the front of the house.

'Can I get you a drink … a glass of water, maybe?' Demeter asked, with a slight frown, taking in his dishevelled state.

'No thanks,' Jace said, finding and sitting in an armchair by the fire before he wobbled and made himself appear weaker than he already felt.

Demeter was sizing him up, which was irritating, but he couldn't blame him. He'd have done the same. He had to push any macho bullshit aside and say what he'd come to say. 'So you and Sasha are a thing now,' he stated, to kick things off.

Demeter went to say something, but Jace held up his hand. 'It's OK, honestly. I'm OK with it.'

Demeter raised his eyebrows quizzically and sat in the chair opposite him. Crossing his legs at the ankle and placing his arms on the armrest, he waited for him to speak.

Jace leaned forward with his elbows on his thighs. 'I'm leaving on tour. I just wanted to make sure you'll look after her.' He looked around him, not sure how to put it exactly. 'Against all this.'

Demeter nodded slowly, clearly hedging at what Jace actually knew and what he meant exactly. He was very intimidating. He'd have hated to come up against him in a negotiation.

'You know … when I'm … gone … If I go … I want to make sure you'll do the right thing by her …'

The guy followed everything he said with those creepy predator's eyes, clearly intrigued.

'Rather than the company.' There. He'd said it. The two things were clearly poles apart in this place.

Demeter continued to study him closely as if he'd surprised him, but he nodded. 'I can tell you care for her a great deal,' he said, eventually. 'She is a unique and rare soul.'

Jace stared at him, trying to read any sinister meaning

between the lines – any inference in his choice of words. He couldn't help it after all the crazy shit that had gone down over the past few days. It came out before he could stop himself. 'Are you as bat-shit crazy as Raz?'

Demeter laughed, with his eyes wide in surprise, as if he didn't know whether or not he should be angry. Thankfully, he opted for the latter and shook his head. He appeared to think about it. 'I suppose it depends on what aspect of life you are referring to.' He shrugged. 'If you mean do I take drugs, and mix with crazy musicians at wild parties, then the answer is no. But if you mean, would I not hesitate to kill someone who crossed my family or me, then I'm afraid my answer would be yes.'

Jace swallowed, not doubting that was the truth for a second. The guy was so cool, delivering his words with such clarity and eye contact that you knew he meant what he said. He also seemed straight and fair and didn't have the sly, devious way about him that the cousins had. He made him feel he could trust him. 'Will you take care of her?' Jace said, getting up shakily and back to the point of his visit.

Demeter rose too, not missing a thing. 'I will.' He said it emphatically, with his no-nonsense look. 'Don't do anything foolish, Jace.' He wasn't trying to scare him; in fact, he looked more concerned.

Jace let out a ragged breath to steady himself. 'Like you, I'll do what I have to for the people that I love,' Jace said, and started to make his way to the door, concentrating on each step. Just before he disappeared, he turned to face Demeter one more time.

The guy narrowed his eyes, looking uncharacteristically on the back foot. Like there was something more he should say.

'Keep her away from the tour,' Jace said.

Demeter frowned, but nodded, sensing correctly that there was no point in asking why.

Sasha escaped to the gardens as soon as she and Demeter got back. The usual shift from warm and attentive to cool and aloof had come over him as soon as he got out of the car. She was getting used to it as part of who he was, but it still hurt.

She needed to gather her feelings and went straight to the maze. It seemed the go-to place these days when she wanted time to think. She quickly found its tranquil centre, now completely familiar with the way.

The bench was empty, thankfully, and she sat down heavily. The fountain soothed her with its calming sound and the weak autumn sunshine warmed her face. Demeter was still a dull ache between her legs and a faint scent on her skin. He was all over her, permeating everywhere, taking over her senses, strengthening his hold. It was getting harder and harder to think clearly whenever she was near him. They'd shared a wonderful weekend, but now it was over, she was all alone. Jace would soon be leaving for months on tour. She had to get her head on straight and work out where she went from there.

She refused to be Demeter's plaything. She'd simply have to insist she work from home. There was no way she could stay. That was all there was to it. She wouldn't make it easy for him. If he wanted to pick her up and drop her, let him come all the way to Pittsburgh.

A rustle made her look up sharply. Her heart thumped at who it might be. Tegan to ruin her peace with veiled threats and cryptic riddles, or Demeter come to ravage her out in the open. Her heart quickened at that. What she didn't expect was Jace, casually walking into her space with his hands in his pockets. Country walks were never his thing.

But when he entered the clearing and came closer, he had to lean on the edge of the fountain to catch his breath. He spat on the floor as if he was going to be sick. The state of him deeply shocked her. He was so thin, so pale and ill-looking. 'Why the hell make me come all the way out here, Sash?' he said, squinting at her in the sunlight.

Sasha immediately jumped up and helped him over to the bench as if he were an elderly man. 'Jesus, Jace. You look terrible.'

'I'm OK … I'm OK,' he said, gingerly sitting and relaxing slowly into the seat as if every part of him ached. He looked up and put his powdery face to the sun.

She studied him; she couldn't help it. He was so gaunt. His eyelids were so dark they looked purple, as if he'd painted them with eyeshadow. His lips looked tinted with carmine. 'You need a doctor,' she said, not hiding her shock. 'Would you like me to get the staff to call one? It's no trouble.' His whole demeanour was scaring her.

Instead of answering, Jace turned to face her and picked up both her hands. Her trusting doe eyes cut him to the quick with their genuine look of concern. Even after everything he'd put her through. The constant neglect and taking her for granted. The many infidelities and she still had his best interests at heart. 'There's not enough time,' he said, more honestly than she would ever realise. 'The bus leaves soon. I just wanted to come and say goodbye properly before I went.'

She nodded; her perfect little eyebrows drawn together in worry. He pulled her closer and kissed her gently right between them in the hope he could smooth her fears away.

'Are you OK, Jace? Really, I mean?' she said, immediately

pulling away to look at him. It made him smile. Even when he'd shown her more affection in an hour than he'd done in a year, she was still only thinking of him. He couldn't help touching the side of her face as he nodded.

'Are you happy?' he asked. Despite the conversation he'd just had with Demeter, he still couldn't equate them being together.

Sasha looked a little uncomfortable with where the conversation was going. 'I don't want to talk about Demeter with you, Jace. It's complicated.'

Jace studied her sadly and drew his hand back as she pulled away from it. It was exactly what he thought. A strong, successful, alpha male, making no promises because he didn't need to. But he was still his best bet to keep her safe in this hellhole. 'I want you to stick close to him, OK, especially here.'

Her eyes darted to his in obvious surprise. It was the last thing she'd expect him to say. 'What are you talking about, Jace? I'm going back to Pittsburgh.'

The feeling of relief those words gave him was immense. 'That's good … that's really good.'

'What is it, Jace?' she said, sitting up straighter and reaching for his hand. 'You're scaring me.'

That was a great question. *What was he doing there? What did he want to say?* Even to him, it sounded ridiculous. The rise in his blood pressure from stress and nerves was making his head thump. He had to get on and say it before he passed out. It took him a moment to get a hold on the contents of his stomach, then he gripped her hands again. 'OK. I'm just going to say it. I need you to listen to me very carefully, Sasha. I want you to let me finish, then you can do with it what you want. But hear me out and know that it is the absolute truth and that I'm not high.' He stopped and thought about that. 'Well, not out of my skull, anyway.'

She rolled her eyes and gave him the small, exasperated smile he was going for. He gripped and shook her hands slightly to get the conversation on track. 'I wanted to say all the things I never realised at the time and should have said to you a very long time ago.' He looked into her eyes at that point to convey how much he meant it. 'You are and always have been my greatest friend, my muse and the love of my life and I am so sorry I couldn't have been more ... more—' He felt suddenly choked, but had to get out what he needed to say. 'More of everything you needed and you deserve. I want you to be happy, but, above all, I want you to be safe and you will never be safe here, Sasha.'

She frowned and shifted in her seat, ready to argue, but he gripped and shook her hands a little harder, forcing her to look at him. 'Pope's dead, Sasha.'

Jace looked intently at her for any glimmer of recognition, but her expression showed only confusion and shock. She had no clue what he was talking about. He felt such relief that he couldn't go on; he was so choked up.

'Dead, how?' she said, sounding devastated. 'He was fine the other day.'

'They killed him. This place ...' Jace said, shaking his head bitterly.

Her face began to cloud, and he knew he was losing her to the assumption that he was being paranoid. 'Ask Zach. Ask anyone in the crew. They'll all tell you the same thing. We were all there. We're in the middle of some Satanic cult here and we all signed up to it. We all agreed to get famous but at a price. A price that was kept quiet from us until we were too far in. Please, Sasha, think. Is your contract in any way tied to ours?' he pleaded, hoping frantically that Demeter's side of things was somehow different and maybe more conventional than Raz's.

She looked concerned and touched the side of his face to

calm him down, like he was being irrational or something. She wasn't getting it. 'Please, Sasha. Don't treat me like a kid. I'm not a kid. I'm a grown man and I don't want anything bad to happen to you,' he said, standing up quickly in his frustration.

'OK, OK, I hear you,' she said, getting to her feet as well.

He pulled her to him and hugged her for all he was worth. She felt warm and safe and so damn familiar. He never wanted to leave that feeling. He burrowed his nose in the crook of her neck and just smelled her for a moment.

'My contract is separate. I stipulated that if you ever left, I could leave as well, if I wanted – come to think of it, it was a weird thing to have to stipulate for an employment contract,' she said, pulling apart.

Jace drew back and watched her frown as she thought about it. It terrified him, but it also gave him hope. He gave her a little shake. 'You must use that clause, OK? If anything happens, you leave, no matter what Demeter says to try to keep you … Promise me!'

She was staring up at him, scared, as if he'd lost his mind.

'Promise me!' he repeated more forcefully, squeezing the tops of her arms. 'I have to know you'll be safe.'

She nodded. 'I promise.'

He hugged her tightly and closed his eyes. 'Always remember I love you.'

She remained silent, but it was enough that she'd listened. He let out a long breath and opened his eyes, just in time to see a flash of clothing disappear back into the maze. It was only a moment. He didn't see exactly who it was or whether it was even male or female. All he could do was pray it wasn't Raz.

·   ·   ·

Once away from the chateau, Jace removed Sasha from his thoughts and gave himself totally to Raz. He had to stay sane and wanted no repercussions for Sasha when he left. Raz had a possessive streak a mile wide. So he finally let go and allowed himself to love her completely, which wasn't hard. She was the whole deal. She was also demanding and needy and completely damaged, but strangely, that made him feel more together than he'd ever felt. She completed him.

They kicked off their sell-out tour in New York. Then, Florida and London, which now felt like a second home. They were meant to be going on to Paris, Munich, Berlin, Madrid, Rome, Malta, Hungary, St Petersburg, various dates in South America and then down to Australasia, back to the US and finishing the tour in their hometown of LA. The schedule was gruelling and relentless. However, by the time they got to London, the cracks were widening in the collective and they were about to implode.

Jace's drug-taking to block it all out had reached gargantuan levels. The newspapers and gossip pages were full of him falling out of clubs, passing out on stage, or asleep for everything else in between. His headaches were so bad that he could no longer perform without vomiting at least once on stage. All captured and streamed for social media. *Rising star crashing and burning.*

Even Raz, who barely noticed anything outside her own sphere of partying and drugs, began to say regularly, 'Do you need a doctor?'

He always kissed her and replied in her ear, 'Nothing a doctor can do, baby.' He knew it would be enough to satisfy her and it always did.

Raz didn't perform with them on tour. Her magic was reserved for the recording studio. She was the Carpathian dirty secret that everyone in the know knew but didn't talk about. Once, when they were stoned, she revealed that her influence was laid down on track level and played back with Hat's beats. There was no more she needed to do.

'What's the point?' he asked. 'Money?' He found it hard to believe that all this could simply be for that.

'The whole world is lying in the power of the wicked one,' she said dreamily one night, sounding particularly wasted. However, she lay down sleepily, with her chin on her folded arms, and talked honestly for the first time. Or at least he took it as that in his own wasted state. 'Our family is very old, ancient, in fact, some even whisper, from the founding of the world. The original sin.'

Jace frowned and lay down next to her, determined to follow what she had to say. 'Like religious, Jesus stuff?' he said, trailing a finger down the side of her face.

She smiled wryly. 'Not exactly. Before that. My cousins know the story better than me. They say the legend goes back to the Garden of Eden and the question our father posed to God himself. The question was free will. Whether people would follow God out of choice. As time went on, it became clear that you had to pick a side. Jesus came and went, making it clear that only those doing the will of God would be saved. But it still came back to that same one question: free will. Would people choose good when the world dangled everything a person could want in front of their faces?'

Jace scratched his head. 'The world?'

'Who rules the world?' she threw back at him.

'The wicked one?' he said, remembering her comment from earlier. This was more than he imagined when he asked her to explain, but he was determined to keep her talking. 'Where does *your* family come into all this?'

She took in a ragged breath and looked awkward. That really made him mentally sit up and listen. It was clearly difficult for her to say. 'Legend says that a dark angel blessed our family to make it the most powerful in the world. I think it was just to control the growing population. It's easy when their god is fame, money and success. You just need to feed everyone's greed. If you're rich enough, you can influence governments, public opinion and that's what my family does. Basically, we keep the general population busy doing anything but what they're meant to be doing.'

'And what are they meant to be doing?' Jace threw back.

'Reading the signs of the times, of course. The whole world is heading for destruction and people are just too busy chasing the dollar or watching reality TV to see it.'

It was all too fantastical for Jace. But Raz clearly believed it. He put it together with everything he already knew: the weird contract, the strange ceremonies, money, the stratospheric heights of the stardom of all those involved. 'And Pope?' That would never sit right with him.

'Sacrifice,' Raz said, leaning up on an elbow to mirror his position. 'Blood must be the cost. Think about it. It's how everything is weighed out in the Bible. Something gained, for something lost. It's always been the way of things.'

Jace wasn't willing to accept that and sat up with his back to her. She scrambled up to sit next to him. 'Think about it, Jace. Once you've done that, you're culpable. Tied in like everybody else.'

That did make sense. All the crazy occult shit aside, it tied them in and made everyone as guilty as the rest of them. It was the perfect NDA. That he understood. 'Do you believe all that shit?' he asked, turning his head to look her in the eyes.

Raz shrugged. 'My power is real.'

He nodded. It was. 'And your brother?'

She shifted moodily, jumping to the connection to Sasha. 'He handles the greed side of things.'

'Does he have to kill people?' His mind was on Sasha

before he could help himself, risking exposing his concern to Raz.

She narrowed her eyes, 'Not sure, exactly. I don't get to see his side of things. I think they kill themselves … if they can't handle it. I don't know.'

He let out a single breath of mirthless laughter. That'd be right.

She was hedging deliberately, and he didn't want to anger her by pursuing it. She had answered a few good questions, though. Whether he believed any of it or not was a different story. What was important was that they did. It was real enough for it to be happening in this day and age. *Astonishing.*

He had to remember that all the while they were touring, they were away from the chateau and had a reprieve. 'How often do they hold those sacrifice ceremonies?'

She shrugged now, closing off from him. 'Whenever they feel like it.'

He backed off after that, not wanting to ruin any chance of her opening up to him in the future.

The UK leg of the tour continued after that. He started to notice just how insecure and volatile Raz was. He had to walk a fine line between being accessible to his fans and not being overly friendly. Raz would lose her temper and assume everyone was a groupie.

It was as if she knew, deep down, that she was inevitably going to lose him. But it was more than that. He was watched by Steve, her personal bodyguard and the guards that always surrounded her. For her cousins, probably. He was trapped. Hemmed in by them and the gruelling timetable. No time to even make fresh music. He was away from any news of home or the real world. Which meant Sasha. It was a treadmill he knew he'd never get off.

They were in London. The last date before they left the UK. A feeling of deep sadness and nostalgia came over him.

In his heart of hearts, he knew he would never be coming back there. It felt like his last connection to everything he loved: the music before big business got involved, and Sasha.

To make matters worse, the pressures of the tour were taking their toll on the collective and tempers were boiling. It came to a head at their hotel in Piccadilly.

They congregated in Zach's room for a final pep talk before they left. The roadies had loaded up and their bus was waiting for them outside. It wasn't unusual for Zach to use the opportunity to fire them up and motivate them, but it was getting harder the longer the tour wore on. Honestly, it would be flagging even if Jace didn't feel like death.

'Come on, guys!' Zach shouted. 'We've come so far in the short time we've known each other. I know you're tired. Burnt-out. On edge. Angry and hurt at our loss.'

Jace noticed the shared angry looks. No one had forgotten Pope.

'It's understandable,' Zach continued. 'But never forget we achieved a dream. We have an album that hit number one right out of the gate. A world tour and we get to party with our friends every night.'

Jace listened, watchful of the others, all swapping furtive looks between them. They weren't becoming happy or moti- vated by Zach's words. Just the opposite.

Raz snaked her arm around his neck and kissed the top of his head from her standing position next to him.

'Let's go out there tonight and thank Pope and dedicate this performance to him!' Zach said, finishing on a rousing crescendo.'

A few said, 'Yes!'

'Let's do this for Pope!' Zach said, realising he finally had them.

For Pope!' they all said, raising their cans and beer bottles.

'For Pope,' Jace repeated quietly, taking out and popping a

couple of double-strength codeine and a Xan, knowing he'd need the strength for what was coming.

THE SHOW that followed went great. They all kept their promise and sent it upwards to Pope. At least that's how it felt. Jace spaced out during much of his performance. He remembered falling into the crowd and hugging Duo emotionally during 'Hellraiser'. The crowd loved that.

'You will always be my friend,' Jace said into his mic.

'And you mine,' Duo said back, getting caught up in it and openly crying.

Something felt very final about the show. Jace wasn't sure how he knew, but he did. One last great show for Pope. And despite all the friction between them, he wanted Duo to know how he felt about him hadn't changed.

After their encore, Jace thanked every single one of their collective and hugged them, saying, 'I'll never forget you.'

Most humoured him, many looked at him strangely as if he'd truly lost his mind, wasted and lovey as some often got. The truth was, he was tired. So terribly tired.

They took their final bows to thunderous applause, cheering and stamping of feet and the crowd chanting TRHBDor, over and over. They went into a last encore, but Jace had nothing left to give. He'd barely eaten in days and what he had, he'd thrown up. His liquid intake had been beer and his only solids had been painkillers. His tank was very definitely on empty.

He managed to be at the front of the queue to get on the bus and got the corner seat at the back, which he loved. None of the others fought him for it, clearly sensing his need. He put his feet up and sparked a joint, watching the high spirits of the others. It had been a good show. The hour and a half to the airport would pass without much effort from him.

Raz sat, looking at him strangely. She did that a lot lately. There was no baiting him for an argument today. He felt cocooned and warm and he smiled back lazily.

She frowned, looking him up and down. 'You sure I can't get you anything?'

His eyelids were almost closed. 'I think I'm gonna sleep for a bit,' he said, dreamily. He knew he should be comforting her, but sleep was drawing him down and it felt so damn good. 'Remember, you don't have to do what they tell you,' he said, thinking of the cousins. 'You have the power. You can do whatever you want.'

A warmth entered his chest, like someone had poured hot water on him. His head hurt badly for a moment, and then it was gone. For the first time in ages, he couldn't feel a thing and he felt happy as he slipped quietly away.

CHAPTER 25

'Oh no. Honey, you need to come and see this,' Sasha's mom's voice came from the other room.

The TV volume was turned right up, which brought Sasha from the kitchen into the living room. Her mother was pointing at the TV at the picture of Jace, smiling, taken years ago, before he'd got many of his facial tattoos.

An ice-cold chill rippled through her body as the news-reader delivered the words she'd dreaded ever since she'd known him.

'Breaking news … Death of emo-rap star, Lil Jace. Early eyewitness reports say he was due to leave for the next leg of a world tour from London's Heathrow airport. Attempts were made to revive him, but he was pronounced dead at the scene. Tributes from his many friends, in a who's who of the music industry, have already started flooding in.'

Sasha couldn't move. She remained frozen as they did a quick bio that said absolutely nothing of the cute, kind guy he was. All she could think, over and over, was: *the day has come … the day has come … he's gone.*

That was the state her mind was in as she said it to her mother, 'I knew he would, Mom. I knew he'd go like this.'

Her mother steered her through the hallway and up the stairs to bed.

'He's gone, Mom,' she said, staring up at her bedroom ceiling.

Her mother tucked her in and promised to come back with some hot, sweet tea for the shock.

IT FELT like she hadn't moved, but it was morning when her mother opened the curtains.

'I had a terrible dream,' Sasha said, snapping awake with a start.

Her mother came over to the bed, soothed her feverish brow and pushed the damp hair from her face. 'It wasn't a dream, honey, he's really gone. All that confusion and hurt and he's finally at peace.'

Strangely, that was the thought Sasha clung to that got her through those first few days. It shouldn't have been such a shock; he'd been committing slow suicide for years. Now he'd simply gone.

The collective, or the career he'd left, hadn't entered her head. Until after three days, Demeter arrived at the house.

Sasha was out of bed, lying on the sofa, looking like she was fresh out of the asylum. She hadn't washed, was wearing the same nightshirt she'd been in for days and hadn't put a comb through her hair.

Demeter didn't say a word, simply gathered her in his arms and held her while she sobbed. For some reason, seeing him unlocked everything deep inside, and it all came tumbling out. Her mother came in, gave a swift about-turn and quietly left them to it.

Eventually, she pulled away and blew her nose with a box

of tissues her mother had left for her. Demeter sat quietly watching her, waiting until she was ready to speak. 'Thank you,' she said, grateful he wasn't trying to say inane words.

'I wanted to come personally and let you know the arrangements,' Demeter said, maintaining eye contact. 'There is to be a big funeral in LA next week. The body is being flown back. There will be an autopsy. Don't worry. It's perfectly normal. Do you want to come back with me now? Or shall I leave you here till then?'

For just a moment, Sasha imagined lying in Demeter's arms for days until the funeral, but the reality of her probably spending them completely alone soon came crashing in. 'No, I'll stay here. My mother will want to come to the funeral.'

Demeter nodded and stood up. He regarded her thoughtfully with his hands in his pockets. 'I'm truly sorry for your loss,' he said.

Sasha flopped back into the sofa and brought her knees up to her chest. 'But? Go on, say what you want to say.' She flashed her eyes at him and stared ahead of her, waiting.

'It couldn't have come as too much of a surprise.'

She finally looked at him properly. He was frowning and his look was completely unapologetic as he held her gaze. 'No, but I never expected it to be now,' she snapped, angrily, her voice wavering and tears stinging her eyes again.

'Look, there is something else.'

She rolled her eyes, determined not to make things easy for him after his insensitive comment.

'You must be careful of my sister. She has become … unstable.'

That was it. She was on her feet in an instant. 'What? You're only just seeing that now? What the hell is her problem?'

Demeter shrugged and looked a little defeated as if he

totally got what she was saying. 'She's just hurt, angry, looking for someone to blame.'

'Oh my god,' Sasha said, closing her eyes and trying to get a hold on her temper. 'Blame … How about she takes a good, long, hard look in the mirror. She did nothing but enable Jace since she met him. How about she starts there!' Tears were streaming down her hot face and she pushed Demeter hard in the chest. 'Go back and tell the mad bitch that!'

Demeter caught her hands after the second shove and pulled her in to him, probably to stop the shoving. He trapped her arms and held her so she couldn't move to hit him either, but he spoke gently into her hair. 'Listen to me very closely, Sasha. Your contract with me is now void because of your little caveat, which means you have no protection from the company. Raz will come at you, do you hear me?'

Sasha stopped struggling and now stood still, listening, in his arms, absorbing what he said and remembering that last, strange conversation she'd had with Jace.

Demeter slowly let her go but held the tops of her arms, so she had to look straight at him and see just how serious he was.

She scowled at him, not sure what to do with a piece of information like that. 'What about the others? she said, suddenly thinking of their friends.

He bobbed his head. 'They, too, are free of their obligation, Jace saw to that. They are travelling back to LA for the funeral.'

He gripped her arms more tightly to bring her attention back to him. 'But for you, that's not good. You need my protection.' He released her after a hard stare and pulled out a folded manila envelope from his breast pocket. 'Here … I have drafted a watertight contract. All you have to do is sign it.'

Sasha took it from him cautiously, with Jace's last words burning in her ears. 'I need to read it first and think about it.'

He looked a little exasperated with her, something she rarely saw. He was always so confident about everything. He sighed and turned, heading for the door. 'OK, but please don't take long. Sign it and call me on the number on the envelope, but do it quickly. Don't go anywhere or meet anyone you don't know or trust. Do you hear me?'

She had heard him, but she was looking down at the envelope with the Carpathian logo on the front.

'Sasha!' he said sternly, making her jump and look up. 'Have you understood the importance of what I just said?'

She nodded, feeling numb, not knowing what to think. There was so much conflicting information going around her head. He was the same handsome, powerful, wildly attractive guy, sensible and driven in business, but there was also the anguish in Jace's last conversation with her, talking of devils and evil waiting to trap her. She knew who sounded more credible and that made her feel disloyal. She was all over the place. 'OK … I'll take a look at it,' she said weakly. It was the best she could come up with to buy some time.

'Tonight!' Demeter said forcefully, hand on the door handle.

She smiled noncommittally. 'I'll do it as fast as I can.'

He narrowed his eyes as if he knew she was stalling, and, with a final shake of his head, he disappeared out the door. She could hear the soft tone of her mother's voice saying goodbye and his deep, indiscernible reply from the hallway and the street door closing.

Sasha put the envelope down, unopened, on the coffee table and curled up in a ball on the sofa. Silent tears stole through her body until she finally fell asleep.

Her mother came in some time later with a bowl of hot soup. 'Please eat something, dear. I'm getting so worried about you. Your friends keep calling, and Demeter is worried, too. He just called

It all just flowed over her with everything else, in one long stream of misery, until she took the tray from her mom, nodded and pacified her with a few mouthfuls of soup.

She lay her head back on the cushion while her mother's voice continued in the background, and her eyes rested on the envelope, creased down the middle, where Demeter had stuffed it into his pocket. He'd gone to a great deal of trouble to have that prepared and come all the way there. The collective no longer existed as far as the Carpathian Group was concerned, not in any way they wanted to represent, so it meant she wouldn't be designing for them. There was no Jace for her to babysit – not that she'd done much in the end. They'd only ever really wanted Jace, so why tie them all? Why had Jace felt the need to make sure they were all free before he went? Why had he begged her to use her own get-out clause and not listen to Demeter's pleas to keep her? Why had she needed to include one?

Then, Demeter turned up right after it had happened, with a contract already drawn up and with Jace's warning still fresh in her mind; none of it made sense. Demeter was genuinely worried about her, and she couldn't accept that he had no regard for her at all. That would make him some kind of monster.

Sasha reached forward, picked up the envelope and slid her finger under the sealed end and ripped it open. She pulled out the sheets of yellow paper and scanned the cursive old-fashioned ink. She was looking for anything that stood out in the handwritten contract. Anything different from the last one she'd signed.

Everything appeared the same except for the very last paragraph:

The undersigned, Sasha Victoria Bond, will remain solely the

employee of Demeter Lucian Carpathian and will be retained for perpetuity. The undersigned agrees to have no connection in business, in either person, proxy, or secondary company, with the Carpathian Group or any of its subsidiaries. Nor endeavour to work nor engage in any competing design entity in the USA, Australasia, UK, or any European country. The undersigned will not work for or design for any other artist in or outside the music industry. In recognition of the loss of income, the employer, Demeter Lucian Carpathian, agrees to pay the salary of $1,500,000 (one point five million dollars) per annum.

Sasha's eyes remained glued to that part. One point five million for doing nothing. It made no sense. Was Demeter offering to set her up as some sort of kept woman? It was absurd. She couldn't sign this. She wouldn't. Why would he possibly want her to? Unless he got off on control.

Her mother came back in with a tray. 'What's that?' she asked, pointing at the papers.

'Demeter's idea of a joke,' she said, bitterly, throwing the papers down on the table. 'He wants to keep me as a pet.'

Her mother stooped and gathered them neatly together again. 'Do you mind?' she said, holding them up.

Sasha shrugged moodily. 'Knock yourself out.'

She watched her mother's eyes moving across the page, from left to right, as she carefully read the contract. She raised her eyebrows and sighed, putting it back in the envelope. 'That's a lot of money, Sasha. Too much money. Why would Demeter want you to sign a contract for perpetuity? He's such a nice man; there must be a reason. Maybe copyright or something.'

Sasha laughed. 'OK, Mom. I know you're a fan.' He really had schmoozed her mother.

Her mother rolled her eyes, a little irritated with her. 'Well, at least get a lawyer to look it over. What about your cousin, Jack? Aunty Rose's boy.'

'Jack's an intern, Mom. He's not even a real lawyer. Anyway, it doesn't matter because I'm not signing.' Jace's emotional plea flashed into her mind and threatened to make her cry all over again. 'I'm not doing or thinking about anything to do with it until after the funeral.'

TRHBDor HELD a midnight vigil for Jace and Pope in downtown LA, in the street in front of their old loft. It was perfect and their old landlord, loving the publicity and their celebrity status, allowed them up on the roof to use it as a platform.

They were expecting a couple of hundred hardcore fans, but more like two thousand showed up in the end. All carrying candles and wearing Jace's flamboyant style of clothes, leather and fake fur in pastel pinks and yellows. Many wore Jace's steampunk goggles around their necks, bandanas over their mouths, or the TRHBDor T-shirts that Sasha had designed. The small shrine that had started by their old street door grew to the length of the building and all over the sidewalk. Many were crying and comforting each other, while they sang one of Jace's most popular songs. Ironically, it was about his love for her and how he wanted to tell her how he felt, because he would never reach twenty-five. How truly prophetic those words were.

Sasha looked down at the sea of heads and felt like this was his real send-off. Just the collective, all their real friends and the fans. Jace would have loved it. Tomorrow's big industry affair would be celebrities and journalists and very few who really knew or appreciated him.

Sasha's mother had stayed back at their hotel, so Duo and Tears held each of her arms and swayed with her to the singing below. It was a deeply moving experience. Each member of the collective took the mic and said a few words.

Duo, who kept breaking down, spoke next and his words were the most poignant of all.

'I was lucky to have spent the last two years with Pope and Jace, and being with them, especially Jace, my best friend…taught me that y'all – you fans down there, and the music, are what's important. Not deals…not interviews and all the bullshit that the business brings with it.'

The crowd whistled and cheered at that. They could all imagine Jace saying something like that.

'We found out something today and it told me just how special and close a friend Jace really was. Because of Jace's passing, he made sure we are all free from our watertight contract with Carpathian Music. We are free to do whatever we want and to take other contracts if we want to. A year ago, we would have called him selfish, but now we see him for the genius he was and the great gift he's given us. Keep spittin' those bars, my friend. And thanks to Pope, his friendship and films he made, you are immortal. We love you and we'll never forget you. Jace and Pope!' he finished, tears streaming down his face, holding up his beer can while everyone cheered.

Sasha was crying too; she couldn't help herself. She and his sister, Tears, both hugged him while he sobbed into her shoulder. The crowd started singing another of Jace's songs, holding up their candles. It was one called 'Diamond of mine', and was one of his earliest songs. The air literally carried their emotions upwards. It proved they'd been with the music right from the beginning and it was very moving. There wasn't a dry eye anywhere.

However, Duo's words reverberated through Sasha long after he'd finished speaking. She had no idea the collective had wanted out of their contracts. Jace had fought so hard to get them in. Every one of them knew Jace had been on a course of self-destruction and that he'd been on it for a long time, but the wording he'd insisted on in the contract had set his friends free, as if he'd known ahead of time that something was wrong and had contrived to end the whole thing. It left a lot of unanswered questions. Jace's warning resonated again.

There was talk that there had been a full autopsy and how ill he'd been in the end. Some were saying he shouldn't have gone on tour. She was troubled by that as they wandered back inside their old loft, given over to them for the occasion.

She accepted one drink. She wouldn't stay long. No doubt the party would go on through the night, as Jace would have expected, and she wanted to get back to her mother. One drink to be polite and then she'd be off. Many were hitting the tequila already. Old friends, reminiscing about times spent with Pope and Jace and the legendary drinking and drug-taking that went on.

'Raz not here?' she said, scanning the room, as Duo came up to her shoulder.

He was subdued too and shook his head rapidly as if the idea repulsed him. It surprised her; she imagined they all got on. 'No, she's a great musician, but she was no good for Jace. We all knew that.'

'You were his real partner,' Ballistik said, eavesdropping on the conversation.

'Yeah, that's true,' Brains said, nodding as well.

Sasha smiled sadly, deeply touched, but as hard as it was to admit, she and Jace were relative strangers in the end.

'We wanna get as far from that place as possible now we're out,' Duo said with a shudder.

This was all news to her. She would have thought they would have been climbing over themselves to re-sign for solo careers.

'I still can't believe he managed that for us.'

It was all so weird and disturbing; nothing was making any sense. Unless she took into account Jace's final warning. 'Mine finishes too,' she said, thinking aloud, frowning. 'They only got me in to look after him, really – a lot of good that did.' She shrugged. 'But I'm nothing to do with the music side of things.'

'Doesn't matter,' Duo said, sounding overly excited, literally jumping on her words. 'You've got a chance to get out of there. You have to take it.'

She studied his anxious face. He sounded so much like Jace. His sister, Tears, was nodding manically next to him. They were all acting like they'd escaped a jail term with Hannibal Lecter or something. 'Demeter has offered me another contract. It's a lot of money. I've got to at least consider it.'

'No! No! No!' several of them said, jumping on her words and crowding around her. She blinked, backing up, trying to look at them all, bewildered. 'Why? I don't understand.'

'Listen,' Duo said. 'If you go back, none of us will be safe. That is no ordinary company.'

'They're not regular people,' Tears added, fearfully.

'They're evil aliens or demons or something,' Ballistik said.

She was just about to call a halt on the ridiculous conversation and put it down to magic mushrooms or something, when Duo finally said, 'They killed Pope, Sasha. And loads of others…right in front of us.'

She was still gaping at the terror in Duo's eyes when Brains pleaded, 'You can't go back there…you can't. For you … Our sake … Jace's memory.'

Sasha felt attacked on all fronts. She didn't know what to think. They were all so forceful in their arguments, but it had the hallmark of a bad trip. Jace had been with them. Maybe they'd done bad drugs together.

'Please, Sasha. Promise me you won't sign anything,' Duo pleaded. 'I wouldn't be a friend to Jace if I didn't at least try to stop you.'

She smiled weakly at that low blow. But it worked as she assured them she'd do nothing before the funeral. She finally said her goodbyes, already rationalising the crazy comments in her mind. Demeter was the straight-talking businessman and her friends, though lovable, were the huge drug-takers. But the contract was real enough and strange, and so was Demeter's urgency for her to sign it.

THE FUNERAL WAS A HUGE AFFAIR, held in a cemetery at dusk, among the graves of huge stars. It was so Jace, he would have loved that part – everyone dressed in red and black leather and lace. Not so much the guest list, who happened to be everyone in the music industry who barely knew him. They all wanted to be seen paying their last respects to a star who'd burned brightly and crashed too young. Plus, they'd get their faces on all the glossy magazines and TV.

She guessed this was what Jace meant when he'd spoken of the hypocrisy in the business. It was more about being seen and who with, and less about the music they made. Ironically, despite the cool venue, if he'd been alive, he wouldn't have come. Well, not in the conventional sense. He'd have been holed up in one of the mausoleums with a select few friends, having their own little party and not giving a shit who was there. That was what made him so much cooler and everyone clamber to be part of his inner circle. Sasha swallowed down the lump in her throat that seemed to have taken root these days. Her mother squeezed her hand.

Zach was there, ecstatically happy. Flitting about like a butterfly, far too upbeat for the occasion. His dilated eyes and jittery demeanour pointing to some sort of class-A stimulant.

'Dodged a bullet,' Duo commented, nodding as he watched the same thing.

It made her frown and think of their wild story all over again. She had noticed that there wasn't a single representative from his record company or the Carpathian Group.

Something nudged her arm. A young man she'd never met passed her a folded piece of paper. She thanked him, opened it and read: *Must see you, meet me in the parking lot, Dem.*

Sasha's heart quickened. Demeter had come. She knew he wouldn't let her down. She made an excuse to get some air, slipped out of a side gate, and followed the path around the main building to the closely guarded car park. It was tightly packed with expensive cars and limos.

She stood for a moment, looking around to see if she could see him anywhere. A driver in full chauffeur's uniform stepped forward from one of the waiting limos. 'Miss Bond?' he said, holding open a door for her.

She looked behind her to check no one saw, then she rushed forward and jumped straight into the leather seat, expecting Demeter to be waiting for her. Instead, she found a Carpathian guard. Another got in the other side of her and the door closed. The driver hopped immediately into the driver's seat and the car pulled away.

'I can't go,' she said, frantically trying to reach for the door.

Her hands were grabbed, and she was pushed calmly, but forcefully, back into her seat. 'Where's Demeter?' she said, with an ice-cold fear constricting her heart, speeding up in her chest. Something was very wrong and she went to shout for help, but a guard put up a warning hand to stop her. It worked as she froze before a word came out of her mouth.

'Please, Miss Bond. Do not be alarmed. We're taking you to him,' he said, in perfect accented English. 'He cannot be linked to a music artist in this way.'

'But he said to meet him in the parking lot,' she said, ignoring the rationale, trying to turn to see out of the back window. But it was too late and the rear window too small to see anything.

'Please be calm, Miss Bond. You will see him shortly. You are under the protection of the Carpathian family. No harm shall come to you.'

The words, meant to put her at ease, felt like an ice-pick to her heart after all the warnings she'd received. Her mind was all over the place. She didn't want to leave the funeral. It had barely started and everyone would soon give their eulogies. She'd be missed. 'My friends will be looking for me. My mother!' she remembered as an all-consuming blow. 'You'll have to take me back,' she said, frantically in a last-ditch attempt to get through to them, but she already knew it was hopeless. He was under orders.

'No need to be concerned. We have already made your excuses and your mother will be looked after.'

That was no comfort. Her mother would definitely worry and she was away from home and barely knew her friends. This wasn't right. Demeter would never do anything like this unless something was gravely wrong. 'Is Demeter OK?' Suddenly, she was imagining scenarios, all of which ended with him in the hospital, and her heart was constricting in fear.

'Everything will be explained to you shortly,' the guard said calmly, facing front, as if they were just going for a Sunday drive.

Sasha knew she wasn't going to get any more out of him and shrank back into her seat. There was no point in asking any more questions. She just hoped the journey would soon be over. She was sweating and her heart kept racing in fear. The busy shopfronts changed to retail outlets, then sprawling industrial lots. It was hard to tell exactly through the smoked glass. Then they slowed at a barrier that she recognised. 'This is the airport. I'm not getting on a plane,' she said, her voice rising in panic.

She scrambled for the door handle, but one guard grabbed her hands and the other yanked her back to sit back in her seat. Something soft covered her mouth and the world receded to black.

CHAPTER 26

Sasha awoke and blinked up at the familiar ceiling a few times. She allowed herself to come to slowly with patchy memories. Jace, the funeral, the note, then the scuffle in the car. She sat up with a start. She was forced to hold her head. Her brain swam while it caught up with the rest of her. She felt slow, dizzy and sick, as you would expect if you'd been drugged.

She gritted her teeth, furious. She knew exactly where she was. She was back in her old room at the château. How dare Demeter kidnap and bring her here against her will. She'd missed the funeral – *oh my god*. She suddenly remembered her mother, all alone there. She grabbed the phone next to the bed.

A friendly female voice answered on the other end. 'Good morning, Miss Bond. How can I be of service?'

Sasha tried to calm herself so she could think straight. It had to be the next day with the flight and time difference and everything. 'Can you get Demeter for me? And tell him to get his ass here, please.'

'Of course, Miss Bond. We will convey your message as soon as he is home.'

Sasha's heart stalled. 'He's not here?' She couldn't believe he'd snatched her from her dearest friend's funeral, forced her to abandon her mother and not even had the decency to be there when she arrived to explain. She was struck dumb with rage.

Then a cold finger of dread began to rise up her spine as a horrible suspicion crept over her. 'Is Raziah home?' Her throat tightened to barely a squeak.

'Yes, of course, Miss Bond. Would you like me to arrange for her to come and see you?'

Sasha's heart plummeted to minus fifty. Her brain now functioning on pure hatred. 'No, it's OK,' she said, putting the phone down slowly, while the woman was still talking. She could barely swallow. She had to think.

She got off the bed and had to hold onto a wall to steady herself for a moment. She looked down, only just realising she was still in the red lace dress she'd been in when she left the funeral. Only her black shoes had been taken off. She stepped back into the only pair of court shoes she owned, went over to the door, and, unsurprisingly, found it locked. Things were beginning to make a horrible kind of sense to her.

She didn't like Raz. She didn't even really know her. However, she knew enough to know she wasn't exactly stable. And here she was, the ex-girlfriend of the man Raz loved and recently lost, as an unwilling guest in her house. It certainly didn't feel like a safe place for her to be right then. She had to face the horrible notion that maybe Demeter hadn't kidnapped her at all. And scarier still, that maybe he had no idea she was there.

Her purse was in a heap at the foot of the bed. She quickly picked it up and rummaged, but swore in disappointment.

They'd never make the mistake of leaving her with a phone. Then she had one wonderful eureka thought: *Margaret.* She went back to the phone and quickly punched in the extension to her room.

She picked up right away. She was about to blurt out everything, but something made her hold back at the last minute. Margaret herself had warned her about them listening in on conversations. 'Hi, Margaret. It's me, Sasha.'

'Oh, hi, sweetheart. I was so sorry to hear about Jace.'

Tears immediately filled her eyes at the mention of his name and it felt like she was a million miles away from where she should be right then. 'Can you come to my room, please?' she said, unable to hide the wobble in her voice.

'Of course, darling, I'll be right there.'

Sasha began pacing up and down as she waited, trying to work out what she wanted to say. Then a slow, icy thought occurred to her. There was no surprise in Margaret's voice to find her there at the chateau. No enquiry about the funeral that she missed.

She shook her head. She was just paranoid.

Her thoughts went up and down like that until Margaret finally knocked on her door about ten minutes later. She waited for any comment about the fact that it was locked and a guard was stationed outside, but there was none. Tentacles of suspicion made a slow journey through her veins as she fought not to launch into a thousand questions and accusations. Perhaps it was more than her job was worth and maybe she could use Margaret's trusted position. She did seem genuinely pleased to see her.

Sasha threw herself at the only friendly face she'd seen since the funeral and hugged her tightly. Margaret's arms immediately came around her, and she patted her back soothingly. 'Hey, it's OK. Oh, darling, I'm so sorry,' Margaret said.

Sasha found herself trying not to cry again. 'Can we go for a walk?' she said, pulling away to gauge the woman's eyes for discomfort. She wanted to trust her; she really did. She wanted her to be the friend she always thought she was and not part of any of this. Maybe she was and she was just over-wrought. 'I'm stifled in here. I could do with some air.'

Sasha watched Margaret, who looked a little uncertain at the door, still making no comment about the security. Then she went over, opened it and said something in another language. 'It's OK. He can escort us,' Margaret explained cheerfully after.

Sasha frowned, unsure what to think. Her behaviour was so confusing. All she could do in the end was nod and smile, and just be glad to get out of the room.

The guard held out his arm for Margaret and Sasha to lead the way. They walked at a pace down the hallway and trotted down the stairs. It felt like some sort of escape. 'Where to?' Sasha said, glancing over her shoulder at the guard a few feet behind.

'Maze,' Margaret said, widening her eyes, giving Sasha hope that she might still be on her side.

It took no time at all to reach the mouth of the maze with Sasha half walking, half running next to Margaret's much larger strides. 'Wait here,' Margaret ordered the guard.

He frowned and went to take a step forward and ignore her, but Margaret stood her ground. 'No! I said stay here. We can't exactly go anywhere, can we?'

To Sasha's relief, he gave her a black look and finally nodded. 'Don't be long.' Then, after looking up and down the driveway, he stood sentry in the gap.

Margaret picked up her hand and led her through the avenues that turned into tunnels of foliage, until they eventually came out to the clearing in the middle.

Sasha still couldn't get over the fact that she was under

armed guard. It was easy to kid herself in the room, but not when he refused to let her out of his sight. And what was more, Margaret might have helped her, but she hadn't questioned it.

They immediately went over to the bench facing the fountain and sat down. It occurred to her that all the secret conversations were held there because even if they planted a bug, the fountain would muffle the sound.

Sasha leaned forward and put her head in her hands. It was the first time she felt she could relax. She let her arms fall away and looked sideways at Margaret sitting next to her. 'Do you know what all this is about?' Sasha asked.

Margaret shook her head. 'No, I was as surprised as you were to find out you were here. What happened?'

So she knew it was an impromptu visit. Sasha explained the chain of events that led to her being there. 'I have no idea why I'm guarded. Do you know where Demeter is?' That was the real test of Margaret's honesty, because she always knew where Demeter was.

'He was called to New York to sort out some messy acquisition. That was the last I heard. A couple of days ago.'

'Before that?'

'He was in LA. What he was doing there, I wasn't sure.'

Sasha studied her. She appeared to be telling the truth. 'Did you know Demeter came to see me in Pittsburgh? He brought a new contract with him. One point five million dollars' worth, tying me to— Carpathian for life.' She had wanted to say, him, which was the truth, but for some reason, she changed it to Carpathian, at the last minute. Something made her hold back that information from a possible ex.

Margaret whistled and shook her head in amazement. 'He certainly wants to keep you. You really must have got under his skin,' she finished with a hard glint in her eye and a wry smile. It made her relieved she'd softened the blow. 'Maybe that's what all this is about?'

Sasha studied the innocent look on her face. 'I don't know what the big deal is, though. I haven't made up my mind what I want to do yet.'

Margaret's look turned skeptical.

'I would have just continued the old contract for the time being. I don't understand the rush. Do you know why?'

It was the first direct question she'd slipped into conversation, and she eyed Margaret closely for any giveaway tells that she knew what was going on.

'I have no idea, I'm afraid. All I know is that Dem can be ruthless and stop at nothing to get what he wants.'

'And what about Raz, does she stop at nothing?' She watched her closely again.

It caught Margaret off guard, and she frowned, but Sasha cut in before she could come up with excuses. 'Someone drugged me and brought me here against my will, Margaret. And I'm not sure about you, but that's a felony where I come from. I need to know who is responsible and why.'

Margaret looked uncomfortable, but nodded. She sat back in her seat as if she were thinking about it. She shook her head. 'This wouldn't be Dem, it's not his style.'

Sasha nodded with a huge sense of relief. Relieved she could still trust Demeter, and, by the looks of things, Margaret as well. 'That just leaves Raz or the cousins.' It seemed unlikely that they'd be working together on something like this.

Margaret sat straighter and shook her head. 'Not the cousins. Tegan would just get you to sign some nondisclosure agreement and he probably wouldn't even bring you here for that. If he wanted rid of you, you'd simply disappear.'

Sasha stared at her, shocked. As scary as that was, she was

probably right. This was the big leagues, where billionaires did whatever they wanted. She'd be thrown in some hole with concrete poured over her and be part of the foundations of a building somewhere. This seemed a lot more personal. That just left Raz. She was definitely unhinged enough.

Sasha sagged back into her seat. She still couldn't discount Tegan. Maybe her old contract was no longer legally binding and he didn't want her walking around like a loose cannon. It had much more of a ring of truth about it than deranged ex-girlfriends.

Margaret seemed to follow her train of thought. 'Raz has no freedom, remember, without Jace. She's pretty much a prisoner here, like you are.'

Sasha's gaze shot to hers. It was still unclear who Margaret thought it was. But what was most alarming was her use of the word prisoner. So matter of fact. As if Margaret was used to it and not outraged by it at all. 'So they've done this kind of thing before?' she said flatly.

Margaret immediately realised her slip and looked uncomfortable, but she quickly recovered and said moodily, 'Look, Sasha. These people are billionaires. Normal rules don't apply. I guess when you've worked for them for a while, you grow another skin to it, in a way.'

Sasha studied her for a full minute after she finished speaking. Maybe she was being a little unfair on her. She was only voicing what her niggling conscience had told her right back in the beginning when she was suckered in. She could hardly blame her for it now. She let out a slow breath and nodded. 'What do you think I should do then?'

'As your lawyer or as a friend?' Margaret said, studying her sympathetically.

'Both, I guess,' Sasha said with a shrug.

'As your lawyer, I'd tell you to sign an NDA or anything

else they want you to sign because they will silence you one way or another.'

Sasha opened her mouth to protest that Demeter would never allow it, but Margaret cut right across her. 'Demeter, while gorgeous, is still a Carpathian. Never forget that. He seems all lone wolf and everything, and to an extent, he is.' Margaret seemed to see something in the middle distance, a memory or a daydream, but she snapped herself out of it and looked directly at her again. 'But he will protect his family and his company at all costs.'

The strength in her vehement words shocked Sasha into silence for a moment. She swallowed, unsure what she could possibly say that was worse than that. 'And as a friend?'

Margaret smiled regretfully. 'I'd still sign an NDA. Then, at your first opportunity, run and keep running. Because if you don't work for them, they won't trust you to keep quiet.' Sasha stared at her, unsure what the friend part of that was. 'And Demeter...all of this?' As she said the words, she knew she was being foolish and that he had to know. A man like him would know everything about the company he helped run.

Margaret got up from the seat and smoothed down her clothes. 'Demeter does actually care about you,' she said, not looking her in the eye and acting like that was a surprise to her. 'My guess is that he is trying to tie you in before someone else makes a move.'

Sasha leaned forward with her head in her hands. They already had, hadn't they? Another, far scarier, thought occurred to her. 'What about my mother, my friends?'

Margaret was already heading back towards the opening to the maze. 'Same,' she called back, without even turning her head.

Sasha jumped to her feet. She couldn't believe she was being so blasé about it. 'So that's it? That's all you've got to say?' Everyone she loved was in danger and she was supposed to just leave them like that?

Margaret stopped dead, whirled around and marched back up to her. It made Sasha stand her ground fearfully, preparing for a barrage.

'You still don't get it, do you?' She stepped right into her face and her lips tightened frighteningly. 'There. Is. Nothing. You. Can. Do.' She looked angry and spiteful. Her face was red and her jaw clenched.

Sasha's eyes were wide with fright.

'We're all under bloody contract here, Sasha... The waiting staff. The guard standing outside. No one will step out of line because they know what will happen if they do. Is that clear enough now, Sasha? Do you understand?' Her eyelids lowered with contempt and she turned and walked off after she got the terrified nod she was after. 'Come on... before you're missed,' she called without turning.

Sasha finally breathed, got her legs to move and followed. She was in complete shock at Margaret's outburst. Her heart was still beating with fear. She was in real shit here. No one knew where she was and no one could help her for fear of the same reprisals. *Fuck!* She didn't even know where she was for certain. If she disappeared, no one would even know where to start looking.

Tears streaked down her face while she walked silently back to her room.

CHAPTER 27

Sasha had been there for days and still no sign of Demeter. In fact, except for that one time with Margaret, she hadn't seen a soul except for the guard and the maid. Maybe it was a bad sign, meaning he knew where she was. He would always check in with her, normally. Except she didn't work for him anymore. That scared her the most of all. She was cast adrift in all of this.

After three days, a maid brought her some clean clothes and she was taken to the boardroom with her guard still in tow. Margaret was already there and gave her a small, regretful smile that said it all.

Tegan strode in with his two brothers and indicated for her to sit with an impatient hand. He took the papers from Margaret and slid them across the polished table. 'Sign, please,' he said, simply.

A guard pulled out a seat for her to sit and an ink pot and quill were placed next to her, without further explanation. Sasha sat slowly, glancing at Margaret and when she didn't meet her gaze, finally looked down at the paperwork. She skimmed the highlights. It seemed like a typical NDA. It said nothing about her working for them anymore. Only to keep her mouth shut. Of what, she didn't know. She knew very little and even less about the music side of things.

However, a little voice at the back of her mind told her to hold off. If only it had spoken louder the first time. She shook her head. 'I won't sign anything until I've had a chance to speak to Demeter.'

Margaret hid a smile by pursing her lips. Tegan's eyes went wide and he grinned in genuine surprise. 'You expect Demeter to be your white knight.' He turned to his brothers and laughed.

Sasha's distrust turned into open dislike. He was such an arrogant asshole. 'No, but he gave me a job offer that I've been considering. I want to talk it over with him before I decide.'

Tegan couldn't hide his genuine surprise and he looked accusingly at Margaret, who obviously hadn't shared. It was gratifying as it showed she was loyal. She simply shrugged it off as if it were news to her. It also proved that Demeter made his own decisions independently of the cousins.

His face was thunderous when he snatched up his briefcase. 'Very well. We will call Demeter and we will see which contract you will sign.' Then he marched out of the room, looking furious, with his brothers following behind him.

Although it felt like a small victory, Sasha recognised there was no option not to sign anything at all. She was now left alone with Margaret and the guards. Margaret stood and began gathering the papers and putting them back into her briefcase.

Sasha went to say something, but Margaret quickly shook her head. She flashed her eyes in warning and left through the same door as Tegan. Then the guard nudged her and tilted his head to the door they had come from, and she went thoughtfully back to her room.

Sasha sat on the bed and brooded. She went over and over the previous conversation with Margaret and her behaviour today. It was obvious she was as fearful and trapped as she was, and Demeter must be aware of that.

She prayed Demeter would get there soon to answer some questions. Now that she'd mentioned the contract, they must have contacted him. It did feel like Tegan was right about one thing; she was probably looking to the worst one of the lot to save her.

SASHA THOUGHT she would spend another long and lonely night alone when the door knocked. Her heart quickened. There was only one person it could be. She jumped up from the bed and ran over to answer it. She threw the door open, ready to throw herself into Demeter's arms, when she stopped and caught herself and 'there you are …' died on her lips.

There, with all her denim-clad attitude and swagger, was the perfect Miss Punk-Pixie, Raz.

'Oh, it's you,' she said, before she could help herself.

Raz rolled her eyes and pushed past her. 'Sorry to disappoint. Can I come in?'

'Why not?' Sasha said, letting her arms flop to her sides in exasperation.

Raz stopped and turned in the large space at the foot of the bed, taking everything in. It was like she'd never seen one of the many generic bedrooms before.

'What can I do for you?' Sasha said on a tired exhale. She'd barely had a conversation with her while Jace was alive. She couldn't think of a single reason to start now.

Raz was still being nosy when she finally answered. 'I thought I'd better come and check you were alright. It's been remiss of me, I know, but I have been kind of devastated about Jace and everything.'

Sasha had no idea how to respond. She watched her put a shaking hand to her forehead as if she was pulling herself together and felt instantly bad. She'd never seen any real emotion on the girl before, except anger and possessiveness over Jace. Of course, Raz would be upset if her boyfriend had just passed away, even if a part of Sasha blamed her for it.

Sasha reached out a cautious hand and gave Raz's shoulder a sisterly squeeze.

'He didn't see a doctor. I told him over and over to go and see one,' Raz said, with her voice wavering.

Sasha felt for her. She carried guilt around about that, too. But in the end, it had to come down to Jace. 'If it's any consolation, Jace was always going to go this way. As devastating as it is, there is nothing you could have done,' Sasha said, thinking how tiny and small-boned her shoulder was as she pulled back her hand.

However, instead of being soothed by her kind words, Raz's hand dropped from her face and she fixed her with those strange, piercing eyes. Then they narrowed with so much hatred that Sasha shrank back away from her. 'You're glad, aren't you,' Raz said, turning to face her squarely. 'Because he didn't want you.'

Sasha almost choked; she was so shocked. 'I'm sorry, what did you say?' she said, blinking rapidly.

Raz took a step towards her and poked her in the shoulder. 'I think you hated it because Jace was with me. So you turned to my brother in consolation and found out he'll never really want you, so you're glad. Glad we're all as miserable as you are.'

Sasha's jaw fell open. It wasn't so much the words but the venom behind them. There was no point in her even replying to a girl as clearly deranged as this. 'I want to go home. You can't hold me against my will like this,' she finally said, gathering herself together.

Raz's scowl suddenly changed to a bright smile as if someone had pressed a button. 'You can't leave until after the next honour ceremony, which I've arranged for tonight. Then you'll be leaving whether you like it or not,' Raz finished with a spiteful smile. She was already heading for the door.

Sasha felt a mixture of emotions, but mostly sadness and exasperation. Raz understood Jace so little. He would have hated them fighting like this. 'Jace really loved you, you know.'

Raz stopped with her hand on the doorknob.

'He said you made him feel serious and grown up and the most responsible he'd ever felt.' It was the truth. He'd finally met someone more chaotic than he was.

Raz slowly turned, but, instead of looking comforted, her eyes narrowed as if she would kill her. 'You think you're really that special, don't you, to have conversations with him like that. I saw you. The day he left. I heard him feel sorry for you and tell you he loved you.'

Sasha's mind was thrown back to that last fateful conversation. The one in the maze. She'd wondered if they'd been overheard. Well, it appears Raz had, of all people. *Great.* 'As a friend,' Sasha said wearily. She desperately wanted to salvage something out of this, for Jace's memory, if nothing else. But she had to admit that even she'd taken it to have meant more than that. It had gone through her mind a thousand times since Jace's death, and she'd put it down to his lost, first honest declaration of love. It must have been devastating for Raz to overhear and then to lose him before she had the chance to get closure about it. 'Jace was ill ... and I've moved on and developed feelings for Demeter since splitting with Jace. He just wanted to make sure I was OK, that's all,' Sasha said as a last-ditch attempt to get through to her.

Sasha held her breath as Raz stalked right up into her face again. 'You think you can try to own my man and toy with my brother, a son of the most powerful family on earth. He destroys powerful people without even breaking a sweat.'

Raz spoke low and deliberately, and appeared remarkably calm. Sasha swallowed, not wanting to anger her. This was far more intimidating than when she was ranting about her taking the man she loved. There was truth to her words and nothing she hadn't thought herself.

'There is no use waiting for him. Demeter won't come. He doesn't even know you're here.' Raz's lips twitched with a hint of a smile.

Sasha felt a certain amount of relief that Demeter knew nothing about it, but her heart sank with the confirmation that he wasn't coming to her rescue. 'He wants me to sign a new contract,' she said lamely, in a small, broken voice.

Raz's smile grew spiteful. 'Yes … he wants to own you. He does that – collects people like interesting knick-knacks. I've decided, you'll belong to me instead.'

Sasha's eyes went wide and her blood began to pump. *Over her dead body.* This went way beyond NDAs and job offers. This was something else entirely. Jace's outlandish claims and warnings flashed through her mind and didn't seem so fantastic now. Whether they were real or imagined from this girl's deranged head, Jace believed them enough to scare him half to death, just like Raz was doing to her right now. She tried to keep the terror out of her voice and spoke as reasonably as she could. 'Just let me go, Raz. Then you'll never have to see or hear from me again. I promise.'

'I know I won't,' Raz said, smiling, looking more crazed than ever with her hideous grin and penetrating eyes. Then she shocked her by turning on her heel and walking towards the door, her mood switching completely. 'Later. I've decided to honour Jace and you will be TRHBDor's last nomination before I disband them forever. You should be glad,' she said, looking over her shoulder just before she went out. 'You'll be the parting gift. Perfect,' she said, laughing, like she couldn't contain it.

'Wait!' Sasha called. 'Gift to who?' she shouted angrily

'My father.'

Sasha remained stunned. *Father?* The girl was completely unhinged. Raz had heard her last conversation with Jace and already had a problem with her. Then Sasha being involved with her brother, on top of everything else, did seem like she was rubbing salt in the wound. However, Raz had hinted that she might leave tonight. That was something, so she clung to that. She just had to get through the last few hours and she could go home and never come back here again.

THE DRESS that came later was bridal white lace. Sasha held it up. It was beautiful, but obviously a joke. Raz was making fun of her. She had half a mind to wear the red dress she'd arrived in, but didn't want to anger her.

Sasha dressed and smoothed it down in the mirror. It was figure-hugging, fishtail and looked far from virginal, except that it was white. That and the fact it was lace meant no underwear could be worn underneath it. She sighed, resigned. She literally had nothing else to wear.

She put on what little makeup she had and asked the maid to help her put up her hair. She arrived with pins and by the time they'd finished, she looked quite unlike herself. But not half bad, if she did say so herself.

At last, it was dark and the maid came back and asked her

to follow her down. Her stomach swirled with a mixture of excitement and nerves. Excitement that she was almost at the point where she could leave and nerves that a guard was still stuck to her tail. There was no need for it. Still, she was glad to be out of that room.

The sounds and the spectacle were the same as last time, except this time, Demeter wouldn't be whisking her away. The party was loud. Raz was on the stage, like before, with some young rock group and there was a similar array of huge stars from the music world lounging about on the floor.

She would never get used to it. Jace took it all in his stride, but it was never her. She picked her way through the sprawling crowd, apologising and not wanting to make eye contact. Then she recognised the same area Jace and her friends had occupied the last time and an overwhelming feeling of sadness came over her. It was devoid of people. There were no friends and, more devastatingly, no Jace.

The maid indicated this was as far as they went, so Sasha thanked her and sank into the very same beanbag that Jace sat on the time before. She wanted to cry. The party didn't feel happy; it felt grotesque and over-the-top. There had to be at least five hundred people and she felt utterly alone.

'It's Sasha,' someone said.

'Oh my god, it is,' a female voice said right after.

She brought her head around immediately and found familiar faces all staring at her. She scrambled in the tight dress to her feet and suddenly she was swamped with familiar faces, tight hugs and sloppy kisses. Duo, Tears, Brains, Ballistic, Sensei, they were all there. Every one of them except Jace and Pope. Even Zach looked pleased to see her and made a fuss, asking what had happened to her at the funeral. All she could say truthfully was all she knew. 'They brought me back here.' He looked angry as he marched off, determined to get answers.

She sat back down and they all did the same, congregating around her with worried and concerned faces. 'It's her,' Duo said, looking angrily at Brains.

'It has to be,' he replied, sadly.

Sasha looked between them, not understanding at all.

'What exactly did they say to you?' Duo asked.

'Demeter wanted me to resign with him, then they brought me here, and I think they want me to sign an NDA or something,' Sasha said, thinking that if they offered it to her again, she'd sign it.

'Same as us,' a couple of them said.

'Well, not the Demeter part,' Tears added.

'Did they offer you a new contract … after Jace?' she said, feeling the lump rise in her throat again.

'No,' they all said, shaking their heads quickly, as if she'd offered them live eels.

'Never again,' Duo said. 'None of us realised until after, what a big thing Jace did setting us free. The last thing we'd do is chain ourselves again. That's why we couldn't understand why Zach wanted us here.'

Zach was walking back towards them, looking flustered and severely pissed off, like he'd been arguing. He looked her up and down, taking in her ridiculous dress and then leaned down and kissed her cheek. Then he looked around at the others waiting for him to tell them what was going on. He looked heavenward. 'It's her, you know that, right?'

They all nodded guiltily, not looking her in the eye.

'We need to get her out of here, now!' Zach said angrily.

They were all immediately on their feet, pulling her up out of the bean bag. 'What's me?' she said, trying to get someone to look at her.

'How though,' Duo said to Zach, as if she hadn't spoken at all.

'I dunno. Let's get out of this room first,' Zach said, grabbing her hand and pulling her along towards the door.

She went to pull back, but the others swarmed around her and all looked so scared, ushering her along, that she went along with it. Her heart was pounding as she gauged their frightened faces. All she could think was, thank God they were there. She'd be hopeless otherwise. Especially when she remembered their positions had to be as precarious as hers. She was now positive that Jace had freed them deliberately. A tear trickled down her cheek. It was so foolhardy and totally him.

They were almost at the door when a change rippled through the crowd. All the waiting staff began to file out of the room through the various exits.

'Quick, Zach shouted to everyone behind him. 'Before they lock the doors.'

'Lock the doors?' Sasha squealed, breaking into a jog, as she was swept along. The others half lifted her off the ground as she was too slow in the ridiculously confining dress. She was tripping over and treading on people, their annoyance and swearing dying behind her before she could apologise.

They were almost there when the double doors were slammed shut and locked with a loud clank, as the security bar was pulled across the outside. Sasha looked around them wide-eyed and terrified, not understanding why they were totally locked in.

Zach shook the handle and pounded his fist against the wood. The others soon joined him. 'Let us out!' they all shouted. 'We want to get out!'

'These kids aren't contracted,' Zach said, which made Sasha gape at him at what possible difference that could make to their situation. All she could think was that it was true. Jace had freed them all.

The crowd hushed behind them, making their group gradually stop banging and turn around. A male voice came over the mic. 'It's almost time, people. We have a truly special honour ceremony tonight.'

The others stood quietly, their worried faces now riveted to the stage. The whole thing began sinking into the floor and a huge circular one was rising in its place. There were small podiums all the way around the outside and one larger one in the middle.

Suddenly, guards were around them, herding them away from the doors and around the edge of the room.

'OK, OK, we'll go and sit down.' Zach was saying, trying to brazen it out and gain control of the situation.

But they weren't going in that direction. They were being steered towards the stage.

The male voice finished and Raz's clear voice echoed. 'Give it up for TRHBDor, everyone.' The whole room began clapping, standing up and cheering them to get up on the stage.

'Not been with us for that long,' Raz was saying. 'But have achieved so much!'

A guard was now holding her arms behind her, like a criminal. She looked behind her frantically, but it was happening to the others, who began to resist and wouldn't walk forward towards the stage.

'Come on up. Don't be shy,' Raz said. 'This is your night.'

Sasha was nudged roughly to go up the steps to the stage. She almost fell over with the confinement of her legs in the dress. She got to the top and looked around her. It was like some awful nightmare. Her friends looked wide-eyed and terrified, like captured animals. The guards looked angry and purposeful, and the audience seemed overexcited and manic. The sound merged into a single ugly din as she was pushed towards the podium in the middle. She felt naked and conspicuous in the stupid dress, right in the middle of the stage. A guard literally picked her up and put her on the centre podium, and she felt her hands being roughly pulled and tied behind her. She watched, immobile with shock, as all her friends, including Zach, were treated the same on the podiums all the way around the edge. Some were trying to fight, but there were too many guards and they were soon overpowered.

Raz got serious and calmed down the crowd by flattening her hand. 'Listen, guys. Tonight is a solemn occasion. As you know, the love of my life passed away recently. His album just went platinum. Close to ten million plays on YouTube. Right now, he is the biggest star on the planet and it's because of you guys. It's your energy that makes it possible. Give it up for yourselves,' Raz said, clapping her hands in the air, while holding the mic. The crowd went wild, cheering and whistling.

Sasha didn't understand what was happening. It was like she'd slipped into some parallel universe. *What was wrong with these people? Why were they cheering?* Were they so lost in showbiz that they thought they had any kind of effect on a single thing anyone else did, especially Jace? What's a platinum disk to someone who's dead? It was ridiculous and disrespectful to his memory. It was as though Raz were the master of ceremonies for some huge bad-taste joke.

'Tonight, we offer up thanks for Jace. His music and his life. Showing how much we loved and appreciated him by sending him the energy of the people he loves.'

Her friends were all shouting and screaming for help. Ballistik and Sensei were scuffling with the guards and were jumped on and punched, until they submitted and were handcuffed to the posts behind them. Sasha watched in horror, frozen in fear. They were all terrified and fighting for their lives. Except some, like Brains, who were paralysed in shock and Tears' legs were shaking so badly she had two guards holding her up.

Raz began a slow, dramatic walk around the stage, like the host of some grotesque game show. 'Now time for the choice.'

CHAPTER 28

Raz flashed her mad gaze at Sasha and grinned. It was one of satisfaction, borne from the confidence that she had in her no matter what. 'I'm talking to you guys,' she said, addressing them as a group again. 'I know you're a tight-knit group, but if you nominate, there need only be one sacrifice.' She pulled the mic away from her mouth so only those on the stage could hear. 'Then you can sign your NDAs and simply go home.'

'Don't believe her!' Duo shouted.

'We're not contracted for any of this,' Zach called out from the opposite side of the stage, where he was still struggling with his guards. 'We're all free. Jace's clause saw to that … Don't say anymore. She can't do it, she's not allowed.'

Raz was clearly furious with him, forgot herself, and spoke into her mic. 'Not for suicide, Zach. You should always read the small print.' She grinned spitefully and twirled, pointing at them all. 'You're all still tied.'

'Why are you trying to get us to sign new NDAs then?' Sasha shouted. 'Isn't that in the existing contract?'

'She'll do it anyway,' Brains cried, unable to keep himself together.

Sasha was watching the others, terrified. Everyone was facing outward toward the crowd and couldn't see beyond the person next to them. They were unable to see the maniacal hatred in Raz's eyes, but she could. Brains was right. This wasn't about them; it was about her. There was no way she would be going free tonight. Raz was simply using the collective to sentence her. There must be some rule that stopped her from doing it herself. That look. The hatred in her eyes. She would never forgive her for being Jace's first love. Even if she knew deep down, they were platonic in the end. She would never allow her to leave.

A smile of satisfaction settled on Raz's face when she knew she got it. 'Margaret!' she called over the mic.

Margaret came onto the stage, looking awkward in her heels and rust-coloured business suit. She looked out of place, carrying a bunch of papers. 'Get each of them to sign and you can go.'

Sasha strained against her restraints, but she was firmly tied now. The audience had grown restless. There had been a shift and they were no longer cheering. They were bored and uncomfortable, sensing something was wrong.

Sensei, Brains, Tears, and even Duo were released by their guards. One by one, they jumped down from their podiums and bent over their papers. Sasha could clearly see a knife tucked into their ribs. An extra precaution, hidden from the crowd. Each one scribbled and scurried off, and Sasha's heart sank a little lower. They couldn't look at her. Except for Duo. He looked at her wretchedly, mouthing the word, 'Sorry,' before he left too. She couldn't blame them. They had no choice. It was obvious she was doomed no matter what. They all did as they were told until she was the only one left. Just her, Raz and Margaret.

It wasn't clear why Margaret was still there. She looked frozen in fear. Raz looked between them, clearly following her thought process until the penny finally dropped. Her stomach sank so low; she could barely breathe. Margaret had her own reasons for wanting her out of the way: *Demeter*. She should have known. The signs were all there. She'd loved him first.

The guy in the white priest's robes came back onto the stage carrying a huge knife.

This was happening. It was really happening, Sasha thought, struggling wildly against her restraints. A warm, wet stream trickled down her leg. 'Margaret … Please,' she pleaded. She was a smart, educated woman. This wasn't her. 'I'll leave and I'll never come back. I promise.'

Margaret closed her eyes and turned her back on her. At least it wasn't easy for her. She couldn't believe the one person she thought she could trust had thrown her to the wolves like this. 'Demeter doesn't know, does he?' Sasha began to shout. 'What do you think he will do when he finds out?' she screamed, as Raz and the priest were closing in.

'Do it! Raz barked, glaring at the priest. 'I want to watch her blood fall.'

When Margaret moved right away, out of earshot, all was lost. Something still and dark settled over Sasha. She guessed it was the dull fog of resignation. Not bravery. Simply a foolhardiness or loss of reason. She began to shout so as many people as possible in the crowd could hear her. 'No, you're just a sore, spoiled brat and a yellow-bellied coward.' Sasha began to laugh in a shrill, maniacal way. So much so that it was causing ripples in the first few rows of the audience. No one ever spoke to their cosseted princess like that. They were already unsure of what was happening and began to boo. The priest was looking between them now, becoming unsure.

Raz gave the priest a shove. 'Get on with it, you idiot!'

'There's no sacrifice in this,' Sasha screamed, laughing.

The priest looked fearful from one to the other.

'DO IT!' Raz screeched.

'Didn't you hear her?' Sasha mocked. 'She wants her rival got rid of. Don't you, Raz? Can't stand the competition, can you? All that talent and looks and you still couldn't get Jace away from me.'

'SHUT UP!' Raz bellowed and shoved the priest, so he almost stabbed Sasha when he stumbled into her, but he still held off.

Sasha became aware of loud banging and commotion coming from somewhere else. Perhaps the audience was revolting and trying to get out. Still, she wasn't so stupid as to take her eyes off Raz, the demon in front of her. She was red in the face and the veins were sticking out on her forehead in her temper. She lowered her voice so only Raz could hear her. 'You have no idea of the real world, do you? Playing guitar and looking good were never enough for Jace. He was surrounded by that all the time.'

Raz's face blackened while commotion sounded like it was going on all around them. Shouting and violence were erupting throughout the room. She couldn't pinpoint it exactly; she was so intent on exposing and ripping to shreds the pampered girl in front of her.

Raz finally lost it and snatched the knife, pushing the priest over and kicking him till he scurried away. Sasha kept her eyes on the blade as Raz passed it between her hands, feeling its weight. Then she slowly approached with a widening grin.

The crowd were now all on their feet, shouting. Something was happening, but she had no time to take notice.

She should have shut up; she knew she was baiting a crazed animal, but she couldn't help herself. It was so liberating. After months of putting up with her open hatred of her and misuse of Jace, it all came tumbling out. 'You were just the one person in the whole world worse off than him, so he babysat you.'

That was it. Raz let out a high-pitched scream and ran at her. Sasha flinched, curling up as much as her bonds would allow and closed her eyes.

The crowd shouted 'NO!'

Then silence.

Nothing.

A can clanged on the floor.

Sasha stayed frozen in her cowering position, as if someone had stopped time and she was the only person aware. There was complete quiet. A cough. Whispers. Until she slowly opened her eyes and straightened up to see Demeter standing there, gripping Raz's raised wrist of the hand holding the knife.

He snatched it from her and threw it to the ground. Raz's face was still red and contorted with rage as she glared at her brother. Both stared at each other in some kind of weird standoff. Taking in the anger in each other's faces. 'You did this to me,' Raz said, venomously.

Demeter bobbed his head slightly, not confirming or denying either way.

'This is nothing to do with you, Demeter,' Raz was saying.

'It is when you're about to break sacred law as well as secular law. In a room full of fucking witnesses,' Demeter hissed, just managing to keep a lid on his temper.

'But I haven't,' Raz said with a smirk of satisfaction. 'Her collective signed an agreement and nominated her.'

Demeter adjusted his stance impatiently, still holding onto her wrist. He looked around as if he was only just noticing the gawping crowd, now quiet, waiting on his every word. He turned his head to a guard a few feet away. 'Get them out of here. Send them straight home and tell them they will be compensated.'

The guard nodded and hurried off. 'Open the doors!' the guard shouted to a colleague. The crowd began to murmur and gather their things. Sasha was still tied to her podium, figuring that with Demeter between them, it was still the safest place for her to be.

Demeter looked down at his sister again, dangerously. 'She is mine. You know that,' he said low and ominously.

'But she hasn't signed anything, that means she's fair game,' Raz whined.

Sasha could see she was trying his patience and he was fighting the urge to swipe her across the face or throttle her. Instead, he looked up to a group of onlookers, reluctant to leave. 'Go home, vultures,' he said. 'NOW!' he shouted when they didn't move fast enough. They jumped and grabbed their things and went off through the now almost-empty room.

Raz tried to use his change of focus to struggle and get away, but he simply grabbed her around her small neck with his other hand. He was fast and incredibly strong.

She croaked. 'You're hurting me. That's not allowed.'

Demeter brought her right to his face and narrowed his eyes at her terrifyingly. 'You are not expendable, Sister,' he said as if she disgusted him. 'The Star Child lives on, but the sister is interchangeable. Our father will send another, then another. FREE HER!' he barked at the priest, hovering fearfully nearby.

The priest quickly went behind Sasha and she felt the cords loosen around her wrists. After rubbing the chafed skin, she finally stepped down off the podium.

'YOU!' he snapped at Margaret, also trying to sidestep into the background. She jumped as if he'd hit her. 'Go and get Sasha's real contract, now!'

She hurried off the stage without argument.

'Don't, Demeter, please,' Raz squeaked through her restricted airway. Her demeanour had now completely changed to a young child knowing she was in big trouble and scared that she'd pushed her big brother beyond the point where he was only just holding onto his temper.

Tegan, Rollo and Taj nonchalantly stepped up onto the stage and Margaret was with them, carrying an envelope. The rest of the room was now empty except for around twenty guards. Sasha wondered whether the cousins had been deliberately absent or clueless about the whole thing. It was hard to believe it had been organised without their knowledge. Or maybe just her part. They approached the group and the guards looked at each other nervously, obviously not sure who had seniority there.

'What are you doing, Demeter?' Tegan said, in a soft voice as if he was talking down a desperate felon in a hostage situation. 'Let's all go to the boardroom and talk.'

'Give me Sasha's contract,' Demeter said, clicking his fingers and beckoning Margaret closer. 'Sasha will sign it and then I'll deal with this spoiled bitch.' Every time he moved, Raz went with him like a rag doll hanging from his hand. It would have been funny if Sasha hadn't been in so much shock.

Tegan stepped in front of Margaret before she could hand it to him. 'You shouldn't manhandle her like that, particularly in front of guests,' he said, now starting to look nervous as if one little slip and their little cash cow was no longer. She couldn't imagine it was for any sentimental reason. He just didn't seem to have that in him. 'Demeter, these are ancient rites, practised for centuries. There is nothing you can do about them. It's simply the way it is … how it has always been,' Tegan said, trying to reason with him.

Demeter straightened and Raz yelped as he tightened his grip, clearly the one who held the power.

Tegan immediately held up both hands and stepped back. Demeter's temper was hanging by a thread and he was just baiting the tiger. Demeter took a menacing step after him, dragging his gurgling sister with him, now clawing at his hand to let her go. He gave her another little shake to make her quit. 'She was about to murder Sasha herself, in front of a roomful of baying witnesses. You need to stop treating her like a pet and start teaching her some manners.' He took another dangerous step into Tegan's space.

Rollo went to intervene, but Demeter put up his other hand to stop him.

Sasha was looking on, wild-eyed, holding her breath. She'd never seen Demeter like this. Terrifying, but easily outnumbered. His next words completely shook her, all the more in their menacing, reasonable, quietness. 'Never forget who I am. I'm the eldest son. The firstborn of every generation. His representative on earth. You can't ignore it. You certainly can't escape it. I can't escape it. It's marked all over my fucking body. So I don't care about traditions or ancient rites and I don't care if you are on the other side of the business, and you get off on all this shit. You listen to me, and my word is law. Do you understand?' he finished, staring menacingly into Tegan's eyes, mere inches away.

'Raz was gurgling, trying to prise his fingers off. He'd obviously tightened them in his temper. She was going a great shade of purple.

The three cousins immediately stepped back and bowed their heads. It was bizarre. Sasha had never seen anything like it. Like he was some kind of king or something.

Demeter nodded, like that sealed it, and Margaret appeared in front of her. 'Sign!' he ordered, looking straight at Sasha. His eyes now looked bloodshot and deadly, and the snap in his words made her jump and grab the pen and papers. Margaret held her gaze in apology, but she was too shaken to think about her part in everything. She bent her head and quickly found the dotted line and paused a moment before signing. If she did this, she was putting all her trust in Demeter and going against everything Jace had warned her about. However, she'd seen enough to know Demeter had saved her life today. She hurriedly signed her name and put the contract back in Margaret's waiting hands.

'Show me!' Demeter said, and Margaret held it in his line of sight. 'Date it!' he said, focusing on Sasha again, looking the most frightening she'd ever seen him.

Margaret jumped as well and held it, shaking, whispering the date, while Sasha scribbled.

Demeter gave his sister another shake, making her croak. As if he was reminding everyone she was still there. She didn't look well. He pointed at Sasha. 'She is mine.' He glowered at the entire company. 'If ever any of you go after anything of mine, I will end you in the most final kind of way. Do you understand?'

Raz couldn't move to say either way.

The cousins looked at each other and nodded.

'Do you understand?' Demeter shouted, making them all answer up. 'My sister is a sociopath and you let her roam free with that boy, which led to his premature death. From this day, the Star Child will never leave the chateau.'

Tegan stepped forward, nonchalantly. 'The boy's death was a suicide …' He shrugged, 'albeit an unintentional one. Technically, they are all still bound to their contracts owing to the small print added to their clause, which clearly states, 'except in circumstances of suicide. Making this evening completely legal, if not somewhat theatrical.'

Small print? It was news to her.

Demeter looked stonily at his cousin. 'It was not suicide.' He turned his head to Sasha. 'I will explain later.'

Raz began to sob. 'Don't, Dem. Forgive me … please … I'll die here,' she rasped and croaked.

'Yes, you will.' His eyes tracked to Margaret. 'As for you … I will decide what will happen to you tomorrow. For now, take her to her room.'

Margaret nodded, quickly, as if she was scared half to death.

Then his eyes landed on her. 'I will find you later and explain. Rest. We'll talk.' His features hardened when they landed back on his sister, and he dragged her with him to the steps down into the dark, cavernous space below the stage.

'No, Dem … Please don't … I'll be good. I'll be good.' Followed by a shrill scream as they disappeared from sight.

Sasha looked at Margaret, terrified. She shook her head, widening her eyes so that she would not say a word. 'Come on … don't think about it.' Margaret linked her arm through hers and steered her from the stage towards one of the doorways. Guards averted their gaze from her, as if they were now scared. She briefly locked eyes with Tegan, who inclined his head in respect, as if she'd achieved a great thing. What that could possibly be, she had no idea. All she could do was run along next to Margaret, glancing at her face, not knowing who was more scared out of the two of them. 'What just happened?' she whimpered.

'Whatever you're putting out of your mind as ridiculous is true. Believe me, you don't want to know.'

'What did he mean about Jace?'

'I have no idea.'

They reached her door, and the guard who was already stationed there opened it for them. Margaret allowed Sasha to go in first and she immediately went in, turned and waited for some sort of explanation. 'For what it's worth, I am sorry about tonight,' Margaret said. 'Nobody will bother you again.' She turned and walked off.

Sasha rushed to follow in her frustration, but the guard barred her way. 'Wait … I need details. I need to know what's going on, Margaret … What do you mean?' she asked, calling after her.

But Margaret kept on walking as if she couldn't hear.

The guard forcefully ushered Sasha back into her room and shut the door in her face.

CHAPTER 29

Sasha was left standing in shock, looking at her door, unsure how to process what had happened that evening. *What would Demeter do to Raz? What did he mean about Jace's death not being suicide? Why was everyone looking at her weirdly like that at the end? Was she still a prisoner?*

It was several hours before Demeter came back. She'd managed to calm down enough to shower and lie down on her bed to rest. Somewhere during that time, exhaustion must have dragged her into sleep. She woke up in the lamplight to Demeter's wonderful cologne and him kissing her forehead.

She basked in his affection for a few moments before she remembered the events of earlier. She hitched a breath and went to sit up. 'Shh, stay there,' he said, resting a hand on her shoulder. He kicked off his shoes, stretched out his long legs next to her, and leaned up on an elbow. He was studying her face while she did the same. 'Are you OK? Did she hurt you?' he asked, eventually.

She shook her head. 'I'm fine. The others, are they OK?'

'They are all safely on a plane back to America, nicely compensated. They were more concerned about you.'

Sasha breathed easier and nodded. She was glad and didn't blame them. 'What happened tonight?' she asked, watching his expression closely.

He raised his eyebrows and let out a slow and weary breath. 'I finally took the mantle of my birthright… and you helped me do it,' he said, poking her in the stomach and narrowing his eyes shrewdly. But he was smiling as if he were playing with her.

She smiled up at him, not sure what the difference was. She thought he already ran his side of the company. 'So you're CEO now or something?'

He laughed, resting a caring hand on her stomach. He leaned down and kissed her gently. 'Something like that.'

'I'm sorry about your sister,' Sasha said, running her finger across his lips. 'She tricked me. I thought I was coming to you.'

'Shh,' he said, kissing her fully, languidly, drugging her to completely open to him. He let out a long sigh and looked deeply into her eyes. 'What had you planned to do … before my crazed sister kidnapped you, that is? Would you have worked for me again?'

'Is that what this is?' she said, smiling. 'Why does it always have to be contracts with you?' She went to sit up and out of the circle of his arm, but he held her still.

'Stop deflecting, Sasha. You know as well as I do that the contract saved your life.'

'Why, though?' she said, starting to get impatient with him. She deserved to know after everything she'd just been through. He couldn't just smooth it over with the comfort of his arms and a few kisses. There was something truly sinister going on there. 'It isn't normal. None of this is normal, Demeter.'

Demeter slowly sat up so she could do the same, but he continued to regard her closely.

'Jace freed us all – well, he thought he did. And we all let him down tonight. Every single one of us. All of us re-signed at the first sign of pressure.'

Demeter looked at her sardonically. 'Hardly a little pressure, Sasha.'

Nothing he could say would make her feel any better about it. She felt wretched. It had all been for nothing. 'I'm sure he had no idea a suicide didn't count.'

He was studying her with that assessing look he had. Like she continued to surprise him. 'It wasn't self-inflicted – not all of it, anyway. It was the reason I've been away for so long. I wanted to go through the autopsy results with the coroner, which meant we had to go back into Jace's medical records.'

'But Jace almost never went to a doctor. The only time was when he broke his ankle falling off a friend's skateboard, when we were about fifteen. I went with him to the ER room.' Her heart was speeding up, dreading what he would say next. Her mind was already speeding through all the symptoms he'd had over the last few months and thinking the worst.

Demeter nodded. 'You're right. His record contained almost nothing.'

She swallowed. 'What did he die from then?'

'Subdural haematoma, probably sustained from a fall or a blow to the head.'

Sasha was confused and shook her head. 'In English?'

'A haemorrhage – a brain bleed,' he said.

Sasha stared ahead of her, racking her brain to remember any time that might have been. She guessed he could have fallen any time when he'd been wasted. They hadn't exactly been joined at the hip during the last year. 'An autopsy? I thought it was cut and dry with his lifestyle and everything,' she said, utterly bewildered.

'It's usual when something like this happens – especially when it happens to a celebrity like Jace.'

Sasha studied his face, looking back at her, filled with concern. He really cared about all this. But it still didn't explain Jace's stark warning. He'd wanted her and all their friends away from this place. 'The NDAs … The others signed. Is there any catch or something to be worried about?' she asked, suddenly suspicious.

He smiled a little. 'Not if they don't break it … It is normal in business, Sasha,' he said, laughing slightly at her startled expression. 'Damaging stories could be sold to the media for money. We are a powerful family,' he said, as if it were the most reasonable thing in the world. She guessed that if his mad sister hadn't just tried to kill her, it probably was.

'And if they don't?' she said, holding her breath.

'I'll grind their bones to make my bread – what do you take me for, Sasha?' he said, laughing. 'I'll take them to court and take them for every penny, of course.' He softened a little at the obvious confusion on her face. 'The idea is not to let it get that far.' He waggled her chin with his hand and shook his head, smiling at her.

She smiled reluctantly. She still couldn't stop thinking about Jace's condition and the obvious pain he must have been in. 'And mine?' she said on an exhale. 'I blindly signed something, and I have no clue what was in it.'

Demeter laughed seductively and pulled her over to sit across his lap. He kissed her deeply and ground her down onto him, where she felt his hardness already growing. Her breathing became laboured in seconds when he began to bite down the side of her neck and her nipple through her night shirt. 'It says you will remain in my bed,' he said between nips. 'Where you will service me on demand, daily.'

She half laughed, half groaned as he lifted her shirt and pulled it up over her head and from her shoulders. All smoothly and adeptly, while he circled his hips and blew gently across the bare skin of her breasts.

'Only letting you out when I'm good and ready,' he added, gently sucking the hard peak and toying with her with his teeth.

'What about work? Does it say anything about work?' she said, breathlessly.

He ripped her lace panties with a loud tear when he couldn't get to where he wanted to go. He lifted her for a second, like she weighed nothing, and pulled the confining material from her legs. She was left looking at the discarded heap on the floor where the ruined panties joined the nightshirt.

She faced him again. His eyelids were low and her heart was racing at what he would do next. A part of her, even then, knew it was a complete distraction from what she wanted to know, but every nerve ending in her body was tingling and aching for his next touch.

He lay back and, keeping eye contact with her the whole time, he undid his belt, his button and the zipper on his pants. When he was free in front of her, he opened the buttons of his shirt, revealing his smooth, tattooed chest. The ones that identified him, he'd said. 'What do they say?' she asked, running a finger down the intricate line on his stomach.

He narrowed his eyes, and for a moment, it was clear he warred with what to say. But then his gaze became stony and dead. 'It says, I'm the harbinger of death ... the bogey man mothers warn their kids about.' All the while he spoke, he pulled her closer instead of pushing her away. Her breathing stopped and her heart rate doubled, until he blew noisily into her neck to make her laugh. Another deflection. As if he couldn't go through with the serious revelation.

However, she was ticklish and couldn't help laughing. 'Will you still have me design all your clothes?' she said, running her hand across the inked skin, becoming serious again.

'As long as you work naked, every day, wearing only baby oil.' Even he had to laugh at the ridiculousness of that. He'd decided that was enough chatter and threw her over onto her back. He was on top of her before she could take another breath. There was no preamble. No more talking. He plunged into her deeply. Relentlessly and mercilessly, he pushed away her questions, on and on, until he owned every inch of her.

Somewhere in the recesses of her mind, it felt like the sealing of the real contract. The small print. That was just as binding. She had no idea what she'd really signed up to. But with every push he made into her, every sensation, every moment, made her let go. Until she had only one thought: how utterly powerful he was.

In the restless hour before dawn, while he slept peacefully next to her, the reality of her situation became clear.

Raz was nowhere to be found and no longer a threat. The cousins were put in their place. Demeter was now head of a multi-billion-dollar corporation and everyone's silence had been bought. Jokes aside, without a single vow or declaration of love, she *was* tied physically and figuratively to his bed, for as long as he wanted her. If every thrust hadn't chipped away at her senses, she might have even credited him with a kind of marriage, or at the very least, a master stroke.

CHAPTER 30

*O*ne *year later*

Sasha adjusted her backpack and followed the line of pilgrims on the windy path to the temple. She had to catch her breath and mop her brow a few times in the Cambodian humidity. The heat was gathering momentum even though it was still early in the day.

At last, she reached the summit where the red temple was built into the hillside, and she reaped her reward of the view of patchwork paddy fields laid out in the terraces below. She breathed in the morning air, filled with the scent of wild blossoms and the vague smell of incense from the temple behind her.

Today marked a year since she'd signed with Demeter at the chateau. It had flown by because she was happy. Her life was stress-free, unrecognisable. No more worrying about Jace. No more music business. Just her dream life of travelling the world.

After tying her into an iron-clad contract that really did enslave her for life, Demeter had set her free. Always vague in his explanations, he'd simply said, 'Go do what you must do. Take one year. The business isn't going anywhere in that time.'

It still brought tears to her eyes when she thought about the kindness of it. The only thing he'd stipulated was that she keep in touch with little cryptic clues on social media and postcards sent to his London office. It seemed he was aiding and abetting her escape and the only person he wanted knowing her whereabouts was him. He advised her to keep moving, so she never stayed in one place for longer than a few weeks. She was enjoying learning about textiles and natural dyes for a new sustainable clothes line she wanted to start, named 'Devil-may-care,' causing Demeter to raise an eyebrow. At first, she'd been sad to have to say goodbye to the Vaggabond brand, but Demeter had reminded her it was legally tied to the collective and Jace and all the implications and painful memories of that. Better to start anew, with just the right marketing to hint at her past to ensure its success.

He had a habit of dropping in from time to time. His excuse was that he was keeping an eye on his investment. Bringing news that the collective had picked up where they'd left off in LA with limited success. They never seemed to get the traction now Jace and the Carpathian connection had gone. Sasha couldn't understand why any of them would want to even try, now that they knew what went on behind the scenes. 'The industry is a den of vipers that eats sensitive artists alive,' Demeter once said, and he was right. She thought sadly of Jace. Being sensitive and all for the music was never enough. You must have no conscience and a thick skin to succeed, both of which meant Jace had always been doomed.

Sasha never saw or heard from Raz again. In fact, Demeter never even mentioned her since that fearful day. She'd only ever broached the subject once and he'd simply said she was gone and never to worry. And so she never did.

She certainly didn't need the limelight. She never had. She had a new identity, thanks to Demeter: Florence Perrenne. She thought it sounded very chic and French. Demeter insisted it was for her anonymity and therefore her safety, which did give her a little concern, but as usual, he smoothed it away.

He also bought her mother a new condo and changed her name to Perrenne. It did terrify her that the paparazzi and crazed TRHBDor fans could actually seek to do them harm. Demeter explained that it had more to do with her association with him and her special place in his life, which she never fully understood. She guessed his family was powerful, and she'd exposed a weakness he shouldn't have.

She took another deep breath and turned and trudged the last few feet to the temple. She was almost there when she spotted a smarter-than-average man, sitting in a carved red chair. He looked completely relaxed in his aviator sunglasses, navy blue slacks and Wedgewood blue shirt. It was left unbuttoned at the neck – his only concession to the heat. His dark, tousled hair perfectly framed the tanned, chiselled face, and his smile immediately melted her insides. *Demeter,* she thought, with the usual punch to her gut.

Seeing him always took her breath. Not just because he always surfaced in the most unlikely places, but simply because of the sheer magnetism of the man. She was hopelessly hooked. And despite not seeing him for months, she was instantly pulled back in.

He stood immediately, showing off his perfectly trim physique that always seemed to show in the cut of his clothes. Without a care for the tourists around them, he pulled her into his body, drew in her scent and kissed her neck. It always quickened her heart, the way he did that. He smelled the same as ever, his signature cologne and the scent of pure him. 'How did you get here?' she asked, looking down at his expensive shoes.

'Helicopter,' he admitted, kissing her forehead. 'There is a plateau big enough just over there,' he said, nodding his head to somewhere past the temple.

It was lovely to see him, but it was a lot of effort to come just to say hello, and her butterflies soon changed to nerves. 'I can't believe you're here?' she said, a little hesitantly.

He squeezed her hand. 'Shall we?' he said, taking a step towards the temple. She nodded and smiled, a little relieved and secretly thrilled that he wanted to see it with her. They wandered the avenues, he leaning in and kissing her on occasion, just like any other happy, affectionate couple. Using any excuse to touch and get close. It made it easy to get caught up and forget who he was and why he was probably there. They spent a wonderful couple of hours, even tying little plaques to the laden prayer tree.

'What do you think of this religion?' she asked, looking up at the temple.

'Buddhism?' he shrugged. 'Better than most, I guess. For those not lured by greed. They are all distractions. I guess enlightenment in any form can only be a good thing for the individual.' But his look was wicked. He always made her think he was being sarcastic and making fun of her when he said things like that. She gave him a playful shove.

He laughed and brought his arm around her and kissed the top of her head.

The time had come and she couldn't put off the question any longer. 'Why have you come, Dem? It's a lovely surprise, but I know there is a reason. I can feel it in you.'

Demeter studied her face as if she were the most beautiful creature on earth. It was like payday. She absolutely loved the way he did that. But the hint of sadness in it told her all she needed to know. 'You've come to take me back, haven't you?'

His smile was regretful as he tilted his head to the side and gently touched her cheek. 'I bought you one year of freedom and now the year is up.'

She swallowed. Fear rose in her chest, her heart thrashed, and panic seized her for a moment, until she could finally tamp it down.

He allowed her the time, solemnly, and hugged her to him as if he understood. Of course he did. 'You are and always will be my greatest sacrifice,' he said, almost crushing her as he spoke into her hair.

Sasha pulled back to examine his face after the unmistakable declaration of love. She relaxed, resigned as she slowly understood and nodded. This day was always going to come.

'I love you, Sasha Bond. Know that in any other life, I would give you everything you ever wanted.'

She smiled wanly up at him, taking in the intensity and the love in that mesmerising gaze.

A sharp bee sting caught her in the neck and her eyes went wide to his in a last moment's panic as she felt herself falling backwards, ever backwards. *Not then...not right then.*

CHAPTER 31

'Welcome to the Metal Beats show, where we bring all the music, news and views from LA and around the world. I'm Trent Derby and I would like to welcome Zach Bennington, former manager of the very successful, talented and tragic collective, TRHBDor and one of the surviving, much-loved founder members, Duo Tempo. Welcome, guys.'

'Hi, Trent. Glad to be here. It's been a beat,' Duo said.

'Certainly has and a lot's happened. It's hard to believe that a year has passed after the tragic passing of Lil Jace, Pope... and now the tragic loss at sea of Sasha Bond. It's so awful. Was it suicide? We know so little. There's been huge speculation that she quit the collective following the loss of Jace.' Trent spoke straight to the camera. 'In case you don't know, Jace and Sasha were childhood sweethearts.' Then, facing across the table to his guests again, 'Can you shed any light, Zach? I know you knew them both really well.'

'Yes, Trent. I did. Can I just say that they weren't together in the end, but their love and friendship were undeniable. Both will be hugely missed.'

'Is it true they've posthumously put together a new fashion line in her honour of all her unmade designs?'

'Yes it is. She was working on a collection called Devil-may-care. One hundred per cent sustainable,' Zach said.

Trent clapped, along with many of the crew. 'So that was what she was doing when she sadly passed?'

Duo nodded. 'She was in Cambodia and it wasn't suicide.' He shifted uncomfortably in his seat. 'And they never found a body.'

'So you're saying she could still be alive?' Trent said, pouncing on the possible headline.

'Unlikely, given where the boat was last seen,' Zach cut in before Duo could answer. 'But we live in hope, you know?'

'So sad,' Trent said, shaking his head. 'People are starting to talk about the curse of the TRHBDor. Does that worry you?'

Duo and Zach caught each other's eye and nodded. 'Every day.'

'You believe in the curse, then?' Trent asked, seizing the opportunity for a great line of questioning.

Duo and Zack shrugged.

'It's certainly hard to ignore … Is it true that you've all now gone your separate ways because of it?'

Duo let out a long breath. 'Well, we all got our own things going on, you know? Brains has written a book. I've been producing some exciting new talent.'

'What about your sister?'

'She's getting married now she's got a baby son.'

'Jynskie, Ballistik and Lil Sensei?'

'They doin' their thing, you know.'

Sounds like all of you are happy to take a step back from the business. So is TRHBDor finished?'

'Never say never,' Zach said, sitting forward more enthusiastically. 'There's actually been talk of a benefit concert this year for famine relief.'

'So you aren't afraid to get out there again?'

'I'd say it's not us who have to worry, it's the new up-and-coming artists,' Duo said.

Trent sat up, interested. 'And what words of advice would you say to some of our new budding stars, about to embark on their journey?'

Zach put his hand on Duo's arm as if to stop him, but he brushed him off.

Duo called the cameraman to him and made him zoom in on his face. 'Enjoy the early days. Get everything out of it you can. Because when you get noticed and big business comes knockin', it's the Devil and no one else … It saps the soul right out of you until there's nothing left. Yeah, you have the money and everyone knows your name, but love, friendship, even your art dries up and is left hollow and meaningless.'

'Wow,' Trent said, wild-eyed and shaking his head. 'And if you had your time again, you'd have turned down that level of fame?'

'In a heartbeat.'

Zach hesitantly nodded along.

'I would have stayed with my loyal fans, doing our thing in those small club venues, with my best friend – with all my friends, having the best time of my life.'

CONTACT T

To receive your two 21st Century Sirens Novellas, and be the first to know anything relating to T's books, leave your details here: https://mailchi.mp/d18c89c14f50/tstedmannovellas
And please don't forget to leave a review wherever you bought your book, I really appreciate the feedback.

Much love
T

www.tstedman.com
Facebook
X
TikTok

ALSO BY T STEDMAN

Dark Valentines Collection

The Watchers

Diablo

21st Century Sirens Series

Soul Breather **(Free to download)**

Blood Sister

Shield Maiden

Tiger Lily

Night Goddess

Darkly Begotten

The Novellas (Free to download)

Protector

Lost Moon

The YA Novels

Young Atlanteans

Two Tribes

Cross Heirs

Night Shades Novels

The Blackwood Curse

Demon in the Attic

TinBoiz

Entanglement

Non-Fiction

My Migraine Story

www.ingramcontent.com/pod-product-compliance
Lightning Source LLC
Chambersburg PA
CBHW060739190726
48285CB00001B/279